D0412041

Should I
Forget You

By the same author

Wives and Mothers
The Long Way Home
Oranges and Lemons
This Year, Next Year
The Lost Daughters
Thursday's Child
Eve's Daughter
King's Walk
Pride of Peacocks
All That I Am
The Happy Highways
Summer Snow
Wishes and Dreams
The Wise Child
You'll Never Know. . .

Should I Forget You

Jeanne Whitmee

ROBERT HALE · LONDON

© Jeanne Whitmee 2009
First published in Great Britain 2009

ISBN 978-0-7090-8778-6

Robert Hale Limited
Clerkenwell House
Clerkenwell Green
London EC1R 0HT

www.halebooks.com

The right of Jeanne Whitmee to be identified as
author of this work has been asserted by her
in accordance with the Copyright, Designs and
Patents Act 1988

2 4 6 8 10 9 7 5 3 1

SCOTTISH BORDERS LIBRARY SERVICES	
007756147	
Bertrams	31/07/2009
	£18.99

Typeset in 10/13½pt Palatino
by Derek Doyle & Associates, Shaw Heath
Printed in the UK by the MPG Books Group

SCOTTISH BORDERS COUNCIL

LIBRARY &

INFORMATION SERVICES

CHAPTER ONE

'I can't keep this one no longer! She ain't no dratted use to man nor beast.'

Mrs Fenning's strident voice rang out across the village hall, temporarily in use as the village billeting centre. She stood in the doorway, looking like the angel of doom in her long black coat, one claw-like hand clutching the collar of nine-year-old Kathleen O'Connor's shabby brown coat. As she spoke she gave the child a shove, sending her stumbling forward into the hall.

'I don't know what parents teach their kids nowadays,' she said, looking at the little girl with an expression of disgust. 'She ain't got no idea how to milk a goat. She can't even draw a bucket of water from the well.'

Maureen Kendrick, the vicar's sister gathered her wits together. 'These children come from London, Mrs Fenning,' she said with as much patience as she could muster. 'I don't suppose the poor child has ever seen a goat – or a well either if it comes to that. And after all, she's only been with you for two days. I'm sure she would soon learn your ways – with a little kindness and patience.'

But Mrs Fenning was not to be fobbed off. 'If I'm to take some strange child into my home it'll have to earn its keep,' she snorted. 'I weren't never molly coddled as a child and it never done me no harm. Any o'these 'ere vaccies what gets dumped on me had better make up their minds to work for a living never mind no *kindness and patience.*' She spat the words out as though they were a bad taste.

It was a week since the evacuees had descended on Beckets Green. Far more had arrived than had been expected, much to the dismay of Maureen and her little band of helpers. The village school was full to overflowing. Children were seated three to a desk in every room as well as crowded into the hall; and makeshift classes were being held throughout the village: In the scout hut, the old timber village hall which was due for demolition, even at the back of the church, and the moment Maureen had completed all the necessary paperwork the new village hall was due to be requisitioned too. It helped that some of the teachers had come from London along with the children, but even with the extra staff classes had swelled to impossible numbers.

Kathleen O'Connor was the third child that had been allocated to the widowed Mrs Fenning. None had been to her liking. She had alleged that the first, a boy of thirteen, was 'ungodly' and had sworn at her, the second had wet the bed and now Kathleen had fallen short of her expectations as a skivvy. Maureen was almost at the end of her tether.

'These children have not been sent here to be servants, Mrs Fenning,' she said. 'She should be at school anyway. Why haven't you sent her?'

'She can go t'school when she's done her jobs like I told her,' the woman said, folding her arms.

'And have you taken her along? Does she know where to go?'

'No I ain't! What d'you think I am – some kind of nursemaid?'

Maureen went to the little girl who stood by the wall, the regulation gas mask in its battered cardboard box dangling from a length of string around her neck. She looked forlorn and tearful as she clutched the brown paper carrier bag containing her few possessions.

'It's Kathleen, isn't it?' The child nodded. 'Well, pop along to the kitchen, Kathleen,' Maureen said gently. 'Mrs Harris is in there, she'll give you a drink of cocoa and a biscuit.' She put a finger under Kathleen's wobbling little chin. 'And don't worry dear,' she whispered. 'We'll find you somewhere nice to stay.'

'Yes, miss.' Kathleen made her way towards the door at the back of the hall. In the kitchen plump, motherly Joan Harris had the kettle on. She beamed at Kathleen.

'Hello my duck,' she said. 'And what do they call you?'

'Kathleen – Kathy, miss – er – missis.'

'And what can I do for you, Kathy?'

'The lady out there said you'd give me some cocoa and a biscuit,' Kathy said.

'And so I will. Just sit you down.' Joan eyed the little girl thoughtfully. Her clothes were shabby and outgrown and she looked small for her age and far too thin by Joan's standards. She took in the stringy hair and pale, tear-stained face and her soft heart melted. 'Got no one to stay with my duck?' she asked.

Kathy's eyes filled with tears. 'The lady where I was staying said I was no use to – to man or beast,' she quoted.

Joan bridled. 'Saints alive! What a thing to say! Why was that then?'

'It was because I didn't know how to milk her goat and I couldn't turn the handle on the well.'

Joan Harris nodded. 'Ah – I wouldn't mind betting that were old Mrs Fenning,' she said.

Kathleen stared at her. 'How did you guess?'

'She's a hard old nut to crack. Don't you worry about her,' Joan said. 'The Arch Angel Gabriel 'imself'd have his work cut out trying to please Lizzie Fenning an' no mistake.' She put a steaming mug in front of Kathleen and took the lid off a tin of biscuits. 'There you are my duck. You get that down you. And don't you fret. If anyone can find you a nice home it'll be Miss Kendrick.'

Kathy drank the hot sweet drink with relish and gobbled down the biscuit. She'd been sent to bed last night without any supper because she hadn't been able to milk the goat. The creature had terrified her, staring menacingly at her with its strange colourless eyes. It had seemed to sense her fear and had kicked out viciously the moment she went near it with the bucket.

Noticing the ravenous way Kathy demolished the biscuit, Joan pushed the biscuit tin closer. 'Are you hungry luvvie? Here, help your-self.' There was something heart-wrenching about this little one. She wished with all her heart she could take her home with her but she knew it wasn't possible. She had four children of her own and with the three evacuees she had impulsively volunteered to take in, her tied cottage was full to bursting point. It was a good job that her Fred was easy-going and fond of kids.

Kathy munched her biscuit, her tummy rumbling in appreciation. She had never seen a place like Beckets Green before and when she had arrived here and stepped down from the bus with all the other children she had looked around her in wide-eyed amazement. There were hardly any buses or cars on the narrow roads and the houses were so funny, many of them built out of roughly cut stones and roofed with thatch. Mum used to keep her hankies in an old chocolate box with a picture of a thatched cottage on the lid, but Kathy had always believed that they only existed in fairy tales or on chocolate boxes. Yet here they were with people actually living in them as though it was normal. There were lots of trees and fields full of green grass with horses and cows. There was a little church with a squat grey tower and a school shaped like a gingerbread house nestling besides it. She could hardly believe her eyes. She might as well have been transported to another planet, so strange was it all.

It smelled different too. In London the air smelt of soot and petrol and the rotting fruit and veg from the barrows and the market stalls. They were the smells Kathy was familiar with. Here it was different. She wasn't sure what the smells were – apart from Mrs Fenning's goat – or whether she actually liked them. Not that she'd had much time so far to find out.

Mrs Fenning's cottage had a thatched roof but it was neither pretty nor romantic. It had a parlour whose door seemed to be permanently locked; a living-room with a stone flagged floor and a black, smoking range. A draughty lean-to kitchen led onto the yard where the goat lived. Upstairs there were two bedrooms. The one she had slept in was at the back. It was cold and cheerless, furnished with a single iron bedstead with a lumpy flock mattress, a chair and a wash-stand. There was no mat on the floor and the one small window looked out on the back yard which the goat shared with a few scrawny chickens. The only lavvy was in the yard too and Kathy had to pass the goat every time she wanted to go. Twice the beast had butted her as she tried to sidle past, propelling her painfully into the wall.

The two days that Kathy had spent there had been like a nightmare. The old woman had expected her to scrub and clean every room in the cottage as well as tackle things she had never done before such as milking the goat and winding the bucket up from the depths of the seemingly bottomless well. There had been very little to eat or drink and no time to go to school. But perhaps the worst thing for Kathy had been the fact that she hadn't been able to wash.

'You wanna wash you'd better get out in the yard and draw yerself a bucket'o water,' Mrs Fenning had told her, knowing full well that the child wasn't strong enough to turn the handle. 'Anyway, I don't hold with too much washing. Everyone knows it's weakening to the body.'

Kathy had felt deeply ashamed at having to go dirty. Mum had always been so particular about cleanliness. When the old woman had decided to take her back to the billeting centre she felt relieved.

She paused and looked up, aware that the nice fat lady was speaking to her.

'I expect you miss your mum, duck.'

Kathy nodded. 'She'll be all on her own now,' she said.

'Ah, Pa gone off to the war then, has he?'

'No. He's dead.'

Joan's face fell. 'Oh my dear Lord. I'm sorry duck.'

'It's all right,' Kathy assured her. 'He wasn't my real dad. I've got two step-brothers but they're in the army now.'

Charlie and Bill had been called up as soon as the war began. They had both been in the Territorials and that meant they were the first to go. Kathy had been glad to see the back of them. Mum had married Jim Brady, their dad five years ago. They were big boys even then and had made Kathy's life a misery with their cruel teasing and sadistic practical jokes. Since their father had died, falling under a bus in a drunken stupor one Saturday night, they had become almost uncontrollable: noisy, dirty and disobedient. Their stepmother, at the end of her tether, had finally gone to her parish priest for help and it had been Father Gerard at St Jude's who had talked them into joining the Territorials, painting a rosy picture of the rough and tumble camaraderie whilst hoping that the discipline would do them good. Since the outbreak of war when they had been called up Kathy and her mum had been happy, free to enjoy one another's company and a bit of peace and quiet. Mum had always had to work long hours to keep food on the table and a roof over their heads. Their small flat on the sixth floor of Halfpenny Buildings was always neat and spotless, even if they didn't have much money but things had been easier since the boys had left.

'She'll be missing you too,' Joan said, shaking her head. She couldn't imagine the anguish it must have caused those city mothers having to part with their precious kiddies, sent off to God only knew where. 'Any chance she might be able to come and join you here once things are more settled?'

Kathy smiled wistfully. 'I don't know. I wish she could.'

The door opened and Maureen Kendrick looked round it. 'If you'd like to come with me now Kathleen, we'll go over to the school,' she said. 'It's all right. Mrs Fenning has gone,' she added, seeing Kathy's apprehensive look. 'I'll introduce you to the teachers and maybe you'll see some of the other children who came with you. It's playtime now so they'll be having a break.' Kathy got down from the table.

'Thank you for the cocoa and biscuits, missis,' she said, remembering her manners.

Joan smiled. 'I'm sure you're very welcome my duck. Don't forget your bag and your gas mask – horrid thing. And I hope you find a nice place soon.'

Across at St Mark's Church School the children were out in the playground energetically letting off steam with noisy games. One or two of Kathy's old school mates called out to her as she followed Maureen Kendrick through the door.

'Wotcher, Kath!'

'Gonna come and have a game with us?'

She waved, shaking her head and following the vicar's sister into the school.

Inside Maureen tapped on the door of the head's office where the teachers were having their mid-morning cup of tea. 'Can I come in?' She took Kathy's hand and drew her inside. 'Mrs Fenning has brought me yet another reject,' she said with a sigh. 'I'm afraid the old lady is a bit of a lost cause. I shan't try her with another child unless I'm really pushed.' She put a hand on Kathy's shoulder and urged her gently forward. 'This is Kathleen O'Connor. Does anyone know of a kind soul who'll take her in? She's not very big and I'm sure she's a good girl, aren't you, Kathleen?'

Kathy nodded solemnly. 'I like being called Kathy best,' she said quietly.

Lena Spicer who took what was known as the 'scholarship' class of ten to eleven year olds put down her cup and smiled at the child. 'How old are you, Kathy?'

'Please, miss, I'll be ten next month,' Kathy said.

'I've got a little girl the same age as you,' Lena said. 'And I've got a boy who is twelve. How would you like to come and stay with us? We live on a farm.'

Kathy looked worried. 'Would I have to milk a goat?' she asked fearfully.

All the teachers laughed and Kathy blushed. 'No,' Lena said. 'We've got a man who does that for us except that we have cows, not goats.'

Maureen was looking at her doubtfully. 'What about the Smith boys?' she asked. The Spicers had been allocated five-year-old twin boys a week ago. 'Won't you be terribly crowded?'

Lena smiled. 'Their mother arrived from London the day before yesterday in floods of tears and took them home with her,' she explained. 'I can't say I blame her. The boys were very young and very traumatized at being uprooted and parted from their mother. So you see it would be ideal.' She smiled at Kathy. 'That is if Kathy would like to come.'

Realizing that all eyes were upon her Kathy blushed and nodded. 'Thank you, miss.'

Another teacher spoke. She was quite young and had fair hair and kind blue eyes. 'You'll be in my class, Kathy,' she said getting up from her chair. 'I'm Miss Hart. So if you'd like to come along with me now I'll show you where to hang your coat then we'll find you a desk.'

Kathy looked at Mrs Spicer who nodded. 'At lunchtime you can come home with me and see your new home.'

Kathy was seated next to a girl with auburn hair who, she soon learned was Elaine, Mrs Spicer's daughter. After playtime the lesson was arithmetic, which was Kathy's favourite. She'd always loved numbers, the figures seemed to dance in her head and fit neatly together like the pieces of a puzzle. It fascinated her. By the time the bell went for lunch she was feeling decidedly happier. Mrs Spicer was waiting for her at the door. She took each girl by the hand and together they walked down the lane.

'We live at Magpie Farm,' Mrs Spicer told her. 'It's only about half a mile away. If you look you can see the roof of the farmhouse from here.' She pointed to a red tiled roof with two gables that could be seen above the treetops.

Elaine had been quiet, eyeing Kathy speculatively, she was very small and quite scruffy really, she even smelled a bit, but she'd been grudgingly impressed by the other girl's enthusiasm and skill in the arithmetic lesson. They'd just started doing fractions and Kathy seemed to pick things up really quickly and she could do 'mental' in a flash – something Elaine struggled with. She hoped this new girl wasn't going to outshine her. She'd always been close to the top of her class. It would never do to have an evacuee doing better than her.

They soon reached the farm. Mrs Spicer opened the five-bar gate and they crossed a well scoured yard, pausing to pat a black and white dog chained up to a kennel near the back door.

'This is Fly,' Lena told Kathy. 'He's a sheep dog really but we haven't got sheep any more so he helps Fred, our cowman herd the cows and bring them in for milking.'

As soon as the back door was opened a rich smell of cooking assailed Kathy's nostrils, making her mouth water.

'There's a casserole in the oven.' Mrs Spicer said, taking off her coat and hanging it up in the small lobby. 'The others will be in shortly. Lay the table Elaine, will you?'

Kathy looked round the big farm kitchen. It was a large room with a quarry-tiled floor scattered with rugs. A big dresser stood against one wall, laden with willow pattern plates; cups hanging from its shelves by little hooks. Under the window there was a big chintz-covered sofa. Warmth and delicious aromas emanated from a cream enamelled Aga range in an alcove. In the centre of the room was a large round table on which Elaine was busy spreading a blue and white checked tablecloth. Mrs Spicer smiled at Kathy.

'Hang up your coat in the lobby and make yourself at home, Kathy,' she said. 'Elaine will show you where you can wash your hands. Are you hungry?' Kathy nodded eagerly. 'Good. Hurry up then. After we've eaten I'll show you where you'll be sleeping.'

When the girls came back to the kitchen two men had joined the group. Both wore overalls and had left their muddy boots by the back door. Both smiled at Kathy.

'This is my husband,' Mrs Spicer said, pointing to the tallest man who had brown hair and twinkling blue eyes. 'And that is Mr Harris – Fred, who takes care of our cows. You probably met his wife, Joan at the hall this morning.' Kathy nodded, watching with fascination as Mrs Spicer began ladling out the casserole. The gravy was rich and brown and it had carrots and onions in it as well as meat. 'I think you had better call us Auntie Lena and Uncle James,' she said. 'Most of the evacuees are calling their hosts 'auntie and uncle', though at school of course it had better be Mrs Spicer.' Again Kathy nodded. The anticipation of imminent food was making it almost impossible for her to concentrate.

The plates were passed round and a dish of fluffy mashed potatoes offered. Kathy began to eat. She tried hard not to bolt the food but she was so hungry that it was hard not to. She was unaware of 'Auntie Lena's' watchful eyes on her.

'Would you like some more?' she asked as Kathy finished scraping her plate.

Kathy blushed and glanced round at the others. Mum had always taught her that greed was a sin. Lena smiled. 'It's all right,' she said. 'There's plenty to go round.' She held out her hand and Kathy passed her plate.

At playtime that afternoon the other London children gathered round Kathy.

'Where you been then, Kath?'

'We thought you'd gone back to London,'

'Someone said you got billeted on a witch and she'd got you locked up in a cupboard.'

'Where you stoppin' now then, Kath?'

'At Magpie Farm,' Kathy said proudly. She already knew that she was lucky to have been chosen by Mrs Spicer, or Auntie Lena. The dinner she'd eaten was a real treat and when she'd been shown the pretty little bedroom she was to have all to herself she could hardly believe her luck.

'With that teacher from the top class – that Mrs Spicer?' One of the boys looked at her with disdain. 'Aw, she's gonna be a teacher's pet,' he announced to the others. 'You wanna be careful of her now. She'll *tell* on yer.'

'No I won't!' Kathy protested. 'I don't tell tales.'

'You will do,' the boy insisted. 'Grass – grass – kick you up the arse!' he chanted, dancing a grotesque jig around her. Some of the others joined in but Sheila Brown who had always been Kathy's best friend at Spencer Street Elementary in Hackney took her hand and drew her away.

'Take no notice,' she said. 'They're only jealous.'

Kathy had noticed that Elaine had her own group of friends. She hadn't invited Kathy to join them and for the duration of the break they had ignored her. Sheila drew Kathy's attention to this unwelcome fact.

'Is she a bit stuck up?' she asked jerking her head in Elaine's direction.

Kathy shrugged. 'A bit.'

'I 'spect she thinks she's the cat's whiskers with her mum bein' one of the teachers.'

'I don't think she likes having me to live at their place,' Kathy said. 'She don't like her mum bein' nice to me.' She knew already that it wasn't going to be easy getting Elaine to like her, but she knew she would have to be careful not to make an enemy of her. She didn't want to cause trouble and – horror of horrors – get sent back to Mrs Fenning.

After school when they got back to the farm Auntie Lena took Kathy upstairs and helped her to unpack her few belongings.

'Is this all you've brought?' she asked as she hung the meagre collection of crumpled clothes in the wardrobe. Kathy nodded.

'There wasn't much time and Mum didn't have a proper case to put things in. Anyway. . . .' She caught her lower lip between her teeth. 'I ain't – haven't got many clothes.'

'Mmm. The colder weather will soon be here. You're going to need some warmer things.' Lena looked thoughtful. 'Elaine is growing fast and you're a little smaller than she is. I'm sure I can find you some of the things she's outgrown.' She looked at Kathy. 'If you wouldn't mind wearing cast-offs.'

Kathy shook her head. 'I don't get many new things,' she said resignedly. 'Mum gets a lot of clothes from jumble sales. She always washes things and mends them before she lets me wear them though,' she added quickly.

'Right. We'll see what we can find.' Lena looked at Kathy as she closed the wardrobe door. 'There's plenty of hot water, would you like to have a bath before tea? And if you like I'll wash your hair for you.'

Kathy looked up in delight. 'Ooh, yes please. Mrs Fenning wouldn't let me have a wash. She said too much washing made you weak.'

Lena hid a smile. 'I'm sure we don't need to worry about that.'

Bathing in the big bathtub in the Spicers' bathroom and submitted happily to Lena shampooing her hair was a delight. For Lena's part she was relieved to find that Kathy had no nits. Many of the evacuee children had and it had caused problems in the village as they spread like wildfire through the school. Kathy's hair, when it was clean proved to be glossy with a natural curl which sprang up under the brush as Lena dried it. She found her a blouse and a little pleated skirt and cardigan to match. It was a very different Kathy who appeared in the kitchen at teatime.

The only person in the kitchen was a big boy with a thick thatch of fair hair that flopped over his forehead. He wore grey trousers and a dark green blazer and he was sitting at the table bending over his homework.

'This is Kathleen O'Connor,' Lena said. 'She's from London and she likes to be called Kathy. She's come to stay with us. Kathy, this is Christopher, Elaine's brother.'

The big boy looked up with a smile. 'Hello, Kathy. I hope you like Magpie Farm,' he said. 'And I like to be called Chris by the way.' He got up and solemnly held out his hand. 'I'll show you round the farm later if you like.' As his mother moved away he lowered his voice and added. 'You make a nice change from those two awful kids. Always whining and spilling their milk. Good job their mother took them back home if you ask me.'

His blue eyes sparkled into Kathy's and she knew in that moment that she was destined to adore him.

That night Kathy slept in a warm, comfortable bed and wakened refreshed. To her delight Joan Harris was in the kitchen when she went downstairs.

'Hello my duckie,' she beamed. 'Well now, I must say you're lookin' a lot better than the last time I saw you.'

She put a fresh new-laid farm egg on the table in front of Kathy along with homemade bread cut into 'soldiers'. 'Get that inside you,' she said. 'We'll soon have the roses back in them cheeks.'

Kathy set off for school with Elaine and Auntie Lena in good spirits. Her happy mood was to be short-lived however when, after prayers and Assembly the first lesson was English. Kathy's writing and spelling left much to be desired and her punctuation and grammar were almost non-existent. Elaine was secretly relieved.

'Haven't you done any of that at your old school?' she asked in a whisper as she saw Kathy struggling, her tongue poking out from the corner of her mouth.

Kathy shook her head. 'I had to have a lot of time off when Mum was poorly last year,' she explained.

Hearing the sibilant murmur Jenny Hart looked up. 'Who is talking instead of working?' she asked.

Elaine spoke up. 'Kathy can't do it, Miss,' she said, unable to keep the note of triumph out of her voice.

Kathy looked up, her cheeks scarlet. 'I – it's just – different. Miss,' she stammered.

'Bring your book to me,' Jenny said gently. 'Let's see if we can sort the problem out.'

As Kathy went reluctantly up to the teacher's desk there was a buzz of interest from the rest of the class. She dragged her feet, feeling wretched at being the centre of attention.

'The rest of you can get on with your work,' Jenny said. She took Kathy's book and looked at it. She could see at a glance that the child had a problem. She was puzzled. She had been quite outstanding at arithmetic yesterday yet from the look of this, English grammar seemed almost like a foreign language to her.

'Don't you like English, Kathy?' she asked.

Kathy bit her lip. 'I like stories, Miss,' she said. 'But I can't do the spelling and the punc – punc.... I never know where to put the comics.'

'Commas,' Jenny corrected.

At that moment the bell went for playtime. Jenny looked up. 'You may all get your milk and go out to play,' she said. 'Except you, Elaine, I would like to talk to you and Kathy for a moment.'

'To *me*, Miss?' Elaine looked up in surprise.

'Yes. I think I know how you and Kathy can help one another.'

Coming to stand beside Kathy, Elaine turned to look her up and down.

'You are quite good at English, Elaine,' Jenny said. 'Whilst Kathy is good at arithmetic. If I set you both a little exercise each night English for Kathy, arithmetic for you, Elaine, you can help one another as you both live in the same house.' She smiled at the two girls. 'It will help you to get to know one another and become good friends.'

The girls looked at each other. Neither of them shared their teacher's optimism.

As soon as they were out of the teacher's hearing Elaine turned to Kathy. 'I'll show you how to do your English if Miss says I have to but I don't need you showing me how to do sums.'

Kathy shrugged. 'OK.'

'Anyway, you've got my blouse and skirt on,' Elaine pointed out.

'I know.' Kathy swallowed hard. 'Auntie Lena said they didn't fit you any more.'

'Perhaps they don't, but I don't remember you saying thank you for them.'

Kathy coloured. 'Yes I did!'

'Not to me, you didn't.'

By this time they were in the playground and Elaine's friends had gathered round. 'What did Miss want you for, Elaine?' one asked.

The other girl tossed her auburn head. 'I've got to help her with her English,' she said, pointing at Kathy. 'She called a comma a *comic*.' They all laughed. 'Look at her,' Elaine went on, encouraged by the laughter. 'She's even got to wear my old clothes because her own are in rags!'

Kathy's eyes filled with tears of humiliation as all the other children stared at her. Suddenly a voice rang out from the steps.

'Elaine Spicer! Come here, please!'

Lena Spicer, who was on playground duty began to walk down the steps, her eyes flashing with anger as she looked at her daughter. 'How dare you treat Kathy like that!' she said. 'She is away from her home and her mother and she is a guest in our house. You will treat her with respect and kindness. I'm ashamed of you. Apologize at once.'

One or two of Elaine's friends had started to snigger. She turned to Kathy, her cheeks scarlet. 'Sorry,' she muttered.

'*Properly*. Say it as though you mean it,' Lena insisted. 'As for the clothes you have grown out of, I can't believe that a daughter of mine could be so mean as to make Kathy feel uncomfortable about it. Perhaps I should make you go on wearing them, even though they are too small for you. Is that what you want?'

Elaine shook her head. 'No.'

'As for thanking you, she will be repaying you amply by helping you with the arithmetic you are having difficulty with. Isn't that so?'

Elaine hung her head. 'Yes.'

The other children had turned away now, nudging one another, their hands over their mouths to hide their amusement.

'I think you had better make up your mind to be Kathy's friend,' Lena said firmly. 'She may be with us for quite a long time and surely it's nicer to be pleasant and helpful than be mean and nasty. Don't let me hear any more of your bullying, Elaine.'

And without waiting for a reaction from either girl Lena raised her whistle to her mouth and blew it for the end of playtime.

Lena always stayed on at four o'clock to prepare the following day's lessons so the girls were left to walk home together. Kathy expected reprisals from Elaine who had been silent for most of the day so she was surprised when the other girl said goodbye to her friends and came across to Kathy in the cloakroom.

'Want to walk home together?' she asked. 'I know where there are some blackberries. We could get some for Mrs Harris to bake in a pie.'

Kathy smiled uncertainly. OK. If you like.'

Elaine started off at a run. 'Come on then.'

CHAPTER TWO

Kathy loved the High Street at Beckets Green with its collection of shops – all so different to the ones in Hackney. There was the butcher's where fat Mr Johnson in his striped apron stood in the doorway every morning, a smile and a joke for the children on their way to school. There was the baker's which always smelled deliciously of fresh bread. At the back of the shop there was a big bakehouse where many of the village people took their dinners to be cooked in the big ovens for a few pence each day. Kathy would often see the children collecting the steaming dishes covered in a cloth as she walked home at dinner time.

The sweet shop was called The Cosy Corner and was kept by Miss Jolly, a little old lady with rosy cheeks and glasses; only now that there was a war on sweets were in short supply. At the end of the High Street was the Co-op where Auntie Lena went every week to collect the rations for the family; next to that was the Turf Cutters' Arms, which had leaded windows and smelled like pubs always smelled when you walked past. That was the one smell that reminded Kathy of home.

But best of all was the post office-cum-general store which faced the village green. Kathy had never seen anything like it in Hackney. A large ginger cat always lay curled up in the window soaking up the sunshine, surrounded by packets of cocoa powder and pyramids of tins of peas, none of which he ever seemed to knock over. Kathy loved to go in though the green painted door that made a loud *ping* when you opened it and marvel at the amazing variety of things Mrs Trent, the post mistress sold.

The shop was divided into two. One half sold stamps and postal orders and did all the usual post office things behind a metal grille, while the other half sold what seemed to Kathy like everything you could possibly think of. As well as porridge oats, something called pig nuts and bundles of firewood there were cards of knicker-elastic; reels of cotton and packets of needles; skeins of knitting wool; writing pads; combs and hair grips. It seemed there was no end to the range of goods on sale. And the mixture of smells was magical. Kathy would stand breathing it in and trying to analyze it. There was paraffin oil; cheese; bacon; floor polish. It was as diverse as the stock.

Kathy wrote home to Mum every Sunday evening and Lena posted the letters for her on the way to school on Monday morning. Mum wrote back, but the letters were infrequent and usually only a few lines long. She wrote that she had a full time nine-till-five job now that she was on her own, working at the local Food Office. It was much easier than the early morning cleaning jobs, which were all she could do when she had a family to care for. She was the 'tea lady' and seemed to do a bit of everything. She liked the company but she said she missed Kathy and she always sent a sixpence wrapped in a scrap of tissue paper in the letter, which was signed off with her love and three big XXX's.

Autumn turned to winter and the weather grew cold. Lena gave Kathy the coat Elaine had worn last winter, now outgrown. It had a little fur collar and was very snug and warm. The swapped homework exercises that Miss Hart set Kathy and Elaine were proving effective. The two girls had formed a truce over the shared work and although they had not become close they had begun to respect one another, each of them recognizing her own shortcomings. Chris was the bond in their tenuous relationship. He was an easy-going, good natured boy, taking everything in his stride and when he saw that the girls were having difficulty in communicating he took charge, teaching them how to laugh at themselves and at each other without malice.

Kathy continued to adore him.

Lena suggested that Mary O'Connor might like to come and spend Christmas with her daughter at Magpie Farm. Kathy was thrilled by the idea and Lena wrote and invited her, but Mary wrote back thanking Lena but saying that sadly it wouldn't be possible. Both Brady boys were to get leave for Christmas and she would have to be at home for them.

'After all,' she wrote, 'who knows where they'll be by this time next year. And I know my Kathy is safe and happy with you.'

Kathy tried hard to hide her disappointment but in the privacy of her little room she cried herself to sleep on the night the letter came. She imagined she kept her feelings hidden, but Lena was all too aware of how upset the little girl was and one Saturday morning in mid-January when she took the farm pick-up truck and drove off into town she refused to tell the children where she was going. At dinner time, coming in from a walk to the village with Chris and Elaine, Kathy was riveted by the sound of a familiar voice as she took off her outdoor clothes in the lobby. Opening the kitchen door she stood, speechless with excitement at the sight of her mother sitting at the table drinking tea with Lena.

Mary got up from the table to envelop her daughter in a hug.

'Well, well, just look at you. You've grown so you have, and you've got such lovely rosy cheeks. Sure I'd hardly have known you.'

That afternoon Kathy showed her mother everything: she proudly escorted her round the farm and took her down to the village to see all the places she had come to love, not to mention her school.

'You're lucky to get a nice place like Magpie Farm,' Mary remarked. 'You are happy here, aren't you, love?'

Kathy nodded. 'Auntie Lena is lovely. She made me a special tea on my birthday and Mrs Harris made me a cake with ten pink candles on it.'

'And you get along all right with the other children?' Kathy nodded and Mary smiled and nudged her. 'Especially that Christopher, eh? Sure and isn't he the handsome lad? Ah – I can see you think so.'

Kathy blushed. 'Oh, Mum – don't tease me!'

'And do you ever get to Mass?'

Kathy shook her head. 'There's no Catholic church here,' she said. 'But I do try to remember my prayers.' She looked up at her mother with big blue eyes. 'You don't think Jesus will forget me, do you?'

Mary smiled and put an arm around her daughter, hugging her close. 'How could he forget my Kathy?' she said. 'Just remember at the end of your prayers to say, *please don't forget me* and I'll be sure to light a candle for you every Sunday. Jesus will understand. For now that will have to do, love.'

That night when the children were in bed and James had gone down to the Turf Cutters' Arms for his weekly Saturday evening pint and game of darts Lena and Mary sat together in the cosy sitting-room. As

Lena poured them each a glass of sherry Mary thanked her hostess for all she was doing for her daughter.

'I can't tell you what a relief it is to know she's safe and happy,' she said. 'And she looks so well.' She sighed. 'It was so terrible hard to part with her. Till she was five it was just the two of us and you get very close to your child when you bring her up alone.' She lowered her eyes. 'I know I did wrong in having her when I wasn't married. Her father came from the next village. He was already married when he courted me, though he forgot to mention it at the time. I lived in a village much like this one in County Limerick, and when I found I was expecting his child I had to leave to save my family from the disgrace. That was when I came to London. It was hard, scratching a living with cleaning jobs here and there – finding someone who'd look after Kathy when I wasn't there. When I married Jim Brady I was run down and close to desperation.' She shook her head. 'Little did I know I was jumping out of the frying pan into the fire! His two boys were in their early teens then. Talk about a handful! And Jim was no better. Not so bad sober but when he was in drink. . . .' She threw up her hands. 'The devil incarnate! The one good thing was that he knew how to keep the boys in line. He'd only to start unbuckling his belt to bring them to order. But once he'd gone and I was left alone with them they went wild. I couldn't do nothing with them. Into everything they were – thieving; getting into fights; knocking round with a rough crowd. I was at my wits' end. And poor little Kathy. They made her life a misery, God love her.'

'You've had a hard life,' Lena said.

Mary shrugged. 'Oh, no worse than a good many women where I come from, I dare say,' she said. 'All I hope is that the army will put the lads on the straight and narrow. After the war things will be better. They'll get good jobs and Kathy and I can start thinking about making a better life for ourselves.'

Privately Lena thought Mary was being over optimistic. After all, they had the war to win first. The news wasn't good. Everything was in Hitler's favour. He had a vast army and air force and seemingly endless resources whilst England was so ill-prepared. The future looked bleak.

'Why don't you leave London and come here to be with Kathy till the war's over?' she suggested.

Mary shook her head. 'I'm earning better money now that I can work full time,' she said. 'And with the lads gone I can put a bit away each week. When the war's over I want to make a better home for Kathy – maybe if she passes the scholarship exam I'll let her stay on at school and get a good education.' She opened her handbag and produced an envelope. 'Please, I want you to get her some winter clothes and maybe buy her a present from me; shoes too. I know how fast she grows out of them. You've been ever so kind, passing things down to her from your own girl. Nicer things than I could ever afford.' Lena shook her head.

'There's no need, really.' But Mary was adamant.

'I could have brought some of her other clothes with me,' she said. 'But I guessed she have grown out of them by now.' She looked at Lena. 'Between you and me, there's a desk job going at the Food Office. I've put in for it and I reckon I've a good chance. Just because I've always been a cleaner doesn't mean I'm stupid. My da' made sure I went to school regular until I was fourteen. I know I can do it. If I get it I mean to get my Kathy the best, to make up for all she's had to go without, so please take this for now and I hope there'll be more to come.'

Touched, Lena took the envelope. 'I'll do as you say,' she promised. 'But I know that you have nothing to reproach yourself with. You've been a good mother and always done your best. No one can do better than that.'

The weekend visit was over all too soon and on Sunday afternoon Kathy drove into Northampton with Lena in the farm truck to see her mother off on the London train. Kathy clung to her as the train drew in.

'You will write, won't you, Mum?'

' 'Course I will, darlin'.'

'And you won't forget to light a candle for me like you said?' she whispered.

'I won't forget.'

Kathy waved till the train was out of sight and Lena had to swallow hard at the lump in her throat as she took Kathy's cold little hand in hers.

'Come on, dear,' she said. 'It's cold here on the platform. Tell you what, why don't we go into the buffet and have a cup of tea and a bun?'

*

When Hitler failed to invade England or send bombs or poison gas attacks to annihilate London's population many of the children went home, collected or sent for by relieved parents. Things quietened down in the village as the spring of 1940 came in and although many of the evacuees remained and the school was still full beyond its capacity, outside classes were no longer necessary.

James and Lena Spicer listened avidly to the news every evening after the children had gone to bed. Things looked bad but they did their best not to let their family see how worried they were. In late spring the weather was good. Not so the war news.

In May both Belgium and Holland surrendered to Germany and soon after came the devastating British defeat at Dunkirk. Mussolini declared war on the Allies and threw Italy's lot in with Hitler. And the pictures in the national newspapers of German troops parading down the Champs-Élysées sent shivers of dread down Lena's spine. She knew then that what she had been dreading closer to home would happen and a few days later her worst fears were confirmed.

'I'm going to volunteer,' James declared one evening as he turned the wireless off. 'I can't stay here when everyone is out there fighting for our country.'

Lena reached out a hand to him. 'I know how you feel, but you're doing valuable war work here on the farm.'

'There are plenty of people who can do it just as well as me. Fred's going. He'll be called up anyway soon. I'll find a farm manager – maybe an older chap, and I'll apply to the Min' of Ag' for some land girls,' he told her. 'There's even talk of extending the school holidays so that the children can help with the harvest and potato picking so farm work won't suffer.'

Lena sighed. 'You've got it all worked out, haven't you?'

He nodded and pulled her close. 'I know you'll hate it but I have to do it darling. I'll only despise myself if I don't. We all have to pull together in times like this. My conscience just won't let me sit back.'

But when James came back from the recruiting office later that week Lena knew by the look on his face that he'd been turned down. She tried hard not to let him see the relief she felt.

'Was it because of the farm?' she asked.

He shook his head. 'A heart murmur,' he said bitterly. 'I had a medical and would you believe it that fool of a doctor said I had a heart murmur. It's ridiculous. I've never had a day's illness in my life. I'm as fit as the next man – fitter!'

'Nevertheless, I think you should go and get it checked by our own doctor.'

'Rubbish!' He stood up abruptly and strode out of the room. 'There's nothing wrong with me,' he growled over his shoulder as the door slammed behind him. Lena sighed. Why were men so stubborn when it came to their health?

In the end, as a compromise, James joined the Home Guard and took it in turns with the other members to keep watch for parachutists in the scout's hut all night, armed with the rifle he used on the farm for shooting vermin.

On July the first there was even more worrying news: Germany had invaded the Channel Islands.

'My God! They're almost here,' Lena whispered.

James shook his head. 'The Islands are closer to France than to us,' he said, trying to sound reassuring. 'Because they speak our language doesn't mean they're part of England.'

But Lena wasn't convinced, especially when in August the Luftwaffe began daring raids on British airfields.

The Spicer children and Kathy helped with the harvest when school broke up for the summer holidays. All the family worked late into each evening in the extra daylight 'double summertime' gave them.

Kathy discovered that she loved working in the open air, and the sunshine and fresh air seemed to make her blossom. Her skin turned golden brown from the fresh air and sun, her eyes shone with health and she put on weight. Lena saw with satisfaction that her young charge was turning into a strong, hearty child and losing the pale, pinched look she had arrived with.

The day came when Fred Harris had to leave his job and family to join his army unit. Looking strange and uncomfortable in his uniform, he came to say goodbye to everyone at the farm on the morning of his departure. All that day Joan was unusually silent, dabbing away the occasional tear as she went about her work. All three of her evacuee children had gone back to London.

'We'll be rattlin' round that cottage like peas in a colander now that my Fred's gone too,' she complained. 'I'm sure them cows won't milk nearly s'well for them slips of girls as they did for my Fred.'

She was referring to the land girls, three of them allotted to Magpie Farm by the Ministry of Agriculture to help generally on the farm. Jane, Phyllis and Pat arrived on their bicycles early every morning from the hostel where they lodged and, contrary to Joan's dire warnings, the cows seemed to perform for them well enough.

When the new term began Elaine and Kathy moved up into Mrs Spicer's class and prepared for the 'scholarship' examination, which would take place the following March. It seemed strange to Kathy to have 'Auntie Lena' as her teacher, but she soon learned that in class as Mrs Spicer, Lena was a totally different person from the 'Auntie Lena' she knew at home. She was strict, but fair and kind and made lessons seem interesting and exciting, Kathy soon grew used to the situation and enjoyed being taught by her.

It was soon after the beginning of the term that the first devastating air raid on London took place. Lena would have preferred to keep the news of it from Kathy but there was no chance of that. All the children at school were full of it. It took place on a Saturday and two of the London children had gone home to spend that weekend with their families. Neither returned and the rumour quickly spread that they had been killed in the raid. Next morning at Assembly Miss Weller, the headmistress broke the news as gently as she could to the children that their schoolmates had indeed lost their lives along with their families in the bombing.

Kathy was deeply shocked and upset. One of the children had been Sheila Brown, her best friend.

All that day she was quiet, keeping her tears at bay but at home time she hurried out of the classroom and set off along the lane alone. After a few minutes she heard running footsteps and looking round she saw Elaine trying to catch her up.

'Wait for me.' The other girl arrived at her side panting breathlessly. 'What's your hurry?' She looked at the tears on Kathy's cheeks. 'What's the matter – why are you crying?'

'Sheila's dead. She got – got killed,' Kathy choked. 'She was always my best friend. She lived near us at the "buildings" and we started school on the same day.'

'Oh – I'm sorry.' A subdued Elaine walked along beside her for a few minutes, glancing at her sideways from time to time. 'If you like I could be your best friend now,' she ventured at last.

Kathy turned to stare at her, her eyes huge and tear-filled. 'But – you don't even like me,' she said.

'I helped you with your English, didn't I?' said Elaine, stung.

'Only because Miss Hart said you had to.'

'You helped me too – with my arithmetic so that makes us even.'

'Yes, I know, but. . . .'

Elaine put her hand in her pocket and produced two squares of chocolate. She passed one to Kathy. 'D'you know what?' she said. 'I've always wanted a sister. Oh, Chris is all right but I've always thought a sister would be fun.' She munched thoughtfully on her chocolate. 'I like you being here now. We could pretend to be sisters if you like, couldn't we?'

Kathy was astonished. She couldn't speak for the lump that filled her throat. 'I always wanted a sister too,' she said.

'That's all right then.' Elaine took her hand. 'Come on, let's go and see if Mrs Harris has made scones for tea.'

It had been decided at the beginning of the school year that St Mark's Church School would put on a concert for Christmas, the proceeds of which were to go to the war effort and plans began to take shape as soon as the children returned to school.

Miss Hart was to produce the show. She was musical and always played the piano for Assembly as well as taking a dancing class on Saturday mornings. Everyone in the village was roped in to help. James and Chris Spicer volunteered to paint scenery and Joan Harris promised to be there on the night to provide refreshments in the interval. Lena was to be wardrobe mistress and other teachers were to provide some of the scripted material. The principal performers were chosen for their singing and dancing talent but all of the children were to take part, from the smallest infant up to the older ones.

Elaine and Kathy were delighted to be chosen to do a Laurel and Hardy sketch; Elaine's slim figure padded out as Oliver Hardy, whilst Kathy took the part of willowy Stan Laurel. They were to sing 'The Land of the Lonesome Pine' and perform a slap-stick cookery act involving much flour and water. Watching them practice it at home, relegated to the farm yard so as not to make a mess indoors, Chris – watching through the kitchen window, almost split his sides laughing.

And when he saw them wearing the costumes Lena had made for them, with bowler hats and baggy trousers he was almost speechless.

Everyone put in hours of work after school each day and the dress rehearsal took place on the day before Christmas Eve in the Village Hall.

Mary had been persuaded to join them for Christmas this year but they kept the concert a secret from her. She arrived on the afternoon of Christmas Eve and after tea she was taken along to the hall and seated mysteriously in a front row seat, reserved specially for her. She was entranced by the whole show and clapped till her hands stung at the Laurel and Hardy sketch. At the end when all the children assembled on stage for the finale and sang 'The White Cliffs of Dover' her eyes filled with tears and her throat was too tight to join in the chorus with the rest of the audience.

Later she was full of praise for the effort everyone had put in. As for Kathy, she could hardly believe that her shy little daughter could have found the confidence to stand on the stage, acting and singing in front of all those people.

'She's growing up,' she said to Lena later with a hint of wistfulness in her voice. 'You've done wonders with her so you have.'

Fred Harris was home on leave for Christmas, sporting a lance corporal's stripe on his sleeve. James guessed that it meant he was due for embarkation overseas shortly but he kept the speculation to himself. On Christmas Day the four Spicers, Kathy and her mother and the Harris family all sat down to Christmas dinner together. One of the largest turkeys Kathy had ever seen, specially fattened on the farm sat in the centre of the big kitchen table to be ceremoniously carved by 'Uncle James' There were crackers and a rich, delicious plum pudding made by Joan Harris, who had been saving dried fruit for it all year. After dinner they all went into the living-room where there was a big log fire and a Christmas tree bedecked with coloured baubles and a present for everyone.

But in spite of the fact that Mary clearly enjoyed herself, Lena was worried about her. She looked so drawn and weary. When they were alone, sharing the washing-up in the kitchen Lena asked how she was coping with the bombing. Mary shrugged.

'Much the same as everyone else, dear,' she said. 'It's bad but it's the same for all of us and we all help one another. You can't beat the spirit of the East Enders. It'll take more than a little German house painter with a moustache to break the people of London.'

She was able to stay for four days and Lena made sure she had plenty of good food and rest while she was there. Seeing her onto a troop-packed train on the Sunday afternoon, where it was clear that she would have to stand for the whole journey she squeezed her arm.

'Mary – do think again about joining us at Beckets Green,' she whispered, quietly so that Kathy wouldn't hear. 'Kathy worries about you, especially since her little friend Sheila was killed.' Mary shook her head.

'I'm so tempted,' she said. 'Especially after the lovely time I've had with all of you, but I'm determined to try and stick it out now that I've got a better job and I'm earning good money. Even old Hitler can't keep it up this bad for ever. This is the first chance I've ever had to put a bit of money away for the future. If my Kathy gets that scholarship I mean to let her stay on and get the education she deserves. God knows we have to try and get some good things out of this wicked war.' She looked at Lena. 'I've been thinking – will you start a building society account for her here with the money I'll send you? I don't want my hard-earned cash going up in smoke if the London banks get bombed.' She smiled and kissed Lena's cheek. 'Thank you so much for everything, darlin',' she said. 'And I'll try to reassure Kathy that I'm safe when I write.'

All winter long the blitz raged relentlessly. The Luftwaffe was bombing all of England's major cities now as well as London. More evacuees arrived and were squeezed in where ever possible. Joan was glad to have more children to care for and the school wasn't as overwhelmed as it was at the beginning of the war.

Mary continued to write Kathy cheerful letters. She passed on the news that Charlie and Bill Brady had been sent out to North Africa so they wouldn't be coming home on leave again for some time. She told of how she and all her neighbours at the flats would get up when the siren went and go down to the underground station to sleep. She urged Kathy not to worry because it was very safe down there, so deep under ground. She wrote of how some people would organize sing-songs and other entertainment and how much fun and comradeship there was. She didn't mention the overcrowding and the lack of sleep, nor the gruelling tiredness that most people suffered. She didn't tell of walking to work in the morning, dizzy from lack of sleep to find your place of work bombed out or emerging from the shelters to find your home and belongings reduced to a pile of rubble.

Lena wrote to her, urging her once again to get out of London. She invited her to stay at the farm until she could find work and a place to live. But Mary's reply was always the same. London was where she belonged. She sent the promised postal order every week for Lena to buy whatever Kathy needed, the rest to go into the building society account.

Don't worry about me, she wrote. *This is my chance to build for a better future for Kathy and me.*

During the weeks preceding the examination all the 'scholarship' children worked hard under Lena's guidance. She had a good record at St Mark's School for getting a high percentage of the children through. Not all of them chose to take up their places at the grammar school. Although the school places would be free, some parents could not face the expense of keeping their child on at school for at least another three years, especially those who had large families. Often Lena's heart ached for the wasted opportunity of a particularly bright child who was withdrawn from school, but year by year things seemed to be improving and more places were taken up.

She gave all the children homework each evening, concentrating individually on each child's weakest subject. This year she was especially keen for Kathy to do well. She and James could afford to pay for Elaine to attend the girls' high school privately if she failed the exam and it was a foregone conclusion that they would take up that option if necessary. She hated the thought of Elaine going without Kathy. In spite of the rocky beginning when Elaine had resented sharing her family and home with an evacuee she and Kathy now seemed to be good friends, in fact Kathy became more and more like a member of the family as the months went by.

On the day of the exam both girls were nervous. Joan insisted that they both ate a good breakfast.

'You can't expect them brains o'yours to work proper-like on empty bellies,' she told them. 'That old tractor out there don't go if it don't 'ave no petrol in the tank, do it?'

The girls laughed at Joan's homespun simile but neither of them felt hungry. However, Joan stood over them until they had eaten enough to satisfy her.

Lena left for school early to make sure that the classroom was ready for the exam, the girls following half an hour later. As they passed the bus stop outside the post office they passed Chris who was waiting for the bus to school.

'Good luck!' he called out. 'In September you'll be waiting for the bus with me.'

'As if I'd be seen waiting for the bus with you!' said Elaine, walking on haughtily. Kathy hung back a little.

'Do you really think we'll pass, Chris?' she asked.

' 'Course you will.' He put a hand in his pocket and held something out to her. 'Here,' he said quietly, glancing up and down the road. 'Quick, take it before the others come. It's my lucky penny – to bring you luck.' He pushed it into her hand, his cheeks turning pink and then turned away abruptly. Almost too surprised to speak, Kathy muttered thanks and walked on, the penny still warm in her hand. He had shown her the lucky penny with a hole in it once before. He'd found it, he told her, turned up by the plough in one of the fields a long time ago. He always made sure he had it with him when he took his exams, and he'd lent it to her – his precious lucky penny. He'd chosen *her* and not his sister. He must like her a bit then, mustn't he?

The classroom looked odd with the desks rearranged to seat one pupil per desk and the twelve candidates filed in and sat down with fluttering hearts. Suddenly it was time to turn over the first paper and begin and after that nerves were forgotten as concentration took over.

The morning passed quickly with a short break in the middle, during which they were told not to discuss the exam papers with each other. Kathy found each of the subjects brought its own challenge, though she found it less daunting than she had expected. Even the English paper presented no insurmountable problems. At last the teacher who was invigilating looked up.

'Time is up, children,' she said. 'Put down your pens and turn your papers over. The exam is now finished.'

Kathy had just completed the last sentence of the grammar section. She heaved a sigh of relief, carefully blotted her paper and turned it face-down on the desk.

In the cloakroom she and Elaine faced each other. 'How did you get on?' Kathy asked.

Elaine grinned. 'Better than I thought. What about you?'

'The same. I'm glad it's over though.'

'Me too. It's nice that we've got the afternoon off,' Elaine said. 'What shall we do?'

Kathy buttoned her coat and reached for Elaine's hand. 'Someone said there are primroses out in Hayford Wood,' she said. 'Let's go and see if we can get some for Auntie Lena, shall we?'

In the week before St Mark's Church School broke up for the summer holidays it was announced at Assembly that eight out of the twelve children who had sat the 'scholarship' examination had been successful. Two boys had won places at the Boys' Grammar School and six girls were to go to St Ursula's High School. As they stood side by side Elaine reached for Kathy's hand and squeezed it hard as the names were read out. Elaine's name was second on the list, Kathy turned to smile at her. Five more names were read out by Mrs Weller, the headmistress. Kathy's heart sank, convinced that she was going to be one of the four who hadn't passed, then Mrs Weller looked up with a smile.

'And I have great pleasure in announcing that the final place has been won by one of our evacuees, Kathleen O'Connor.' Her eyes sought out a pink-cheeked Kathy and she smiled. 'Well done, Kathy and congratulations to you all.'

'Mum must have known already,' Elaine said as they filed out of the hall to their classrooms. 'Fancy making us wait!'

But Kathy knew that Auntie Lena would never have done anything as unfair as to have told them in advance. She was still reeling with a heady mixture of excitement and disbelief. Just wait till Mum heard. She'd be so proud of her clever daughter. Secretly, though, Kathy was convinced that it was nothing to do with cleverness, it was all down to Chris's lucky penny.

CHAPTER THREE

The first term at St Ursula's school was a revelation to Kathy. She was now in a 'form' instead of a class and in the evenings she did 'prep' instead of homework. Playtime was now 'break' and arithmetic: 'maths'. She loved it all, especially the smart new uniform of navy gymslip and white blouse, not to mention the navy blazer and hat with its distinctive purple and yellow band.

At morning prayers in the great hall most of the teachers stood on the platform wearing caps and gowns.

'It shows that they've graduated from university,' Elaine told her. 'The ones who don't wear them have just been to teacher training college. I asked Mum and she told me.'

Both girls were in the same form and at the end of term Kathy was surprised to find that she had achieved top place. Elaine, who came second, was slightly resentful.

'I should have been top,' she said, her lower lip thrust out. 'My mum is a teacher.'

'I only got two more marks than you,' Kathy pointed out. 'For my arith ... er – maths.' She had found the new subjects of algebra and geometry exciting and challenging and had picked both up quickly, whilst Elaine still struggled. 'You got lots more marks than me for English.'

In December came the momentous news that Pearl Harbor had been bombed which resulted in America joining Great Britain and the allies against Germany and Japan. James Spicer learned that part of his farm land was to be requisitioned for an American air base and in the spring of 1942 the Eighth Air Force arrived in the village and Bomber Command began its relentless raids on German industrial sites. At last the news was encouraging.

That summer the days were long and warm. The children helped get the harvest in once more, pausing to lean on their pitchforks at dusk to watch as the American 'Flying Fortresses' took off in great roaring waves, flying off on their nightly missions to unknown destinations. Most of the airmen were very young and many, especially the country-bred boys were homesick. With the help of Joan Harris, whose soft heart went out to the boys so far from their homes and families, the Spicers entertained the American boys in twos and threes to Sunday tea at the farm. Occasionally there would be faces missing after a big operation. There was no need to ask questions but Lena never quite got used to their abrupt departure.

James enjoyed comparing notes about farming methods, especially with two of the boys who came from Kansas farming families. But the three children were fascinated by their glamorous accent, hitherto only heard at the cinema, and they certainly enjoyed the treats they brought; things that were rarely seen in the shops now: tinned fruit, sweets and chewing gum and, delight of delights, the occasional tub of ice cream, now unobtainable in England.

Mary joined them again for Christmas 1942, hardly able to recognize her daughter, grown so tall and smart in her school uniform. Lena noticed that Mary looked even more tired than before, although she insisted that she was fine.

'We're all in the same boat,' she said. 'And the spirit is wonderful – everyone helping their neighbours.' She smiled. 'You know, it sounds awful but in a lot of ways the war has brought out the best in folks,' she said. 'People who've never spoken to their neighbours before have taken them in when they were bombed out. And look at me. I'd still have been a cleaner if it hadn't been for the war, yet here I am working as a clerk and earning good money. Never thought I'd see the day.'

Lena sighed. 'Well, now that the Americans have joined forces with us we won't have long to wait before it's all over.'

James, overhearing the conversation, said nothing. Church bells may have rung out in November to celebrate the victory in El Alamein but as far as he could see the allies still had a huge task on their hands. Fred Harris, now a corporal, had been one of the survivors of the disastrous failed Dieppe offensive in August. He was lucky to have escaped with minor injuries. Now the Japanese were a force to be reckoned with in Burma. In James's opinion they would have to wait a long time for the longed-for peace.

In July 1943 Kathy and Elaine celebrated the end of their first year at St Ursula's School. The uniform that Kathy had worn with such pride was taken off with relief and hung at the back of the wardrobe. There were to be two weeks' extra holiday this summer so that children could help with the farm work.

In October Kathy would be fourteen, and already the signs of approaching adulthood were beginning to be apparent. Her body was changing. Although still slender she could see the changes every time she undressed. At first she felt like a freak and tried to hide her burgeoning womanhood until she realized that Elaine was going through all the same changes. Lena gently encouraged both girls to take pride in their new femininity. She talked to both girls frankly about the facts of life, although, living on a farm most of these things came naturally.

'I thought all that was just for the animals,' Elaine remarked.

Lena laughed. 'We're all basically animals,' she said. 'But human beings are civilized. We have pride and dignity and we should show respect for one another as well as ourselves and our bodies.'

Kathy and Elaine spent long hours shut up in Elaine's bedroom, sprawling on the bed and talking about their hopes and dreams – what they wanted from life and what they would do when they left school. Elaine wanted to be a teacher like her mother; Kathy hadn't yet made up her mind. The one thing she was sure of was that she would not make the same mistakes as her mother, falling in love with the wrong men and spending her life struggling to pay the price and make ends meet.

Their conversations inevitably included boys, although being at an all-girls school the only boys they came into contact with were grammar-school boys they met at the bus stop and the friends Chris sometimes brought home, most of whom ignored them completely.

'Chris is getting very good looking, isn't he?' Kathy remarked casually one afternoon.

Elaine sat up and stared at her. 'Chris? My brother, Chris, you mean? You *must* be joking!'

Kathy turned away to hide her reddening cheeks. 'No. I think he's very handsome.'

Elaine laughed. 'Kathy O'Connor! I do believe you've got a crush on him! Just wait till I tell him.'

'*No!*' Kathy sprang up, her heart beating wildly. 'Promise me you won't say anything – *please!*'

'Oh, all right. Keep your hair on.'

'I only said I thought he was quite nice looking.'

'OK – if you say so.'

'So – promise not to tell?'

Elaine cast her eyes up to the ceiling. 'Well – what's it worth?'

'I've got a bar of chocolate in my drawer. You can have that.'

'Mmm.' Elaine slowly shook her head. 'I'd give anything to see his face when I told him. A bar of chocolate won't do it.'

'No – please.' Kathy searched her mind for something Elaine might consider worth her silence. 'Look,' she said at last in desperation. 'You can have the silver bracelet Mum gave me for Christmas.'

Elaine looked surprised. 'Ooh! You *are* worried, aren't you? OK then, let's have a look at it.'

Reluctantly Kathy went to her room and returned with the bracelet. Elaine slipped it onto her wrist, holding it out to look at it. 'OK. It's our secret,' she said with a grin.

It was true that Chris was good looking. Now sixteen, his shoulders were broadening and he was growing tall like his father. He was doing well at school having just passed his school certificate examination with distinctions. His ambition was to go to university to study law. James was infinitely proud of his son; disappointed of course that he showed no interest in taking on the farm when the time came for him to retire, but happy that good-natured Chris was always more than willing and happy to help with the work when ever he could.

This summer he could see so many changes in his son. The hard physical work had developed his muscles and strengthened his long straight back. Working long hours in the open air had bleached his already fair hair golden and his eyes shone a brilliant blue against his tanned skin.

'Won't be long before our Chris is breaking a few female hearts,' he remarked to Lena one evening over their bedtime drink.

She smiled, keeping to herself the fact that she'd noticed one partic-ular female heart that was already beating faster on his account. She'd noticed how eager Kathy always was to work beside Chris; how quick she was to fetch him a drink of water when he was hot and how she always managed somehow to wangle a seat beside him when Lena took their midday lunch out to the fields. For his part Chris was as blissfully unaware of it as James clearly was. But then that was men for you, she told herself with a smile.

'What are you smiling at?' James asked her.

'Nothing.' Lena took the mugs to the sink and rinsed them. Just you chaps and the way you never see what's right under your noses, she added to herself.

All too soon the end of the extended summer holidays approached and Lena dug the uniforms out from the back of the wardrobes and checked them for fit. The girls' gymslips needed letting down and she could scarcely believe how short Chris's uniform trousers were when he tried them on for her. He had spent all summer in shorts and she hadn't realized how much he had grown. His blazer was tight and too short in the sleeves too. She would dearly have liked to buy new for them all, but with clothing coupons and fabric shortages most mothers were reduced to attending the pre-term sales that most of the schools had organized when outgrown but not outworn uniforms could be recycled.

Both girls were promoted to the next form and were to begin the two-year study for school cert'. Kathy liked their new form teacher. Mrs Raye was young and recently married with a husband serving in the Navy. She was popular with the girls who admired her pretty face and slender figure and tried hard to model themselves on her.

It seemed hardly any time at all before half-term arrived. Mary had promised to get a few days off to visit and Lena had all kinds of plans for Christmas, which included some of the American boys who had become firm friends. On the first afternoon of the break Chris and the girls had gone into Northampton on the bus to the cinema as a special treat for Kathy's birthday. Lena had promised a special tea when they returned.

The moment they let themselves in through the back door Kathy sensed an atmosphere. It was unusual for the kitchen to be empty and as they passed through the hall a low buzz of voices came from the sitting-room. The girls went upstairs to take off their outdoor things, and as they started back down again, the sitting-room door opened and a grave-faced Lena stood at the bottom of the stairs.

'Elaine, will you go and put the kettle on, dear?' she said. 'Kathy, you have a visitor who wants to speak to you. Come in, please.'

With a quick glance at Elaine, Kathy followed Lena into the sitting-room. In the doorway she stopped, startled to see the dark-suited figure of Father Gerard from St Jude's sitting in the chair by the fireplace. When he saw her he stood up.

'Kathleen, my child.' He held out his hands. 'It's good to see you after all this time.' Taking her hands in his he glanced at Lena. 'Perhaps you would be kind enough to stay, Mrs Spicer.'

Lena nodded. 'Of course I will.'

Sensing that the priest had brought bad news Kathy's heart began to thump. 'Father – what is it – what's wrong?'

'Sit down, child.' Very gently Father Gerard drew her down onto the settee beside him. 'Kathleen – the day before yesterday there was a daylight air-raid warning in London. As it happened it was a false alarm, but people hurried to the Underground for shelter. Something happened – no one can be sure – someone must have tripped and fallen. Others fell on top – then more, like a human avalanche.' He shook his head. 'A terrible, tragic accident. A great many people were killed and injured without a single bomb being dropped.'

Kathy's hand flew to her mouth. '*Mum!*'

The priest pressed her hands between his. 'I'm afraid so, my child. I'm so sorry to be the bearer of such terrible news. I had to make the journey myself. I couldn't leave it to come through the usual channels. I would have come before but it took time to identify all of the...' He glanced at Lena. 'All of the casualties.' He took Kathy's stricken face between his hands. 'Kathy, your mammy was a good Catholic. Never a Sunday went by that she didn't attend Mass no matter how bad the bombing was. And she always stayed to light a candle for you. I know she'd have wanted me to come and tell you in person. It was the least I could do.'

Kathy was sobbing now. Lena sat beside her on the settee and drew her close. Looking over her head at the priest she said, 'Can I offer you a meal and a bed for the night, Father? It's getting late.'

He shook his head. 'Thank you, no. It's kind of you to offer but I have to get back to my parish. There is so much to do; so many people who need me and so many. . . .' he shook his head sadly and lowered his voice. 'so many funerals to arrange.'

'You'll let us know when – when it is to take place?' Lena asked softly.

He looked surprised. 'You'll bring her?'

'Of course,' Lena said. 'There's no question of that.'

The Spicer family sat round the tea table in silence that evening. None of them had any appetite for the food Lena had prepared. Kathy seemed numb, her face white and her lips trembling with shock. Later Lena took her a drink of hot milk and tucked her up in bed.

She slept for a while, waking with a start in the hope that it was all a bad dream and when the bleak realization crept back the tears began to flow. She tried to say her prayers like Mary had always taught her but it seemed to her that no one was listening tonight. '*I asked you not to forget me,*' she whispered. '*Mum said you wouldn't, but you did. You took Mum from me. Why did you have to do that? She never forgot you. It's not fair!*'

Anger and grief racked her body, making her throat and chest ache till she thought they would tear in two. To stifle her sobs she buried her head under the covers but after a few minutes she heard the door open softly. She felt the covers being drawn back as Elaine slipped into bed beside her. Neither of them spoke, but Kathy found a deep comfort in the other girl's closeness and, after a while, she slept. When she wakened in the morning Elaine had gone, but as she drew back the covers to get out of bed the morning sunlight glinted on something round her wrist. Somehow Elaine had slipped the little silver bracelet onto her arm when she was asleep. It was her way of saying what she could find no words for.

Father Gerard telephoned the following day to say that Mary's funeral would be in two days' time at St Jude's church, Hackney at two-thirty in the afternoon. Lena promised that Kathy would be there.

James was deeply concerned about Lena's intended visit to London.

'I know you feel you have to go for Kathy's sake,' he said. 'I know it's important for the child to be able to say a last goodbye to her mother, but you have your own family to think of.'

'I am thinking of you all,' Lena told him. 'I'm thinking that I'm so lucky to have you all with me. How lucky we all are here at Beckets Green. We've only had to get up for an air raid warning a few times when the German planes flew over to bomb the Midland cities. There's been hardly anything to disrupt our family life at all. This is something I can do to help. It's surely such a little thing when there's so much suffering in the world.'

James slipped to his knees beside her chair and took her hand. 'I know I don't often say this, Lena, but I love you more than anything else in the world. The idea of trying to live without you is unthinkable.' He pressed her hand to his cheek. 'If you were to be caught in another air raid. . . .'

'I have to go with her, James,' she said quietly.

He sighed. 'I know you do.'

'And Kathy will have to stay here with us now. She has no one else.'

'Naturally. That goes without saying, but we can talk about that later.' He stood up and raised her to her feet, holding her close and kissing her. 'I love you,' he whispered. 'so very, very much, and I'm proud of you, my darling. Never forget that.'

Kathy was quiet and tense in the train on the way to London. Joan Harris had picked flowers from her own garden, brightly coloured dahlias and chrysanthemums, tying them into a posy for Kathy to take to the funeral. She sat clutching it tightly in her hands.

They arrived at Euston Station and took the Underground to Liverpool Street. Lena noticed the signs of the nightly occupation that Mary had described on the platforms and she wondered if Kathy would be affected by them but the girl made no comment. It was only when they came up into the street and Kathy saw the devastation caused by the bombing that she showed any sign of emotion. She took in the bomb sites; the great expanses of fenced open ground where once here had been busy streets and the heaps of uncleared rubble, and her jaw dropped. Turning huge frightened eyes up to Lena, she whispered,

'It's horrible. It's all looks so different – like a place I've never been to before.'

As they walked they passed a half demolished house with shreds of wallpaper still fluttering from its broken walls in the breeze. There was half a staircase, going nowhere – a door hanging from its hinges. Looking at it felt like an intrusion. For some reason that Kathy didn't understand, it made her feel ashamed.

They found a café and Lena ordered them each a sandwich and a cup of tea, one of its two windows was criss-crossed with blast tape, the other, boarded up making the interior dim. They were only halfway through their snack meal when suddenly the siren sounded. The blood-curdling wail turned Kathy's knees to water and she looked at Lena with panic in her eyes.

'What shall we do?'

The other customers left quickly and the café owner, a middle aged woman in a print overall came out to fasten the door. She looked at them. 'Are you visitors?'

Lena nodded. 'We're here for a funeral.'

The woman nodded. 'Well, you're welcome to share our shelter,' she said. 'We always go down the cellar. There's only me this time o'day. The kids are at school. It's this way.'

They got up and followed the woman through to the living accommodation at the back of the café. She opened a door at the back of the staircase and switched on a light illuminating a flight of stairs. In the cellar there were chairs and bunk beds, a primus stove and cooking utensils. Lena looked round.

'It looks as though you've spent a lot of time down here,' she said. The woman smiled wryly.

'Home from home, you could say. The kids thought it was fun to start with – all an exciting game. They're sick of it now, like we all are.' She indicated the chairs. 'Have a seat. There's nothing for it but to sit it out.' She looked at her watch. 'What time's your funeral?'

Lena glanced at Kathy. 'Two thirty.'

'Where?'

'St Jude's Church, Hackney.'

The woman pursed her lips. 'Unless they hold it up I doubt if you'll make it,' she warned. 'Hackney's a way from here and it takes a while for the buses to get going again.' She caught sight of Kathy's face and added quickly, 'Let's just hope Jerry's in a hurry this time, eh?'

The raid was terrifying to Kathy. Although they were underground, they could hear the whine and impact of the bombs dropping. One or two seemed very close at hand, the bangs so loud that she clapped her hands over her ears, her heart racing wildly as she felt the ground tremble beneath her feet and bits of plaster from the ceiling fell into her hair. How could Mum have stood this night after night when she didn't have to stay? Lena put an arm around her and held her close.

'Try not to worry. It'll soon be over.'

Watching them, the woman, asked, 'Someone close, is it – the funeral, I mean?'

Lena nodded over the top of Kathy's head. 'Her mother,' she mouthed.

The woman nodded. 'Oh. Well, I hope Jerry hurries up and lets you get there in time.'

But by the time the 'all clear' sounded it was almost three o'clock. As the woman let them out through the café door she pointed. 'There's a bus stop on the other side of the street. Good luck. I hope you're not too late.' She smiled apologetically at Lena. 'I daresay I must seem hard to you, but we've lived with bad news and funerals for the past two years. The fact is, you get used to it in the end.'

St Jude's Church had been bombed twice. There was a hole in the roof, now covered by a tarpaulin and the bell tower and gallery at the back of the church had been so badly damaged they were out of use. A warning sign had been placed at the bottom of the stairway. The church was empty but they went in and sat in a pew at the front. Father Gerard appeared through a door at the side wearing his long black soutanne and biretta. He hurried over to them.

'I'm so sorry,' he said. 'We had to carry on with the service, raid or no raid. We always do. I take it you took cover?'

Lena nodded. 'I'm glad you did.'

He looked at Kathy, still clutching the now wilting posy. 'Were those for your mammy?' She nodded, tears welling up in her eyes. He patted her shoulder. 'I'm so sorry you missed the requiem mass, Kathleen. Wait there while I get you a little vase. You can put your flowers at the feet of Our Lady and then you can light a candle for your mammy. How's that?' Kathy nodded managing a smile and he hurried away to return a moment later with a small vase filled with water. As Kathy went off to perform her little ritual he slipped into the pew next to Lena.

'It was good of you to bring her,' he said. 'I'm sorry you were too late. We have so many funerals that we have no choice but to carry on, regardless of the bombs. If we didn't we'd never get anything done.' He sighed. 'It's a terrible business, this war.' He nodded towards Kathy. 'What will happen to her now?'

'She'll stay with us,' Lena told him. 'At least for the duration of the war. After that we'll have to see.'

He sighed. 'Poor child,' he said. 'Just at the age when she needs her mother. Ah well, there are so many more like her. All we can do is pray for them all.'

Kathy knelt in front of the statue and looked up into the serene face. She put the flowers into the little vase and then took a candle from the box and lit it. But the words she knew she should be saying just wouldn't come.

You let her down, a voice inside her accused. *She trusted in you and you let her down. She came every Sunday and she said her prayers to you every day. And I asked Jesus not to forget me, but he did. And you did too!* Getting to her feet she walked back to where Lena and Father Gerard sat.

'Can we go home now, Auntie Lena?' she said.

Later as they sat in the train on the way home, Lena asked Kathy, 'Why did you never tell us you were a Catholic?'

Kathy shrugged. 'Mum said not to when we were evacuated,' she said. 'There are some people who don't like us. Mum always said it was only because they don't understand, but that it'd be better not to mention it.'

Lena took her hand. 'Surely you knew that we weren't bigoted?'

Kathy shrugged. 'I didn't to begin with – not at first.' The ghost of a smile lifted one corner of her mouth. 'I bet Mrs Fenning was though.'

'Well, from now on we'll see that you get to your church on Sundays.'

Kathy shook her head. 'No,' she said firmly. 'I've decided. I don't want to go any more.'

It was late by the time the train arrived at Northampton. Lena went to a telephone box and rang James at the farm.

'I'll be there as soon as I can,' he said.

They waited in the cheerless waiting-room, shivering in the chill of the autumn night. After half an hour Lena suggested they move out to the forecourt and a few minutes later James arrived in the farm truck. As they got in, squeezing together on the front seat he looked at his wife over Kathy's head.

'Everything all right?'

She nodded, mouthing, 'Later.'

'I expect you're hungry. Joan made lentil soup and there's a casserole keeping warm in the Aga,' he told her.

But Kathy was too exhausted to eat anything when they got back to the farm. She managed a little soup before Lena tucked her up in bed with a hot water bottle and was asleep almost as soon as her head touched the pillow.

Downstairs in the kitchen as they sat opposite each other at the table James reached for Lena's hand. 'I'm glad you're back safe and sound.'

'There was a raid,' she told him. 'We had to take shelter and we missed the funeral.'

'Oh, no! So it was all for nothing?'

She shook her head. 'Not quite. We went to the church and Kathy said her goodbye and laid her flowers. I'm afraid her faith has taken a blow over this, but she'll recover. She needs us, James. We have to be here for her now.'

He squeezed her hand. 'And so we will be,' he promised. 'For just as long as it takes.'

CHAPTER FOUR

Kathy threw herself into her school work and received an excellent report at the end of term as well as coming top of her form again. Lena was pleased, though slightly worried that the girl was working too hard. She was afraid of a delayed reaction to her mother's death and sure enough the inevitable backlash came the following spring. One morning at breakfast Kathy suddenly rose from the table, her face chalk white.

'I – don't feel very. . . .' She got no further, her knees buckling under her. Chris leapt up from the table, tipping his chair over as he rushed to catch her before she hit the floor. He looked at her mother.

'What is it? What's wrong with her?'

Lena shook her head. 'She'll be fine. It's just a faint. Put her on the settee and don't crowd her.'

Kathy came round quickly, surprised to have created such concern. 'What happened?' she asked as Lena held a glass of water to her lips. 'I felt awful then everything went black.'

'You fainted,' Lena told her. She motioned to the others to leave them alone. 'Kathy, I think we should have a talk dear. You've been working too hard. I've noticed your bedroom light on far too late at night.'

'I must pass my school cert,' Kathy said. 'Mum would have wanted me to. I can't let her down.'

'And that's another thing.' Lena sat beside her on the settee. 'I don't think you've allowed yourself to come to terms with your mum's death. You haven't let yourself grieve properly.'

Kathy frowned. 'I didn't think you'd want me weeping all over the place.'

45

Lena shook her head. 'That's not what I mean. Grieving doesn't necessarily mean shedding buckets of tears. It's accepting that some-one has gone from your life, but allowing yourself to think about them, appreciating the relationship you had and remembering all the good times you had together. It's creating their memory if you like; making a little place in your heart where they'll always be waiting for you and you can visit and talk to them at any time. It's not shutting the door on them. I think that's what you've been trying to do, darling. It's painful and it doesn't work as you've just proved.'

Kathy looked at Lena for a moment then the tears welled up in her eyes. 'I miss her so much, Auntie Lena,' she said. 'If only she'd come to live with me here when you asked her to she'd still be alive. It was so hard to begin with. I was angry with Mum for staying in London when she didn't have to. It was as though she'd abandoned me and it hurt so much I just tried not to think about it, but I can see that what you say is right. I'll try and do it your way.'

'That's my good girl.' Lena drew her close and hugged her. 'I know one thing for sure: your mum wouldn't want you working so hard that you made yourself ill. So no more midnight oil, eh?' She looked into Kathy's face.

'No more midnight oil,' she promised.

'We're losing two of our land girls soon,' Lena reminded her. 'So as soon as you break up for the summer holidays it'll be Backs to the Land, as the government leaflets say.'

Kathy smiled, greatly cheered at the prospect. Working on the farm meant being close to Chris all day. If anything would cheer her up, that would.

As June began the news of D-day buoyed up everyone's spirits. School broke up in July and the Spicer family plus Kathy got down to plenty of hard work with the harvest along with Phyllis, the remaining land girl. Once Kathy adjusted her thoughts and came to terms with her mother's death she felt better. She began to look better too, especially when the fresh air and sunshine did their work on her pale skin and brightened her tired eyes.

For the first time Chris began to see her as an attractive girl and not just a likeable 'kid'. True, she was only the same age as his younger sister, but ever since the morning she had fainted over breakfast and he had caught her in his arms and carried her to the settee, he had felt something different for her. She was as light as a feather and had felt so soft and vulnerable in his arms. It made him feel strong and protective towards her. He was slightly embarrassed and ashamed of this new found softness in his nature. It made him gruff and off-hand with her. It also brought a blush to his cheeks when ever she was near; something that Elaine was quick to pick up on.

'You like Kathy, don't you – quite a lot.' she teased one day when she sat down next to her brother under a hedge out of the heat of the midday sun to eat their sandwiches.

He shrugged. 'She's OK I suppose.'

'Come off it!' She laughed. 'Just "OK" doesn't make you turn as red as a beetroot when ever she comes anywhere near you!'

'Don't talk rubbish!'

'There! See what I mean? You've gone scarlet again.' She pointed to his face and he got up quickly. 'Don't be such a stupid little kid,' he flung over his shoulder as he walked off in disgust.

Kathy joined Elaine and flung herself down on the ground. 'Phew! It's hot.' She glanced over to where Chris had settled some yards away. 'What's the matter with Chris?'

Elaine grinned. 'I think he's in love.'

Kathy's face dropped. 'Is he? Who with?'

Elaine tapped the side of her nose. 'Ah – wouldn't you like to know!'

The harvest was still in full swing when suddenly there was a new word in the air: Buzzbombs. It was the nickname Londoners gave to the V1 weapon that some said was Hitler's last ditch attempt at over throwing the allies. The new robot weapons certainly took their toll of war-torn Londoners who had considered the worst to be over. Once again all the 'safe' towns were inundated with evacuees. Lena moved the two girls in together and took in a small boy of eight who cried himself to sleep every night. His mother came down to Beckets Green most weekends but this only seemed to make young Stanley's homesickness worse. On one momentous evening one of the pilotless planes missed its target and flew over Beckets Green. The Spicer family, hearing the strange low throb of the engine went outside to see what was flying over. Looking up at the unfamiliar black shape they suddenly heard the engine stop abruptly and saw the red tail light go out. It was directly over the farm house and James shouted, 'My God, it's a V1! Inside everyone – under the stairs!' And a moment later as they huddled together in the capacious cupboard under the stairs they heard the crash. Later they discovered that the V1 had landed in one of the newly harvested fields, young Stanley trembling with fear in Lena's arms. The following Saturday his mother decided to take him home.

'Strikes me we ain't safe nowhere,' she said morosely. 'If your name's on it you're gonna get it wherever you are. We've already lost Stan's dad at Dunkirk and if we've gotta go too we might as well be together.'

In September a new robotic rocket weapon, the V2 was launched. This one was silent, which meant that there was no warning. Londoners were once again in the thick of it, but James was optimistic.

'The allies have liberated Rome and Paris this year,' he said. 'Hitler's finished and he knows it. This time next year we'll be celebrating victory. I'd stake my life on it.'

Just before Christmas Kathy and Elaine were summoned to the head-mistress's study just before 'home time'. Both stood outside the door in fear and trepidation and when her secretary opened the door and invited them both in together they were slightly mystified. Miss Redfern sat behind her desk, smiling reassuringly.

'I asked to see both of you together because I wanted to see how you felt about something I have in mind for you,' she said. 'There is no need for you to look so apprehensive. You are not in any kind of trouble. You may sit down.'

With relief both girls took a seat, sitting on the edge of the chairs the secretary pulled up for them.

'I am confident that you will both do well in your school certificate examination,' Miss Redfern went on. 'And I think you are both promising teaching material.' She leaned forward, clasping her hands together and searching both girls' faces. 'How would you view the prospect of studying to be a teacher? Does it appeal to you as a career?'

Elaine nodded eagerly. She had always wanted to be a teacher; Kathy had not been so sure – but that was before she met Mrs Raye. The young teacher had inspired her and made her see the profession in a different light. She looked at Elaine now and both girls nodded in unison. Miss Redfern smiled.

'That is very encouraging. Well, perhaps I should explain the situation to you. Depending on how many credits you get in your school certificate you will be entitled to go either to teacher training college or, if you were to receive a distinction, on to university where you would study for a degree. That, of course would take three years and so the choice would be up to you. Either way I would like you to think about it over the holiday.' She stood up to indicate that the interview was at an end. 'I am sure you will want to go home and discuss the prospects with your parents.' She put a hand on Kathy's shoulder, holding her back for a moment. 'I daresay you will prefer the quicker way my dear, under the circumstances,' she said quietly. 'And there are some very good scholarships available. You can be sure that St Ursula's will do all it can to help. Either way, a very rewarding career in teaching is highly recommended for you both. Good afternoon girls.'

Elaine chattered excitedly about the interview all the way home in the bus; Kathy, on the other hand, was quiet. Even if she did get one of the scholarships Miss Redfern had mentioned she could see no prospect of going to college. She had always known, even when Mum was alive that if she was lucky enough to get her school certificate she would have to leave and begin working for her living right away. The Spicers had been more than generous to her but she could not expect them to go on supporting her.

When they arrived home Elaine rushed into the kitchen like a whirlwind, her satchel flying one way, hat and scarf another. She poured out a garbled version of the interview the girls had had with the headmistress to her mother, her words tripping over each other in her excitement. Lena, who had already spoken to Miss Redfern, hugged her.

'Congratulations darling. Now you have something to work towards. You must be sure to study hard between now and the exam.' She looked over her daughter's head at Kathy who stood taking off her outdoor things. 'What about you, Kathy? Aren't you excited too?'

Kathy shook her head. 'I can't go to college,' she said.

Elaine turned to stare at her in amazement. '*Not go*? You never said. Why ever not?'

Kathy began to unpack her books from her satchel. 'I'll need to find a job if I'm lucky enough to get my school cert,' she said. 'I'm on my own now and I'll have to earn my own living.'

Elaine shook her head bemusedly. 'But you *can't* not go! Well, I'm not going without you, so that's flat. If you don't go then neither will I!'

Lena looked at her daughter. 'Go upstairs for a while, will you darling? Get your homework done before supper. I need to talk to Kathy.'

Elaine looked inclined to argue, but the look on her mother's face stopped her 'Oh – all right.' Reluctantly she picked up her satchel and left the kitchen.

Lena held out her hand to Kathy. 'Come and sit down,' she invited. Kathy sat down opposite her at the table. 'Don't you want to go to college, Kathy?' Lena asked gently. 'Don't you fancy teaching as a career?'

'It's not that. I'd love it.' Kathy met Lena's eyes. 'You and Uncle James have been so kind to me – to Mum too. You couldn't have done more if you'd been my own family, but I can't go on taking from you.'

Lena reached across the table and took her hand. 'Kathy – listen. One of the reasons – the *main* reason your mother stayed on in London through the blitz was to put money by for your future. Obviously she planned to share that future with you but sadly it wasn't to be. She asked me to open an account for you and she used to send me money from her wages every week. Some I used to buy you clothes and things you needed for school; she insisted on that. The rest was put away in the building society.' She got up and went to the dresser. Opening a drawer she took out a small blue pass book and gave it to Kathy. 'All that money is yours,' she said. 'It has gained in interest and I think there would be enough to see you through two years at college if you were careful.' She smiled. 'There's always work for you here on the farm in the holidays and a home to come to, of course.' She smiled. 'So – what do you say?'

Kathy looked at the weekly figures paid into the account and the final total. She had never seen so much money in all her life. She looked up at Lena.

'Mum saved all this – for me?'

'She was so proud of you – proud to be in a position to provide for you at last. She wanted to make up for all the things you went without as a little girl. She was so keen for you to do well and have a better start in life than she had. So you see, Kathy, you owe it to your mother's memory to go to college. This is your chance to make her efforts for you worthwhile.'

Kathy threw her arms round Lena, tears pouring down her cheeks. 'Thank you, Auntie Lena,' she mumbled, the lump in her throat almost choking her. 'Thank you so much.'

Christmas 1944 at Magpie Farm was the best Kathy could ever remember. Once again the decorations, carefully put away last year, were brought down from the attic and festooned all round the house. Lena complained that some of them looked the worse for wear, but nevertheless they were colourful and festive. James and Chris brought in fresh evergreens and a six foot fir tree which the girls trimmed with the glass baubles and some decorations they had made themselves. Finally James produced a bunch of mistletoe from one of the apple trees in the orchard and hung it triumphantly in the hall, grabbing Lena as she passed and kissing her soundly under its pale leaves and pearly berries.

This year Lena's parents were able to visit. They lived in Dorset where travel had been restricted for most of the war so it was something of a reunion. Margaret and Tom Lovell were delighted to be able to join in the festivities with their family once again. They could hardly believe how much their grandson and daughter had grown and welcomed Kathy to their family as though she was another granddaughter.

Over supper on the evening they arrived, they insisted on hearing all about their respective schools and what plans they all had for the future. Elaine told her grandparents about Miss Redfern's suggestion that she and Kathy apply for teacher training college. Then Chris, who so far had been quiet, spoke up.

'Another few months and I'll be able to join up,' he announced.

The remark was certainly a conversation stopper, everyone stopped eating to stare at him. James was the first to find his voice as he looked down the table at his son. 'If you get a place at Cambridge you'll probably get a deferment.'

Chris shook his head. 'I'd rather go as soon as I'm old enough and get it over with. Besides, I'd like to get in there while there's still some action going on.'

'You haven't even applied for a place at university yet,' Lena reminded him. 'I'm sure you'll get a place. Anyway, the war might soon be over. Everyone says it can't last more than another few months.'

'I read that all young men of eighteen will still be conscripted for a spell of National Service even after the war's over,' Chris told her.

'For how long?' his grandmother asked.

'Two years.'

'*Two years!*' Lena looked horrified. 'That's a terrible slice to take out of a boy's life just when he's studying for a career.'

'I'd soon catch up,' Chris told her mildly. 'Anyway I'd probably get the chance to go abroad – see places I've never seen before. I'm looking forward to it.'

His enthusiasm put a damper on the meal, the rest of which was a subdued affair.

It was early evening on Christmas Day before Kathy had a chance to give Chris the present she had bought for him. It was a pen and pencil set. She had wrapped it carefully and tied it with a green ribbon, but she hadn't put it under the tree with the rest of the presents because of Elaine's teasing. Instead she hid it in her coat pocket hanging in the hall, hoping to find an opportunity to catch him alone. She was coming downstairs just after tea when she saw him taking his overalls out of the hall cupboard ready to help his father with the evening milking. This was her chance. Her heartbeat quickening, she cleared her throat.

'Chris.'

He looked up. 'Yes?'

'I – I've got something for you.' She slipped her hand into her coat pocket where it hung on the hall stand and brought out the small parcel. 'I wanted to wait till I saw you alone because – because of. . . .'

'Because of my revolting sister,' he finished for her. 'I'm glad you did.' He looked down at the oblong parcel she thrust into his hand. 'What is it?'

'Open it and see,' she said. 'I – I hope you like it. It's to help – it's to use for your exams.'

He tore open the paper and opened the box. His cheeks coloured. 'Kathy! It's smashing. You shouldn't have. It must have cost an awful lot.'

She felt her cheeks colouring. 'That's all rig.

'Look – I wish I'd got something for you.'

'It doesn't matter – honestly. I wasn't expectir.
He was looking up at something and she followed
tipped up her face he suddenly bent and kissed her. F.
soft on hers and her heart drummed so fast that she w
hear it. He smiled down at her.

'That's what you're supposed to do, isn't it – under the
Christmas?' She was too overcome to reply and he looked a   .r
thoughtfully for a moment, then, 'But that was for Christma . This is
for my present.' He kissed her again, this time putting his arms around
her waist. She reached up to touch his cheek and felt the soft prickle of
his new beard against her fingertips. She thrilled at the feel of it. Then
the kiss was over and he was taking a step backwards and laughing
self-consciously.

'Better get these overalls on and get out to the milking parlour,' he
said, backing away. 'Dad'll wonder where I've got to.'

For the rest of the evening Kathy felt as though she was walking on
air. When James and Chris came in from milking they played charades
and roasted chestnuts round a fire blazing with fragrant applewood
logs. The girls were only allowed lemonade to drink, much to Elaine's
disgust, but James offered Chris a hot whisky toddy along with the
adults. It was a sure sign that he was now considered a young man.
Although Kathy stole the occasional glance at Chris, he refused to meet
her eyes. She wondered if he regretted kissing her, or whether he was
just embarrassed.

When she was getting ready for bed Elaine came in and sat on the
bed, watching Kathy brush her hair. 'Where did you get to after tea?'
she asked.

Kathy paused to look at her through the dressing table mirror. 'I
went upstairs.'

'Mum and I began to wonder if you were all right. You were an
awful long time.

'Was I?'

'You know jolly well you were.' Elaine paused. 'Chris was missing
too. Funny, that.'

'Chris was getting ready to help Uncle James with the milking.'

'Oh, you saw him then?'

He was getting his overalls out of the hall cupboard as I came downstairs.'

'Are you saying you didn't speak to him?'

'No, of course we spoke.'

'*Spoke*. Is that all?' The grin on Elaine's face stretched from ear to ear. 'Come off it, Kathy. He kissed you under the mistletoe, didn't he?' She waved a dismissive hand. 'Don't bother to deny it. I was coming to find you. I opened the sitting-room door and saw you, so I...' She pursed her lips and assumed a superior tone. 'I withdrew tactfully.'

Kathy turned to look at her. 'So – what do you want to keep quiet about it this time?'

Elaine laughed. 'Nothing, silly. I think it's sweet. I wish I had a boyfriend.'

'Chris isn't my boyfriend,' Kathy protested. 'He's more like a brother. Anyway, you and I have more important things to think about for the next few weeks.'

Elaine groaned. 'Ugh! Rotten exams you mean.'

Kathy nodded. 'Exactly, rotten exams – if you're serious about wanting to go to college.'

But in spite of her protests it wasn't exams that filled her dreams that night. And as for her thinking of Chris as a brother – nothing could have been further from the truth.

When the spring term began, Kathy, Elaine and Chris hardly had time for anything else but work. After the Easter break exam time arrived and there was the usual flurry of nerves and anxieties. Had they done enough? How hard would the questions be? Suppose they failed? This last thought was anathema. In order to attain the school certificate it was necessary to get pass marks in both English and maths. If either of those subjects was under par the whole exam would be null and void regardless of how good their marks were in other subjects. Both Kathy and Elaine worried over the prospect and each knowing their weakest subject they decided to revert to Miss Hart's suggestion that they help one another. Nevertheless, on the morning of the exam both were so nervous that they could hardly breathe as they stood outside the examination room, pens and rulers clutched in shaking hands as they waited to be admitted.

No sooner was the exam over than the end of the war was declared;

a double cause for celebration in the Spicer household. Plans had been in progress for the village festivities for weeks. There was to be a bonfire and fireworks on the village green and a tea for the children in the church hall which would be contributed to and supervised by all the village mothers. Later there would be a dance; the bar would be laid on by the landlord of the Turf Cutters' Arms and the refreshments organized by Joan Harris. Fred Harris had been quite badly wounded at the Rhine crossing and had been in a military hospital in York ever since. Joan, in her usual uncomplaining way had soldiered through it all. She had made the journey north to see him twice, taking the children at Christmas and staying over to be with him. Now she and her family were excitedly preparing to have him home again.

After the fireworks, during which an effigy of Hitler was tossed onto the bonfire amid loud cheers, the children were taken home to bed, meanwhile the village hall was cleared and local musicians prepared to play for the dancing. Some of the American airmen came to the dance and Kathy and Elaine were allowed to go, under Chris's guidance, with strict instructions to be home by eleven and no later. As they sat waiting for the dancing to begin Elaine nudged Kathy.

'See that boy over there?' she nodded. 'That's Nigel Oliver, Doctor Oliver's son. He's been away at a really posh school, Harrow, I think. He used to be a bit of a twerp when we were little kids at St Mark's together – skinny with knock-knees and specs but look at him now.'

Kathy followed her gaze and saw a tall, dark-haired boy of about seventeen with broad shoulders and flashing brown eyes. 'He doesn't look much like a twerp now,' she said with a smile.

'He doesn't, does he? He's not half bad and if he doesn't come and ask me to dance I'm going to ask him,' Elaine said.

Kathy laughed. 'You can't!'

'You reckon? Just watch me.'

The band struck up 'There Goes That Song Again' and Elaine waited a few seconds and then got to her feet. 'Right, that's it, I'm off,' she said, walking resolutely across the floor to where Nigel Oliver sat.

Kathy watched with amusement as she saw her friend bend down and whisper something in the boy's ear. Then she saw him smile and stand up, holding out his arms to her. A moment later as they quick-stepped past Kathy Elaine gave her a knowing wink over Nigel's shoulder.

She was still laughing when Chris arrived at her side. 'I thought you might like a drink,' he said handing her a glass of lemonade. 'What are you laughing at?'

'Your sister. She wanted to dance with that boy but he didn't ask her, so she asked *him*.'

He smiled and sat down beside her. 'That's Elaine for you. She's always known what she wanted.' He took a sip of his drink and Kathy noticed that it was a half-pint of lager. 'Actually, Nigel's not a bad chap,' he went on. 'I've just been talking to him. He's going to study medicine – plans to be a doctor like his dad, but like me, he's looking forward to doing National Service. We could even be in the army together.'

Kathy shuddered. 'It sounds horrible, but at least there'll be no more fighting.'

He turned to look at her. 'We're still fighting the Japs, you know.'

She turned horrified eyes on him. 'You mean you could be sent out to Burma or somewhere like that – to the jungle?'

He looked amused. 'Would you really worry about me?'

She blushed 'Well – I wouldn't like you to get hurt. I mean – I wouldn't like *anyone* to get hurt.'

'Oh – now you've spoilt it,' he said.

'Stop teasing me.'

'OK.' He finished his drink and looked at her. 'Do you want to dance? I warn you, I'm hopeless at it – two left feet.'

She smiled. 'I'll risk it.'

As it happened, Chris wasn't a bad dancer at all. Kathy enjoyed dancing with him. It was nice, having his arm around her waist and their steps seemed to fit together perfectly as they circled the floor to a romantic tune. When the lights were lowered so that 'spot prizes' could be won she raised her face to his.

'This is nice,' she whispered as they stood in a shadowy corner. 'You said you had two left feet, but you're really good.'

'And this is even better,' he said bending his head to kiss her softly.

The four of them walked back to the farm together, Kathy and Chris secretly holding hands in the dark. Nigel was only home for the week-end, but Elaine could talk of no one else for days afterwards. For her part Kathy remained silent on the subject of Chris.

Harvest that year was good. Kathy, Elaine and Chris all helped, working hard from early morning till dusk, glad to have plenty to do to take their minds off the approaching exam results. James still retained his two huge shire horses, Bunter and Butch, and to save precious petrol he used them for ploughing and at harvest time for pulling the big cart that transported the harvested hay and sheaves. Kathy loved to ride on top of the sweet-scented hay with Elaine or sometimes Chris and occasionally, when no one was looking he would steal a quick kiss. These were moments she cherished.

When in early August the dramatic news that the Americans had dropped an atomic bomb on Hiroshima, culminating in the surrender of the Japanese, there was renewed celebration, but all Kathy could really think of was that Chris would not have to fight them after all.

When the long brown envelopes arrived by post one morning soon after VJ Day, Kathy and Elaine looked at each other across the breakfast table, turning the envelopes over in their hands, neither wanting to be the first to know their result. At last Elaine said,

'Let's swap and open each other's.'

Chris looked at the girls. 'Oh come on you two. Let's see what kind of a hash you've made of it.' He looked from one to the other. 'Well – what are you waiting for?'

Solemnly they swapped envelopes. Kathy opened Elaine's, drew out the contents and looked up. 'You've passed,' she said, her eyes bright. 'You're on your way to college.'

Elaine let out a whoop, then remembering, she slit open Kathy's envelope. There was a pause then she looked up, the corners of her mouth drawn down. 'Oh dear! I'm sorry old thing but it looks as if you slipped up on your English paper.'

Kathy's hand flew to her mouth. 'Oh *no!*'

Chris reached across the table and snatched the letter from his sister's hand. 'You poisonous little monster,' He said. 'She's having you on,' he told Kathy. 'Of course you've passed – with flying colours, too. Here read it for yourself if you don't believe me.'

Lena insisted that the three of them go into town to the cinema to celebrate. Taking the money from her purse and pressing it into Chris's hand she said, 'And take the girls out for tea afterwards,' she said. 'You've all worked so hard this year. You deserve it.'

They went to see *Rebecca* at the Exchange cinema and they enjoyed it immensely. Afterwards they went to the cinema café for tea.

Chris studied the menu. 'They've got fish and chips,' he said. 'Mum's given me enough so shall we have that?'

Both nodded in agreement and when the waitress came for their order Chris ordered for them all with all the authority of a man-about-town.

'Hark at Lord Haw-Haw,' Elaine giggled when the girl had gone. 'Behaving as though he's treating us. I wonder what she'd think if she knew it was your mum's money you're spending.'

Chris shrugged. 'And I wonder what she'd think if she knew I have to put up with a cretin for a sister,' he countered.

Kathy broke in. 'Oh shut up, you two. We've had a smashing day so don't spoil it by quarrelling. This is a day I won't forget for a long time.'

Later she was to remember those words.

When they arrived back at the farm Lena was in the kitchen. 'You have two visitors, Kathy,' she said.

Kathy paused in taking off her coat. 'Visitors – me?'

'They're waiting to see you in the sitting-room.' Kathy looked at Lena but she could not read the expression in her eyes. Chris and Elaine were looking at her too.

'Who is it?' Elaine asked her mother.

'That is for Kathy to find out. They've been here for some time, Kathy, so don't keep them waiting any longer.'

As she went through to the hall Kathy felt apprehensive. Who could possibly be visiting her? No one from London had ever known where she was except Mum. There was nothing for it but to find out. She ran her damp palms down the sides of her skirt and turned the door handle.

Two young men sat opposite each other in front of the fireplace. On the coffee table between them were two empty cups. Lena had obviously made them tea while they waited. Kathy looked from one to the other. The taller of the two stood up.

'Kathy?' He shook his head. 'Blimey! I'd never have known you gel.'

She frowned in disbelief. 'Is it – it's not Charlie, is it?'

'Sure is!' He smiled. ' "Large as life and twice as natural" as they say. And this is Bill.' She stared speechlessly from one to the other and Charlie went on, 'It's a few years since we last clapped eyes on one another. A lot of water's gone under the bridge since then, eh?'

The other man stood up now and Kathy saw that Bill was thinner and shorter than his brother just as he had always been. Both had short-back-and-sides army haircuts and wore ill-fitting civilian suits. The three of them stood staring awkwardly at one another.

'Are you out of the army now then?' Kathy asked.

Charlie nodded. 'Yeah. First in, first out.' He held his arms out sideways. 'What d'you think of the clobber? De-mob suits they call 'em. Rubbish but better than flamin' khaki, eh, Bill?' His brother nodded. 'Just wait till we get settled though,' Charlie went on. 'We'll get some proper gear then.' He raised a hand to touch his head. 'We won't be having any more of these bleedin' awful haircuts neither.' He looked around the room. 'Nice gaff you've got here, Kath. Fell on your feet, eh?'

Kathy swallowed hard. 'Mum got killed,' she said.

'Yeah.' He nodded. 'Yeah – we heard. We couldn't get to the funeral.'

'No.' The feeling of apprehension she had felt initially was growing inside her and she said suddenly, 'Why are you here, Charlie? What do you want?'

Charlie glanced at his brother. 'We've come to take you home, Kath. You're our little sister and we reckon families should stick together.'

Kathy suddenly felt as though a cold hand had clutched her stomach. 'What home?' she asked. 'There's no home any more.'

'That's where you're wrong,' Charlie told her. 'We salvaged everything we could from the flat at the buildings. Part of it was bombed, but our old flat was hardly touched and most of our stuff was still there. We've bought a little shop. Remember Fisher's fruit and veg in Kemsley Street.'

Kathy stared at him. 'You're going into the greengrocery business?'

He shrugged. 'Maybe – maybe not. We might start up something different. Thing is, there's a flat to go with it. Three bedrooms. We're gonna fix it up real nice and cosy, Kath. You'll love it.'

'But I'm not your sister,' Kathy pointed out. 'I'm only your stepsister.'

'We're still your next-of-kin, Kath. And till you're twenty-one I'm responsible for you. I'm your legal guardian.' He looked at his silent brother. 'I *am*. Ain't that right, Bill?' He frowned. 'Come on mate, for Christ's sake open yer bleedin' gob, can't you!'

'Yeah – yeah, that's right, sure enough,' Bill said hastily.

'See, we thought we could all work together and you could run the house for us.'

'But – I'm still at school,' Kathy told him. 'I'm going to college when I'm eighteen.'

For a moment Charlie looked nonplussed then he laughed. 'Well, the Smoke might've been bombed to hell and back but the last time I looked there were still a few schools around,' he said. 'Nothin' to stop you carryin' on with yer schoolin if that's what you want.' When she didn't reply his smile vanished. 'Look, Kath, as I see it you ain't got no choice. These people you've been staying with – you can't expect them to keep you forever. They're strangers and we're your family. The war's over. You've gotta come home now.'

CHAPTER FIVE

Kathy awakened as usual to the rumble of traffic. The shop in Kemsley Street was close to the corner of Hackney Road and the traffic noise never ceased, day and night.

When she had first arrived here almost a year ago it had kept her awake all night. She thought she would never get used to it after the deep silence of the countryside nights, but now it didn't bother her – except for that moment when she first woke in the mornings. That was when the realization that she was back in London broke into her dreams, pulling at the thread that still connected her to the Spicer family and reopening the yearning pain of homesickness in her heart.

Charlie and Bill had turned what used to be a greengrocer's into a tobacconist's and sweet shop. In truth they had already started to put their plans into motion before they came to take her back to London, though Charlie hadn't mentioned it at the time. Once Kathy was living here she could see why. The tiny office at the back of the shop was used by Charlie as an illegal betting shop. He warned Kathy not to talk about it, although, he added hurriedly, plenty of people were doing it. The customers would come in for cigarettes and pass their bets across the counter for Bill to pass to Charlie in the back office with his telephone.

The same men seemed to place bets day after day, calling in later for their winnings – if there were any. Kathy soon learned that it wasn't only horse racing that the customers gambled on. It was anything from the winner of the three-thirty at Doncaster to the result of the general election that took place that July. She often wondered how their wives felt about the housekeeping money being frittered away but when she expressed this thought to Charlie he laughed.

'Their loss is our gain, gel,' he said. 'No sentiment in business. No one forces 'em to gamble their hard earned dosh, do they?'

Charlie had made quite a name for himself in the army as a boxer and he augmented their income with bouts at the local drill hall, two or sometimes three nights a week. To Kathy it was brutal and violent and she hated to see him on the days after a fight when his face would be swollen and bruised, even though he nearly always won his fights.

'It looks so painful.' she had commented more than once. He always laughed at her concern.

'I've had worse than this hangin'on the backs of trucks in the old days,' he told her.

'I remember.' It was true. She recalled the skinned knees and blistered hands that Mum was always having to deal with. Oddly enough though, it was inevitably Charlie who came a cropper. Bill was lighter and more agile and seemed to get away with it more often than not as she reminded him now.

'Ah, but I box heavyweight,' he told her. 'That's more about packing a punch than dancin' about.'

'But why do you do it?' she asked.

'For the only reason I ever do anything – 'cause I like the lolly,' was his reply. 'One o'these days I'm gonna make the big time. Just you wait and see.'

The flat above the shop was a far cry from the house at Magpie Farm. True, she had a room to herself on the top floor and as much privacy as she wanted, but the roof needed mending and when it rained water dripped through her ceiling. There was no bathroom, so weekly bathing had to be done in the kitchen, which was on the ground floor at the back of the shop. The boys were respectful over this and provided her with a screen to cut out the draughts. They usually made themselves scarce on her bath night too, so that she could lock the door.

Charlie was full of plans. 'Just you wait,' he told her. 'Soon as we've made enough dosh we're gonna build on a proper bathroom at the back of the kitchen.'

'Won't you have to apply for a building permit?' she asked. 'And won't it be difficult to get the materials?'

Charlie laughed. 'Not when you know the right people,' he told her, tapping the side of his nose. 'There's loads o'stuff that was salvaged from some of the posh hotels Up West that was bombed. Bathroom suites, fridges – all sorts. Just you leave it to yer Uncle Charlie. This place'll be a proper little palace by the time I'm done with it.' He made no mention of getting the roof fixed though.

Bill, for his part, said very little. As far as Kathy could see he just did whatever Charlie told him to do, working behind the counter in the shop, an endless fag between his lips; running errands and being a general dogsbody.

Kathy had given up the idea of going back to school. As far as she could see none of the local schools came up to the standard she was used to. A large percentage of the pupils seemed to play truant, hanging around the street corners and getting into trouble with the police.

Miss Redfern had been disappointed to hear she was to leave and had made her promise to continue with her education. For the first few months Kathy had attended evening classes as a compromise, but somehow it was not the same. Somehow there seemed to be no point and at the end of the second term she gave up. Charlie did nothing to encourage her to stay on.

'Never could see the point of education meself,' he said. 'Learn to read and write and reckon up, yeah. That's all I ever needed. Not passing exams has done me no harm.' He swiped at his brother's head. 'Nor Bill neither, eh, Bruv?'

Kathy doubted whether Bill could actually read words of more than two syllables. It was all he could do to reckon up the price of more than two items in the shop, but she said nothing, resigned to her fate. She told herself that if she hadn't been evacuated she would probably be as ignorant as her stepbrothers by now, so she might as well be thankful for what education she had managed to benefit from.

She remained in touch with the Spicers, looking forward to the letters that Elaine wrote her every other week. They were full of news about the farm and the family. She was looking forward to starting at college now and her letters were full of it. Although Kathy loved to read them they made her long to be back at Beckets Green with her friends; to be going to college with Elaine. Now that she was back in London the prospect of training for a proper career seemed like a half forgotten dream. Although Charlie was generous, she refused his offer of pocket money. She longed to be independent and told Charlie that she intended to look for a job. He always put her off.

'There's no work round 'ere for an educated gel like you, Kath,' he told her. 'You'd be wasted in some clothing factory or servin' fish and chips. You ain't got no worries about money. Anything you want – just ask. I'll see you right.'

But being reliant on her stepbrother was not what Kathy wanted. She had withdrawn the money her mother had carefully saved for her, keeping it in a large brown envelope under her mattress and drawing on it whenever she needed anything. Sometimes she felt guilty about it, knowing it was not what Mum had intended but she could see no alternative.

Elaine wrote that Chris was in the army doing his National Service. He had been posted to Germany and already had a commission. Second Lieutenant Spicer sounded very grand. As far as she could gather from Elaine's letters he was thoroughly enjoying the life. Kathy wondered if she would ever actually see or hear from him again. She was sure he would have forgotten her by now – he'd probably met another girl. She tortured herself with images of him with a beautiful blonde on his arm or perhaps a glamorous redhead. Of one thing she was sure: she would never forget him – nor would she ever love anyone else.

When she first joined the Brady boys Kathy had wondered what it would be like to have to live on rations alone. As she would be in charge of the housekeeping she imagined she would probably find it difficult. At the farm there had always been Joan's home made bread, butter and jams and fresh new laid eggs from her chickens. There was always plenty of meat from the farm in the form of chicken and pork and an abundance of home grown vegetables of course. Oddly enough, though, they did not go short in London. Charlie seemed to be able to obtain all kinds of things other people couldn't get. When Kathy asked where they came from his reply was always the same, tapping the side of his nose he would say, 'Ask no questions – hear no lies.'

She soon realized that he was in the habit of using the goods for bartering; men would come into the shop and a pound of butter or a dozen eggs would be exchanged for petrol coupons, or a side of ham for some clothing coupons which she had overheard him selling at an inflated price. One day she asked Bill where his brother got all the luxuries he brought home. Bill shrugged, shifting the cigarette he was never without from one side of his mouth to the other.

'Down the docks,' he said laconically. 'He knows some geezer down there and bungs 'im a few quid when a boat comes in.'

It was Kathy's introduction to the black market.

Lena had been deeply disturbed about letting Kathy go back to London with her stepbrothers. She'd had many a sleepless night worrying over it.

'I didn't care for the looks of them,' she confided to James. 'What do they want with a young girl like Kathy anyway? She isn't even related to them except by marriage.'

'The older chap says he's her legal guardian,' James reminded her. 'We have to respect that. At least he's taking his responsibility seriously. Anyway love, I don't think there's anything we can do about it.'

But that only made Lena worry even more. 'She's been with us for almost six years,' she said. 'We've brought her up like our own daughter. She isn't used to the kind of life they obviously live. You should see what the East End of London is like, James. I was really shocked when we went up for poor Mary's funeral. It's in ruins; filthy, run-down and polluted. A breeding ground for crime, I shouldn't wonder.' She looked at him, her eyes wide and frightened as a horrifying thought suddenly occurred to her. '*James* – you don't think they plan to introduce her to a life of – of *vice*, do you?'

James put his arms around her. 'Lena – darling, you're letting your imagination run away with you. Kathy herself wouldn't let that happen. She's a sensible girl with a good head on her shoulders. You told her she could always come back here if things didn't work out, didn't you? And she's got the money her mother saved for her.'

Somewhat placated, Lena nodded. 'I suppose you're right,' she sighed. 'Though I do think it's a shame when she had her whole future mapped out.'

Knowing that Elaine would show them to her mother, Kathy's letters to Elaine were somewhat sparing with the truth. She told of how the boys were good and generous to her, which was true. She described how Charlie was refurbishing the bomb-damaged house and installing a bathroom and how the shop was flourishing. She avoided mentioning Charlie's boxing or the black market deals he was obviously mixed up in, or the fact that Charlie had begun to spend long hours away from the shop 'on business' as he called it. When she asked Bill what business his brother was doing during these long hours of absence he gave her a sly smile and said, 'It's – er – I reckon you could call it a kind of insurance.'

Kathy looked puzzled. 'Insurance?'

'Yeah. He likes to make sure that the other business folks round here don't get any trouble.'

'Why would they get any trouble?' Kathy asked him.

Bill leaned one elbow on the counter. 'You gotta remember that this is the East End, Kath,' he said. 'There are some very funny people about. Charlie likes to take care of people – make sure they're OK, see?'

Kathy didn't *see* but she knew she would have to be content with Bill's oblique explanation. Some inner instinct prevented her from quizzing Charlie about his business. She had already guessed that he liked to play his cards close to his chest and she was beginning to learn that it was better to remain ignorant about some things.

On her seventeenth birthday Charlie took her Up West and insisted on buying her some new clothes, and in the evening the boys took her out to dinner at a smart restaurant. Two months later, at Christmas, Charlie presented her with a fur coat. She gasped with surprise when she took the lid off the box, lifting one of the sleeves and burying her face in its softness.

'Oh, Charlie,' she breathed. 'It's lovely!'

'Well – go on, try it on, let's have a decko.'

She lifted the coat from its box and was surprised to find it quite light. It was a pale milk chocolate colour and as she snuggled into it and turned up the collar she caught sight of Charlie's beaming face through the mirror over the fireplace.

'You look like a millions dollars, gel,' he said smiling and nodding appreciatively. 'I knew you would. You know, you're getting to be a real looker, Kath.'

Kathy blushed with pleasure. 'But it must have cost a fortune. You shouldn't have.'

He waved a dismissive hand. 'You're worth it, gel. But sit down, I've got a little proposition for you and I'd like to see what you think.' When Kathy was seated he lit a cigarette and took a long drag, assessing her face through the smoke.

'No need to look scared. It's nothing you can't do. I've noticed how quick you are with figures when you help out in the shop occasionally. As you know, Bill's a bit of a dead loss when it comes to reckonin' up. The books are a mess and he's losing me money hand over fist. You've mentioned a few times that you'd like a job and there's nuthin' like keepin' it in the family, so what d'you reckon to taking over the shop – runnin' it for me? I'll pay you well – make it worth your while.'

'I don't know. What about Bill?'

'Don't you worry about Billy boy. I've got other plans for him. I have to be out more and more these days and he could place the bets for me over the blower. I reckon he could just about manage that. Then there's other ways he can make himself useful. He might look like a seven stone weakling but he's wiry and quick.' He frowned suddenly. 'I mean, he'll be useful for humping stuff about too.'

'Won't he resent me for taking his job?'

Charlie laughed. 'Resent you? If I know anything he'll be so relieved he'll wanna kiss your feet. As for the punters, it'll make a good impression, 'avin' a bit of class to look at instead of Bill's ugly mug.' He lit another cigarette from the stub of the first one. 'There's somethin' else. We've got an old army mate joinin' us in a couple of weeks' time. Jeff Slater's his name.'

Kathy was immediately on her guard. 'Oh, is he going to move in here?'

Charlie shook his head. 'Nah! Nothing like that. He's got a really posh gaff somewhere down in Surrey. It's just that I'd like you to be nice to him – invite him round for a meal and stuff like that. He might put a bit of money into our business.'

'Would that be the shop?' Kathy asked. 'Or the insurance business?'

Charlie's head snapped up and he stared at her for a moment, his face suddenly stony. '*Insurance*? What d'you mean?'

She shook her head. 'Bill said you run an insurance business,' she told him. 'Looking after local businessmen – so that they don't get any trouble.'

'Oh yeah?' His eyes narrowed. 'What else did he tell you?'

'Nothing – just that. He said there are some nasty people about and that you like taking care of people.'

He relaxed visibly. 'Oh well, yeah, that's right.' He stood up. 'You will wear the coat, won't you, Kath? I want folks to see what a smashing sister I've got.'

'Of course I'll wear it.'

'And you'll take the job?'

'OK, Charlie. I'll take the job. Thanks for the offer.'

She had been in bed for some time that night when she was woken by a crash and a cry from downstairs. As she lay awake she heard Charlie's raised voice. He sounded very angry.

'Get up and stop whining! What the bleedin' 'ell's the matter with you? Either you don't open yer gob at all or you spew out stuff you're supposed to keep shtum about. Sometimes I think you ain't got nuthin' between them ears but stuffin' like a bloody toy monkey.'

Bill's reply was barely audible. 'You got no call to hit me, Charlie. I. . . .'

'Shut up!' Charlie broke in, 'I'm tellin' you, Bill – if you was anyone but my brother I'd have kicked your arse into the gutter long ago. From now on I'm gonna make sure you're where I can keep an eye on you. Don't do or say nuthin' unless I tell you to. Not to Kath or any other bugger, right – savvy?'

'Right. I never meant nuthin', Charlie,' Bill whined. 'I never said nuthin' that'd let on to her about. . . .'

'*You don't say nuthin'*!' Charlie thundered. 'Understand? *NUTHIN*! Kath's no fool, Bill. She's not thick like you. She's a good kid but she knows how to put two and two together. The least she knows, the better, or before you know it she'll be askin' awkward questions. Just keep it buttoned from now on. OK?'

Kathy lay awake for a long time, wondering just what it was she was better off not knowing.

Jeff Slater arrived about three weeks later, towards the end of January. Kathy had taken over from Bill in the shop after New Year and in spite of her misgivings she had picked it up quickly and was quite enjoying the work. It was good to feel she was earning her living. She cleaned the shop and arranged the merchandise more attractively. A bonus was that the customers seemed to appreciate the changes she made.

When the stranger walked in one afternoon she knew at once that he was not one of the regulars. He wore a camel coat over a well cut suit and the leather driving gloves he put on the counter looked expensive. And there was a sleek little red sports car parked at the kerb outside which she guessed was his.

'Can I help you?' she asked.

'You certainly can,' he smiled.

His hair was very dark, almost black and well tamed with brilliantine. He had an olive skin and dark brown eyes that gave him a slightly Mediterranean appearance. Although he wasn't as tall as Charlie, his broad shoulders gave the impression of strength, but his hands, Kathy noticed, were soft and well manicured, and a diamond winked in the heavy gold signet ring he wore on his little finger. She thought he looked quite interesting.

'Excuse me, but – have we met before?' He was smiling enquiringly at her and she realized suddenly that she had been staring at him like a silly star-struck schoolgirl.

'No, I. . . .' She bit her lip hard as she felt her cheeks colouring. 'I think I know who you are though. Charlie's friend, Mr Slater?'

'Got it in one, though I prefer to be called Jeff. And you are?'

'Kathleen O'Connor. Charlie and Bill's stepsister.'

'Of course. I've heard all about you from Charlie. Is he about?'

'Yes, but I think he's busy on the telephone at the moment. He shouldn't be long.' She lifted the counter flap. 'If you'd like to come through to the back I'll make you a cup of tea. I think Bill's about somewhere.'

Bill was in the kitchen reading the Racing News, he had his feet up on the table and the predictable cigarette stub between his lips. When Kathy came in with their guest he jumped guiltily to his feet, removing the stub and flicking it into the sink.

'Oh – er – *Jeff*! Wotcher mate.'

Jeff held out his hand. 'Good to see you again, Bill.'

Kathy filled the kettle and lit the gas. 'Will you make Mr Slater some tea, Bill? I'd better get back to the shop.'

'Wait.' Jeff held up his hand. 'Surely Bill can mind the shop for a bit,' he said. 'I'd like to get to know the little sister I've heard so much about.' He looked at Bill. 'You don't mind, do you?'

Looking as though he minded very much Bill said, 'What, me? No mate.' As he made for the door Kathy said,

'Let Charlie know there's someone to see him, will you?'

Bill shot her a truculent look. 'You know he don't like bein' interrupted when he's on the blower.'

Jeff smiled at Kathy as the door closed. 'Brother Bill doesn't change much, does he?'

She shrugged. 'They're not really my brothers. My mum married their dad when I was little. I didn't see them all through the war when they were in the army. We hardly knew each other when we met again.' She poured him a cup of tea and passed him the milk and sugar. 'Help yourself. I think there might be some biscuits somewhere.'

'Don't worry. I never touch them.' He spooned sugar into his tea and stirred, looking at her speculatively. 'So – you must've been a young kid when the war started.'

She nodded. 'Ten. I was evacuated to a little village in Northamptonshire. Beckets Green. I lived on a farm with a nice family. I loved it there.'

'Mmm, must've been quite a wrench to leave when the time came,' he observed.

'It was. The East End isn't the prettiest place to live. I still get quite homesick for the country at times. But Charlie and Bill have been very kind.' She chuckled. 'They've changed quite a lot since we were kids.'

He laughed with her. 'A right pair of little tearaways, I bet.'

'Oh, they were,' she told him. 'Always in trouble. After their dad died they used to run rings round my mum.'

'Your mum?' he cocked his head enquiringly.

'Killed in the blitz.'

'Oh, that's a shame. I'm sorry to hear that – Kathleen, is it?'

'That's right, though I like Kathy better.'

They talked for some time. Jeff told her about his house in Surrey. 'I was an East End kid too,' he told her. 'But like you I lost my folks in the blitz while I was away in the army. My dad was in the rag trade and he left me everything. Well, all that was left after the Luftwaffe had bombed the factory and our house to smithereens. First thing I did when I got demobbed was buy this little place in Virginia Water. It's a lovely spot. D'you know it?' She shook her head. 'I put most of the cash into bricks and mortar. I reckoned that was the best move at the time.'

'So what do you do now?' Kathy asked.

'I'm back in the rag trade.' He said. 'It's all I know – what I grew up with. I've got a little place over in Bethnal Green with a dozen machinists. The building's due for demolition but the business is ticking over nicely and it'll do for a start. Once clothing rationing comes off I should be able to get the business cracking again.'

'It must be hard for people coming out of the services,' Kathy said. 'Picking up the threads again and trying to make a go of things.'

He smiled. 'Oh, there are ways and means of taking up the slack. I do have other irons in the fire.'

She was still trying to work out what he meant when he asked her, 'So – what about you? Is this what you do all the time – work in the shop?'

'I run it,' she told him proudly. 'Charlie asked me to take over from Bill. He wasn't really suited to it.'

He grinned. 'I can imagine. Is it something you've always fancied then – running a shop?'

'Well. . . .' She hesitated. This stranger was so easy to talk to. She didn't want to be disloyal but it was tempting to tell him about the opportunity she had missed and still regretted. 'I was still at school when the boys came to bring me back to London,' she said. 'I'd already got my school cert' and I was hoping to go to teacher training college.'

'And you passed that up for this?'

She shrugged. 'I didn't really have much choice. I thought I might be able to continue but the schools round here are. . . .'

'Rubbish?' He laughed. 'Go on, you might as well say it. What about night school? Or you could always go further afield. There are better schools in the suburbs. You seem like a bright girl to me.'

She felt her cheeks warming. 'Oh, I don't know. I'll be eighteen this year. It feels as though it's a bit too late.'

Jeff regarded her for a long moment. 'So where do you go from here? Where do you see yourself in, say ten years from now? You'll still be a young woman.' He smiled. 'Or maybe you've set your sights on marriage and motherhood.'

Kathy hadn't thought that far ahead and the notion pulled her up sharply. She shook her head. 'I – don't know – haven't really thought.'

At that moment the door opened and Charlie's furious face came round it. 'What the 'ell is Bill doin' behind the counter, makin' a bleedin' pig's ear. . . ?' He stopped short. 'Oh, *Jeff*, mate!'

'Hello there, Charlie. Good to see you.' Jeff stood up and shook Charlie's hand. 'Don't blame the lovely Kathy for deserting her post. It's my fault.' He looked at her. 'And can you blame me? You never told me your kid sister was this beautiful.'

Embarrassed, Kathy stood up. 'Now you're here I'll get back to the shop, Charlie,' she said. Suddenly she remembered what he had asked her to do and turned to Jeff. 'Oh – perhaps you'd like to have a meal with us one evening?'

He smiled. 'Home cooking? I'm not going to pass on that. I get sick of eating in restaurants. Thanks very much.' He looked at Charlie who quickly added,

'Yeah, good idea. What about tomorrow? We could talk about that bit of business afterwards. Are you free?'

'You bet.'

They both looked at Kathy and she guessed that they were leaving it to her to suggest a time. She did some quick calculations. The shop closed at six. She'd need at least an hour and a half. 'How about eight o'clock?' she suggested.

Both men nodded. 'Eight o'clock it is.' Charlie clapped Jeff on the shoulder. 'I'll come out to the car with you,' he said. 'I take it that snazzy little number out there is yours and I wanna know where you got it.'

As they went through the door Charlie turned and gave Kathy a sly wink of approval from which she gathered that she had done and said the right things.

If Kathy was wondering what she would provide for the following evening's dinner party she needn't have worried. Halfway through next morning Charlie came in laden with carrier bags. Behind the counter of the shop he showed their contents to Kathy. There was steak, the best fillet; fresh fruit and vegetables and something black in a tub that smelled fishy. She sniffed it and looked enquiringly at Charlie.

'Caviar,' he told her. 'It's what the toffs have. You have it on little bits of toast before the main course.'

Kathy wrinkled her nose. 'Are you sure?'

He puffed out his chest. '"Course I'm sure. Old Jeff is used to that kind of nosh.' He opened the other bag and drew out three bottles of wine, one red, one white and another round fat bottle. He grinned at her. 'Brandy,' he said. 'For after.'

'This lot must have cost you a fortune,' she said. 'Anyway, what about the meat ration? Where did you get it all?'

Charlie tapped the side of his nose in the characteristic gesture. 'Ah, that'd be tellin', gel. Let's just say I called in a few favours.'

'You're going to an awful lot of expense just for an old army pal,' she observed.

'I know what I'm doin',' Charlie told her. 'Jeff's loaded. I want to make a good impression. He's worth cultivatin'.'

'As a friend?' she asked.

'A friend and business colleague.'

Kathy gathered up the bags of food. 'These need keeping cool,' she said. 'I'll put them down in the cellar if you give me the key.'

The cellar door, which led off the kitchen was always locked. She held out her hand but Charlie shook his head.

'You don't wanna go down there,' he told her. 'It ain't safe since the bombing, ankle deep in water half the time. And rats too.'

Kathy shuddered. 'Oh! No place for food then.'

'You said it gel.' He took out his wallet which she noticed was stuffed with notes and peeled off a handful. 'Here – take the afternoon off and go Up West. Get yourself somethin' sexy to wear,' he said. 'Have your hair done too. I'll take over in the shop for once.'

Kathy stared at him, then at the money. 'No, Charlie, I couldn't.'

'Yes you could.' He took her hand and folded her fingers round the notes. He raised an eyebrow. 'Got enough coupons?' She nodded. 'Right. Do yerself proud then gel, you deserve it. Oh and, Kath. . . .'

'Yes?'

'Put a bit of make-up on, kid. You know – lipstick and stuff. It'd suit you.'

She shrugged. 'OK – if you say so.'

Kathy didn't ask any more questions. She did as she was told, travelling up to the West End and buying herself a smart little black dress that she considered very sophisticated. She had her hair cut too, in a very short style that made the natural curl frame her face, giving her features an elfin look. She guessed that Charlie was hoping Jeff would invest some money in whatever 'business' it was that he was running, though from what Jeff had told her his own business was a small-time clothing factory. Surely that couldn't bring in much money.

Later that afternoon in the kitchen she looked at all the food spread out on the table. Charlie had already explained what to do with the caviar. The steak would be the main course. Charlie had suggested making chips to go with it, accompanied by fried onions, mushrooms and peas. They were to finish the meal with the fresh fruit.

Upstairs in the living-room Kathy did her best to make the table look nice. She arranged the fruit tastefully in a large glass bowl she found and put it in the centre of the table. When she had done as much as she could towards the meal she changed into her new dress and brushed her hair.

Jeff arrived on time, bringing with him a bottle of champagne for the boys and a bouquet of flowers for Kathy. He looked smart and handsome in an elegant dark grey suit and crisp white shirt. Charlie and Bill looked smart too. It hadn't escaped Kathy's notice that both boys had acquired a whole wardrobe of smarter clothes just as Charlie had predicted, and this evening she noticed that Charlie was sporting a heavy gold identity bracelet on one wrist and a splendid new watch on the other.

Much to her relief the meal was a great success. Jeff announced that the steak was grilled to perfection, smiling at her over the rim of his wine glass.

'Where did you learn to cook?' he asked.

'At the farm where I lived all through the war,' she told him.

He nodded. 'Didn't go short of much there, I'll bet.'

'I suppose not.'

All three men had drunk freely throughout the meal, but Kathy had only had a few sips of wine. Now Charlie brought out the brandy.

'I always think a drop of the old Napoleon helps with the business talk,' he said, looking pointedly at Kathy. He made to put a glass in front of her but she shook her head.

'Not for me.' She stood up. 'I'll do the washing up – leave you to your business talk.'

Charlie helped her carry the last few dishes down to the kitchen. 'Clever girl,' he said with a smile. 'You know when to make yourself scarce. I like that in a woman.'

As he closed the door Kathy tied on an apron and ran water into the sink. She couldn't help feeling a little resentful. After all, she ran the shop, didn't she? Wasn't she part of the business? Didn't she have the right to sit in on the business talks?

She had just finished the washing-up when the door opened and Jeff came into the kitchen. He was wearing his overcoat and scarf.

'I'm just off,' he said. 'Wanted to say thanks for a lovely meal.'

She hurriedly dried her hands. 'Oh, that's all right.'

He closed the door. 'I was wondering – would you let me take you to dinner one evening next week?'

Taken aback, Kathy stared at him. '*Me?*'

He laughed. 'Yes, you.' He took a step towards her. 'I own a little club. It's called The Starlight Room – just off the Edgeware Road. It's only small but I've got a good chef and there's a little five-piece band for dancing to. So – how about it?'

Kathy could feel her face turning pink. 'Well. . . .'

'Of course if you don't want to. . . .'

'Oh, I *do*.'

He smiled. 'OK then. Next week – say Friday. I'll pick you up at about eight. 'Night, Kathy.'

And he was gone, leaving her staring open-mouthed at the closed door.

CHAPTER SIX

Kathy wore the little black dress for her dinner date with Jeff. Over it she wore the fur coat that Charlie had given her. Jeff's look of admiration when he picked her up assured her that she had made the right choice.

The Starlight Room was, as Jeff had said, quite small and intimate, but the Mediterranean décor and the comfortable furnishings gave it an exclusive atmosphere.

When they arrived it was still only half full. The band was playing a popular tune and a few couples were circling the tiny dance floor. The head waiter ushered them to the table Jeff had reserved in an intimate corner where he immediately ordered a bottle of champagne.

'I hope you're hungry,' he said, pouring her a glass. 'The menu's very good if I do say it myself. Champagne all right?'

Kathy took a sip and tried not to shudder. She didn't like the taste and the bubbles stung her nose. 'Yes,' she said. 'But I don't really drink.'

He laughed. 'I'll have you know, young lady that this champagne is the best that money can buy. And all you can say is that you don't really drink.'

She blushed. 'I'm sorry. You shouldn't have. . . .'

He smiled and covered her hand with his. 'Relax, Kathy. I'm teasing. Champagne is something you'll easily get used to I promise you. Drink it up. You'll be surprised how good it makes you feel.'

And he was right. Kathy drained her glass and felt herself beginning to relax at once. She did not protest when Jeff refilled her glass. He ordered dinner for her and when the food came she found it delicious.

As the evening wore on the lights were lowered and the band

played soft music. Jeff asked her to dance, but she found it very different from the village hall dances at Beckets Green. The floor was
crowded and there was hardly room to move. Jeff held her very close.
He was wearing a spicy scented cologne which she found quite heady
and after they had circled the floor a couple of times she laid her head
against his chest.

'Tired?' he asked, his lips against her ear.

She shook her head. 'Not really – just a little bit dizzy.'

He chuckled softly. 'I think I'd better get you home,' he said. 'Don't
want to get into trouble with the big brothers for getting their little
sister drunk, do I?'

'Oh!' She raised her head to look up at him, her eyes round. 'I'm *not*!'

' 'Course you're not. Let's just say you're not used to it.'

In the car she snuggled into the soft leather seat. She felt pleasantly
sleepy. 'I've had a lovely time, Jeff,' she said. 'Thank you for taking me
out.'

He reached across and cupped her chin. 'No, thank you sweetheart,'
he said. 'It's a long time since I was with a girl as sweet and innocent
as you.' He bent forward and kissed her very gently on the lips. She
sighed.

'Mmm. That was nice.'

He straightened up and switched on the ignition. 'Er – yes – I think
I'd better get you home before we both do something we'll be sorry for
in the morning.'

It was the first of many dates that Kathy had with Jeff. Their Friday
evenings became regular. Sometimes they would go to Jeff's club;
sometimes Up West to a theatre, cinema or restaurant. Charlie encouraged the relationship and seemed pleased with Kathy, and for her part,
she always enjoyed herself in Jeff's company and looked forward
eagerly to Friday evenings.

Charlie's business obviously flourished. He had the roof mended
and had a smart new bathroom put in with materials he said a mate
had got for him from a bomb-damaged source. It certainly made the
living accommodation more comfortable. He continued to buy himself
smart clothes too and he gave up the boxing, saying in a half joking
way that it was 'ruining his looks'.

As spring turned to summer Jeff would sometimes turn up early and
suggest a run down to the coast on warm summer evenings to

Southend or Margate. To begin with Kathy would hesitate about deserting the shop but Charlie would urge her to take the time off and go,
assuring her that Bill would fill in for her for a couple of hours.
Occasionally instead of eating in a smart restaurant they would walk
along the beach eating fish and chips and laughing like children. On one
of these evenings Jeff invited Kathy to sit down on the sea wall, it was
a beautiful evening, the air warm and mellow and the sun just setting.
The sea was smooth with hardly a ripple and the sky was streaked with
pink and gold. Jeff took something from an inside pocket.

'Here – something I thought you might like.'

Kathy took the oblong box from him, looking up at him. 'What is it?'

'Why not open it?'

Inside the box, nestling against a bed of white velvet was a pearl
necklace. She gasped.

'Oh, Jeff, it's gorgeous. Are – are they real?'

He assumed an expression of mock horror. 'Would I give my girl a
string of fake pearls?' He took the necklace from its velvet bed and
undid the clasp. 'See this?' He held out the little jewelled clasp. 'Those
are diamonds.' He put the necklace around her throat and fastened it.
'There,' he said, looking at her with approval. 'I knew they'd suit you,
your lovely skin brings out the sheen on them. You're class, Kathy.
Nothing flashy for you.'

She was touched. 'Thank you so much, Jeff. I've never really had any
jewellery before.' She held out her wrist and touched the silver bracelet
her mother had given her that she wore every day. 'Only this.'

He picked up her wrist and pulled off the bracelet. Before she could
stop him he had tossed it on to the beach. 'There,' he said. 'That old
thing is rubbish. You deserve better and you shall have—

'*Hey*! What are you doing?'

Kathy had jumped down from the sea wall and was frantically
searching in the sand for her bracelet. 'My mum gave me that,' she
cried. 'It was the last present she ever gave me before she was killed. It
must have cost more than she could afford and it's the only thing I've
got to remember her by.'

'Oh Christ! Kathy, I'm so sorry. I didn't know.' He joined her, scrab-
bling in the sand in a vain attempt to find the bracelet.'

'*Stop it!*' she shouted. 'You're making it worse. We'll never find it
now.'

He grasped her shoulders. 'Kathy – look, calm down sweetheart. It's got to be here somewhere. You sit down and let me look for it.'

But half an hour later he still hadn't found the bracelet. The tide was coming in. Already it was lapping at the soft suede of his hand made shoes.

'Leave it, Jeff,' Kathy said. 'It's gone. You'll never find it now. It's getting chilly. Let's go.'

She was silent in the car on the way back to London; her eyes downcast and her shoulders drooping. Jeff kept on glancing at her. 'You all right?'

She nodded. 'Yes.'

When at last they drew up outside the shop in Kemsley Street he turned to her. 'Kathy – look, love, I've said I'm sorry. I know you're upset but you need to get things in proportion. I know you thought a lot of the bracelet but when all's said and done it was only a bit of metal. You're not going to forget your mum because it's gone, are you?'

'No, of course not.'

'If I'd known I wouldn't have done – said what I did. You do know that?'

'Of course.'

'Then – are you going to stop punishing me – please?'

She sighed and turned to him, making herself smile. 'I'm not punishing you, Jeff. I realize you didn't know.'

'Good.' He took her shoulders and drew her close. 'Because there's something I need to tell you, Kathy,' he said. 'I think – well no, I *know* that I'm falling in love with you.'

His words shocked and slightly dismayed her. 'Oh – Jeff.'

'It's not something that happens easily to me, Kathy, and when I fall, I fall like a ton of bricks. What I need to know – what's important to me is – how do *you* feel – about *me*? Where do I stand?'

Kathy swallowed hard. 'You're so good to me, Jeff. I love our Friday evenings and. . . .'

'That's not what I'm asking.' His hands on her shoulders tightened. 'For Christ's sake, Kathy! You know what I want to hear. Look, I know I'm a lot older than you – at least ten years, but you've got under my skin. I can't stop thinking about you. You're on my mind all the time. Is it the same for you?'

The dark eyes that were only inches away from hers smouldered with passion. How could she say that she didn't really know how she felt?

'I – er – yes, Jeff. Of course I love you.'

'Oh Kathy – my darling!' He crushed her close and kissed her. This kiss was different from the kisses they'd shared before. His tongue probed her lips until they parted and then explored her mouth. One hand began to unfasten the buttons of her dress and a moment later she gasped as she felt his hand close over her breast. As she felt a shudder of desire convulse his body she began to panic.

'Oh, Kathy, *Kathy*, I want you so much.'

She began to push him away. 'No, Jeff. I can't. Not – not now.'

'So – when?' He took her face between his hands, searching her eyes hungrily. '*When*, darling?'

'I – I don't know.'

His expression hardened, then suddenly the tension in his arms and hands relaxed. 'OK, OK. It's all new to you and I shouldn't try and rush you. You're only a kid really and I know I have to be patient, but don't keep me waiting too long sweetheart, will you? I'm not made of stone you know.' He got out of the car and came round to her side to help her out. At the door he pulled her close and kissed her again, deeply and lingeringly.

'Goodnight, angel,' he said at last. 'I've got to go away for a few days – a bit of business to attend to.' He kissed her again. 'I'm really going to miss you, but at least it'll give you time to think. I hope it'll be a question of "absence makes the heart grow fonder".' He tipped up her chin with one finger. 'I'll see you when I get back eh? I can't wait.'

She watched until the car turned the corner of the street and then took out her key and let herself in, her mind in turmoil. What had she let herself in for?

Jeff's declaration of love and the sudden acceleration of their relationship troubled Kathy seriously. She liked him a lot. She was grateful to him for the enjoyable outings he had taken her on and she enjoyed his company. But *love*. . . ? The trouble was, she hadn't any experience to draw on. True, she'd imagined herself in love with Chris Spicer but they had been no more than children that Christmas when they had kissed under the mistletoe. By now he would surely have met other girls – had lots of experience of what falling in and out of love was like.

As for her, she still thought of him with a girlish longing that she knew to be unrealistic. It was a bit like having a crush on a film star. They were poles apart and even if they ever met again it would be under very different circumstances. Knowing that she had to talk to someone older and more experienced she decided at last to speak to Charlie. She chose an evening when Bill was out on an errand.

'Charlie – can I talk to you?'

'Sure.' He looked up. 'What about?'

'It's Jeff.'

'What's he done now?'

'Nothing. At least – he says he loves me, Charlie.'

He laughed. 'That all? Nuthin' wrong with that, is there?'

'It's just that I don't feel the same. I feel awful, Charlie. He's been so good to me and I've enjoyed it all, but now. . . .'

'Now he's callin' in the debt?'

She winced. 'You make it sound horrible – like some kind of business arrangement.'

'Just the same, I'm right – yeah? He reckons it's time he got something back?'

She was shocked. 'I'm sure he didn't mean it quite like that.'

'Just the same, it's what it boils down to.'

'The thing is Charlie, what should I do?'

'I dunno.' He grinned. 'What do you wanna do?'

'I don't want to do anything.'

'Well, maybe you should make yourself want to.' He wasn't smiling now. 'Come on gel. It can't be that bad a deal, can it? Jeff's not a bad lookin' geezer and you have had a good time. He must'a spent a fortune. It's gotta be worth a bit of slap and tickle, surely?' Seeing the look on her face he added, 'You might even get to like it and I'm sure Jeff wouldn't let. . . .' He lifted his shoulder. 'anything happen – if you know what I mean.'

Kathy did know what he meant but it didn't help. Charlie was really saying that she should go along with what Jeff wanted.

He leaned forward. 'Listen, Kath, Jeff's important to Bill and me. We've got a good thing goin'. I wouldn't want anything to 'appen to chuck a spanner in the works if you get my drift.'

His 'drift' was all too clear. He was saying that he wanted her to co-operate – keep Jeff sweet. Was that why he had pushed her towards him in the first place? The thought made her feel cheap. As she got up to leave the room, Charlie caught her arm.

'Kath – you're not a kid any more. You're a woman, a very attractive one too and it's time you grew up. If you're clever you'll learn how to use the assets you've got to your advantage.'

She pulled her arm from his grasp. 'What are you suggesting?' she said. 'Do you want me to be like one of those girls I've seen picking up men outside the Prince of Wales.'

' 'Course I don't!' He looked angry. 'You're my sister. D'you really think I'd want that? You're a bright girl – clever as well as pretty. You've got a good head on your shoulders and if you play your cards right you can make it work for you.'

'I'm not sure I want to.'

'You want a good life, don't you? Nice things and all that?'

'Only if I work for them.'

He laughed. 'It's a question of findin' out what work you have to do,' he said. 'And I suggest you learn quick.'

Kathy tossed and turned all that night, unable to sleep for the thoughts that plagued her mind. The one consolation was that she would at least have a short respite. Jeff was to be away for a week. She hoped and prayed that some solution would miraculously present itself to her before the time was up.

For some time Kathy had been puzzled about the amount of money Charlie was spending. She ran the shop and she knew that it barely broke even. He no longer earned anything from his boxing bouts so where else did their profits come from?

Normally Charlie did the weekly shopping. She had offered to do it many times but he had always refused and she guessed that he had 'business arrangements' with various shopkeepers. She was proved right in this assumption one day when he had to be away for the day and they ran short of food. She asked Bill which shops they were registered with for their rations. He laughed.

'Charlie don't bother with any of that,' he said. 'Just go anywhere and tell 'em you're Charlie Brady's sister. Everyone knows us.'

Amazingly he was right. The local shopkeepers seemed only too happy and eager to provide her with anything she wanted. In fact many of them had already put aside some of the scarce delicacies they knew Charlie liked and the fact that she had no coupons to offer was brushed aside. Even when she offered to pay her offer was brushed aside. When she expressed her surprise to Bill later as she unpacked the laden shopping bags he laughed.

'It's called shopping under the counter,' he told her.

'But why should they treat us any different to anyone else?' Kathy asked. 'It's illegal. They could get into trouble. Charlie must be very popular.'

'Oh, he is' Bill could hardly speak for laughing. 'The most popular geezer in the whole of East London I reckon.'

The week was over all too soon and Jeff telephoned to tell her he was back in town and longing to see her.

'I'll pick you up about seven,' he told her. 'I thought we might have a bite to eat somewhere and then run down to my place. You haven't seen it yet, have you?'

Kathy agreed that she hadn't. She tried to sound enthusiastic, but she knew what spending time alone with Jeff at his house would mean. Charlie would be all in favour of it. In fact he would urge her to co-operate. There was no one she could turn to for help or advice. She would just have to hope that an appeal to Jeff's better nature would prove effective.

They ate at a small restaurant about halfway to Virginia Water. Kathy wasn't hungry and only picked at the food. Jeff seemed to have little appetite either and soon they were back in the car and on their way again. It was a beautiful late summer evening and as they drove into leafy Surrey Kathy wound down the window to breathe in the fresh air.

'It's nice countryside down here,' Jeff observed. 'Away from all the traffic fumes. I'm planning to spend more time here once I get all my business deals up and running.' He turned to look at her. 'How would you like to live down here? Better than Hackney, eh?'

She nodded. 'Yes.'

'You're very quiet.' He put a hand on her knee. 'Not nervous, are you? No need to be scared, sweetheart. You know, I can't wait to see you against the setting of Maple Lodge, I'm sure you're going to love it.'

At last they were there. Jeff drove through double, wrought-iron gates and down a tree-lined drive. Jeff's house, Maple Lodge, stood back from the road, concealed by mature trees and shrubs. Kathy's eyes widened. She had seen nothing like it except on the films. It had timbered walls and the latticed windows gleamed and winked in the evening sunlight.

'Manderlay,' she said softly under her breath.

Jeff looked at her. 'What's that?'

'Manderlay. The house in the film, *Rebecca*,' she said with a smile.

He looked at her blankly. 'Not much of a one for films, me,' he said as he helped her out of the car. Taking out a key, he unlocked the studded oak front door and as they stepped inside Kathy caught her breath. The floor was of polished oak, strewn with rugs in rich colours. An elegant staircase curved up two sides of the hall to reach a circular galleried landing above. At the turn of the staircase was a tall window with lozenge shaped panes of alternate pink and green glass. Evening sunlight streamed in throwing pink and green pools of light across the hallway.

'It's beautiful,' she breathed.

Jeff put his arms around her. 'And it's all yours,' he told her. 'Just say the word.'

On the ground floor was a large drawing-room, sumptuously furnished. The floor was fitted with thick wall to wall carpet and there were draped and tasselled curtains at the French windows which opened onto a sweeping lawn with flowered borders. Also on the ground floor was a dining-room with dark oak furniture and an inglenook fireplace; a study furnished with a large mahogany desk and swivel chair, and the largest, most luxuriously equipped kitchen that Kathy had ever seen.

'Who looks after it all?' she asked him. 'It must be an awful lot of work.'

He waved a hand. 'There's a local woman who comes in to clean, and a gardener. I like to potter about myself when I'm here. I've always been keen on growing things.' He took her hand. 'Come and see upstairs.

Again Kathy was dazzled by the opulence. Four bedrooms led off the landing, most of them with a view of the garden and all luxuriously furnished. The master bedroom had its own adjoining bathroom and also a dressing-room, one wall of which was made up of wardrobes with sliding mirrored doors. Kathy stared at the four poster bed with its muslin drapes and pale gold satin quilt. Jeff slipped an arm round her waist.

'Like it?'

'It's gorgeous.' She looked at him, suddenly aware of the fact that they were standing in his bedroom. He smiled.

'Shall we go down and have a drink?'

In the drawing-room he opened a cocktail cabinet. Inside was an array of bottles. He looked at her. 'What would you like?'

She shrugged. 'I don't know – anything. You know what I'm like when it comes to drinks.'

He poured her something colourless. When she took a sip she found it was tasteless too apart from the lemonade he had added to it. She drank it quickly and Jeff took her glass and quickly refilled it. He sat down on the sofa and patted the seat beside him.

'So – you like my humble home then, do you?'

She laughed. 'I don't know about humble. It's the most luxurious house I've ever seen.'

He slipped an arm round her shoulders. 'And, like I told you, it's all yours for the taking.' He raised an eyebrow at the empty glass in her hand. 'You must have been thirsty. Want another?' Without waiting for her reply, he got up and replenished her glass again. 'So – how do you feel about coming to live here?' he asked as he sat down beside her.

'By myself?'

'No, with me of course.'

'Oh.'

'What does "oh" mean?' He took the glass from her hand and pulled her into his arms, kissing her deeply. 'Oh, Kathy, having you living here with me would make it all perfect. When I bought this place I thought all my dreams had come true, but there was always something missing. I know now that something was you, so what do you say?'

Kathy sighed. She felt very peaceful – almost drowsy. What Jeff was saying sounded very inviting and when he kissed her again she relaxed in his arms.

'It's your birthday soon, isn't it?' he whispered. 'Why don't we make it your birthday present – moving in here with me?' He was on his feet now, pulling her to her feet. When she managed to make her eyes focus on him she saw that his face was flushed and the pupils of his eyes were large and black 'Let's go upstairs,' he whispered.

She frowned, trying to remember why going upstairs wasn't a good idea and Jeff laughed gently as he scooped her up in his arms and made for the staircase.

'I think you're a tiny bit drunk, my darling. Maybe a little lie down will help.'

She had no idea how long she had slept. When she woke it was dark outside and she found herself under the covers in the four poster bed. She raised her head and saw that Jeff was beside her.

'What – where. . . ?'

He raised himself on one elbow and pushed her gently down again. 'Take it easy, sweetheart. I shouldn't have given you that third drink. You passed out cold on me.'

'How long did I sleep? What time is it?' She tried to raise her head again, but the room swam a little and she sank back again.

'You slept for an hour or so, but don't worry, the boys aren't expecting you home tonight anyhow.'

She frowned. 'They're not. . . ?'

He leaned across and kissed her, his hand moving down her body and it was only then that she realized that they were both naked. He smiled into her eyes.

'I had to take your things off. Didn't want you to ruin that pretty dress, did I?' He kissed her again and moved one leg across her body. She tried to resist but his leg was heavy and she found that she was too weak to resist. His hands were everywhere, stroking squeezing, fondling; his breath was hot and rapid against her cheek. Then, moving on top of her he pushed her legs apart determinedly.

'Jeff! What. . . .' Her protest got no further. The next moment he entered her swiftly with one brutal thrust. He silenced her cry of alarm and pain with his mouth in a passionate kiss. She pushed at his shoulders, twisting her head this way and that, afraid she would suffocate, but his mouth clung to hers like a limpet.

What he did seemed to go on for ever. She squeezed her eyes tightly shut and prayed for it to end, her arms outstretched and her hands clenched into tight fists. The pain and humiliation were indescribable. At last he rolled away and lay breathing heavily beside her, staring at the ceiling. Eventually he turned and looked at her. Silent tears were running down her face to soak into the pillow.

'Sorry about that, sweetheart,' he said casually. 'It'll be better next time. It's like that for some girls the first time.'

Some girls! How many others had he seduced, she wondered. She turned away from him and rolled herself into a ball. 'I want to go home,' she said. 'Take me home – please.'

'I can't. Not now. It's too late.'

She sat up, pulling the sheet up over her nakedness. '*I want to go home.*'

'Well you *can't!*' he said angrily. 'I'm not driving back to London at this time of night. What are you making such a fuss about anyway? You've been asking for it for weeks with your teasing eyes and your half promises.'

'*Asking* for it! Asking for *that!*' she shouted. 'It was horrible! Like my worst nightmare!'

'Thanks! Do you think it was any fun for me?' He got out of bed and began to throw on some clothes. 'Get dressed then and be quick about it. You're damned lucky I don't throw you out to find your own way home.'

She gathered up her clothes and went into the bathroom, locking the door. Tears streaming down her cheeks, she showered away the traces of her ordeal and dressed. When she came out of the bathroom Jeff was nowhere to be seen. She composed herself, combed her hair and picked up her bag then went downstairs. She found him in the kitchen making coffee.

'You'd better have a cup,' he said. 'Black. It'll make you feel better.'

'I'd rather just go.'

He ignored her, pouring two cups and passing one to her. After a moment he said. 'It wasn't meant to be like that. If you'd just relaxed. . . .'

'I'd rather not talk about it.'

'It's like I said. Sometimes the first time is hard for. . . .'

'*Some girls.* Yes, you said.'

'Well – so I've been told,' he replied. He took a sip of his coffee. 'Seems I can't do or say anything right for you.'

She put down her cup. 'Can we go now?'

In the car he glanced at her. 'Are you trying to give me the brush-off?'

'I've said, Jeff: I don't want to talk about it any more tonight.'

'Does that mean you might want to talk about it tomorrow?'

'No. I don't know.'

They didn't speak for the rest of the journey but when he pulled up in Kemsley Street he turned to her. 'Kathy, seeing that you feel the way you obviously do, you'd better tell Charlie I'll be in touch with him tomorrow.'

'All right.' She made to open the car door but he reached across and put his hand over hers. 'You see if you're really giving me the old heave-ho, I don't think I can bear to be around here any more,' he said. His face was close to hers and although his tone was light there was a hard glint in his eyes. 'It's only fair that Charlie knows I'll have to dissolve our partnership. I warn you – I'm afraid he might be very upset.'

She stopped as the words sank in. She allowed her eyes to meet his and recognised the gleam she saw in their dark depths as triumph. He had played his trump card. She was trapped.

He smiled. 'If you'd like some time to reconsider just let me know,' he said smoothly. He stroked her cheek with one finger. 'You shouldn't be too hasty, Kathy. You may not have enjoyed tonight, but I promise you I could make you happy if only you'd let me try.'

As she turned away he added chillingly. 'I mean, when you think about it, things could be a whole lot worse.'

Dawn was breaking as she slid between the cold sheets of her bed. She lay there shivering, unable to sleep. Jeff was virtually blackmailing her into becoming his mistress; his *property* – to do with as he wished. She closed her eyes, reliving her ordeal at his house and shuddered. How could she ever have imagined him an attractive man? He was a monster. Tonight he hadn't cared anything for her feelings. He had taken what he wanted with no more thought than he would have given to a newspaper, read and then thrown away. She remembered how he had pulled the gift her mother had given her from her wrist, calling it rubbish and throwing it away. That should have warned her of the kind of person he was.

When she went downstairs Charlie was in the kitchen. He looked up in surprise as she walked in.

'Oh. I thought you were staying over at Jeff's place,' he said.

'Which is more than I did.' She filled the kettle and set it on the gas then turned to look at him. 'What kind of man is Jeff, Charlie?' she asked. 'And what kind of partnership have you and Bill got with him?'

For a moment the colour left Charlie's face. 'It's a business partnership of course,' he said.

'What business though? I know it has nothing to do with the shop, so it must be this mysterious insurance business that Bill mentioned.'

Charlie looked angry. 'It's nothing for you to bother your head about,' he said. 'Stuff you wouldn't understand. Better if you forget anything Bill might've said.' He looked at her keenly. 'Kath – you haven't had a row with Jeff, have you?'

'Charlie. . . .' She laid a hand on his arm. 'I don't want to see him any more.'

'Why not?' He looked alarmed.

'Last night – at his house, he gave me something to drink; too much of it. I passed out and when I woke up – he forced me to. . . .'

'Oh surely not!' Charlie laughed. 'Come off it, Kath. You're not a kid. You must've known what was goin' on.'

'I knew I had to be careful, but after I drank the stuff he gave me everything went out of my head. I want nothing more to do with him after what he did.'

He drew a long breath and rubbed his hand across his eyes. 'Christ, Kath, you're puttin' me in an impossible position. I can't cross Jeff. If I do. . . .' He looked at her. 'Tell you what. Let me talk to Bill about it. We'll come up with something, just leave it with me.'

Charlie explained what it was that he and Bill had come up with later that morning when Kathy was in the kitchen making coffee during a lull in the shop.

'There's something we'd like you to do for us,' he said. 'It's just a little practical joke we wanna play on a mate. You game for that?'

'What kind of joke?' she asked.

'Come down the Prince of Wales with us tonight and get talkin' to this geezer we'll point out to you.'

'You know I don't like pubs.'

'It's just this once. Get talkin' to this bloke. By nine o'clock he's bound to be half cut anyway so you offer to walk him home, right?'

'Won't he wonder why?'

'Nah! Take him round by the bombsite where Mason's warehouse used to be. If he starts askin' questions you can make him believe you're up for a bit of 'ow's yer father.'

She shook her head. 'I don't like the sound of it.'

'You'll be quite safe,' he assured her. 'Me'n'Bill will be followin' we'll be right behind you and we won't let nuthin' 'appen to you.'

'I said no!'

Charlie's face grew hard. 'Look, Kath, you want me to fix things for you with Jeff, right? Well just do this one little thing for us and I will. If you're gonna be awkward you're on your own.'

'There must be something else I can help with. After all, you say this is just a practical joke.'

'So it is, but it's important. This geezer needs teachin' a lesson. He's played one too many jokes on us and enough's enough if you know what I mean.'

'So what are you going to do?'

He affected a laugh. 'Oh, we thought we'd take 'im for a little ride. Dump 'im off somewhere where he don't know where he is. Let him find his own way 'ome. That'll teach 'im.'

'And that's all I have to do?'

'That's all.'

Kathy hated the atmosphere in the bar at the Prince of Wales. You could hardly see across the bar for smoke; the tables and chairs were greasy and the whole place smelled of stale beer, cigarettes and unwashed people.

Standing just inside the door Charlie pointed out a man seated at the bar. He was about thirty, with greasy dark hair in need of cutting. He wore a belted gabardine mackintosh and a cloth cap lay in front of him on the bar. The pint he was in the act of sinking was clearly not the first of the evening.

Bill chuckled. 'Ugly bugger, ain't he? Funny that 'cause he thinks he's God's gift to birds. If you ask me he's ripe for the pluckin' too. Been boozin' since openin' time by the look of him.'

Charlie gave Kathy a nudge. 'We'll wait outside. Don't want him to spot us together. Take your time, gel. Good luck.'

Kathy grabbed his sleeve as he was leaving. 'And you promise to make Jeff leave me alone if I do this?'

Charlie looked irritable. 'For Christ's sake. I've said so, ain't I?'

When they'd gone Kathy sidled up to the bar. Her heart was beating fast as she hoisted herself onto a stool next to the man. With a flash of inspiration she nudged his elbow causing him to spill a little of his drink. He turned on her angrily.

'Watch out, you dozy cow. . . .' His eyes rested on her for a moment and his expression changed. 'Oh, sorry miss. I thought you was someone else.'

'I'm sorry I made you spill your drink. Let me buy you another.'

'No, let me get you one. What'll you 'ave?'

'Thank you. A shandy would be nice.'

Kathy watched the man as he ordered the drinks and paid for them. He had a sallow skin and shifty blue eyes. His nose had been broken at some time and not set properly. Its crookedness gave him a lop-sided appearance.

'Ain't seen you round 'ere before,' he said as he pushed the glass towards her. 'Where're you from?'

'Northampton,' Kathy said, thinking on her feet again.

'Right. Just 'ere for an 'oliday, are you?'

'Something like that,' she said. 'Visiting friends.' She looked at him. 'Are you a boxer?'

'What?' He looked surprised then his hand went up to his crooked nose. 'Oh, you mean the conk. Yeah, done in a fight I s'pose you could say.' He smiled. 'Nuthin' wrong with your boat though an' no mistake.'

She frowned. 'Boat?'

'Boat race – *face*!' He laughed. 'Easy to see you ain't from round 'ere. Cockney rhymin' slang. Like I said, you're a good lookin' bird – sorry young lady.' He held out his hand. 'I'm Gus by the way.'

'Thank you.' She shook the hand. 'I'm – Molly. So – tell me more about this rhyming slang.' Kathy knew all about rhyming slang, having grown up in the East End, but she was glad of a way of making conversation with someone as unpromising as Gus. He warmed to the subject and as he was regaling her with the variety of rhyming words and phrases he sank two more pints of ale after which his words became slurred. Seeing the barman eying him doubtfully, Kathy seized her moment.

'It's time I was going,' she said. 'I don't suppose you'd do me a favour and walk with me. I'm not all that sure of the way.'

The barman leaned across the counter and spoke to her softly. 'If you take my advice, miss you'll leave Gus to his own devices.'

She gave him what she hoped was a confident smile. 'It's all right. I can handle him.'

She helped the man down from his bar stool and together they left the pub, Gus weaving slightly. It was almost closing time and very dark out in the street, lit only by one dim lamp on the corner.

'Where d'you live then, love?' Gus slurred.

She took his arm. 'Just along here. It's not far.' As they walked she tried out some of the rhyming slang he had taught her, purposely getting it wrong so that he would laugh and correct her. They reached the corner of the street that led to the bombed-out warehouse. Gus paused looking puzzled.

'Can't be down 'ere, love,' he said.

'Yes. It's a short cut.' Kathy hoped Charlie and Bill would soon put in an appearance. She wasn't sure how much longer she could carry on fooling Gus. He was drunk but not so drunk he didn't know where he was going.

The ground was strewn with rubble, and jagged sections of the broken walls of the old warehouse were still standing throwing the whole place into a maze of light and deep shadow. Gus stumbled and almost fell.

'Bloody 'ell! Call this a short cut? You could break your bleedin' neck. . . .' Two figures suddenly emerged out of the shadows, both carrying some kind of club. ' 'Ere what the—' Gus got no further. One of the figures raised his club and landed a blow on the side of his head sending him sprawling to the ground. Kathy staggered back in horror and began to scream. An arm came round her neck from behind and a hand closed over her mouth.

'Shut it, Kath. You done OK but better bugger off 'ome now and leave it to us. This ain't no place for you.'

She recognized Bill's voice. He let her go and she stumbled back against the wall. Both men continued to rain blows on the defenceless man on the ground, kicking him in the back and ribs and landing more blows with their clubs. His cries of fear and agony made Kathy's heart thud and she felt physically sick. This was no 'practical joke,' it was a deadly assault on a powerless, drunken victim. There was nothing she could do to stop it, and when she realized that she had been the decoy she felt sick with horror and shame. Turning away and covering her ears to shut out the man's pitiful cries, she stumbled away.

CHAPTER SEVEN

Kathy was in bed when Charlie knocked on her door.

'Kath – can I come in?'

She covered her head with the sheet and hoped he would go away.

'Kath – look, I'm comin' in anyway.' The door opened and she held her breath, hoping he would think she was asleep and give up. He didn't.

'Kath!' He shook her shoulder.

Throwing back the sheet she glared up at him. 'You tricked me,' she said. 'You tricked me into leading that poor man to the bombsite so that you and Bill could attack him. Do you call that a practical joke?'

'You don't know him, Kath,' Charlie said. 'He's pure shit – into drugs and guns and everything crooked you can think of. He's not worth your sympathy. He had it coming. He done the dirty on Bill an' me – owed us a packet and he's been laughing at us for months, thinkin' he could get away with it.'

'What have you done to him? Is he – dead?'

Charlie laughed. 'Dead – Gus Norris? You bet yer sweet life he ain't dead, not that anyone'd miss 'im if he was. It's like I said. He needed teachin' a lesson and that's what we done tonight. He'll have a few bruises and a bit of an 'eadache tomorrow, but he'll think twice before he plays around with the Brady brothers again.' He patted her shoulder awkwardly. 'Just you get some kip and don't worry your 'ead about him no more.'

'So what about Jeff?' she asked as he made his way to the door.

He turned, paused for a moment then came back to sit on the edge of her bed. 'Yeah, I've been thinkin' about Jeff. You know, Kath, he ain't a bad bloke and he really fancies you. If you was to play your cards right you could have anything you wanted.'

'There's nothing I want from *him*.'

'You could do a lot worse. There's that smashing gaff of his down in Surrey. He owns a couple of night clubs and other businesses as well. He's really in the money. You could live like a real lady.'

'Not without my self respect I couldn't.'

'Look – I 'ad a word with Jeff yesterday. He's sorry he rushed things like he did. He never meant to put you off, 'cause he really likes you. He said he couldn't help himself – you drove him mad with them eyes of yours and your smashin' figure and—'

'*Stop it*!' Kathy put her hands over her ears. 'I don't want to hear any more. You promised to make him leave me alone if I did what you wanted. Well, I kept my part of the bargain.'

'I know, and I know what I promised, but it's easier said than done with a bloke like Jeff. He's used to getting what he wants. If he doesn't then someone's usually in for a packet of trouble.'

She frowned. 'Are you saying that he threatened you? Are you afraid of Jeff, Charlie? Are you using me to keep him sweet?'

' 'Course I'm not.' He said unconvincingly. 'It's just – well – Jeff knows people – powerful people.'

Kathy felt as though a cold hand closed over her heart. It seemed there was no one prepared to be on her side. 'If – if I were to go to the police . . .' she began.

'Don't even think about it,' Charlie held up his hands. 'Jeff's got certain members of the local fuzz in his pocket. Going to the old Bill'd be a *really* big mistake.'

Kathy felt trapped. 'So – what am I to do?'

He shrugged apologetically. 'Well – like I said – just go along with it. It probably won't last long anyway. Jeff soon gets bored. Maybe in a couple of months some other bird'll take his fancy.'

'And in the meantime. . . ?'

'In the meantime you might as well make the best of it,' he said. 'Live it up a bit – enjoy yourself. Jeff can be generous to people he likes. It's one of his good points. Get all you can out of him while it lasts – why not?'

He made for the door again, but Kathy stopped him.

'Charlie. What kind of hold has Jeff got over you?' He turned to look at her.

'Hold? Wotcher mean, *hold*?'

'What *is* the connection between you? I know it's nothing to do with the shop, or your bit of bookmaking. And how is it that all the shop-keepers round here are willing to let you have anything you want off ration – off money too, half the time?'

'I daresay some of them remember the old days, before the war, when we was kids and lived round 'ere.'

'Do you think I'm stupid, Charlie?' she asked. 'If they remembered you and Bill as kids they'd remember the way you used to pinch stuff from under their noses and throw stones at their shop windows when they told you off. You two didn't store up any happy memories for the folks round here. So just what are you up to?'

He closed the door and crossed the room swiftly to stand looking down at her. His eyes narrowed menacingly but behind the threat she saw something else – fear – alarm? 'Listen, Kath, just take my advice and keep it buttoned, right? You don't wanna go sticking your nose into trouble. The less you know, the better, see? Just leave it. We didn't bring you back here to start asking questions.'

'That's another thing: why *did* you bring me back here, Charlie?'

He stared at her for a moment. 'You're our kid sister, ain't you? Like I told you, I'm your legal guardian – next of kin. You know East End folks. We look after our own.'

'Did you think I'd be useful for doing the kind of thing you got me to do last night?' she asked him. 'Did you think you could rent me out to your friends so as to put yourself in a good light with people like Jeff?'

He looked shocked. 'I'm gonna make out you never said that, Kath.'

'I'm not really what you expected, am I, Charlie? I may have been just another East End kid when I left here, but Mum always brought me up to be decent. And the people I was evacuated with made me see that there was a better way of life.'

'So there is,' he said lightly. 'That's what I'm trying to tell you. You'll learn how to get it too, if you stick around long enough. Look, Kath, if you live with Bill and me you'll have to accept us the way we are.'

'What you mean is that I'll have to accept that Jeff and men like him are part of the package.'

He ran a hand through his hair exasperatedly. 'Oh – why the hell can't you just take what's on offer and be grateful like any other bird?' he said irritably. 'If you know what's good for you you'll keep your trap shut.'

'Is that a threat?'

'Let's call it a warning.'

When he'd gone, she thought about all that had taken place. It was clear that Jeff was mixed up in something crooked. Two suburban nightclubs and a run-down clothing factory obviously didn't bring in enough to fund the kind of lifestyle he enjoyed – with enough left over to invest in Charlie's business – whatever that was. Charlie was clearly afraid of Jeff. He'd hinted that she should be afraid of getting on his wrong side too, but why?

In spite of the events of the previous night and the turmoil in her head, she managed to get a few hours' sleep. When she went downstairs next morning, the post had been and there was a letter with a Northampton postmark, addressed in Elaine's neat hand. She tore it open eagerly.

Her friend wrote that Mrs Weller, the headmistress of the village school, had retired and Lena had been appointed in her place. James had been ill and had been diagnosed with angina which meant he had to take on extra help on the farm. Fly, the redundant sheep-dog had died and that James had bought the family a Labrador pup which they had christened Winston, after Mr Churchill.

Elaine went on to say that she had been awarded a place at teacher training college and the best part was that she would only be going as far as Wellingborough and so would be able to come home every weekend. This was especially good because she was courting Nigel Oliver, the doctor's son. Nigel was at university studying medicine and hoped to take over his father's practice when he qualified. They were planning to get engaged on her next birthday. Last but not least, Elaine wrote that Chris's National Service was almost at an end. They were all looking forward to having him home again soon.

Kathy laid the letter down with a sigh. It evoked strong nostalgic memories of life at Beckets Green; a life so sweet and uncomplicated. Elaine still sounded so young and carefree; so full of life and vitality. It made Kathy realize how fast she had had to grow up since her return to London and she yearned to be back where she could enjoy that easy, straightforward life again. It was only when she was folding the letter that she noticed that Elaine had written a P.S. over the page.

P.S. I enclose a letter that Chris has asked me to send on to you. Funny he's never sent you one before. I wonder what can be in it. I'm bursting with curiosity so do let me know next time you write. E.

Kathy looked inside the envelope and found another envelope with her name written on the front. She tore it open eagerly and read:

Dear Kathy
It seems ages since you went back to London with your stepbrothers. I hope you are happy and have made a good life for yourself. My time in the army is almost over. I've enjoyed it far more than I ever thought I would and in some ways I shall be quite sorry to leave. I've enjoyed seeing places I might never have seen if I hadn't been in the army. Nevertheless it will be good to see the family, Beckets Green, Magpie Farm and all my friends again.
My plans for going to university may have to be shelved. Elaine might have told you that Dad has heart trouble. He's still too young to retire and I know it would break his heart to sell the farm, so I've decided to stay and help him and maybe even take over from him when he retires.
I hope you will visit us soon, Kathy. I may not have kept in touch but I've thought of you a lot. I found the enclosed trinket in an antique shop in Berlin. It made me think of you. I hope you like it.
Hoping to see you in the not too distant future.
Love, Chris.

Kathy looked inside the envelope and found a tiny silver heart-shaped locket engraved with the letter K. It was suspended from a fine chain. Her eyes filled with tears as she fastened it round her neck.

Chris's letter touched something deep inside her. His words stayed with her all morning. She was not the girl he remembered. How would he feel about her if he knew what she had become; if he knew the shameful thing that had happened between herself and Jeff and the part she had played in the attack carried out on Gus Norris last night?

Suddenly it was as if her mother's voice spoke inside her heart and she knew what she must do. Telling Charlie she felt the need of some fresh air she asked Bill to cover for her in the shop. Going upstairs she put on her coat and went out.

*

S Jude's Church looked much better than the last time she had been here. The bomb damage had been repaired and the surrounding houses had been tidied up too. She scanned the notice board outside, wondering whether Father Gerard was still the resident priest or whether he had moved on. But to her relief; his name was still there. *Father Michael Gerard SOJ.*

She went inside and slipped into one of the pews. It was peaceful and quiet, smelling faintly of flowers, incense and wax polish, the familiar smell that brought back childhood memories. Sunlight streamed through the stained glass window over the altar, throwing pools of colour across the floor of the chancel.

It wasn't the official time for confessions. All the boxes at the side of the church were empty. She knew that if she rang the presbytery bell Father would happily come and hear her confession, but suddenly she felt shy and reticent. It was years since she had been to church – not since her mother's funeral in fact. She had no right to expect Father to put himself out for her.

She knelt and closed her eyes, waiting for the words to come into her head; desperate to know what to do about the dilemma she was in. Suddenly she felt a hand on her shoulder and a soft voice asked,

'Can I help you, child?'

She hadn't heard his footsteps, but she recognized the voice. Opening her eyes and looking up she saw the familiar face of Father Gerard and was overwhelmed by a feeling of relief.

His eyes widened as she looked up. 'Kathleen! Is it Kathleen O'Connor?'

'It is, Father.'

'My dear child! How long have you been back in London?' He slipped into the pew to sit beside her.

She held her breath. 'Two years, Father.'

'Two years, is it? And why has it taken you so long to come and see me?'

He didn't say 'come to church', but 'to see me'. It was so like him and she loved him for it. 'I'm afraid I've been a bit lost,' she said.

'Well, never mind, you're here now and that's the important part.' He took her hand and looked into her eyes. 'But you're troubled, child.'

'Yes, Father. I was going to ask you to hear my confession.'

He smiled. 'I think a cup of tea in the presbytery would be better on this occasion,' he said with a smile. 'Just this once.'

In his study he fiddled with an electric kettle. 'It's my housekeeper's day off today,' he explained. 'She always leaves me a casserole in the oven and a tray set out with all the necessary makings for a cup of tea.' He looked at her. 'Do you like biscuits?'

'Yes please, Father.'

She drank the tea he made her, grateful for the respite to gather her thoughts.

'So what made you want to come back to London?' the priest asked, taking his seat opposite her. 'I thought you were happy in the country.'

'I was, but the war ended,' she said. 'I couldn't expect the Spicers to keep me there for ever.'

'They expected you to leave?' He frowned. 'And you all alone with your mammy gone? I am surprised. I got the impression from Mrs Spicer that the family had grown very fond of you.'

'They were fond of me – still are. We're still in touch. I'd just passed my school certificate too, and I had plans to go on to college later. Then Charlie and Bill turned up one day to bring me home.'

The expression on Father Gerard's face changed. 'The Bradys?'

'Yes. Charlie said he was my next of kin; my legal guardian and it was his duty to look after me. He said I had to come home with them.'

'And was that what you wanted?'

She shrugged. 'All the evacuees had to go home when the war ended. Some were happy to go – some not.'

'And you?' He reached across and took her hand. 'Kathleen – what is it you've come to tell me this afternoon? What has happened to make you so unhappy, child?'

Slowly and painfully she told him about Jeff; how Charlie had encouraged her to be friendly towards him. She glossed over what had happened that night at his house but she knew that he guessed at the truth. Finally she described what had happened to Gus Norris the previous night and the unwitting part she had been persuaded to play in his brutal assault in return for a solution to her unwanted association with Jeff.

When she had finished he poured her another cup of tea and passed it to her silently, waiting until she had drunk it before he spoke.

'Kathleen, you can't stay in London,' he said gravely. 'Get out before they drag you down with them.'

'But where would I go?'

'Go to your friends, the Spicers,' he said. 'I'm sure they'd be only too glad to have you, if they knew what you were becoming involved in. Do it, child, before it's too late.'

'Charlie would come and take me back,' she said. 'I'm in his care until I'm twenty-one.'

'I doubt that very much,' he said with a shake of his head. 'Charlie Brady is no blood relation to you. Whatever he has told you I'm sure he would not have been given guardianship of a sixteen-year-old girl. I don't care to think why they wanted you with them, but I urge you to get away before it's too late.' When he saw her uncertain look he leaned forward. 'Kathleen – a priest hears many things; some of which he may not reveal because of the confidentiality of the confessional, but I can tell you without infringing my vows that the Brady brothers are almost certainly running what is known as a protection racket.'

Kathy shook her head. 'Protection – but isn't that good?'

'The way it works is this: the shopkeeper pays money to be left alone. If he fails to pay, bad things happen.' He paused. 'They are into the black market too and illegal gambling; I've heard it said that they handle stolen goods, too. But although a lot of people know about their illegal activities nothing has been proved. So far they've got away with it.'

Kathy gasped. Suddenly so many things were clear, Charlie's long absences 'on business' and his mysterious income; the way that local shopkeepers ingratiated themselves. It was all out of pure fear, and she had unwittingly been part of that too by accepting their gifts. She felt sick. Then another thought struck her. The cellar – the way the door was always locked and Charlie's discouraging remarks about flooding and rats. Could they be hiding stolen goods down there?

'The man you call Gus Norris,' Father Gerard went on. 'I don't know him but it's my guess that he probably tried to muscle in on the Bradys' patch and had to be taught a lesson.' He leaned forward. 'As I said, they've managed to get away with it till now but it's only a matter of time before the law catches up with them. Meantime, obtaining money by the use of threat and menaces only leads to violence. What they're doing is ugly and dangerous and I hate the thought of you being involved in it.'

Kathy closed her eyes. In her head she was hearing again the sickening thuds as the relentless beating was carried out; the pitiful cries of the man as he lay on the ground being mercilessly kicked and beaten about the head. 'Oh my God,' she whispered. 'What can I do, Father?'

'Do as I say. They've already begun to involve you. If you don't leave soon you'll be asked to do even worse. I guarantee it.'

'Charlie would never let me go.'

'Then don't tell him. Just go.'

'He'd guess where I'd gone. He might even come to Beckets Green to get me back again. I'd die rather than make trouble for the Spicers. I wouldn't even like them to know what's been going on.'

'Leave him a note. Tell him you've found out what he's doing and that you'll get in touch with the police if he ever comes near you again.'

'I don't think he's afraid of the police.'

'Then threaten to tell me.'

'*You*, Father?'

'Charlie Brady might think himself a hard man; he might not have come near a church since he was a child, but he was brought up to fear God as a Catholic. It's bred in the bone in the Irish village his parents came from. Hellfire and damnation. Call it superstition if you like, but what does it matter if it works on men like him?'

Privately Kathy couldn't see Charlie being afraid of Father Gerard, but she didn't say so. He walked with her to the pavement and pressed her hand warmly.

'Remember what I said, Kathleen,' he said. 'And don't ever feel you are alone. I'm always here if you need me.'

That night she lay in bed trying to form a plan. She knew that Father Gerard was right; she had to get out before something worse happened, but how was she to do it? The three of them lived in close proximity. To run away she would have to do it in the middle of the night, when Charlie and Bill were asleep. But they kept late hours, sometimes not coming in until the small hours of the morning. It wasn't going to be easy.

She was in the shop next morning when two men came in. She looked up, surprised to see that one of them was in police uniform 'Good morning. Can I help you?'

The elder of the two addressed her, 'Miss Brady?'

'O'Connor,' she corrected. 'Kathy O'Connor.'

'You're not the sister of Charlie and Bill Brady then?'

'Stepsister.'

'I see.' The man took out a warrant card and showed it to her. 'I am DS Smithson and this is Police Constable Duncan. Can we have a word in private, Miss O'Connor?'

'I can't leave the shop,' Kathy said.

'Then I advise you to close up for a few minutes.'

Something about the gravity of his manner made her heart miss a beat. Going to the shop door she turned over the 'open' sign and dropped the latch.

'What is it about?' she asked.

'Do you know a man called Gus Norris?'

The name made Kathy's stomach turn over. Her mouth suddenly dry, she shook her head.

DS Smithson went on. 'The man whose name I've just mentioned was found on a bombsite near here badly beaten and unconscious yesterday morning. He was taken to hospital and has been in a coma ever since. You might have heard a report on the wireless.'

'No – no, I haven't.'

'The doctors have operated to remove a blood clot from his brain but he must have lain there for hours and his heart isn't strong. The prognosis isn't good.'

Kathy's heart missed a beat. 'I told you. I don't know him,' she said.

'And yet you were seen with him the night before last in the bar of the Prince of Wales.' He looked at her closely. 'Are you trying to tell me that you weren't in the Prince of Wales the night before last?'

'No. I – was there,' She noticed that the uniformed P.C. had taken out a notebook and pencil and begun to take down her replies. 'It was crowded,' she went on. 'I knocked a man's elbow and made him spill his drink.'

'This man – what did he look like?'

She bit the inside of her lip. Why were they asking her all these questions? Something inside told her she must keep calm. 'Middle aged,' she said. 'Dark hair – greasy and on the long side. He wore a beige gabardine mac and a cap.'

'And you say that until that night you'd never met him before?'

'Never,' she said truthfully.

'Yet according to a witness you were seen leaving together.'

'Witness – what witness?'

'Never mind that. Did you leave with him?'

Kathy took a deep breath. 'As I said, I made him spill his drink. I offered to buy him another but he bought me one instead. We talked for a few minutes and when I said I had to leave he offered to walk with me.'

'So – he brought you home.'

'No.'

'No?' He looked at her. 'But you said—'

'When we got to the corner, I told him I'd walk the rest of the way alone,' she said. 'After all, as I've told you, I didn't know him.'

'Did you see which way he went when you left him?'

'No. I turned the corner and I – didn't look back.'

'You say you talked – what about?'

Kathy's heart was racing. She felt as though the blood had turned to ice in her veins and she was amazed that her voice could sound so calm and normal. 'We – he was explaining Cockney rhyming slang to me,' she said 'You know – apples and pears – stairs; ball of chalk – walk. . . .'

'I am familiar with the idiom, thank you miss,' DS Smithson said quickly. The PC hid a smile as he bent his head over the notebook. 'Did he say anything else? Did he seem anxious? Was he looking around him for instance?'

Kathy shook her head. 'Not that I noticed.'

'And you were at the Prince of Wales on your own?'

'Yes.'

'Would you mind telling me why?' The policeman asked. 'You don't look like the kind of young lady to go to public houses alone.'

'I'm not.' Kathy paused, her mouth drying. 'And I shan't be going there again. It was just that I hoped I might see a friend there.'

'And he stood you up?'

'She,' she corrected. 'There was nothing arranged. I just thought she might be there. It was a friend from the village where I was evacuated. She was going to be in London for the day. She said she'd meet me there if she had time before her train – but she obviously didn't.' Kathy held her breath but DS Smithson seemed at last to be satisfied with the explanation.

'Thank you for your co-operation, Miss O'Connor,' he said. 'We have to follow up every lead, you understand. If this man dies whoever assaulted him will be looking at a murder charge, so you'll realize the gravity of the situation.'

'Yes, of course.'

She opened the door and let the two policemen out then turned the sign back to 'open' again. As she returned to her position behind the counter, Charlie emerged from his office at the back. His face was pale but his manner was unconcerned.

'Well done, Kath,' he said. 'You handled that like a good'un.'

'Gus Norris is in hospital,' she told him. 'He's in a coma. He might die.'

He shrugged. 'He won't die,' he said. 'They were just tryin' to put the wind up you. But you kept cool. I was proud of you.'

'I wasn't proud of myself. I'm not a liar and I don't want to be mixed up in this kind of thing, Charlie.'

He slipped an arm round her shoulders. 'You're a natural, gel; a true East Ender, loyal and true. You could've dropped Bill and me right in it but, you didn't.'

She shrugged his arm off. 'The East End people I remember didn't go around beating people up,' she said. 'Don't ask me to lie for you again, Charlie.'

'I won't. And thanks again, gel.'

That night after she had gone to bed, Kathy heard a loud banging on the street door. She crept out of bed and sat at the top of the stars listening. Charlie walked down the hall calling out, 'All right, *all right*! No need to batter the door down.' Then, as he opened the door, 'Oh! It's you, Jeff.'

Kathy's heart turned a somersault. She heard the street door close then Jeff's voice. He sounded angry.

'What the bleedin' hell did you think you were doing? I told you to rough him up a bit, not half kill him.'

'It was just bad luck, Jeff. We hardly touched him. How was we to know he had a wonky heart?'

'*Hardly touched him*! He was still lying there unconscious next morning for the world and his flamin' wife to find. You must have kicked the shit out of him. I'm telling you, Charlie, if he snuffs it I'm having nothing to do with it. You're on your own.'

'He'll be all right, I know he will, Jeff.' Charlie's tone was whining now. 'The police are just tryin' to put the wind up whoever done it – to flush 'em out. The fuzz asked Kath a lot of questions, but she never batted an eyelid. You should've 'eard her.'

'*Kathy*? What did she have to do with it?'

There was a pause then Kathy heard Charlie say, 'We got her to lure him to the bombsite, Jeff. She was 'appy to do it. We never put no pressure on 'er.'

'You *fool*! Involving a kid like her. The police'll have a field day with her. You think she won't spill when they start putting the pressure on?'

'She won't, Jeff. I promise. . . .'

'Where is she?'

'Upstairs, in bed – probably asleep for all I know.'

Kathy was appalled. So Jeff was part of all this, too. She heard his footsteps coming up the stairs and quickly slipped into her room, jumping into bed and pulling the covers up to her chin. Closing her eyes she feigned sleep. But Jeff was not easily put off, he drew the covers away from her face.

'Kathy. Wake up. I want to talk to you.'

She opened her eyes wide in mock surprise. 'Jeff! What do you want?'

'Don't worry. It's all right.' He sat down on the edge of the bed. 'Listen baby, I'm sorry we got off on the wrong foot. I really like you and I want us to be together. Charlie's told me how upset you were and that you were scared of losing me.' He caressed her shoulder. 'But now there's this thing Charlie and Bill have got themselves into. It was nothing to do with me and he shouldn't have involved you either.' His hand moved to her cheek and it was all she could do not to shudder. 'But I think it might be wise under the circumstances – just for a while, if you and me stopped seeing one another. Once all this business dies down I'll be back for you and you can move in with me just like we planned. That OK with you darling?'

She made herself nod. 'OK.'

He bent and kissed her lips and she forced herself to remain passive. Fresh hope leapt inside her heart. He was going to leave her alone for a while. It might give her the chance she was looking for. His breath was warm and moist in her ear.

'It's so long for a while then, sweetheart. Remember, no phone calls and no letters. It's sad I know, but I'll be in touch as soon as the coast's clear again. Till then be good.' He stood up and a moment later he had gone. Charlie was clearly waiting for him in the hall and she heard him say,

'Everything all right, Jeff?'

'It better be. Look I had nothing to do with Gus Norris. I never heard of the bloke – got it?'

'Got it, Jeff.'

'If I hear that you or that snivelling brother of yours has dropped me in it you'll wish you'd never been born – right?'

'Right. You know I'd never let you down, Jeff.'

'And you better hadn't or it'll be the worse for you. I'm going to keep my head down for a while and I advise you to do the same. If there's anyone else in on this you'd better warn them. Right. I'm off. No getting in touch, Charlie. From now on you're on your own. Now, stick your head out and make sure there's no one about.'

Kathy heard the street door opening, Charlie's voice affirming that the coast was clear and a few moments later the door closing again.

Moments later she heard voices in the hall again. Charlie and Bill were about to go out. The door opened and closed. She waited for a moment in the ensuing silence then got up and went downstairs. Her mouth was dry and she needed a drink of water. Charlie had promised to make Jeff leave her alone if she helped with his plan but he'd had no intention of keeping that promise. He'd led her to believe that he and Bill were about to play some kind of joke on the unfortunate Gus Norris when all the time he knew that they were about to beat him half to death. He was a liar and a cheat and heaven knew what else. If he could involve her in this what would it be next?

In the kitchen she saw that his jacket was draped over the back of a chair. On impulse she felt in the pockets. Both side pockets were empty but feeling in the breast pocket her hand closed over something hard, a key. She took it out and looked at it. It was an old key and she was fairly sure it was the key to the cellar door. Holding her breath she inserted it in the keyhole. It fitted. Very carefully she tried it. It turned easily as though it had been in regular use. Opening the door she saw that steps led down into the cellar. On the wall was a switch which illuminated the area below. Briefly, she thought about the rats Charlie had mentioned, but she steeled herself, making her way carefully down the steep fight of stone steps.

The sight that met her eyes when she reached the bottom was an even greater shock than the rats would have been. Pulling the cover off a clothing rail she discovered dozens of fur coats. Kathy remembered the one Charlie had given her as a present and realized with horror that she had been wearing a stolen coat. There were boxes stacked four and five high containing wireless sets and other electrical appliances. She opened a steel filing cabinet that stood against the wall and found a wealth of jewellery stowed away inside; expensive looking rings and bracelets, watches and necklaces, earrings and cufflinks. Gold, silver and precious stones.

She stood looking around her, rigid with shock, hardly able to move. There must be thousands of pounds worth of goods here; stolen goods. And here she was living right on top of it. She had managed to convince the policeman that she knew nothing about the attack on Gus Norris, but who in their right mind would ever believe she knew nothing about all this? Father Gerard had been right. She had to get away – and it couldn't be too soon.

CHAPTER EIGHT

After Kathy's discovery in the cellar, she knew there was no time to lose. She dressed and packed as quickly as she could. The only luggage she had was the small cardboard case that Auntie Lena had given her when she returned to London with Charlie and Bill. She crammed as much as she could into that and the rest of her belongings into brown paper carrier bags. She wrote Charlie a quick note, leaving it in her room. With luck they wouldn't discover her absence till morning and by then she'd be far away.

She left the fur coat hanging in the wardrobe, unable to bring herself even to touch it. She thought with shame of all the times she'd worn it: a stolen fur coat. She left Jeff's string of pearls too, convinced that they too were stolen. Out in the street she shivered against the chilly autumn night air as she made her way to the tube station.

At Euston she bought a ticket to Northampton, asking the time of the next train. She thought the man behind the ticket window looked at her curiously.

'Next one's not till twelve-thirty, miss.' He leaned forward. 'You all right, love?'

She managed a smile. 'Yes, thank you. Which platform, please?'

'Platform twelve.' To her relief he was already turning to the next customer as she moved away. The last thing she wanted was to have attention drawn to her.

She looked at the clock and saw that she had almost an hour to wait. Anxiety stirred in the pit of her stomach. What if Charlie and Bill returned and found her gone? Charlie might guess where she'd be heading and come to find her. Everything depended on how long they stayed out.

In the buffet she bought a cup of tea and a bun and sat in a corner near a window where she could watch the concourse. As the minutes ticked slowly by and there was no sign of Charlie or Bill she began to relax. At a quarter past twelve she picked up her collection of luggage and made her way to platform twelve. To her relief the train was in and she climbed aboard and found a seat by the window on the platform side, watching warily as other passengers hurried past. Again the minutes dragged agonisingly by. The train was almost empty and it looked as though she might be lucky enough to have a carriage to herself. She was promising herself that once they set off she would put her feet up and try to get some sleep when she saw him – Charlie, walking quickly along the platform, anxiously scanning all the windows. When she spotted him he had almost reached her carriage. Her heart in her mouth she pressed herself back into the corner, hastily picking up a discarded newspaper and holding it up to hide her face, but at that moment the doors were heard slamming down the length of the train, the guard blew his whistle and, mercifully the train began to move.

Had Charlie boarded the train? Her teeth clamped to her lower lip, she held her breath, steeling herself to lower the newspaper and take one more look out of the window. As the train gathered speed she saw him, standing back at the end of the platform, a look of frustrated defeat on his face as the train passed. With a huge sigh of relief she fell back against her seat. She'd made it. She was free.

The journey seemed interminable. The twelve-thirty from Euston turned out to be a mail train and stopped at every station. No one came to share her carriage and she tried to relax. She thought about the note she had left. Clearly it had not been enough to deter Charlie from trying to get her back.

Dear Charlie
After what happened to Gus Norris, I can't stay with you any longer.
I've seen what's in the cellar and I know about the other things you are
doing. I don't want to be mixed up in any of it. Please don't try to find
me. If you do I shall tell the police everything I know.
Kathy

She dozed fitfully, her sleep invaded by bad dreams. Charlie had caught up with her and was dragging her off the moving train. Gus

Norris was dead and the police were arresting her for his murder; refusing to listen to her protests. Then, with horrifying realism she dreamed that Jeff was on the train. Suddenly he dragged open the door of her carriage with a rasping sound and stood smiling grimly down at her. She awoke with a terrified cry.

'Sorry, to startle you miss. Can I see your ticket, please?'

Weak with relief, Kathy fumbled in her bag for the ticket and gave it to the ticket collector. As he handed it back he smiled.

'I wouldn't go back to sleep if I was you,' he advised. 'It's Northampton next stop.'

It was just after three when she stepped off the train at Northampton's Castle Station. The platform was empty and she was the only passenger to alight; it was just her and the mail bags which were quickly loaded onto a trolley and rumbled off to a waiting van.

Her mouth was dry and she felt stiff and cold. On the platform a couple of dim lights were burning. It was far too early to try to contact the Spicers and when she tried the handle of the waiting-room door she found it locked. An icy wind blew along the platform and the bench she found to sit on was wet with dew. She'd been sitting there, shivering for about half an hour when she saw a bulky uniformed figure approaching, flashing a torch from side to side. When the beam shone dazzlingly in her eyes, she screwed them up against the glare. She heard a voice say,

'Hello! What have we got here then?'

Kathy opened her eyes and saw the broad shoulders and kindly face of a man in railway uniform. 'I – got off the London train,' she explained. 'The waiting-room's locked.'

'Got nowhere to go then?'

'Yes. I've come to visit friends, but it's too early to telephone them.'

He put a tentative hand on her arm and looked shocked as his fingers came away wet with dew. 'Well, you can't stay out here, miss,' he said. 'You're wet through. You'll catch your death. Better come into the office. There's a stove in there. Come on. I'll make you a cup of tea. You look as though you could do with it.'

Kathy stood up and followed him gratefully. Inside his little cubby hole of an office a paraffin stove threw out a comforting warmth and the kettle that sat on top of it was already boiling. As the man made tea in a blue enamelled can, he surveyed her out of the corners of his eyes. He had a young daughter of his own and he'd have been horrified to find her out at this time of a morning, just off the London train – friends or no friends.

He poured the strong tea laced with condensed milk into two mugs and passed one to her. 'So – what were you thinking of, coming up here to see your friends in the middle of the night?' he asked.

Kathy folded her cold hands gratefully round the warm mug and sipped the hot sweet liquid. 'I went to catch an earlier train last night but I missed it,' she said.

'So why didn't you go home and wait till morning?'

'I – meant to catch the next one. There was an hour to wait so I went into the news theatre on Euston Station and I – I dropped off to sleep; I missed the next one, too.' She applied herself to the tea again, hiding her face in the mug. She hated the easy, glib way the lies tripped off her tongue. Was she becoming an accomplished liar? The thought horrified her.

If the ticket clerk was doubtful about her explanation he didn't show it. Instead he smiled. 'Seems to me you need a good night's kip, girl,' he said. 'Dropping off all over the shop. What are we going to do with you, eh?' He looked at her long and hard. 'Who are these friends you're going to visit then? What's their name?'

'Spicer,' she told him. 'They live at Magpie Farm in Beckets Green.'

'Beckets Green's a good eight miles out of town. I don't know what time the buses start running.' He raised an eyebrow. 'And they're expecting you, are they?'

'Well, no. It was meant to be a surprise. I was evacuated there in the war and I thought. . . .' she trailed off.

He reached across and gently touched her shoulder. 'Not in any trouble, duck, are you?' he asked. 'Not running away?'

'No!' Realizing how sharp the denial sounded she shook her head. 'Nothing like that. I just wanted to see them. That's all.'

'Well look, if they live on a farm they're bound to be early risers. In another half-hour it'll be five o'clock. You can give them a ring from the phone in here if you want. You never know your luck, they might even come and fetch you.' He pointed to the instrument that stood on the desk.

Kathy nodded. 'That's very kind of you. Thanks.'

Kathy learned that the ticket clerk's name was Alf and, as her damp coat hung on a hook to dry he passed the time by showing her snapshots of his family. First there was one of him and his wife in their neat, pretty garden. (*My Ethel tends the flowers and I grow the veg.*) Then his married daughter and her baby boy. (*She was only eighteen – far too young to get married but her young man was in the army and about to be sent abroad so what can you do?*) Then there was his other daughter who was seventeen and worked in Woolworth's on the toy counter. (*A good girl, she is, a big help to her mum. My Ethel's a martyr to her varicose veins you see.*) So carried away with his family history was he, that he didn't notice the time until it was almost five-thirty. When he did happen to catch sight of the clock he was apologetic.

'Well hang me! Look at that time! Here's me going on and on about my lot when you're dying to phone your friends. You should've said, duck.' He stood up and reached for his coat and torch. 'I'm going to take another turn round the platforms before my shift's done so just help yourself,' he told her.

Kathy opened her bag and took out Elaine's last letter. She always wrote on the farm's stationery which bore the telephone number as well as the address. With trembling fingers she dialled and listened to the phone ringing out at the other end. At last Lena's brisk voice answered.

'Magpie Farm. Mrs Spicer speaking.'

'Auntie Lena – it's me, Kathy.'

'*Kathy*! What a surprise. Where are you?'

'I'm at the station – in Northampton. I – I'd like to come and see you if that's all right. Can you tell me what time the buses start running?'

'Kathy, you sound odd, dear. Is there something wrong? What train did you get to arrive so early? Is everything all right?'

The sound of Lena's voice, her kindness and concern destroyed all Kathy's courage in one fell swoop and she found herself perilously close to tears. She swallowed hard at the lump in her throat. 'Not – not really,' she said shakily. 'I just need to see you.'

'Just stay right where you are. I'm coming to fetch you.' Lena sounded as she always had in school, firm and authoritative; Kathy found it infinitely comforting.

'Thanks, Auntie Lena. If you're sure it's no trouble.'

'Of course it's no trouble. I'll be about half an hour. Will you be all right till then?'

'Yes, of course. Thank you and – and, Auntie Lena. . . .'

'Yes?'

'I can't wait to see you.'

His shift at an end, the ticket collector was relieved by his replacement, a surly looking young man who looked suspiciously at Kathy as he took up his position behind the ticket window and watched as she put on her coat. She was glad she'd been lucky enough to have had the company of the kind hearted Alf while she waited.

'I'm off now then, duck,' he said as he wheeled out his bicycle. 'I'm glad your friend is coming to pick you up. When you've got a good breakfast inside you and you've had some sleep you'll be as good as new. Look after yourself.' And he pedalled off with a cheery wave.

It was light now, the sky a pearly grey with a watery sun just beginning to break through low in the east. The new ticket clerk had unlocked the waiting-room and Kathy gratefully took herself off to the 'Ladies' to tidy herself up. She didn't want Lena to see her looking grimy and dishevelled. As the hands of the station clock reached six, she walked out on to the forecourt and a few moments later she was enormously cheered by the sight of the farm pick-up truck turning in at the station approach. Lena drew to a stop and jumped out. She held out her arms and Kathy ran into them.

'Kathy!' Lena held her at arms' length to look at her. 'My dear child you look exhausted. Hop in and we'll get you back to the farm.'

On the drive to Beckets Green Kathy learned that Lena and James were on their own at the farm. Elaine was spending a few days with a friend who would be going to college with her.

'They start next week,' Lena said. 'So they decided to do some shopping together for things they'll need. When she gets back tomorrow we're going to have to start packing for her.'

Kathy felt a pang of regret and envy to think that she too could have been part of all the excitement of starting college. 'And Chris?' she asked.

'Chris is due home at the end of the month,' Lena said. 'He's going to be taking a lot of the weight off James's shoulders, thank goodness.'

'I know. I had a letter from him,' Kathy said.

'We haven't put any pressure on him about helping on the farm. We'd both much rather he was taking up his place at Cambridge,' Lena said with a sigh. 'But it seems to be what he genuinely wants.'

'I'm sure it is.'

'And of course the farm will be his when James retires.'

'Does Uncle James know I'm here?' Kathy asked.

'He does and he's looking forward to seeing you.'

'Yes but – does he mind? I mean, it's a cheek really, isn't it – just landing myself on you like this?'

'We both know you better than to think you'd take advantage.' Lena looked sideways at the girl sitting at her side. She looked so pale and drawn. She'd realized as soon as Kathy telephoned that this was more than just a casual visit. 'Kathy – what's wrong, darling?' she asked. 'Do you want to tell me before we get home?'

Kathy sighed. 'Charlie and Bill are into things I don't want to get involved in,' she said, her eyes downcast.

Lena frowned. 'They haven't – hurt you – haven't forced you to do anything – *immoral*?'

'Oh no, nothing like that. In their own way I suppose they've been quite kind. We were never what you'd call family though. And now – since they came out of the army they – especially Charlie – are into every kind of illegal activity you can think of.'

'Petty crime.' Lena nodded. 'I can't say I'm surprised, but why did they want you to go back and live with them?'

'They've got a shop, a tobacconist's and sweet shop. I've been running it for them.'

'I see. A front for their other activities no doubt.' Lena was secretly relieved. She had feared that the Brady brothers may have had other – more sinister plans for Kathy. Maybe they had. Perhaps she had escaped in the nick of time.

'I found out that Charlie isn't really my legal guardian,' Kathy went on. 'I went to see Father Gerard and he says it would never have been allowed, especially with Charlie not even being a blood relative. So he has no hold on me – he can't make me go back.'

'I was never entirely happy about you going back to London,' Lena confessed. 'I'm so glad you felt you could come back to us. Since your mother died I've always felt that we are the nearest you have to a proper family, Kathy, and I know she would want us to support you in any way we could.'

Kathy nodded. 'I can't thank you enough, Auntie Lena.' She had left out the part about Gus Norris and the way she had been used as a decoy. She hadn't mentioned her shameful relationship with Jeff either, or the stolen goods she had found stashed in the cellar at Kemsley Street. She told herself that the less Lena knew, the better. All she really wanted was to put the last two years behind her and try to start again.

As Lena drew the truck to a stop in the yard, she turned to Kathy. 'I'll have to tell James what you've told me,' she said. 'I'm sure you'll agree that it's only fair that he knows the truth.'

'Yes, of course.'

'But when Elaine comes home tomorrow, and then Chris in a few weeks' time, it will be up to you what you tell them, but it must come from you. I shan't say anything. All right?'

'Thanks, Auntie Lena.'

The farm looked just the same. She might never have been away. The kitchen was warm and once they had taken off their outdoor things, Lena immediately set about cooking Kathy some breakfast. A golden Labrador took up his position next to her as she sat at the table, his tongue lolling in an ingratiating grin.

'This must be Winston,' Kathy said, patting his head. 'Elaine told me about him in her letter.'

Lena looked round. 'That's right. And the biggest con-man you've ever met. When he gives you that pitiful look that says he's starving don't believe him.' She put the loaded plate in front of Kathy. 'While you're eating this I'll go up and make up the bed in your old room,' she said. 'I'll be off to school soon after eight. Joan will be here by then to make James his breakfast when he comes in. I want you to have a good sleep.' She looked at Kathy. 'No arguments now, Miss O'Connor!'

Kathy smiled. 'No arguments.'

'Right then. I'll see you at four o'clock.'

Kathy ate the breakfast hungrily; home cured bacon and new laid eggs. Thick slices of Joan's home made bread toasted golden brown and spread with farm butter. She had forgotten how good country food was.

'There's plenty of hot water if you want a bath,' Lena had said. 'No one will disturb you until you're ready to get up.' She paused to take Kathy's face between her hands and look into her eyes.

'As far as anyone outside these four walls is concerned you are here for an extended visit,' she said. 'What you've told me is strictly between the two of us and James, all right?' Kathy nodded. 'And I've only just remembered something,' Lena went on. 'Today is your birthday. Many happy returns, Kathy darling. And welcome home.'

Kathy's eyes widened in surprise. Her birthday had been the last thing on her mind. In fact she had completely forgotten it. But most overwhelming was the phrase, 'welcome home'. The two simple words were the last straw for her fragile state of mind and she burst into tears.

When Kathy first woke she could not remember were she was. Many times since returning to London she had dreamed of being back at Magpie Farm and for a moment she thought she was dreaming again. Then, slowly the events of the previous night drifted back into her consciousness and she thanked God she was here safe and sound. The afternoon sun was streaming through her window and, looking at the bedside clock she saw that it was three o'clock. Lena would be home before long. She decided to get up, have a bath and dress, so as to be downstairs when she arrived home.

In the kitchen she found Joan, busying herself with preparations for the evening meal which Lena would cook later. As Kathy came into the kitchen she looked up with a welcoming smile.

'Well, as I live and breathe!' She hugged Kathy warmly. 'Mr Spicer told me you'd come back when he came in for his breakfast.' She held Kathy at arms' length and looked at her critically. 'Mmm, you've grown since you left here. You're taller. Too thin though and a bit pale, but we'll soon fix that and no mistake. Now then, what can I get you, girl? Are you hungry?'

Kathy laughed. 'Auntie Lena made me a huge breakfast. A cup of tea would be lovely though, if you've got time before you go home. I want to hear all your news.'

Over a pot of tea Joan told her that her children were all doing well. The two oldest boys were at grammar school and the girls were in Lena's class at the village school.'

'And your husband?' Kathy asked.

Joan pursed her lips. 'As well as can be expected. He's never been quite the same since the war though – only to be expected. His old wound still gives him gyp sometimes, but he's got his job back here on the farm with his beloved cows and that's all he really wants from life.' She refilled their cups. 'Do you know, I still get Christmas cards from my evacuees, bless their hearts. And now here *you* are back again. Beckets Green must have something about it that pulls folks back, though I must say that I thought you'd have been back to see us before now. Still, never mind, you're here now. How long can you stay?'

Kathy shrugged. 'Well – I'd like to stay permanently, see if there are any jobs going and find a place to live. Make it my home.'

'Never settled back in London then?'

'No. It wasn't the same without Mum. . . .'

' 'Course it wasn't, bless you.' Joan got up and cleared the table. 'Only ever went to London once in my life,' she said with a shake of her head. 'Nasty smelly, dirty place; folks all rushing and tearing about. Couldn't wait to get back to Beckets Green again. Never had the urge to go back.'

Kathy laughed. 'I know what you mean, and the blitz certainly hasn't improved it.' She looked up. 'Have there been any changes in the village?'

Joan sat down again. 'Well now, let me think. Miss Jolly at the Cosy Shop has retired and the couple who've bought it have turned it into a baby clothes and toy shop. I reckon the sweet rationing and the tobacco shortage wrecked the business. Apart from that everything's much the same.' She took off her overall and hung it on its hook behind the pantry door. 'Elaine'll be surprised to see you when she gets back tomorrow. And then our handsome young army officer will be marching back home in a couple of weeks. I know he'll be pleased to see you – and you him, I bet.'

'It'll be lovely to see them both.'

Joan grinned. 'I should think so, too.' She fetched her coat from the lobby and pulled it on. 'Well, I'll love you and leave you now. Tell Mrs Spicer I've done the veg and chopped up the meat for the casserole. It's all in the pantry. I'll be off now then. See you in the morning, duck.'

It took Kathy a long time to get to sleep that night. It was true that her sleep during the day had taken the edge off her weariness, but once the lights were out and the house was still she found the depth of the countryside silence disturbing.

She lay there, her body tense as she listened for the slightest sound, her mind clear and active. She found herself comparing the life she had led in London to the simplicity of the day-to-day existence here.

She had persuaded herself that it was better for Lena not to know everything that had happened, but now she knew that she wasn't being completely honest with herself. In truth she was deeply ashamed of the things she had done. She could have refused Jeff's advances. She could have refused to go to the Prince of Wales that night to lure Gus Norris to a horrific beating. The fact that it had been naïvety to trust Charlie and that she could not possibly have foreseen the outcome of her actions passed her by. The fact remained that she was no longer the innocent young girl she had been when she was last at Magpie Farm and the thought of her friends knowing what she had done – what she had become made her shrivel up inside with guilt and shame.

Could she turn back the clock and be the same as before? Was it fair to deceive the Spicers? But when she came down to the bare truth, did she really have any choice? All she could hope for was that somehow she would be able to turn her life around and make up for everything that had gone wrong. If she was to have any chance at all she would have to put the past two years out of her mind and turn her face firmly towards the future.

The following morning on Joan's advice she went for a walk round the village, armed with a shopping list of things needed at the farm. She found few changes apart from the Cosy Shop, which was now called Lullaby. The post office still sold its bizarre assortment of goods and she couldn't resist going in to spend some of her sweet ration when she saw that among the bottles on the shelf behind the counter were her favourite pear drops. Mrs Trent looked hard at her as she weighed the sweets out.

'Don't I know you?' she said as she slid the sweets into their conical paper bag. Kathy smiled.

'I'm Kathy O'Connor. I was evacuated here – to Magpie Farm with the Spicer family.'

The woman smiled. 'Well I'm blowed! So you are. You've grown up a bit since then. Back here on holiday, are you?' She took Kathy's money and put it into the old fashioned cash register with a loud *ching!*

'Well, no, not really,' Kathy said. 'I'm hoping to stay on permanently if I can find a job.'

'Didn't you like being back in London then?'

Kathy shook her head. 'My mother was killed in the blitz. It just wasn't the same without her. I tried for two years but there's nothing to keep me there any more.'

Mrs Trent nodded. 'You're not the only one. A lot of evacuees stayed on you know. Some Londoners had no idea there was such a thing as the country till the war. Once they found it they didn't want to go back to city life.'

Kathy put the bag of sweets into her handbag. 'Well, it's nice to see you again, Mrs Trent,' she said, moving away. 'Thanks.'

She was halfway through the shop door when Mrs Trent called out, 'Just a minute. Did you say you're looking for work?'

Kathy turned. 'Yes.'

'Well – I don't know what kind of work you had in mind.'

'For the past year and a half I've been running a tobacconist's and sweet shop,' Kathy told her.

'Really? Well I'm looking for a young woman assistant. But then I expect you'll be like all the other young girls – wanting to work in town, not stuck out here in a village.'

'Not at all,' Kathy assured her. 'There's nothing I'd like better.'

Mrs Trent looked pleased. 'Good. In that case would you like to come and talk to me about it later today, after closing time?'

Kathy's heart leapt. 'Oh, yes please, I would. I mean that would be marvellous.'

'Good. That's arranged then. Come about six o'clock.'

When Kathy walked in through the back door at Magpie Farm, Elaine was standing with her back to her, talking to Joan. Kathy opened her bag and took out the pear drops.

'Like a sweet?'

Elaine spun round, her cheeks pink and her eyes shining. '*Kathy*! No one told me you were here.' She looked inside the paper bag that Kathy held out. 'Wow, pear drops! You jammy little beast. Where did you get them?'

They both burst out laughing and Elaine threw her arms round Kathy and hugged her tight. 'Why didn't you write and tell me you were coming? How long can you stay?'

Kathy laughed. 'Which question would you like me to answer first?'

Elaine shook her head. 'Come on, let's go upstairs. We've got so much catching up to do.' As she skipped off Kathy hesitated but Joan, who had watched the whole encounter with a big smile on her face nodded towards the door.

'I didn't tell her,' she said. 'Thought you'd like to surprise her. Off you go,' she said, flapping her hand. 'I'll give you a call when lunch is ready.'

Kathy handed her the shopping bag and as she did so her eye was caught by the headline on the morning paper which lay on the table, left by James when he came in for his elevenses. The large black letters seemed to leap out at her with their dramatic message and her blood turned to ice.

ASSAULT VICTIM DIES. HUNT ON FOR MURDERER.

CHAPTER NINE

'What I'm looking for is a girl to help me generally in the shop and the post office,' Mrs Trent said. 'But I'll be honest with you; most of the local girls just aren't interested.'

'I see.'

Kathy was seated with the postmistress in the pleasant little sitting-room of her cottage which adjoined the post office, a tea tray between them on the table. 'Of course it would be a permanent position,' Mrs Trent went on. 'So if it's only temporary work you want you'd better say so right away. It won't upset me. I know you young girls want to see a bit more of the bright lights nowadays. Since the war the young people aren't prepared to live and work in one place like their parents were. Most of them are off into town for jobs.'

'Not me,' Kathy said firmly. 'I like the sound of the job very much.'

'I'm hoping to retire in a couple of years' time and if whoever gets the job is happy and successful they could take up the option to replace me as postmistress.'

'Oh.'

'That would mean a course of training with the GPO and so on.' Mrs Trent cocked an eyebrow at Kathy. 'Would that kind of prospect interest you?'

Kathy nodded enthusiastically. 'Oh yes, it would.'

Mrs Trent smiled. 'Now you say you've been running a shop in London so I take it you'll have references.'

'Oh!' Kathy's heart sank. 'Well – no.'

Mrs Trent looked up in surprise. 'No?'

'It was a family business,' Kathy explained. 'Owned by my step-brothers. We didn't really get on which is why I left and I'd rather not ask them.'

'Oh – I see.' Mrs Trent looked disappointed and doubtful.

'But it was nothing to do with my work in the shop,' Kathy added hurriedly. 'More family matters. And I did get a credit for maths in my school certificate.'

'Well, that's certainly helpful.'

'And I'm sure that Mrs Spicer and Miss Redfern, the head mistress at St Ursula's, would vouch for me.'

Mrs Trent smiled. 'Of course. Would you like to go away and think about it, Kathy? Maybe you'd like to talk it over with your friends at the farm.'

Kathy bit her lip. 'Does that mean you're prepared to take a chance on me?'

'We could see how it goes, yes. We could have a trial period for say a month – on both sides of course.'

Kathy stood up. 'All I have to do now is to find somewhere to live.'

'Yes.' Mrs Trent looked thoughtful. 'Of course when I retire there'll be the cottage that goes with the job, if you were to stay on that is,' she said. 'I've got my eye on a nice bungalow on the Kettering road, but that's looking rather a long way ahead.' She stood up and held out her hand to Kathy. 'Well, let me know what you think, Kathy. Take your time.'

Kathy shook her hand. 'I'll let you know tomorrow,' she said.

As she walked back to the farm Kathy could hardly believe her luck. The prospect of a job and a place to live – even if it was in the distant future was more than she had dared to hope for. Then her heart plummeted as she remembered the headline in yesterday's paper. She had been shocked that Gus Norris had died from the injuries Charlie and Bill had inflicted, and deeply mortified at the part she had played in the attack, however unwittingly. It was something that would weigh heavily on her conscience for the rest of her life. She longed to be able to talk to someone about it, but apart from Father Gerard there was no one she could expect to understand. And now the police hunt was on for his murderer. From now on she would be scanning the papers every day; half of her hoping that the police would catch up with Charlie and Bill; the other half dreading the thought that under questioning they might implicate her in what happened that night. The thought of going to court, giving evidence and – the worst possible conclusion – being charged with being an accessory made her shudder. But even that

wasn't as bad as having the Spicers find out about the kind of life she
had lived in London.

She tried to take comfort from the thought that Charlie would surely
not be inclined to come looking for her with the police on the trail of
Gus's murderer. He'd be far more likely to keep a low profile. She
hoped that the threat in her letter would be enough to convince him
that it would be in his best interest to leave her alone. Somehow over
the coming weeks she was going to have to sit tight – hope and pray
that the worst wouldn't happen.

Back at the farm Lena, James and Elaine were waiting eagerly for
news of her interview and were delighted for her when she told them
about Mrs Trent's offer. Lena agreed readily to give her a testimonial
and advised Kathy to telephone Miss Redfern herself the following
morning.

'I still have to find somewhere to live,' Kathy said. 'I can't stay here
with you indefinitely.'

'You know you're welcome to stay as long as you want to,' Lena
said.

'It's really kind of you, but it's not fair to impose on your hospitality.'

Elaine nudged her mother. 'What she's trying to say, Mum, is that
she wants her independence,' she said. 'Only she's too polite to say so.'
She raised a cheeky eyebrow at Kathy. 'Aren't I right?'

Kathy coloured. 'No, not at all! I'm so grateful for everything you've
done for me but I can't impose on your generosity any longer than
necessary.'

Lena reached out to touch her shoulder. 'We know how appreciative
you are, Kathy, but Elaine is right. You're a young woman now and
you'll be needing a place of your own. And you certainly won't want
to wait until Mrs Trent retires to her dream bungalow.'

James, who had sat in silence throughout the discussion looked up.
'There's always "Shepherd's",' he said.

Lena looked up. 'Of course.' She looked doubtful. 'It's been empty
an awfully long time though, since before the war, when we used to
have sheep.'

'That's a brilliant idea!' Elaine was on her feet. 'We could do it up,
couldn't we? It would be such fun.' She looked at Kathy. 'Don't you
remember "Shepherd's"? It's the pretty little cottage at the end of

Willow Lane.' She clapped her hands. 'Can we go and look at it tomorrow?'

'You've got packing to do, young lady,' Lena reminded her. 'Do I need to remind you that you're off to college in two days' time?'

'But I could help with the renovation at weekends.'

'Just don't get carried away,' James reminded his daughter. 'You're going to have a lot of work to do, so don't make promises you might not be able to keep.' He smiled at Kathy. 'It's certainly worth having a look at the cottage and if it's in a reasonable state of repair I don't see why you shouldn't live in it.'

'We had some vague idea of renting it out as a holiday let,' Lena said. 'But somehow we've never actually done anything about it.'

'I'll pay the proper rent of course,' Kathy said.

'Well, that's something we'll have to think about,' James said. 'You'd be doing us a favour by being a kind of caretaker really. It's a pity to have it standing empty.'

Later, upstairs in Kathy's room, Elaine sprawled on the bed. 'Oh, I wish I wasn't going to college now,' she said. 'It's sick, having to miss all the fun.'

'You're the one who'll be having all the fun,' Kathy told her. 'I just wish I was going to college with you. If only I hadn't wasted two years in London getting nowhere.'

Elaine eyed her friend. 'Actually I've got a bone to pick with you,' she said. 'Why didn't you ever invite me up to stay? I imagined us going shopping in the West End and going to the theatre – having all sorts of fun.'

Kathy turned to her apologetically. 'I wish I'd been able to. But it isn't what you think. Things are getting better all the time, but there's still an awful lot of bomb damage. And where we lived was horrible. You'd have hated it.'

'I'd have loved to see you though. I really missed you when you left,' Elaine told her. 'Then I chummed up with Shirley Mills. You probably won't remember her. She was in a different form to us, but she and I were in the sixth together for two years so we got to know one another pretty well. You'd like her.'

'And that's who you're going to college with?'

'That's right. She saved my life really. As I said I missed you like mad and then when Chris went off to do his National Service it was so deadly dull round here.' Her face broke into a grin. 'But that was before Nigel came back from university. Oh, Kathy, I can't wait for you to see him. He's so gorgeous. You wouldn't believe how handsome he's become. He's doing his pre reg year at Northampton General now so we see quite a bit of each other.'

'So most of your time at weekends will be taken up with him,' Kathy suggested.

'Not always. It depends what shifts he's on. The young doctors have to work terribly hard you know.' Elaine rolled onto her tummy and rested her chin on one hand. 'So – what about you? Don't tell me you've spent two years in London without having a boyfriend – or three.' She giggled.

Kathy shrugged, avoiding her friend's eyes. 'Not really.'

'Go on, pull the other one. I don't believe you. Anyway, you're blushing.'

'Well – there was one.'

'I knew it!' Elaine sat up, her eyes eager. 'Come on then, give. I want to hear all about him.'

'There's nothing to tell. It didn't work out – it was a disaster really.' Kathy was already regretting any mention of her relationship with Jeff. She was trying so hard to put it out of her mind, but Elaine had a way of getting things out of you whether you wanted to tell her or not.

'*How* didn't it work out?' Clearly Elaine wasn't going to let the matter drop. 'Come on, I want to hear all the details.'

'He wasn't what I thought, that's all.' Kathy shook her head. 'I don't want to talk about him. It's all in the past.'

'Oh, get you, woman of mystery!' Elaine laid the back of her hand against her brow. '*All in the past!* You sound like something out of Jane Austen. Go on, misery guts, don't be so cagey. You can tell me. What did he do? Did he two-time you? Did he break your heart?' She swung her legs to the floor and peered closely at her friend. 'Did you sleep with him? Nigel and I haven't – not yet, but—' A sudden rapping on the door stopped her in mid-sentence.

'*Elaine*! Go to bed now, please. Your father has to get up for milking at five, remember and you're keeping us awake.'

Elaine sighed. 'OK, Mum, just going.' She stood up and shot a last reproachful look at Kathy. 'Don't you think I'll forget about it,' she whispered. 'I want the full story so don't imagine you're going to get

away with it. *It's all in the past indeed!'* She grinned unrepentantly.
'Nighty-night. Mind the bugs don't bite. See you in the morning.'

When she'd gone Kathy slipped into bed and switched off the light.
Suddenly in spite of her youth she felt old. Elaine was still so imma-
ture. Life still hadn't touched her. She was still the schoolgirl she had
been two years ago, full of mischief and fun – so confident of the
future. True, her life was about to unfold, with a steady boyfriend,
college friends and taking charge of her own life for the first time, but
at heart she would always belong to her family and life here at the
farm. She obviously adored Nigel and the chances were that she would
become Mrs Oliver, the village doctor's wife and live happily at
Beckets Green for the rest of her days. Kathy wished with all her heart
that her own life could be as uncomplicated and idyllic.

The following morning Kathy went into the village and told Mrs Trent
that she would like to take up her offer of a job as assistant at the post
office. They talked briefly about her wages, hours and duties and it was
arranged that she would start on Monday morning. Then, after a quick
telephone call to make sure it was convenient, she caught the bus into
town and paid a visit to her old school.

Miss Redfern was delighted to see her and very interested in the
prospective new job at Beckets Green post office.

'It sounds like a very good opportunity,' she said. 'Such a pity you
couldn't have stayed on and gone to teacher training college with
Elaine. You were one of that year's brightest pupils. What I would
really have liked would have been to see you get a university place, but
under the circumstances I always knew that was unrealistic.' She
smiled. 'I'll write a letter of recommendation to Mrs Trent this afternoon.' She rose and held out her hand to Kathy. 'Good luck, my dear.
Keep in touch and come and see us again soon.'

At Magpie Farm Elaine waited impatiently. 'Come on, Dad's given
me the key for "Shepherd's". Let's go now before lunch. I've done as
much packing as I can. I'll swear that packing is the most boring activity in the world and I can't wait to get out of the house.'

It was a crisp autumn day and as they walked down Willow Lane
with Winston trotting at their heels Elaine filled Kathy in on the history
of Shepherd's Cottage.

'I was only little when we had sheep on the farm and Ben Grimshaw was our shepherd. He and his wife Molly lived at "Shepherd's" and kept it like a new pin. Molly Grimshaw was a keen gardener. She grew all the old fashioned flowers, you know, hollyhocks and cornflowers and loads of roses. At the back she grew all their own vegetables and she used to win prizes at the village fête most years.'

When they arrived at the cottage Kathy saw that it obviously hadn't been lived in or cared for in years. The hedge was six feet tall and overgrown and the roses that grew round the front porch were straggly and running to briar. The house itself however, a stout little Victorian cottage with a slate roof and leaded windows, looked in fairly good shape.

'I used to come here a lot at lambing time,' Elaine said, unlocking the front door. 'Ben used to bring the motherless lambs home for Molly to rear. She used to keep them warm in the bread oven and she used to let me feed them with a baby's bottle. They were so sweet.'

Inside was a tiny square hall with a stone-flagged floor and a dog-leg staircase leading to the upper floor. On the right a door led into a living-room which looked out on to the front and side of the cottage. At the rear was a kitchen with a cooking range and from there a door lead into a scullery with a sink and cupboards. Flagstones covered the whole of the ground floor. Upstairs there were two bedrooms, one facing front above the living-room and a smaller one at the back, over the kitchen.

Elaine peered up at the ceilings. 'The roof must be sound,' she said. 'No water stains. I bet Dad and Fred Harris will be able to fix anything that needs doing in no time and Mum will help you decorate.' She looked doubtful. 'The lav's outside I'm afraid and there's no bathroom of course. I think the Grimshaws used to lug a tin bath in from the shed and scrub each others backs in front of the range on Friday nights.' She giggled. 'Sounds cosy, doesn't it? Never mind, I'm sure Mum will be happy for you to have a bath at the farm any time you like.' She gave Kathy an excited hug. 'Just think, your own little nest. Aren't you excited?'

'Yes, I am. I think it's lovely.'

'Let's go out and have a look at the garden,' Elaine suggested. 'I bet Chris will give you a hand with that when he comes home.' She gave Kathy a nudge. 'Hey, I bet you're looking forward to seeing him? You used to have a terrific crush on him, didn't you?'

Kathy laughed in spite of herself. 'We were only kids then.'

'Go on! Who's kidding who? Remember when he kissed you under the mistletoe that Christmas? I've never seen such a red face! He even wrote you a letter from Germany, didn't he?'

Kathy's hand went to the little locket which she'd worn around her neck ever since she received it, but she didn't tell Elaine that Chris had sent it. She knew she'd never hear the last of it if she did. 'Yes, he did,' she admitted. 'But then I expect he wrote to all his friends.'

In the garden, in spite of the long grass and the tangle of weeds, it was still possible to see the outline of the beds where Mrs Grimshaw had grown her flowers and vegetables.

'Shouldn't take long to get it straight again,' Elaine said airily.

'I don't know a thing about gardening,' Kathy said.

Elaine laughed. 'Chris does. You'll be able to flatter his male ego by fluttering your eyelashes and playing Little Miss Helpless.'

'I don't think that's a part I'd be very good at.'

'I'm sure you could if you tried,' Elaine laughed. 'Especially to get Chris twisted round your little finger, eh?'

The weeks that followed were busy. It was arranged that Kathy should work in the shop to begin with while she was waiting for a place to come up on the training course Mrs Trent had applied for on her behalf. Many of the local people remembered her and it was pleasant to renew acquaintance with them. To Kathy's delight, Arnold, Mrs Trent's large ginger cat was still alive and took an immediate shine to Kathy, never straying far from her feet under the counter as she worked.

Meantime James had given Fred Harris time off to work on the necessary repairs at 'Shepherd's'. He had replaced the guttering and rusty hinges on doors and windows, swept the chimney and the range flue and given the exterior woodwork a coat of paint. James had arranged for the electricity to be connected again and in the evenings Kathy and Lena went along after dinner with brushes, buckets and brooms, sweeping and scrubbing till the whole cottage shone with cleanliness. But the evenings were pulling in now that autumn was here and the light faded too quickly for decorating.

'We'll have to do it at the weekends,' Lena said. 'I know you have to work on Saturdays but Elaine is keen to help. She can make a start with me this Saturday.'

Kathy shook her head. 'It's so good of you to go to all this trouble for me.' she said. 'I feel quite guilty.'

'Well don't!' Lena said firmly. '"Shepherd's" is our cottage and it really has been criminal of us to have neglected it like this. This is only what we should have done ages ago.'

It took the three of them three weekends to complete the redecoration of the little cottage. Each room was painted a different colour and the old brown paintwork replaced by pristine white. The whole place looked light and airy – and surprisingly, much larger than before.

Kathy came home on the fourth Saturday evening to find that Lena and Elaine had not only lit the range to give the cottage a final airing; they had also unearthed some discarded furniture that Lena and James had stowed away over the years in the attic; wheeling it down the lane to 'Shepherd's' on a handcart and setting out the rooms with the essentials.

'It'll do until you can get something better,' Lena said.

'*Better*? It couldn't be better – it's perfect!' Kathy stood looking around her with tears in her eyes. There were rugs on the floors, old ones, but newly shampooed and vacuumed; a scrubbed-top table and two chairs in the kitchen and a sofa and armchair in the living-room. Upstairs in the largest bedroom there was a single bed, the mattress of which Lena had aired and made up and new curtains hung at all the windows. Kathy shook her head. 'It looks just like a real home,' she said. 'And it feels so warm and welcoming. Thank you so much.'

'It's all a bit basic. The curtains are really just some old ones I've cut down to size, but you'll be able to replace everything in time,' Lena said. 'Of course new furniture is expensive and hard to come by at the moment, but there are always auctions on in town if you watch the local paper.'

'I will.' Kathy nodded. 'And I still have a little of the money that Mum left me put away. Oh, Auntie Lena, I can't thank you enough.'

'That's right, thank Mum!' Elaine protested giving Kathy a dig in the ribs. 'What about *me*, slogging my guts out every weekend? Tell you what – you can thank me by coming into town to the pictures with me tonight. And you can treat me to coffee and cakes afterwards. After all, I'm just a poor impoverished student and you're a well-off career woman!'

CHAPTER TEN

When Kathy's place on the GPO course came up she spent two days of each week going into Northampton on the bus to study at the technical college. By the time she had completed the course and passed the obligatory exam, Christmas was almost upon them and the village post office was busy with people sending letters, cards and parcels to their nearest and dearest. Mrs Trent was really glad her new assistant's studies were over and for Kathy's part the busy days flew past and she found working alongside Mrs Trent easy and companionable.

She had settled into Shepherd's Cottage happily, enjoying the luxury of having the whole place to herself. In spite of the lack of modern toilet facilities, Kathy managed well enough and it became part of her routine to go up to the farm every Saturday evening for a long soak in the bath, a meal shared with the family and sometimes, if Nigel wasn't home for the weekend a trip into town with Elaine to the cinema.

It was late one Saturday afternoon about a week before Christmas when she walked into the farm kitchen to find Chris there. He was in uniform and sat at the table, his back to her, drinking a mug of tea. Momentarily shocked, she stopped dead in her tracks.

'Oh! – hello.'

'Kathy!' His face broke into a smile as he turned and saw her. Getting to his feet he held out his hands.

'Well, well – after all this time! You look wonderful.' He took both her hands and squeezed them, then looked at her wide-eyed, pink-cheeked face.

'What's up? Have I changed that much?'

He had changed. He was taller and broader and so handsome that he quite took her breath away as well as her speech. But she shook her head, hiding her confusion with a laugh. '*You* – change? Of course you haven't. It's good to see you, Chris!'

He laughed. 'Phew! What a relief. I was beginning to think I'd grown another head or something, the way you were looking at me.'

'It was a shock, coming in and suddenly seeing you sitting there.'

'A *shock*? A good one, I hope.'

'Of course it is. I meant I wasn't expecting to see you, that's all.'

'Well, come and sit down,' he invited. 'Mum had to drive into town to meet Elaine – something about new shoes, but they'll be back soon. I think there's another cup of tea in the pot.' He took another mug from the dresser and filled it from the teapot, smiling at her as he pushed it across the table. 'So – tell me all about yourself. We've got a lot of catching up to do.'

Kathy hid her face in the mug. Still slightly flustered and trying to think of a way to avoid mentioning her time in London she said, 'I've got a job at the village post office,' she told him. 'Working with Mrs Trent.'

'So I hear.' He laughed. 'Hardly what you'd call a big career leap.'

She blushed, stung by the remark. 'Actually it *is*,' she said, a little too sharply. 'For me anyway. It's with a view to taking over from her when she retires. I've just finished a GPO training course and in a couple of years I hope to be village postmistress.'

His face fell. 'Oh, Kathy! That wasn't meant to be a put-down. I'm sorry. Being away in the army makes one forget that things move on. All I remember of the village post office is the jumble of things all cluttering the place up and that damned ginger tom asleep on the boiled ham in the window.'

She laughed in spite of herself. 'You mean poor old Arnold and you know perfectly well that he was never allowed near any open food. He's still around if you want to know. And we do still sell everything from a pin to an elephant, though I think it's a bit more organized than it used to be. You'll have to come down and have a look sometime.'

He shook his head. 'Just try and stop me, 'specially now that you're there. I'll be in and out for tupp'ny-ha'penny stamps every hour!'

'You look very smart in your uniform,' she told him. 'But I thought you were out of the army now.'

'Officially I will be tomorrow,' he said. 'I have to go into town and hand in all my gear in the morning. A sort of un-ceremonial passing out ceremony. When you arrived I was just thinking about going up to my room to see if any of my clothes still fit me. Being abroad for so long it's ages since I wore any of them.'

'I think you've grown a bit,' Kathy observed.

He smiled. 'And so have you, very nicely if you don't mind me saying so.' He drew his brows together. 'Oh dear, now I've made you blush again.' He reached across the table and took her hand. 'I like your hair too, Kathy. You're wearing it in a different style, though don't ask me how different! I'm useless at stuff like that. All I know is that it suits you.' She smiled, relaxing a little. 'So – how was London?' he asked. 'And what brings you back to Beckets Green? Didn't you enjoy living with your stepbrothers?'

She shrugged in an attempt to brush it off. 'No. It was all a waste of time. All I did was run my brother's shop and keep house. London's a mess – grey, smelly and dirty. I couldn't wait to get back here.'

'We turned you into a country girl, eh?'

'I'm happy here,' she said simply. 'Did your mother tell you I'm living in "Shepherd's Cottage"?'

'That old place? I'd imagine it must have fallen down by now.'

'Not at all. You should see it, Chris,' she enthused. 'Fred Harris and your dad did the repairs and Auntie Lena and Elaine helped me do it up. It's lovely – so cosy and warm. I'm saving up to buy some more furniture. You'll have to come down and see it.'

'Is that an invitation?'

'Only if you want to come.'

'You bet I want to come.'

At that moment the door burst open and Elaine rushed in, laden with parcels. On seeing her brother she tossed them all in the general direction of the sofa and threw herself into his arms.

'Chris! You rotten beast! Why didn't you tell us you were coming home today?'

Laughing he held her at arms' length. 'I didn't know myself till the last minute. Anyway, it won't be long before you're sick of the sight of me so don't pretend.'

Elaine gave his shoulder a playful punch. 'Don't improve much, do you?' She looked at Kathy. 'You two been catching up then?' She grinned her wicked grin. 'Have you invited him down to see your etchings yet?'

Lena, coming in through the door upbraided her. 'Really, Elaine! Poor Kathy. You're embarrassing her.' She took off her coat and began to bustle round. 'Joan left a pie in the oven. Elaine, can you start peeling the potatoes and perhaps Kathy wouldn't mind setting the table.'

Chris stood up. 'What can I do?'

Lena looked at him. 'Have you been through your wardrobe yet? You look to me as though you've broadened out since you were home last.'

He winced. 'Is that a motherly way of saying I've put on weight?'

Lena laughed. 'Don't worry, a few weeks of farm work will sort out those extra pounds.'

Elaine looked at her brother critically, her head on one side. 'Mmm, don't you mean *stones*, Mum?'

Chris gasped. '*Stones*? How dare you? I'll have you know this is all muscle.'

Lena clapped her hands. 'Stop it you two. You might as well be ten years old again. Doesn't take you long to pick up where you left off, does it? Come on now. Your father will be in for his meal soon.'

Everyone was in high spirits over the meal that evening. James celebrated his son's homecoming with a bottle of his best claret which everyone enjoyed along with Joan's meat pie. Elaine had announced that Nigel would be round to pick her up later. They had planned to go into town to a pre-Christmas dance.

'Why don't you two come too?' she said, looking across the table at her brother and Kathy. 'A foursome would be fun.'

'Great idea,' Chris said. He looked at Kathy. 'That is if you like the idea.'

She nodded. 'I'd love to go. The only thing is I haven't really got anything to wear that's suitable for a dance.'

'What about that rather sophisticated little black number I've seen in your wardrobe?' Elaine said. 'You'd knock 'em stone dead in that.'

Kathy paused. The black dress had been pushed to the back of her wardrobe. It held memories of Jeff that she would rather forget. On the other hand Elaine was right, it was the only suitable dress she possessed. 'Yes, there's that one, I suppose.'

Elaine assumed a nonchalant accent. *'Oh, there's that one, I suppose.* Listen to her, our cosmopolitan socialite. I suppose you think it's too smart for a provincial hop,' she said. 'We don't all wear frilly muslin out here in the sticks, you know.'

Seeing Kathy's uncomfortable expression, Lena broke in. 'Elaine, *really*! What is the matter with you this evening? I know you only mean to tease but sometimes you go too far. I'm sure thoughts like that never entered Kathy's head.'

Elaine had the grace to flush. 'Sorry,' she muttered. 'Look let me come down to the cottage with you and we'll see what you've got.'

Once outside Elaine turned to Kathy. 'You're not cross with me, are you? You know I don't mean anything. I just get carried away. All the excitement about Chris coming home sharpened my tongue. I am quite fond of the wretched boy, whatever it might look like.' She slipped her arm through Kathy's and smiled her cheeky smile. 'You do forgive me, don't you?'

Kathy smiled in spite of herself. 'OK, just as long as you promise not to make a habit of embarrassing me in public.'

'I promise.' Elaine hugged her arm and they walked in silence for a few minutes, then Elaine suddenly said, 'If you want to know the honest truth I'm a bit jealous of you.'

Kathy turned to stare at her. 'Of *me* – why?'

'Well, look at me, still all freckles and carroty hair.'

Kathy laughed. 'You have the most beautiful auburn hair. I'd give anything for colouring like yours.'

Elaine kicked at a stone. 'Yeah – so you say. Fact is – although it cuts me to the quick to say it – you've grown up to be sickeningly attractive,' Elaine said. 'Sometimes I think you don't even realize it yourself. Then there's the fact that you've lived in London – been places – done things; whilst I've never set a foot outside the county.' She looked at Kathy. 'In other words you're far more grown up and sophisticated than I'll ever be.'

Kathy stopped and turned Elaine to face her. 'Just remember that there's a price to pay for experience,' she said. 'Sometimes it's more than you want to pay. And sometimes it's not worth it.'

Elaine threw her hands up in the air. 'There! See what I mean? That is so profound. I'd never have thought of saying a thing like that in a million years! I'm not even sure I know what it means.' She grabbed

Kathy's arm again. Come on, let's get to grips with your wardrobe. I'm in the mood for some light entertainment.'

Kathy wore the black dress. Elaine lent her a pretty crystal necklace and earrings to match and she wore her brightest lipstick. As Doctor Oliver wasn't on call he had let Nigel borrow his car for the evening and the four of them travelled into town in style.

Kathy enjoyed herself enormously. The dance hall was decorated with balloons and streamers and by ten o'clock it was packed with revellers. The dance floor was full and Chris held her close as they moved slowly round.

'I couldn't have wished for a nicer homecoming,' He said into her ear. 'Elaine had written that you were back to stay but somehow I thought you would have changed.'

She looked up at him. 'Elaine thinks I have.'

He shook his head. 'Not to me. You were always a bit special to me, Kathy. You must have realized that.'

She laughed lightly. 'I know you were very kind – well, most of the time. Do you remember lending me your lucky penny on the day I took the scholarship exam?'

His eyebrows rose. 'Good heavens, did I? Obviously you never told anyone or I'd never have heard the last of it. That penny never leaves my pocket.'

'I'm honoured, just as I was then. And no, I didn't tell anyone. I thought it might break the spell. And I passed so it must have worked.'

The band stopped playing and they made their way back to the table where Elaine and Nigel were bubbling over with barely concealed excitement. On the table in front of them were four glasses and a dark bottle wearing a gold seal.

'Hello, what's all this?' Chris asked. 'It's not Christmas for another week yet so what's the celebration?'

'Well your homecoming, naturally,' Elaine said. 'But that's not all.'

'OK, I'll buy it.' Chris sat down, eyeing the bottle. 'You better get on and tell us before we die of thirst.'

Elaine looked at Nigel, but he shook his head. 'No – you tell them.'

Her face aglow she turned to the others. 'Nigel has just asked me to marry him,' she told them triumphantly.

'I know Elaine is still very young and it probably can't be for ages,' Nigel put in quickly. 'And of course I shall ask Mr Spicer's permission as soon as I can, but Elaine has said yes, so as from tonight we're unofficially engaged.'

There were hugs and kisses all round. The champagne cork popped accompanied by their laughter and the evening ended on a high note.

In the back of the car on the way back to Beckets Green Chris slid an arm around Kathy's shoulders and drew her close. 'I've just remembered something else,' he whispered.

'What's that?'

'The Christmas that I got up the nerve to kiss you under the mistletoe.' He put a finger under her chin and turned her face towards him. 'Do you remember that?'

She frowned. 'Erm – I *think* I do.'

'Only think? That won't do. I'd better remind you.'

The first kiss was brief. Chris looked into her eyes enquiringly. 'Ring any bells?'

'Mmm – one or two.'

He kissed her again – a kiss that lasted for quite a long time; a kiss that gave Kathy the distinct impression that her toes were melting. This time it wasn't bells ringing but sparklers fizzing and rockets exploding. Opening her eyes she saw through the darkened window of the car a shooting star high above in the winter sky. And then she knew for certain that she had found the man she would always love.

CHAPTER ELEVEN

Back at home at 'Shepherd's Cottage' that night Kathy lay in bed bathed in a warm glow with Chris's kisses still warm on her lips. But although she tried her hardest to ignore it the small insistent voice inside her head refused to be ignored and finally forced her to face facts.

She was reminded yet again of the part she had played in the assault on Gus Norris and, if anything even worse, her sleazy affair with Jeff Slater. Ruthlessly, she reminded herself that she was no longer the person Chris thought her to be. She had no right to his admiration let alone his love. He had said she had always been special and that she hadn't changed. How little he knew.

The two years she had spent in London with Charlie and Bill had turned her from an innocent young schoolgirl into – into *what*? Could she ever pay enough penance to make up for what she had almost become?

Every day since she had seen the headline, announcing that Gus Norris had died of the injuries he received she had watched the papers nervously for news of an arrest. If the police caught up with Charlie and Bill would they tell of her part in the attack? After all, on the afternoon when the police came she had provided them with an alibi. Realizing that, they were bound to assume she was implicated. She lived in fear and dread of the police turning up at Beckets Green to take her in for questioning. If that happened it would be the end of her job at the post office and any aspirations she might have of one day being promoted to postmistress. The GPO would certainly rule out employing anyone with a police record, especially for this kind of crime?

But gradually as the weeks went by and nothing happened she had begun to relax. It looked as though the boys had got away with this as they had with everything else crooked they involved themselves in. She was torn between resentment and relief.

Turning over in bed she asked herself what she could have done to avoid the events that had taken place. In all honesty she had been power-less, completely in Charlie's hands. Although it had broken her heart to leave Beckets Green and give up her college place, she had felt obliged to go back to London with the boys when Charlie had said he was her legal guardian. If only she had known it was a lie. If only she had gone to see Father Gerard and confided in him sooner. He would have helped her to discover the truth and done all he could to help her to get away.

Then there was Jeff. Naïvely she had been taken in by his sophisti-cated charm, his wealth and the authority he appeared to have. Now she saw it for what it had been – a sham, designed to lure her into his clutches. She wondered for the first time if Charlie had planned it all along, encouraging her to respond to Jeff's advances for – for what? To groom her for a life of vice? She shuddered, remembering the girls she had seen hanging around on street corners, accosting men in cars. Short skirts and too much make-up, bleached hair and behind it all, a dead forsaken look in their eyes. Could she have become one of them? She pushed the horrifying images from her mind. But however much she tried to turn her back on the past two years, it *had happened*; it was part of her past life and nothing in the world could alter that.

Chris deserved better, she told herself. At least he deserved to know the truth. But how could she bear to tell him? She tried to imagine the look of revulsion and disappointment on his face when she told him and it hurt so much that she buried her face in her pillow, the lump in her throat almost choking her. Lena had said that it was up to her how much she told Elaine and Chris. But even Lena didn't know the worst of it. Could she go on living a lie, deceiving the people she loved most in the world so that they would see her in a better light?

What were her options, she asked herself? Tell all and risk losing her job, her home, her best friends and the man she loved, or keep silent and let the past fester inside her like some virulent disease. As she finally drifted off to sleep she made a decision – of sorts. She had to tell the truth and she would – at least some of it – but not yet. Oh, please God, *not yet*.

*

Lena's parents, Margaret and Tom Lovell arrived from their home in Dorset on Christmas Eve. Kathy worked at the post office until they closed at six o'clock after which she had been invited to eat with the Spicers. She was invited to share Christmas Day with the family, too, but she had insisted that she would spend the rest of the holiday at 'Shepherd's', catching up with domestic chores. In actual fact she felt that she should not impose on the Spicers' generosity whilst Lena's parents were staying there. Lena saw so little of them and Kathy felt that it was only fair to let them have time together as a family.

Christmas Day was full of fun. The house looked festive with streamers and evergreens. A huge Christmas tree sparkled in the corner of the living-room, laden with coloured baubles and decorations; Lena had cooked a wonderful dinner, complete with the puddings she and Joan had made and put down to mature in late October and James provided wine from his much cherished cellar. Nigel joined the family after lunch and the day became a celebration of his and Elaine's engagement as well as Christmas.

The Lovells had brought presents for everyone, including Kathy, and when she opened her present on Christmas Day afternoon at tea time – which was the Spicers' traditional present opening time – she gasped with pleasure. A tiny silver brooch in the shape of a Cornish pixie nestled on a velvet bed in a little box.

'Oh, it's lovely,' she said.

Margaret smiled. 'They're said to bring good luck. Cornwall is only a few miles down the road from us,' she said. 'We're right on the border. You'll have to come and visit us sometime.' Kathy handed over her own gifts: a scarf for Margaret and tobacco for Tom. She'd tried hard to think of appropriate presents for everyone. The older members of the family had been easy and she knew that Elaine would appreciate something for her future home with Nigel, but when it came to Chris she was completely at a loss. Scarves, ties and socks were so predictable and in the end she had settled on a pair of silver cufflinks, which she had had engraved with his initials. She kept the little box back till last, putting off giving it to him in front of all the family. She needn't have worried, though, as Nigel produced an engagement ring for Elaine before she had time to hand Chris's present over, saving her any embarrassment.

Elaine was overjoyed as she held out her left hand for Nigel to slip the ring on her finger. A cluster of diamonds and rubies flashed in the firelight as she turned her hand this way and that, admiring the sparkle.

'Oh, Nigel, it's gorgeous!' She threw her arms around his neck. 'All the girls at college are going to be green with envy when they see it.'

James was quick to bring her down to earth. 'Remember now,' he said clearing his throat. 'Nigel has agreed that there's to be no wedding until you have finished your studies.'

'Wait a minute,' Elaine said with a pout. 'I'm the bride-to-be, remember. Don't I get any say in it?'

'Sorry, but I'm afraid you don't,' James said firmly. 'Do I have to remind you that you are still under twenty-one, young lady?'

Elaine tried hard to keep her dignity as a ripple of laughter went round the room. 'Oh all right then. You win,' she conceded. 'But just remember, if I'm to wait I shall expect the poshest wedding Beckets Green has ever seen so you'd better start saving up, Dad!'

After supper when Kathy felt it was time for her to leave, Chris volunteered to walk down the lane to 'Shepherd's' with her, carrying the bag with her presents in it. As she still hadn't given him his Christmas present she was grateful for the chance to do it in private. When they reached the gate she said. 'I haven't said thanks for the perfume.'

'That's OK. I had to ask Mum what you liked. I hope it's all right.'

'It's lovely – perfect. Actually I've got something for you.'

He watched apprehensively as she fumbled in her handbag. 'It's not one of those trick things, is it?' he asked. 'You know, the ones that squirt water at you or give you an electric shock when you open them.'

Kathy laughed. 'I think that's more Elaine's kind of present,' she said, handing him the small square parcel. 'I hope you like it.'

He looked down at it. 'Well, I can't see what it is out here in the dark. Can I come in?'

'Of course.' She got out her key and opened the front door, switching on the hall light. He looked round.

'Wow! You were right when you said you'd made the place nice. It looks really cosy. By the way, Elaine has informed me that I'm to help you get the garden into shape when spring arrives.'

'That would be nice. I daresay I'll need a bit of help.'

'OK. I'm your man.'

She looked at the package in his hand. 'Well – are you going to open it?'

He frowned and shook his head. 'I will in a minute. Meantime a conducted tour would be nice,' he said. 'Preferably followed by a cup of coffee to fortify me for the long walk home.'

'Which is all of two hundred yards!'

'Have a heart. I'm an old soldier remember,' he said. 'The old legs ain't what they used to be.' He clutched his chest and coughed dramatically. 'And me war wound is playin' me up somethin' chronic.'

Kathy laughed. 'Oh, all right then, you poor old thing. A conducted tour won't take long. It's hardly Buckingham Palace.'

On the brief tour of the rooms Chris was impressed by what had been done to the cottage and as he stood watching her make coffee in the kitchen afterwards he remembered his present. Unwrapping the Christmassy paper he found a small square box and opened it to reveal the silver cufflinks. He looked up at her in surprise.

'Kathy! You really shouldn't have. These must have cost you a fortune.'

She shook her head. 'Don't spoil it. I couldn't think what to get you and then I saw these.'

He took one out of the box. 'They're super. My initials on them too. It's the Young Farmers' dinner and dance in February. I shall wear them for that. You will come with me, won't you?'

'Well – we'll see.'

He took a step towards her. 'I don't know what to say. Do I get to thank you in the proper manner?'

She couldn't stop herself smiling. 'I can't think what you mean.'

'Then let me show you.' He kissed her and held her close. 'I'm really glad you came back, Kathy,' he said softly. 'You really are a special girl.'

She felt her heart quicken. 'I'm not, Chris. I'm no more special than the next girl.'

'Well, you are to me. If you hadn't come back I'd made up my mind to come to London and find you anyway. I knew where you lived.' His words made her blood run cold as she imagined how it might have been. He made to kiss her again but she turned away. 'The coffee's getting cold.'

'Damn the coffee.'

'It was you who wanted it.'

He laughed. 'You didn't really believe I wanted to drink coffee, did you?'

She looked up at him. 'Chris – look it's no use, there's something I have to tell you.'

He pulled a face. 'That sounds ominous.'

'It is. I like you so much, Chris. I always have. You know that, which is why I can't let you go on thinking. . . .'

'Thinking what? That the way we both feel might develop – has already developed into something deeper? Is there someone else, Kathy?' He looked at her with troubled eyes. 'That's it, isn't it? You're trying to tell me there's someone else. Elaine told me you said there was someone while you were in London.'

She shook her head. 'No. You know what Elaine is like. She kept on asking so I said it to shut her up.' She swallowed hard. So like Elaine to thoughtlessly make things difficult for her. 'Look, let's take our coffee into the living-room. This isn't going to be easy.'

He looked anxious as he sat down in the little living-room. The fire Kathy had lit that morning was almost out and she put on some kindling and logs, blowing on the embers until they flared up. Getting to her feet she looked down at him.

'All that time I was in London with Charlie and Bill,' she said. 'There were – problems.'

'What kind of problems?'

She took a seat opposite, sitting on the edge of her chair. 'I hadn't been there very long before I realized that my stepbrothers were into something shady. The shop they had – which I ran for them – was just a front for their other activities.'

'What kind of activities?'

'Among other things they were running what's known as a protection racket among local businesses,' she told him. 'Then there was the black market – in everything from rationed food to petrol and clothing coupons.'

'It sounds like petty crime to me,' Chris said. 'There must be plenty of cheap crooks who have been doing the same in cities up and down the country since the war ended. Eventually the law will catch up with them.' Kathy stopped him with a shake of her head.

'It was more serious than that. I found stolen goods in the cellar – fur coats, expensive jewellery – obviously loot from robberies. Charlie had warned me not to go down there. He said it was flooded and that there were rats, but one night I found the key and went to look. Even that wasn't the worst though.'

'Go on.'

'I don't know any details about why it happened; why they did – what they did. All I know is that it ended in a man's death.'

She watched as the colour left his face. 'Oh my God,' he said quietly. 'Are you sure? How do you know this?'

She took a deep breath. 'Because – because I was there.'

He stared at her. 'You saw them actually *kill* someone?'

'No! He didn't die till some time later, in hospital. But it was as a result of the beating they gave him.'

'Do you want to tell me about it?'

'I not only want to tell you, Chris. I *have* to,' she said. 'You have the right to know – because I don't deserve the high opinion you have of me and because if I don't tell someone I can trust soon I'm going to go mad.'

She went on to tell him the story of how Charlie persuaded her to act as a decoy and lure Gus Norris to the bombsite that night.

'He convinced me that it was to be a kind of hoax – to scare the man a bit because he owed them some money and wouldn't pay up,' she added. 'I was stupid enough to believe him. If I'd had any idea what they were going to do I would never have agreed. I was horrified when I saw what they did to him. He was alone, Chris, and there were two of them. It was so violent and so – *sickening*. It turned out that he'd had a bad heart, too. Later when I heard he was in hospital, fighting for his life, I felt terrible – almost as though I was personally responsible. Charlie couldn't have cared less. He said he deserved the beating because he was into all sorts of corruption. Later the police called round at the shop because I'd been seen talking to the man that night. I think I convinced them that I had nothing to do with it. I even gave Charlie and Bill an alibi – mainly because I knew Charlie was in the back room and listening to every word.'

'And that was when you decided to get away?'

Kathy shook her head. 'At that point I was still under the impression that Charlie was my legal guardian. But I couldn't rest – couldn't sleep for remembering what I'd seen that night. Every time I closed my eyes I saw it all – *heard* it all again. In the end I went to see Father Gerard and he said it couldn't be true that Charlie was my guardian. He wasn't even a blood relative and would never have been given guardianship of a young girl. He urged me to get away before anything worse happened. It was after I'd been here a few days that I saw in the paper that the man they attacked had died. So now the police are looking for his murderer.'

Chris reached out and took both her hands in his. 'Kathy – how much of this have you told Mum and Dad?'

'Just about the petty crime and the protection racket,' she said. 'Not about the stolen goods in the cellar or the attack on Gus Norris.' She bit her lip. 'Partly because I didn't want to burden your parents with it all, but partly, I have to admit, because I was – still am – so ashamed. I was afraid they might not want me to stay, knowing the truth.'

He squeezed her hands. 'You have nothing to be ashamed of, Kathy. You are the innocent victim in all this,' he said. 'Mum and Dad should never have let you go back to London with your stepbrothers. They should have made enquiries – looked into it properly. It makes me so angry to think that you could have been saved all this and still kept the place at college you worked so hard for.'

Kathy shook her head. 'Don't blame them. Auntie Lena and Uncle James did what they thought was best. After all, they had no legal right to say what should happen to me. And Charlie can be very convincing when he wants something.'

'I can't think why they wanted you back anyway,' Chris was saying. 'It was vile of them to involve you in their criminal activities. You were just a schoolgirl when they took you away. But I don't think you need worry, I can't see why the police should connect you with this man's death.'

She took a deep shuddering breath. 'I still have nightmares about that night – and about the police turning up to question me.' She looked at him. 'So there it is,' she said bleakly. 'The girl you thought so special is an accessory to a violent crime; one which resulted in a man's death.'

He pulled her to him and held her tight. 'You are nothing of the kind. You were no more than an innocent bystander, drawn into it by two devious men who were supposed to be protecting you. I've a good mind to go up to London and—'

'*No!*' She clutched his arms and looked up at him, her eyes wide with fear. 'Let it go, Chris. I'm trying to put it all behind me and start again and – and now that you know, I think I can begin to do that.'

He kissed her gently. 'My poor little Kathy. You're safe now. I won't let anything hurt you ever again. And as for being special, of course you are; special and unique. D'you know why? Because I love you. I have ever since I was about twelve and I can't think of anything that would ever make me stop.'

She was crying now. Her face was buried against his chest as she wept the tears that she had held back for so long. 'I love you too, Chris,' she whispered. 'I haven't dared admit it even to myself till now because I thought that when you knew about what had happened in London you'd be disappointed in me.'

'Well I'm not. Nothing you could do would ever disappoint me,' he said, stroking her hair. 'From now on everything is going to be fine, so don't worry.'

Later, when Chris had gone Kathy made herself a bedtime drink and sat by the dying fire. It was a huge relief to have confessed to him about her involvement in the attack on Gus Norris. He had told her he loved her and the memory of his arms around her, made her feel safe and warm; his lips on hers gave her a wonderful glow.

She reminded herself, though, that she still had not revealed the truth about her relationship with Jeff and its sordid outcome that terrible night at his house. Surely if he knew about that he couldn't fail to be sadly disillusioned. She pushed the thought away. It was the one thing she dared not risk. There and then she made up her mind to erase all memory of Jeff from her mind. *It never happened,* she told herself. *He never existed.*

She told herself that if she tried hard enough surely – *surely* with time she could make herself believe it.

CHAPTER TWELVE

During the winter Mrs Trent was ill. Soon after Christmas she went down with a bad bout of flu which took several weeks to clear up. For the first few days Kathy ran the village post office and shop as best she could, but at the end of the first week, the GPO sent her a temporary help in the shape of Harriet Ingham. Harriet was a severe-looking young woman of about thirty. She wore unflattering steel-rimmed glasses and scraped her mousy brown hair back into a bun. She was meant to take charge of the post office, leaving Kathy free to run the shop but she seemed to be under the impression that she was in charge of everything.

By the time Mrs Trent was well enough to resume her position behind the grille, Kathy was greatly relieved. Miss Ingham, as she insisted on being addressed had no sense of humour and seemed deeply suspicious of everything Kathy did, from ordering a case of canned peas to changing the window display. She also had an aversion to cats which meant that poor old Arnold was relegated to the icy chill of the back yard until Mrs Trent heard about it and let him into the adjoining cottage to share her fireside.

As February came in all the young people began to look forward to the Young Farmers' dinner and dance. It was the social event of the year and was to take place at the end of the month in the great hall of Greendowne Manor, a stately home about three miles out of Beckets Green. The house was owned and lived in by the Greendowne family whose home it had been since Tudor times. Elaine and Kathy were excited at the prospect of seeing inside the house and looked forward to the event enormously.

As it was a formal occasion both girls had to have new dresses and

Lena went into town with them to help them to choose. Mrs Trent had given Kathy a Saturday afternoon off to make up for all the extra responsibility she had had during her illness.

From the beginning Elaine was in a difficult mood. In the first shop they visited she spied a black satin evening gown with a strapless bodice and clinging fishtail skirt and insisted it was just what she was looking for.

Lena looked at her askance. 'Darling, it's far too old for you.'

Elaine pouted. 'I'm an engaged woman,' she insisted. 'It's not too old for me at all. It's sophisticated, isn't it, Kathy?'

Kathy glanced at Lena and bit her lip. 'Well – I think you might have trouble dancing in it. You know how energetic you like to be.'

But in spite – or perhaps because of the disapproval, Elaine insisted on trying the dress on. When she emerged from the changing-room she looked so like a little girl dressed up in her mother's dress that both Lena and Kathy had difficulty keeping straight faces; a fact which Elaine noticed at once.

'You're *laughing* at me!' Her cheeks went red and she shook her shoulders angrily. 'Well I *like* it. I'm having this one!'

A saleswoman who had been observing from a few feet away stepped forward. 'If you'll forgive me,' she said diplomatically. 'I think I have just the thing for you. You have the most stunning colouring and I rather feel that black submerges it. May I show you?'

Slightly mollified, but unwilling to back down, Elaine shrugged. 'If you like.'

The woman produced a dress of shimmering emerald green taffeta. It had a full skirt, a tiny waist and a smooth off-the-shoulder neckline embroidered with tiny crystal beads. It was clear from Elaine's face that she was taken with it but she tossed her head.

'It's not a patch on this,' she said.

'It's very different, I agree,' the saleswoman said. 'But so much more flattering for you. Why not just try it on?'

When Elaine came out of the changing-room Kathy gasped. 'Oh! You look beautiful,' she said. 'Just wait till Nigel sees you in that.'

Elaine looked at her mother. 'Mum?'

'I agree with Kathy,' Lena said. 'But it's your choice of course.'

To Lena's relief Elaine decided on the dress and now it was Kathy's turn. The same saleswoman was looking at her.

'With your dark hair I think pale pink would suit you,' she said. 'What do you think of this?' She drew an evening gown from the rail. It was of palest cyclamen pink and had a full skirt of delicate tulle scattered with tiny silver sequins, a heart-shaped neckline and tiny puffed sleeves. When Kathy stood in the changing-room and allowed the saleswoman to zip her up she could hardly believe her eyes. The dress was enchanting. Never in her life had she expected to wear anything like it. Her cheeks grew pink and her eyes shone with delight.

Lena smiled and nodded. 'It's perfect,' she said. 'Look at some more though. Don't make up your mind in too much of a hurry.'

But Kathy had already decided that the pink dress was for her. Elaine too was impressed.

'Poor old Chris,' she whispered in Kathy's ear as they left the shop carrying their purchases. 'He doesn't stand a chance. He's going to be completely hooked when he sees you in that.'

On the evening of the dance the two young couples met at Magpie Farm. Kathy had left her dress in her old room and the plan was that she would go straight there after work to dress and get ready with Elaine.

Chris and Nigel were waiting when they came downstairs. Both young men wore dinner jackets and looked elegant and handsome. There were cries of admiration all round when the girls made their entrance. Elaine looked quite stunning in her green dress with her hair a blaze of flame around her shoulders. It brought out the colour of her eyes and made them sparkle.

'You look like a goddess,' Nigel told her holding out his hands to her.

Chris made no comment, but his eyes said it all as he looked at Kathy, and in the back of the car on the way to Greendowne Manor he leaned close and whispered, 'I couldn't say it in front of my green eyed sister, but you're definitely going to be the belle of the ball.' He kissed her cheek and whispered even more softly, 'Love you.'

She turned to smile at him. 'Love you too.'

Kathy wished that the evening could have lasted for ever. The house was like something out of a film with its grand staircase and panelled walls. There were flowers everywhere and a huge log fire burned in the fireplace of the dining hall where dinner was served. The meal was delicious and then, when they repaired to the great hall for dancing to a small orchestra, she was enthralled. She and Chris seemed to float on air as they circled the floor. The music, the perfume of the flowers and the atmosphere seemed to fill her senses and sweep her away. She wished it might never end.

But all too soon the evening came to an end and it was time to go home. Kathy was amazed to discover that it was two o'clock in the morning, but in the car on the drive back to the village she felt her head lolling against Chris's shoulder. Nigel pulled up outside 'Shepherd's Cottage'.

'I'll see her to the door,' Chris said. 'It's all right, Nigel. Don't wait for me. I'll walk home afterwards.'

'After what?' Elaine giggled.

Kathy took her key from the little evening bag that Lena had lent her and gave it to Chris who opened the door for her. He stepped into the hall with her and pulled her into his arms, kissing her until her already spinning head was giddy.

'You look like an enchanted princess tonight,' he said. 'I don't want to leave you in case you vanish when the sun comes up. You won't, will you?'

She laughed. 'When the sun comes up I'll be just plain Kathy O'Connor again,' she told him. 'And that's a promise.'

'I'm glad – though I can't agree about the "plain" bit. Tonight you were the most beautiful girl in the room and I was so proud that you were with me.' He kissed her again then whispered, 'Kathy – can I stay?'

'No! You have to go home,' she said, her heartbeat quickening. 'They're all expecting you. If you don't go everyone will know where you are.'

'Mum and Dad will have gone to bed hours ago,' he told her. 'There's only Elaine.'

'*Only*? You know what she's like. She couldn't resist spilling the beans and she'd never let either of us forget it.'

'I know how to bribe her to keep quiet. Please, Kathy. Let's make it a perfect night.'

But she pushed him gently away. 'No, Chris. We're both tired. And I think you've had just a little bit too much to drink.'

'I won't disappoint you.'

He looked so much like a small boy begging for a treat that she reached up to cup his face and kiss him. 'Nothing you ever did could disappoint me. This just isn't the right time and it has to be perfect.'

'When then?'

Suddenly her heart turned to ice as she remembered a similar conversation and she could barely conceal a shudder. 'Soon,' she whispered. 'But now you have to go home and get a good night's sleep. It's milking at five, remember. That's only three short hours away.'

He dropped his hands to his sides. 'OK, you win,' he said.

One more quick kiss and he was gone. Kathy closed the door and leaned against it with a sigh of relief. All she could think of was that horrible night at Jeff's house when he had plied her with drink and the shameful and humiliating thing that had happened afterwards. Was that what sex was like? Why did they call it 'making love'? She had felt so dirty and degraded. She couldn't bear the thought of it being like that again with Chris. It would ruin everything. She felt sure she would be reminded of Jeff the moment Chris touched her? She knew that somehow it was something she was going to have to come to terms with, but heaven alone knew how.

Mrs Trent's health did not improve. Her chest infection kept recurring and she often had to take time off. Kathy was happy to cope alone, although she found it difficult, especially in the mornings when most of the village housewives did their shopping. Eventually Mrs Trent decided to employ a part-time help for the shop so that she could start work later each day and Maggie Lane, a young war widow with two children, was taken on to help in the mornings while her children were at school. Maggie was a cheerful, good-natured young woman and Kathy got along well with her. Kathy was entrusted with a key so that she could open up in the mornings and Mrs Trent occupied her time, going through the post office paperwork in her cottage and leaving the two girls to it.

Kathy thought that Beckets Green in springtime was the best place in the world to live. Orchards bursting into blossom, new lambs in the fields and the sun shining made her feel glad to be alive. The days flew by; she and Chris saw each other almost every day and life was good. He was helping her with the garden at 'Shepherd's' in the evenings. He had borrowed a rotivator from the farm and ploughed up the back garden. They had decided that half would be a vegetable garden, the other half, nearest the house would be lawn and flowers.

'That can be your department,' he told her. 'I haven't got a clue about flowers, but I can grow you a row of cabbages that'll knock your socks off!'

Kathy laughed. 'I'm not sure I want cabbages that can knock my socks off!' she said. 'They sound distinctly tough and leathery to me. Let's have peas and carrots instead.'

By mid-April Chris had planted the vegetable garden and levelled and sown the pocket-handkerchief-sized lawn.

'You'll have to wait till the frosts have finished before you can plant your beloved flower borders,' he told her. 'I'm glad I've managed to get as far as possible with the garden before this course Dad has insisted on sending me off to.'

James had enrolled his son on a three-week refresher course for ex-servicemen at an agricultural college in Yorkshire.

'I'm really going to miss you,' he said. 'It's too far to get home for weekends.'

'I'll miss you too, but never mind, it's only for three weeks.'

'*Only*! It's going to seem more like three years if I can't see you.'

They were sitting at the kitchen table sharing a pot of tea. At half past seven the failing light had driven them indoors, both of them grubby and pleasantly tired. Chris put down his cup and looked at her with a grin.

'You've got a streak of dirt right across your cheek.'

'Have I? Why didn't you say before?' She made to wipe it off with her handkerchief, but he reached out, catching her wrist.

'Don't. It suits you.' He looked into her eyes. 'I love you, Kathy O'Connor, dirty face and all. By the way, how do you manage here without a bathroom?'

She shrugged. 'I boil a kettle and have an all-over wash.'

'Sounds a bit primitive.' He grinned. 'I like the image it conjures up though; a bit like Venus emerging from the waves.' He raised her fingers to his lips and kissed them. 'When we're married we'll put in a bathroom.'

Her eyes widened as she returned his gaze. 'Who said anything about getting married?'

'It's the obvious conclusion, isn't it?' He frowned. 'You do *want* to marry me, don't you?'

She tried hard not to laugh. 'Shouldn't you have asked me that first?'

'OK – so I got it a bit wrong. I'm not the down-on-one-knee type like Nigel. Well, do you?'

'Do I what?'

'You know damned well what.'

'Mmm. . . .' She paused. 'It's not something I've ever thought about. Maybe I should give it some consideration.'

'Give it some *what*?' He stood up and came round the table, putting his hands under her elbows and pulling her to her feet. 'You'll tell me right now, woman, or I won't be responsible for the consequences.'

'Don't bully me.'

'Then stop teasing.' He was gripping her shoulders and looking intently into her eyes. 'I'm not joking now, Kathy,' he said, his voice husky. 'I know I'm never going to want anyone else and I want – no I *need* to know if you feel the same.'

'You know I love you, Chris.'

'So you say, but is it for *keeps*? Are we going anywhere – together, I mean?'

She smiled. 'I can't imagine going anywhere without you.'

'Then can I take that as a yes?'

'Of course you can, silly.'

Without another word he bent and slid an arm under her knees, scooping her up and heading for the stairs.

When Kathy opened her eyes the room was bathed in moonlight. A full moon was shining in through the window, turning everything in the room to silver. Somehow it seemed so right. Tonight everything in her life was touched with silver.

Her head was resting on Chris's chest and when she looked up at him she saw that he was still asleep, his hair tousled and his mouth slightly open. Very gently she touched his cheek and felt the prickle of stubble under her fingers.

She had been so tense when he first began to make love to her. Although his hands were gentle, his lips tender and loving, she had been so afraid of what was to come – so afraid of her own reaction – that she would hurt and disappoint him, but he had sensed her tension and waited patiently for her to relax.

She need not have worried. When at last it happened it was the most beautiful experience of her life. She had known before that she was in love with Chris, but now she knew that she would lay down her life for him. With all her heart she longed to be his wife – to be together always – to share her life with him.

As though he felt her eyes on him, he wakened. For a moment he looked at her with slightly unfocussed eyes, as though she were still part of his dream, then a smile slowly lit his face.

'Hello there.'

'Hello.'

'Happy?'

'Yes – so very happy.'

'No regrets?'

'Need you ask?'

His arms tightened round her. 'I think we were made for each other, don't you?'

'Mmm.'

'What time is it?'

Kathy reached for her alarm clock and turned it towards the light. 'Ten o'clock.'

He groaned. 'Oh no! Shall I stay here?'

'I'd like that, but I think you'd better go home. You've got a train to catch in the morning, remember, and, knowing you I doubt if you've done any packing yet.'

He sighed. 'I suppose you're right.' He got out of bed and began to dress. Bending down he pulled the covers up round her shoulders. 'Goodnight darling. See you tomorrow.'

'See you in the morning,' she echoed. 'What time is your train?'

'Nine fifteen from Castle Station. Mum's running me into town in the pick-up. We'll be leaving about half-eight.'

'I'll see you to say goodbye before I go to work,' she told him. 'I'll wait for you at the end of the lane.'

He bent and kissed her. 'What a bloody awful time to be going away for three weeks! How shall I bear it? How the hell can they expect me to concentrate on anything?'

'You'll concentrate,' she told him. 'And think how lovely it will be when you get home.'

'I'll write every day.'

'Me too.'
'Goodnight then.'
'Goodnight.'

Next morning Kathy waited at the end of the lane for Lena to come along with the pick-up truck. Chris sat beside her with his hold-all on his knees. Where the lane met the main road Lena stopped and Chris jumped down from the truck to envelop Kathy and a huge hug.

'Take care while I'm gone,' he told her. 'And don't forget me.'

'Of course I won't forget you, silly. How could I possibly?' She lifted her face for his kiss and as he reluctantly let her go and climbed back into the truck she noticed that Lena's half averted face wore an indulgent smile.

When she arrived at the post office that morning she found Maggie waiting outside clutching a newspaper.

'They've got them,' she announced, waving the paper.

'Got who?' Kathy asked, her mind still full of Chris's departure as she took out her key to open up.

'The two thugs who beat that poor man up,' Maggie said, red faced with excitement. 'You know that man in London who died of his injuries.'

Her attention suddenly focussed, Kathy turned to stare at Maggie, her heart missing a beat. 'Really?' She tried to keep her voice steady. 'Is it in the paper?'

'Yes, look.' Maggie thrust the paper into her hand. 'Quite a drama it must have been. The police arrested them – two brothers in the East End of London at three o'clock in the morning. Look…' She jabbed a finger at the page, 'it says here that they raided the house and found loads of stolen goods as well. They sound a right pair of villains.'

Kathy scanned the article briefly. Sure enough it reported that two brothers had been arrested and charged with Gus Norris's murder and been remanded in custody, pending trial. It went on to mention the stolen goods that had been discovered during the search of the premises and the fact that the brothers were also suspected of obtaining money with menaces, theft and fraud.

All morning as she worked, Kathy's mind was on the news of Charlie and Bill's arrest. They hadn't been named, but it was obviously Charlie and Bill. If they were tried and found guilty of murder it would mean the death penalty. She shuddered. There was nothing she could do about it. They should have thought of the consequences, she told herself, before they broke the law.

After lunch Mrs Trent asked her to take the bus into town and go to the chemist for her. 'I forgot to pick up my prescription from the chemist last week,' she said. 'And I've almost run out of my cough mixture.'

'What about the shop?' Kathy asked.

'It isn't pension day so the post office shouldn't be busy,' the post-mistress said. 'Maggie's agreed to come in for a couple of hours while you're away. Her mother will pick up the children from school and if anyone needs the post office she can give me a shout.'

It was a pleasant spring day and Kathy quite enjoyed taking the bus into town as a change from working. She picked up her employer's prescription and treated herself to a cup of tea and a bun at the bus station café while she waited for the bus back to Beckets Green. When she got back to the post office Maggie had her coat on ready to leave.

'I'm glad you're back,' she said. 'I don't like to leave the kids with Mum for too long. She gets tired easily and they're a right little pair of terrors when they come out of school.' She smiled. 'All that sitting still and keeping quiet, I suppose. By half-three they're fair bubbling over.'

When Maggie had gone Kathy took Mrs Trent's cough mixture to her through the door that connected the shop to the cottage.

'Thank you so much, dear,' Mrs Trent said. 'I'll come and help you now that Maggie's gone home.'

'No need,' Kathy told her. 'There's only another hour till closing time. Just put your feet up. I'll be fine. I'll cash up and I'll make sure everywhere is locked before I leave, so there's no need for you to do anything.'

Mrs Trent smiled. 'You're a good girl, Kathy. I sometimes wonder what I did before I had you.'

The final hour before closing was usually quiet and Kathy spent it tidying the shelves and cashing up the shop takings. She slipped through into the post office section and began to cash up the till in there, checking that everything was correct. So absorbed was she that she didn't hear the customer come in and when he spoke the sound made her start.

'Hello, Kath.'

'Oh! I'm sorry I. . . .' The words died in her throat as she looked up and found herself looking into a face she had hoped never to see again. Her heart seemed to freeze into a solid block of ice and she felt the colour drain from her face.

'*Jeff!*' she whispered.

He smiled. 'Yes, love, it's me,' he said with a smile. 'Large as life and twice as natural.'

CHAPTER THIRTEEN

'What are you doing here? What do you want?' Kathy glanced over her shoulder as she spoke.

Jeff laughed. 'I take it you're not pleased to see me.' he said. 'Oh dear, I am disappointed.'

'How did you know where to find me?' she asked, her mouth dry.

'Easy. You told me once that this was where you were evacuated as a kid, remember?' The smile left his face. 'Get your coat, Kath. You're coming with me.'

'No!'

'Don't argue. Just do as I say. Or do you want me to pay a visit to those friends of yours at the farm?'

Kathy's heart was beating so fast she felt dizzy. 'Please, Jeff, don't make trouble,' she begged. 'I've never done you any harm. I can't think why you're here but whatever you want, I can't help you.'

'Oh, but you can.'

At that moment the doorbell pinged as a late customer came in.

'Oh, thank goodness you're still open,' the woman said breathlessly. 'I've just got off the bus and I remembered I hadn't got any bread. Have you got any left?' The woman glanced at Jeff. 'Sorry, I didn't mean to push in.'

'That's all right, love,' he said with a smile. 'Please go ahead.'

Kathy went across to the shop and took a large loaf from the shelf. 'You're in luck,' she told the woman. 'This is the last one.'

The customer stowed the loaf away in her shopping bag and paid Kathy. 'Thanks ever so much, dear,' she said. 'Saved my life, you have. I don't know what my Jack would've said if there'd been no bread for his sandwiches tomorrow.'

Jeff crossed the shop and opened the door, holding it for the woman to pass through. When she'd gone he closed it and turned the sign over.

'Right. Get your coat.'

Kathy stood still. 'Where are you taking me? I warn you, I'll be missed. People will soon start looking for me.'

'Stop panicking,' he said. 'I just want to talk to you that's all. Stop wasting time.'

In the small cloakroom at the back of the shop where she hung her coat, Kathy looked around for some means of escape. With all her heart she wished there was a telephone handy. But who could she ring even if there was one? Lena? The police? And what could she tell them? She realized with a stab of fear that if she didn't want a scene she had no choice but to go with Jeff – hear what he had to say and hope he would let her go afterwards. She certainly didn't want anyone else to see or speak to him. The door handle rattled, making her jump and Jeff's voice demanded to know, 'Come on! What the hell are you doing in there?'

Outside the shop she locked the door while he waited impatiently, then he grasped her arm and hustled her along the street and down an alley between two houses where she saw his car parked at the bottom. He opened the passenger door and pushed her roughly. 'Get in.'

As they drove through the village and out into the countryside, Kathy's heart was in her mouth, realizing that she was completely at his mercy.

'Where are we going?' she asked. 'Why are you doing this?'

He slowed down as they approached a turning and drove for a mile or so down a narrow lane, pulling up under some trees. Switching off the engine he turned in his seat to look at her.

'You'll have seen the papers,' he said.

'About Charlie and Bill being arrested?'

'What else?'

'There's nothing I can do about it.'

'Yes there is. You can substantiate the story their brief will put forward at the trial.'

'I've already done too much,' she told him. 'I acted as a decoy for them – led that poor man to a terrible beating and then I lied to the police for them. I regret what I did with all my heart and I'm not doing any more.'

'If they get convicted of murder they'll hang?'

'Yes, I know.'

'And you know that you may have to give evidence at the trial anyway?'

Her head jerked up and she looked at him with wide eyes. The possibility of being called to give evidence at the trial was something that had not occurred to her. 'No! I won't. *I couldn't!*'

'Oh, you'd have no choice my love. As a crucial witness you'd be subpoenaed.'

She frowned. 'So – why are you here, Jeff? What is it you want me to do? Are you asking me to lie in court?'

For a moment he stared straight ahead out of the windscreen then he turned to look at her. 'I want you to go to the police and give them a statement,' he said. Before she could say anything else, he went on, 'When the boys were arrested they were allowed one phone call,' he told her. 'That's the law. Charlie rang me. He told me to come and find you – persuade you to give him and Bill a get-out. The police already know that the boys were there. Before Norris died he regained consciousness for a few minutes, he said Charlie's name. It's not proof, but the police have latched on to it. It's circumstantial evidence, but it could be incriminating – unless. . . .' He leaned towards her. 'Unless Charlie's brief can put across a strong case for manslaughter – backed up by what you'll say.'

'What can I tell them, though?'

'You can say you were there. That's the truth, isn't it? You can say they roughed him up a bit, but not bad enough to injure him severely.' He grasped her shoulders. 'Listen, Kath, they're going down for a variety of other crimes anyway. If a jury can be convinced that Norris was still conscious when they left him they might just get off with manslaughter.'

'But I don't know whether he was conscious or not. Bill told me to go home I knew there was nothing I could do. I'm not proud of it, but I was scared and I ran home as fast as I could. It was horrible. I still have nightmares about it.' She looked at him. 'Anyway why should you care what happens to Charlie and Bill – unless you told them to do it. Was the beating your idea? Is that why it's so important to you? Are you afraid Charlie will involve you in some way?'

For the first time Kathy saw a flicker of something very like fear in his eyes. 'What you don't realize, Kath, is that Charlie and Bill were only small cogs in a very big outfit,' he told her.

'Run by you! They did this on your instructions and Charlie is threatening to expose you? Is that it?'

'OK – it was on my instructions, yes, but I was only following orders.'

'Whose orders?'

'I can't tell you that. Look, Kath, the less you know, the better. It's like I said, Charlie and Bill are right at the bottom of the food chain. I'm only one step up from them. I have to take orders too.'

She frowned. 'But you own those night clubs – the house in Surrey – the car.'

He gave a dry little laugh. 'You didn't really believe they belonged to me, did you? Christ! How naïve can you get?'

'So – if not you – then who? And if it was someone else's house why did you take me there?'

He sighed. 'That was part of my job, Kath. It's one of the things I'm paid to do.'

'I don't understand.'

'Bloody hell! Do I really have to spell it out for you in one syllable words? The Boss owns the night clubs, gambling casinos and other leisure places as well. They all employ girls – good looking girls. Girls who have – special intimate services to provide for the customers.'

Kathy shuddered as her worst suspicions were confirmed. 'So – Charlie tricked me into coming back to London so that he could – what? Hire me out as a. . . ?' she put her hand over her mouth, unable to bring herself to say the word. 'He was hoping to make money out of me – by *selling* me! And you're seriously expecting me to help get him off the hook?'

'Not just him!' Jeff grasped her hands. 'Listen, Kath, if Charlie pleads guilty to manslaughter you might not be called to give evidence.'

'And if he doesn't? If he tries to get off altogether?'

'You don't get it, do you?' Jeff looked almost desperate now. 'This is serious – far more serious than you can possibly imagine. If Charlie doesn't get the back-up he's asking for he's threatening to turn King's Evidence and expose the man at the top of all this.'

'And so he should,' Kathy said vehemently. 'It'd be the first decent thing he'd ever done.'

Jeff seized her shoulders and shook her impatiently. 'Can't you get it through your thick skull, you stupid little cow! The man we're talking about is no small time crook. He's big – powerful. He's got a lot of people in his pay, including some people in authority. If Charlie shops him it'll blow the whole thing wide open and because I was the go-between the finger will point straight at me. My life won't be worth that!' He clicked his fingers. 'I mean it, Kath. There'll most likely be a contract out on me overnight, and I wouldn't like to describe some of the nasty things that can happen to a grass.'

She looked him in the eye. 'And you think I should care what happens to you after what you did to me? If I went to the police and told them what happened that night you took me to the house and—'

'No one forced you to go,' he growled, his fingers biting into the flesh of her shoulders. 'No one poured drink down your throat or knocked you out to get you into bed. Do you really think anyone would believe a word you said, especially after all this time?'

'You – you *animal*!' She grasped the door handle and tried to get out of the car but he grabbed both her arms and stopped her.

'I can think of one person who might believe *my* version of what happened that night,' he said in her ear. 'That boyfriend of yours – what's his name – Christopher Spicer?' His eyes glinted malevolently and Kathy's heart turned to ice in her chest.

'How do you know about Chris?' she whispered.

'I called in at the post office earlier this afternoon,' he told her. 'You were out, but I had a lovely chat with the plump blonde piece behind the counter. Very accommodating, she was, obviously loves a good gossip. She told me all about how well you'd settled back in the village and your job at the post office. She told me that the village folk were taking bets on how long it'd be before an engagement was announced between you and the handsome Christopher. Childhood sweethearts, she said – went to the Young Farmers' Ball together. So romantic. So *respectable*!' He pushed his face up close to hers. 'What would *he* say, I wonder, if he knew you'd been to bed with the likes of me?' His lip curled in a sadistic smile. 'I've got a very creative imagination, Kath. I'd spin him a good story – spare him no details. By the time I'd finished he wouldn't want to touch you with a ten foot pole!'

'You wouldn't!'

He laughed. 'Do you want to risk it?'

She felt crushed. 'No – please.' Tears sprang to her eyes.

'Then do as I say. I warn you, Kath. My neck's on the line here. I'm desperate enough to do anything to save it and believe me I'll do whatever it takes.'

She felt all the fight drain out of her. 'All right. What do you want me to do?'

'Come up to London with me – now. Go to the police and give them a statement. Tell them you were there and that Norris was still alive when the boys left him. That's all you have to do. I'll sort the rest.'

'I can't go now. I'll have to arrange for time off. I'll have to make up some story about where I'm going. If I don't it will look suspicious.'

'Oh my God!' He passed a hand over his face in frustration. 'OK, OK. I'll pick you up first thing in the morning,' he said. 'And I do mean first thing – dawn – about five o'clock, near that telephone box near the pub on the edge of the village.'

'No. I'll get the train.'

'Oh no you don't. I want to make good and sure you get there. I'll drop you off somewhere in the suburbs and you can get the tube the rest of the way. It'd be better if we're not seen together.'

'I wouldn't ask you if it wasn't serious, Mrs Trent,' Kathy said. 'It's my stepbrother. He's seriously ill and I feel I have to go.'

'Of course you do, my dear,' the postmistress said. 'You were so good while I was ill and put in enough overtime to deserve some time off. Don't give it another thought. Take as long as you need to.'

'How will you manage though?' Kathy asked.

Mrs Trent smiled. 'I'm feeling much better now,' she said. 'And I'll have Maggie to help me. If you have to be away for longer than a day or two I'll ask head office to let me have Harriet again.'

At 'Shepherd's' Kathy wondered whether to write a note for Lena. She wanted to avoid talking to her face to face. Somehow Lena always knew when there was something wrong and she would never be able to convince her that there was nothing wrong. She made several attempts but nothing sounded believable so in the end she decided to leave it. She would take it a day at a time. When the time came for explanations she hoped that something would come to her.

Next morning before the sun was up she packed a bag with a few essentials then set off to meet Jeff at the appointed place.

*

During the drive to London neither of them spoke. Kathy felt weary. She had lain awake for most of the previous night, telling herself that her relationship with the Spicer family, especially Chris would surely be at an end once all this came out. Her life would be in ruins. She'd lose her home, her job and all her friends, not to mention the man she loved – and none of it was her fault. It was all so unfair.

Jeff said he would drop her off when they got to Wembley. On the outskirts he drew onto the forecourt of a transport café and turned to her.

'Want something to eat?'

She shook her head.

'Don't be silly, you can't go all day without food. Come and have something even if it's only tea and toast. Anyway, I've got to make sure you've got the story straight.'

She got out of the car and followed him unhappily into the café where he ordered a full English breakfast for himself, tea and a sandwich for her. As she sat opposite him at the bare table the sight of his plate of fried eggs and greasy bacon and sausage made her stomach churn.

'Now – you know what you've got to do?' he said, his mouth full of food.

She nodded. 'Which police station do I have to go to?'

'Doesn't matter,' he told her. 'Any will do. Just tell them why you're there and ask to make a statement.'

'Then I can go home?'

'Yeah.' He looked up at her. 'Got enough money for the fare?'

'Yes.' She looked at him. Ever since he turned up yesterday something had been bothering her. 'Why was Gus Norris picked on for a beating?' she asked. 'Charlie said he owed them money but there was obviously more to it that than if you gave the orders.'

He shrugged. 'It was to settle an old score. The Boss never forgets an insult. Seems Gus once called him something he didn't like. He decided the time had come to get even.'

Kathy shivered. This man, whoever he was sounded ruthless and sadistic. She was glad Jeff had kept his name from her.

'Right. Drink your tea and eat your sandwich up.' He looked at her with narrowed eyes. 'You wouldn't rat on me, Kath, would you? I need you to keep my name out of it.'

She sighed. 'If you say so.'

'I know you think I deserve it but believe me, it wouldn't be worth it,' he went on. 'If my name was mentioned it'd lead straight to the Boss and I warn you – he's got a long arm. Even you wouldn't be out of his reach and he—'

'*All right*! I get the message.' Kathy ate her sandwich and drank the tea after which she felt surprisingly better. Jeff tossed back the contents of his cup and patted his chin with a paper napkin.

'OK, we'd better get going. I'll drop you at the first tube station we come to.' He leaned forward. 'Kath – after today we won't be seeing each other again and I'd rather you forgot all about me.'

'Believe me it's all I want to do,' she told him wryly.

When Kathy came out of the tube station she asked directions to the nearest police station. There she told the desk sergeant who she was and asked if she might be allowed to give a statement. In an interview room a young policeman interviewed her whist a WPC took down her statement in shorthand.

She told the truth, how Charlie had asked her to go to the Prince of Wales pub that night and engage Gus Norris in conversation, and how she'd asked him later to escort her home and lead him to the bomb-site. She explained that Charlie had told her that the man owed him money and that he and Bill intended only to give him a fright – play a bit of a practical joke on him. (At this the policeman pulled a wry face) Kathy went on to describe her horror when she witnessed the beating, but added that when the boys left she was sure that the man was still alive.

'You stayed until they'd finished?' The policeman looked directly at her.

She bit her lip. 'Well, no. But Charlie told me that the man was fine when they left him. He said they only meant to give him a fright.'

'And you were happy with that?'

Kathy shook her head. 'No! I felt guilty – felt I'd been tricked into it.'

Asked about her relationship with the Bradys, she explained that they were only stepbrothers – how her mother had been killed in the blitz and that Charlie and Bill had come looking for her at the end of the war, insisting that Charlie was her legal guardian. Asked why she had decided to leave London, she explained that she couldn't get used to the city. She also said that she didn't like the Bradys' lifestyle and that the beating of Gus Norris had upset her, especially when she learned that he was in hospital fighting for his life. All she longed for was to return to the good friends she had made in Beckets Green.

A WPC brought her a cup of tea whilst her statement was being processed, then she was asked to read it through and sign it. After that she was warned she might be called upon to give evidence at the trial, but in the meantime she was free to go.

As she was being shown out of the station, the young officer who had interviewed her leaned forward.

'I probably shouldn't tell you this, miss,' he said. 'But another witness has come forward. A woman going home from a late cleaning job took a short cut across the bombsite and she saw Norris being beaten by two men. She hid until they'd gone and she's willing to testify that Norris was still alive when they left him. In fact she ran to a call-box and telephoned for an ambulance, but when they arrived they couldn't find him. Seems he dragged himself some way off, probably trying to get home, which proves he was still alive.'

'Does that mean I won't be called to give evidence?' she asked.

The policeman shrugged. 'Keep your fingers crossed, love.'

When Kathy left the police station, it was half past three. She had intended to find a place to stay overnight but suddenly all she wanted was to get home. She caught the tube to Euston Station and found a train for Northampton already standing at the platform.

When she opened the door back at 'Shepherd's Cottage' there was an envelope lying on the mat. She knew at once that it was Chris's first letter to her. Sitting down at the kitchen table she opened and read it. It was quite brief – about his journey and the college, his room and the other students; how much he already missed her, and at the end he signed off with three words. *I love you.*

Reading them she laid her head down on her arms and wept. She could hardly believe that it was such a short time ago that she and Chris had been together. He would have to know now – all of it. She couldn't live with herself keeping the despicable and shameful secret buried in her heart any longer. And once he knew, everything they'd had would be over.

She carried her bag upstairs, unpacked and put away her unused night things then she washed her face and hands, combed her hair and set off down the lane to see Lena.

CHAPTER FOURTEEN

Lena was alone in the kitchen washing up the supper things. She looked up in surprise when Kathy walked in.

'Kathy! There you are. I dropped in at the post office on my way home this afternoon and Mrs Trent told me you'd taken time off to visit your brother in London because he's seriously ill.' She dried her hands. 'I was surprised you hadn't let us know. What's happened?'

Kathy took a deep breath. 'I had to make up a story. I couldn't tell Mrs Trent the truth. Charlie and Bill have been arrested.'

Lena looked shocked. 'My dear girl! But why did you have to go? You look exhausted. Sit down and I'll put the kettle on.'

Kathy looked round. 'Where is Uncle James?'

'He's gone down to the village for a parish council meeting. There's no one else here but us.'

Relieved, Kathy sat down at the table, realizing for the first time just how tired and tense she was. Lena fussed with making tea, arranging cups and saucers until Kathy longed to tell her to stop – sit down and listen. The sooner she got it all off her chest now, the sooner she would feel better. Eventually Lena sat down opposite her and began to pour the tea.

'Now,' she said, passing Kathy a cup. 'What have those two done to get arrested?'

'It's the worst possible,' Kathy said. 'They're being charged with murder.' The moment she'd said the words she wished she'd found a gentler way of breaking the news. Lena almost dropped her cup and the colour drained from her face.

'Oh, dear God!' she said. 'But how can you possibly be involved, Kathy?'

'There are things I haven't told you,' Kathy said. 'I know now I should have been honest and told you everything before, but when I first came home I was trying to put it all behind me and start again.' As carefully as she could she explained what had happened that fateful night when Charlie had persuaded her to lure Gus Norris to the bomb-site.

'But why didn't you just refuse?' Lena asked.

Kathy hung her head. 'I only agreed because Charlie made me a promise,' she said quietly. 'There's more. It's complicated. There was a man – Jeff Slater. Charlie said he was a friend he and Bill met in the army and they were going into business with him. They invited him round for a meal and I had to play hostess. At first I thought he was nice. He was good to me – took me to nice places and gave me presents. But then...' She paused and looked at Lena anxiously. 'Then it all seemed to be getting out of hand. He seemed to want more of me than I was prepared to give.' She swallowed hard. 'One night he took me to his house. He gave me something to drink and I must have passed out. When I came to. . . .'

'Oh, *Kathy*!' Lena reached across and touched her hand, her eyes full of anguish. 'You don't have to go on. My poor darling. Did you report it to the police?'

'No. I told Charlie but he seemed to think I was making a fuss about nothing. Jeff was a good friend of his and he didn't want him upset. I found out just yesterday that it was Jeff's job to entice girls – to make them fall for him and then induce them to work in the clubs and casi-nos owned by his boss. It was all arranged between them. I was set up.'

'Oh, Kathy.'

'But when Charlie asked me to lure this Norris man to the bombsite, I still didn't know any of this. He told me nothing bad would happen; the man owed him money and he just wanted to scare him a bit. I wasn't happy about it but in the end I said I'd do it if he made Jeff leave me alone. And he promised. A promise I know now he never intended to keep.'

Lena squeezed her hand. 'So you did as he asked. What happened?'

Kathy shuddered. 'It was horrible. I went to the pub that night and talked to the man as Charlie had asked, but when I saw the beating they gave the poor man I was horrified. Bill told me to go home and I went. There was nothing I could do to help the man and I felt so guilty and ashamed that I'd lured him there and then run away. The next day I went to see Father Gerard and told him everything – even about Jeff. He said I should leave as soon as possible – come back here.' She sighed. 'It was like heaven, being back here with all of you again, but I should have realized it couldn't last. You can imagine how I felt a few days later when I heard that Gus Norris had died in hospital and the police were looking for his murderer. I still feel so guilty.'

'But you were tricked into it. You weren't to know how serious the attack would be,' Lena assured her. 'And you only agreed because your stepbrother promised to make this man leave you alone.'

'I know now that he would have promised anything to get me to do it,' Kathy said.

'So – what happened today to make you go to London?'

'Jeff Slater turned up at the post office looking for me.'

Lena looked shocked. 'The man you've just told me about?'

'Yes. I can't tell you what a shock it was, suddenly looking up to see him standing there.'

'How did he track you down?'

'He knew where to find me because I told him once where I was evacuated, but Charlie would have told him anyway. It was Charlie who sent him.'

'What did he say?'

'He made me go with him in his car.'

'*Kathy*! You're telling me you actually went? My God! Anything could have happened to you.'

'He didn't give me any choice, but anyway I soon found out that Jeff had heavier things on his mind,' Kathy said. 'It seems that all of them – Charlie and Bill and Jeff Slater were working for a much bigger organization. When Charlie was arrested he got in touch with Jeff. He threatened to give the police the name of the man at the top unless Jeff came and found me and forced me to give a statement to the police insisting that Gus Norris was alive when they left him. That way they might get the charge reduced to manslaughter.'

'And you agreed to do it?'

'Not at first. I didn't feel I owed any of them anything,' Kathy said bitterly. 'But then Jeff told me he'd been talking to Maggie at the shop, she'd let slip about my friendship with all of you and especially Chris. He said he'd tell him about. . . .' Kathy bit her lip hard to stop the tears that welled up. 'About that night at his house. Except that he was going to make up a lot of lies about me.'

Lena was shaking her head. 'I blame myself for much of this,' she said. 'I told James we should never have let you go with those Brady brothers. To think you gave up your college place and so much else and just for all this. It must have been an absolute nightmare.'

'You couldn't have known,' Kathy said.

'No, but we should have done more to find out. We should have insisted on keeping you with us while we investigated.' She reached across the table to take Kathy's hand. 'We're responsible, James and I. All this is our fault.'

'No.' Kathy shook her head. 'It's useless for you or anyone else to take the blame. It's over and the fact is – I've done it.'

Lena looked at her. 'Done what?'

'Told the truth to the police. Except the part about Jeff ordering the attack. He threatened me with what could happen if I didn't twist the truth and do as Charlie wanted.'

'But you told the truth anyway?'

'About my part in it. I told them I didn't stay – didn't know whether the man was dead or alive when the boys had finished with him; all I knew was that Charlie had insisted the man was all right when they left him. Afterwards the policeman told me that another witness had come forward; a woman who'd been taking a short cut on her way home from work that night. It seems she called an ambulance, but by the time they got there the man had dragged himself away – which proves he was still alive.'

'And that will let the Bradys off the hook?'

'For murder, it might, but it seems that there is enough evidence of other crimes to send them to prison for quite a long time.'

Lena looked at her. 'And this Slater man – you kept his name out of it as he asked?'

Kathy nodded. 'Not because I care what happens to him – because I'm afraid of what he could do.'

'So he's going to get off scott free? It doesn't seem fair.'

'I've no choice. I daren't risk revealing his part in it.' Kathy looked at Lena. 'Now I only have one option, Auntie Lena. I'll have to leave.'

'Leave! Why?'

'I can't risk all of you being dragged into this. Beckets Green is a small village. You'd never live it down. Besides, if the GPO get to hear of my part in this I'll be asked to leave my job anyway.' She stopped speaking and swallowed hard at the lump in her throat. 'You've all been so good to me. You're like my family. I couldn't bear to bring shame on you.' She took a deep breath. 'And then there's Chris,' she said quietly.

'Chris?' Lena was holding both her hands so tightly it almost hurt. 'What about Chris?'

'You must have guessed that I love him,' Kathy said simply. 'He has said that he loves me too, but that was before he knew about me. He doesn't know what I've done – what I've been; doesn't really know me at all. When he does – when he gets to hear about all this. . . .' She bit her lip hard. 'I'm not brave enough to wait around to see the look on his face when I tell him. I'll write a letter for you to give him.'

'I can't let you do this, Kathy.'

'You must. It's the only way.'

'Let me talk to James. We'll come up with a solution.'

Kathy shook her head. 'I don't want to involve you any more. It was bad enough having to tell you. Better if I go now.'

'But where will you go?' Lena grasped her hands. 'Kathy – you said we'd been like your family. We *are* your family. Don't you realize how much we'll worry about you? As for Chris, I think you underestimate his character, if you think he's going to abandon you over something that wasn't your fault.'

'I can't risk it. Chris deserves better than me,' Kathy said. 'I think I always knew it was all too good to be true; the cottage, the job and Chris. Maybe I never deserved to be here with you. After all, I'm just an East End kid. I should never have imagined myself anything else. Perhaps what happened was no more than I deserved.'

Lena shook her head impatiently. 'I'm so glad your mother can't hear you saying things like that, Kathy,' she said. 'She always wanted the best for you. You know that. She worked hard to bring you up to be straight and honest – to be someone who always knew right from wrong. Those Brady brothers tried to bring you down – to corrupt you and now you're letting them win. I can't believe you're giving up like this.'

'I'm not giving up,' Kathy said. 'I'll make a new start somewhere else. I won't let what happened to me affect the people I love.' She stood up. 'I can't thank you enough, Auntie Lena for all you've done for me; for the cottage and for all the happy times you've given me. I'll write a letter of resignation for Mrs Trent but will you please explain as best you can to her – and to Elaine? I'll go and pack now and I'll write a letter for Chris and leave it at the cottage. I'll go first thing in the morning.'

'*Where* though, Kathy? Where will you go? You can't just disappear. If you care about us at all you have to keep in touch.'

Kathy paused uncertainly in the doorway, knowing Lena was right. 'I'll telephone,' she said at last. 'I'll make sure you know I'm all right.' She ran forward and threw her arms around Lena, hugging her tightly. 'I love you Auntie Lena,' she whispered. 'I love all of you – so much. And I'll never *ever* forget you.'

CHAPTER FIFTEEN

Kathy sat on the London train, her mind numb with misery as it rumbled through the countryside. She had risen early and taken the two letters, written last night, down to the farm before she left.

The letter to Chris had been difficult – almost impossible; she had written it again and again before she was satisfied, finally putting it into an envelope and sealing it. Her letter of resignation to Mrs Trent, although easier had been painful. She had been so happy in the job at the post office, with its prospects of promotion and a home of her own. Why was it that every time she thought her future was secure something happened to smash her hopes?

When she had called in at the farm, Joan Harris had been busy bustling round the kitchen making breakfast and Lena had taken Kathy's arm and steered her discreetly through to the hall. She looked pale and tired, as though, like Kathy she hadn't slept much.

'I do wish you'd change your mind about this,' Lena said. 'James and I had a long talk last night when he got back from his meeting. I told him everything and he agreed with me that we should take much of the blame for what happened to you. He wants you to stay as much as I do. He says we'll find a way through it together.'

'It's wonderful of you both, but I can't let you do it,' Kathy said.

Lena shook her head. 'I don't know what I'm going to say to Chris and Elaine. I know they're going to be devastated – especially Chris.'

Kathy handed her the two letters. 'I've written to him,' she said. 'And to Mrs Trent, so if you'd kindly pass them on. . . .'

Reluctantly Lena took the two envelopes. 'What about money?' she asked. 'Have you got enough? Will you be able to manage?'

'Yes. I've got enough to last a little while. I'll soon get some work,'

Kathy assured her. 'I don't mind what I do.'

'Oh, Kathy – I don't like this. I wish it could be different.'

Kathy hugged her swiftly. 'I'd better go,' she said, 'Or I'll miss the bus. I promise I'll ring and keep in touch.'

She was halfway through the door when Lena suddenly remembered something. 'Oh! I almost forgot. The post has been and there's a letter for you.' She picked up an envelope from the hall table and gave it to Kathy, who pushed it hastily into her handbag without looking at it.

'Thanks, Auntie Lena – for everything. Goodbye.'

Her throat was tight as she remembered Lena standing on the step, watching her and waving until she was out of sight. Now, remembering the letter, still unread she opened her bag and took it out. The first thing she noticed was the unfamiliar logo on the envelope. Inside she found a single sheet of notepaper and an official looking form. To her surprise she saw that it was a prison visiting order accompanied by a short letter from Charlie, badly written and misspelled. Charlie had played truant far more than he had attended school as she well remembered and he was no scholar anyway. Her first impulse was to tear up both letter and form and throw them away. Charlie had ruined her life. Why should she want to visit him in prison? But her curiosity won in the end and unfolding the sheet of paper she read Charlie's brief, barely literate note.

Deer Kath

I got a visting order for you coz I wont you to cum and see me in heer. Theres sum stuff I wont too say. Its impornant so I hope yool cum. Plees do

Charlie

She read the note through again, wondering what Charlie could possibly have to say to her. Did he have more plans to make her lie for him and Bill in court? If so she would tell him straight that she was done with all that. She had made up her mind that from now on everything would be above board. No secrets. No lies. Once again she was forced to try to make a fresh start. Each new beginning was harder than the last and it was going to be difficult enough without Charlie making it worse. There was no reason why she should visit him at all. She could just ignore the letter and try to put the past, including her step-brothers behind her. But by the time she stepped off the train at Euston Station, she knew she had to go to see Charlie one last time; if only to let him see that he hadn't broken her; that she was still in one piece with her chin held high and was managing – at least outwardly.

It didn't take Kathy long to find a job and a place to live. To begin with she took the tube to Hackney and walked down Kemsley Street to see what had happened to the shop. It was closed, the window boarded up and police tape across the door. Clearly the premises were still a crime scene and under surveillance . She booked into a cheap bed and breakfast hotel and went out to look for work.

In Charter Street, the newsagents on the corner had a card in the window advertising for an assistant. She went inside to enquire about it. The job was to start at 5 a.m., taking delivery of the newspapers and sorting them for the boys to take out and then working generally in the shop. It was an early start, but the shift ended at twelve, which meant that she could take on a second job if she could find one. The owner, Mrs Kelly, an elderly woman with a wheezy chest, interviewed Kathy and offered her the job on the spot. To her relief she didn't ask for a reference or information about her previous employment.

'Gettin' up at five is beyond me these days,' she confided. 'Can't get me breath of a mornin'. Need someone young and 'ealthy to 'elp me out.' She smiled. 'I think you'll do me nicely, dearie. You'll cheer the place up a treat.'

'I won't let you down,' Kathy assured her. 'I do have experience of shop work.'

Mrs Kelly recommended a house two streets away where she thought there might be a bed-sit to let. Kathy went straight round and found she could just about afford the little room. It was on the top floor of a house and not too far from the shop, which was a relief. She didn't want to have to travel far if she was to begin work at 5 a.m. The following day she found a waitressing job in a café near the tube station; it was from 4 o'clock till 8, which would give her time for a break between jobs. She found a phone box and rang Lena.

'Just thought I'd let you know I'm OK.'

'Kathy, where are you? Are you all right? Have you got a comfortable place to stay?'

'I'm fine,' Kathy assured her. 'No need to worry about me. I'm in

London and I've got two jobs and a nice room.' The word 'nice' hardly described the six by eight room with its lumpy bed, threadbare carpet and wobbly furniture, but Lena wasn't to know that. 'I'll keep in touch. Love to everyone,' she said as cheerily as she could.

The visiting order Charlie had sent was for Friday afternoon at two o'clock which fitted in perfectly. Kathy didn't want to have to ask for time off as soon as she'd started work. Arriving at the prison she joined the queue of depressed-looking visitors, there were mothers, daughters and wives, some with children and some even carrying small babies.

'Who you got inside then, love – dad, boyfriend?' the woman behind her in the queue enquired.

Kathy forced a smile. 'My stepbrother,' she replied.

'Waitin' for trial?'

'Yes.'

'I thinks it's a cryin' shame, bangin' 'em up like this even before they know whether they're guilty or not,' the woman said. She shifted the baby she was holding onto the other hip and regarded Kathy with interest. 'What's he in for, duck?'

'Oh – this and that,' Kathy hedged.

'My old man's in for armed robbery,' the woman volunteered with a dry laugh. 'Armed robbery! I ask you. It's not bleedin' fair. It weren't his idea in the first place and he never ach'lly took part. He only went along to drive the car. How was he to know it'd break down?' She shook her head. 'Can't get a decent car nowadays – not even if you pay for it! The very idea of my Fred thumpin' anyone is laughable! He wouldn't hurt a fly.'

'Perhaps he'll get off,' Kathy said.

'It wants showin' up,' the woman said, taking out a handkerchief and wiping the baby's nose. 'Four years in the army, my Fred done and no job to come out to. I got three more little'uns at 'ome. Gotta make ends meet some'ow ain't yer?' As the queue began to move she thrust the baby at Kathy. ' 'Ere – 'old Pete for a minute, will you? I can't find me visitin' order.'

The queue moved forward while the woman rummaged in her handbag and the struggling baby in Kathy's arms began to wail. His mother snatched him back.

'Come 'ere and shut up you little bugger,' she said affectionately.

'Don't want yer dad to see you with snot all over yer face, do yer?'

For some reason Kathy had expected to see both boys, but it was only Charlie who shuffled in with the other inmates. He looked pale and exhausted, but when he saw her sitting at the allotted table his face brightened a little.

' 'Ello, Kath. I wasn't sure you'd come.'

'Hello, Charlie. Where's Bill?'

He shook his head. 'Dunno. They split us up.' He looked at her. 'You come up from the country today then?'

'No. I couldn't stay there,' she told him. 'Not after what happened. Jeff came to find me and gave me your message. I gave a statement to the police and then I left Beckets Green. I couldn't risk involving the Spicers in something like this.'

To her surprise he hung his head. 'Messed things up for you again gel, ain't I?'

'You certainly have,' she agreed. 'Jeff almost frightened the life out of me. Anyway, I did as you asked – I told the police all I knew, Charlie. I couldn't lie and say I was there when I wasn't, but as it happens there was another witness so they know that Gus was still alive after you left.'

He nodded. 'Yeah, I know. My brief said.' He was silent for a long moment then he looked up at her. 'I've had a lot of time to think while I've been in here, Kath. What we done to you was wrong. I know that now. See – when we was kids we never knew you – not properly. After the war when we got to know Jeff and got involved in what he was into we reckoned up how old you'd be and we thought you'd probably grown up to be a bit of a looker like your ma was once. We thought there was a good chance Jeff might take to you and we thought—'

'You don't have to go on. Kathy interrupted. 'I know what you thought – that I was some stupid girl you could trick into the vice world and make yourself some easy money.'

'That's a bit strong, Kath.'

'It is a bit strong, Charlie; more than a bit strong. You almost wrecked my life. You knew what Jeff had in mind for me the night he took me to that house in Surrey and you just let it happen.'

'At the time I couldn't see no harm in it. Them Spicers brought you up like one o'theirs – classy. We should'a seen that. We should'a known you belonged to a different world. I'm sorry.'

'Sorry?' She shook her head. 'I doubt if you know how to be sorry, Charlie, you or Bill. Even after what happened you still sent Jeff to find me – to get me to lie for you – to threaten me. You must have known how frightened I'd be.'

Suddenly his head came up and he looked at her. 'Kath! Look, I *am* sorry, honest. I never told him to threaten you or scare you. Anyway, you won't be called to give evidence because. . . .' He leaned forward. 'Because I've made up my mind, I'm goin' King's. I'm gonna tell them everything I know – names, places, the lot. Bill don't know yet, which is good 'cause he'd only try and talk me out of it, but I reckon we'll get a lighter sentence if I blow the gaff on 'em all.'

Kathy's blood froze. 'Won't that be dangerous? From what Jeff told me the man at the top is powerful.'

'I've thought of that,' Charlie told her. 'I'll try and make a bargain with the law – information in exchange for protection.'

'Jeff says that if you turn King's Evidence there'll be a contract out for him. That means someone will be hired to kill him, doesn't it?'

Charlie's lip curled. 'You don't wanna take no notice of what Jeff says. He knows how to take care of himself. If he thought that shopping me and Bill would save his skin, he'd do it without a second thought,' he said. 'You don't wanna worry about him.'

'I'm not!'

'Neither am I. Look, Kath, I've had enough of livin' on the wrong side of the law. When I get out I'm goin' straight – maybe take up the boxin' again; make a pile of dosh and a name for meself. Find a nice gel and get married.' The bell sounded for the end of visiting time and Charlie leaned forward again. 'Thanks for coming, Kath,' he said. 'I just wanted to put you in the picture. You won't have to come to court and Jeff and the rest of the gang will get theirs. It's my way of making up to you for what we done. Look at it that way if you like.'

A warder touched Charlie on the shoulder and he stood up. 'Bye then, Kath.'

'Bye, Charlie.'

On the way home, Kathy was thoughtful. Did Charlie really mean what he said? Was he really going to turn King's Evidence and would the law really give him protection? Jeff had told her that his 'boss' had contacts in high places. Did Charlie realize the danger of the risk he was about to take. As for taking up his boxing and making a name for himself: It wasn't very likely; by the time he got out of prison he would surely be too old and unfit to pick up the skill again. And was he really doing all this to make up to her for all that had happened? Somehow she doubted it. Remorse wasn't an emotion that had ever troubled Charlie in her experience.

CHAPTER SIXTEEN

May's Café was usually busy during Kathy's shift. There were twelve tables behind the net-curtained window. They were all covered in oilcloth with the usual condiments and tomato sauce in a squeezy bottle shaped like a tomato sitting in the middle. At first Kathy found it hard work, remembering the orders and waiting at the tables, especially when they were busy. Most of the customers on her shift were male, either on the way home from work or waiting to go on the night shift. Most were quiet, but there would be the occasional boisterous individual who would try to flirt with her.

'You're new, ain't yer love?'

'What time d'yer get off then?'

'You gotta smashin' figure, darlin' This one was usually accompanied by a painfully pinched bottom, which Kathy quickly learned how to avoid.

For the most part, she served them with a cool smile that clearly told them 'hands off' and did her work as best she could.

The café was owned and run by May Gittings, a woman in her forties with a stoic nature. She told Kathy that her husband had been killed in North Africa and that she'd kept the café open all through the raids in spite of being bombed twice.

'It's what my Ken would've expected, dear,' she said. 'We had no windows and no electric one day, but as long as the kitchen was still standin', I carried on somehow.'

Usually by the time Kathy finished her shift, the autumn night was beginning to set in and dusk was falling. After the café closed she usually stayed on to help May with the washing up that had accumulated and to mop the floor and wipe down the tables ready for early morning opening. She was happy to help out. Anything was better than the claustrophobic four walls of her lonely little bed-sit. May usually made a pot of tea when they'd finished and invited her to help drink it, so more often than not it was almost ten before she set off.

She'd been working at the café for about three weeks the first time it happened. She'd started out at the usual time and had reached the corner of the street, when she fancied that hers were not the only footsteps she could hear echoing on the pavement. She stopped walking and glanced round, but the street behind her was empty. She heard the footsteps again the following night. Once just after turning the corner she dodged into a doorway and waited, her heart in her mouth as she watched the street corner. A woman appeared with a dog on a lead and walked past. Relieved, Kathy emerged, but as soon as she continued on her way she was sure she could hear the footsteps again. This time she hurried on, her steps quickening until she was all but running. By the time she reached her destination she was breathless and panicky. Running up the stairs she fumbled in her bag for her key and let herself in. Slamming the door and locking it she leaned against it gasping for breath and waiting for her heartbeat to slow.

She told herself she was being silly, imagining things – being paranoid. She knew these streets. They were where she had played as a child. She had nothing to fear from them. She undressed and got into bed but sleep evaded her. Her mind whirled with the things that Jeff had told her about the mysterious and sinister man he worked for. Had her statement to the police been strong enough? What more could she do? Why should anyone want to hurt her?

At last she fell into a troubled sleep and woke exhausted at half past four to the shrilling of the alarm clock.

Every night that week she thought she heard the footsteps. Every night she told herself she was imagining it, but every time she ended by running the last few yards and flinging herself into her room. She thought of going to the police, but what would she tell them? She had never actually seen anyone following her. They would think she was an over-imaginative, hysterical young woman.

May's was open seven days a week, but the newsagent's was closed on Sundays; old Mrs Kelly had decided a while ago that six days a week was more than enough for her. This meant that Kathy didn't have to rise at the crack of dawn on Sundays, something for which she was deeply grateful. The following Saturday evening she stayed on at the café later than usual. May's daughter, who had married a Canadian airman and gone to live in Canada, had just had a baby and she had received photographs that she was bursting to share. By the time Kathy left for home it was half past ten and almost dark. The summer night was warm and she looked up at the luminous dark blue sky, lit by a sliver of new moon and thought yearningly of Beckets Green, the farm and, most painful of all, Chris. He would be home from his course now. He would have received her letter. Her heart ached at the thought of never seeing him again.

She was still preoccupied when she reached the corner of the street where she lived. As she turned into the circle of light from the street lamp someone stepped out of a shop doorway just ahead of her. A man wearing a trench coat and trilby hat, pulled forward, the brim shielding his face. He turned and stood directly in her path, tipping his hat back. She caught her breath. It was Jeff.

'Later than usual tonight, eh, Kath?'

Through the pounding of her heart she managed to find her voice. 'Wha-what do you want?'

He laughed. 'Aah, did I make you jump? Sorry about that.'

'You've been following me every night, haven't you?'

He assumed an innocent expression and spread his hands. 'Me? Now why would I do that?'

'I don't know. I did as you asked. Why can't you leave me alone? You said we weren't to see each other again.'

'That was before.' His face hardened and he grasped her arm. 'I think we'd better discuss this at your place.'

'*No!*' she tried to shake off his hand but he held her fast. 'I'm not going anywhere with you.'

He scowled at her. 'Oh don't get worked up. I'm not going to touch you, you silly bitch. Why should I bother with you when I can have the pick of real women? No, there are more serious things at stake now.' He gave her arm a vicious jerk. 'Come on, do as you're told.'

She tried to stall him by taking another route, but it was no use. She should have known that he knew by now exactly where she lived. As she tried to cross the road he squeezed her arm painfully.

'Don't make this more difficult, Kath. I know where you live and the sooner we get there and you hear what I've got to say, the sooner I'll leave you alone.'

'I'm not allowed male visitors late at night,' she told him.

'Is that so?' He laughed. 'Too bad. we'll have to be extra quiet then, won't we?'

In her room at the top of the house Jeff turned the key in the lock and pocketed the key. Kathy stood facing him, her heart in her mouth. 'What do you want?'

He took off his hat and threw it onto a chair. 'A cup of tea would be nice,' he said insolently, sitting down on the bed.

'Go to hell!'

He assumed a shocked expression. 'Oh dear, *oh dear*! What would your nice genteel friends think if they heard you speaking to a guest like that? They'd have had the cucumber sandwiches out by now.'

'Say what you have to say and go.' She said, trying hard not to let him see how frightened she was.

'OK. Word on the street is that Charlie's hell-bent on turning King's Evidence no matter what, but then you'd know all about that, wouldn't you?'

'It wasn't my idea. There's nothing I can do about it.'

'Oh, I think there is.'

Her heart froze. 'How can I make him change his mind?'

'Simple, you can pass on a message.'

'I shan't be seeing him again.'

'I think you'd better try if you know what's good for you.' He reached for her hand and pulled her towards him. 'Sit down and listen. I'm not fooling, Kathy.'

'Charlie won't change his mind just because I ask him. He says he wants to turn over a new leaf – go straight when he's done his sentence.'

Jeff gave a snort of laughter. 'Go straight – Charlie? Might as well try and straighten a corkscrew. It's just not in him.' His grip on her arm tightened. 'Now listen! Charlie might not care much about anyone else but he does care about that cretin of a brother of his. More than once he saved his miserable skin when they were in the army. God knows why! You go to see Charlie and you tell him that if he turns King's Evidence, Bill will get it. And I do mean *get it*! They're in different remand prisons so there won't be a thing he can do to protect him this time.' He thrust his face close to hers. 'It won't be pretty, Kath,' he said. 'There are plenty of lags willing to do a little job for the boss if the rewards are tempting enough; plenty of opportunities inside to get even – in the corridors – in the washrooms when the screws aren't looking. Ever seen a bloke get his throat slashed with a razor, have you?'

Kathy shuddered. 'I don't owe Charlie and Bill anything,' she said defiantly. 'I owe you even less. Why should I do anything you ask? Why should I even believe you?'

He began to look exasperated, 'Christ almighty, Kath! I always had you down for a bright kid. Can't you see how dangerous this could be? I can't believe you're being this stupid.'

She rounded on him. '*Stupid?* Oh yes, I'm stupid all right,' she said. 'Giving up all my opportunities – trusting the wrong people; letting my life get ruined. I've had enough of being stupid. How do I know that even if I did as you ask something bad wouldn't still happen?'

'You *don't*! But one thing you *can* be sure of though is, that something bad will happen if you refuse. It won't be me following you home in future. It'll be someone you don't know. He won't want to sit down and talk to you, reasonable like. He'll be someone who means business. And like I said before, it won't be pretty.'

Tears welled up in her eyes. Was this what she had come to; to be threatened and bullied and probably killed in some dark alley by a hired thug. What had she done to deserve it? How had she got into this mess?

Seeing her tears and taking them for raw fear, Jeff's eyes gleamed with triumph. He knew the time had come to play his trump card. 'Or maybe you'd like that turnip-head boyfriend of yours to know what kind of a girl you really are?'

'Don't waste your breath, Jeff,' she told him, swallowing hard at the lump in her throat. 'I've already confessed everything to Chris and the Spicer family. They know all about you and what happened. I've left – walked out of their lives for good so as not to involve them.'

His eyes flickered with indecision for a second then. . . . 'Yeah? I bet you played the whole thing down – made yourself look like the innocent little victim. I could write him a letter – give him some really sweet memories of his dear little Kathy. Let him know what he was missing. I could tell him stuff that'd make his hair curl.'

Inwardly she cringed with revulsion, but she held her chin up and persisted in her defiance. 'Tell as many lies as you like. You might succeed in hurting people you don't even know, but you can't hurt me any more than you already have. And it won't get you what you want either.'

She began to turn away and in an instant he was on his feet. Grasping her shoulders he pushed her against the wall and held her there. One hand round her throat, his face inches away from hers he said, 'You were really rattled when I followed you home this week, weren't you? You ran the last few yards and threw yourself through that front door like the hounds of hell were after you. How would you like to be looking over your shoulder every time you ventured out? The difference would be that next time the person who follows you will catch you up real quick. What he'll do will be swift and silent – and *final*! And the best bit is that you'll never know when it's coming.'

Terrified, she opened her mouth to scream. The time had come to admit she needed help. His other hand clamped over her mouth, hard and hot, bruising her lips against her teeth.

'*Shut up*! You get anyone up here and I'll tell them you're on the game and I'm one of your punters. D'you want to get chucked out on the street?'

Her eyes wide, she stared at him.

'No – thought not. Just calm down, Kath, and listen.' He pulled her across to a chair and pushed her into it. 'All you've got to do is get yourself over to the prison and make it clear to Charlie that he'd better keep his mouth shut – OK? Tell him what'll happen to Bill if he doesn't. And make it convincing.'

'And – and if he doesn't believe it? After all, he says they'll get a shorter sentence if he turns King's Evidence.'

Jeff laughed dryly. 'Oh, they'll get a shorter sentence all right. In fact the pair of them'll be lucky to live long enough to get as far as court.' He stood up and walked to the door. 'I'll leave you to think about it, Kath,' he said. 'But don't take too long, time's running out for Charlie and Bill – for you, too, unless you co-operate.' He picked up his hat and put it on the back of his head, smiling down at her as he took the key out of his pocket. 'I've a good mind to keep this,' he said, tossing it up into the air and catching it. 'It'd be nice to be able to come and see you when ever I fancied a nice chat, wouldn't it?' He laughed at the horror stricken look on her face. 'That made you sit up and take notice, didn't it. Here – catch.' He threw the key at her, watching her scrabble for it as it landed at her feet. ' 'Night then, Kath. Sweet dreams. Sleep tight. Mind the bugs don't bite.'

When he'd gone, Kathy rushed to the door and turned the key in the lock then leaned against it, sighing with relief. She was trembling uncontrollably and her heart was beating like a drum. Jeff had really scared her; he was all smiles one minute, evilly brutal the next; this was nothing like the man who had courted her so convincingly. She knew she had no choice but to do as he asked. She had to try and stop Charlie telling the police all he knew. They would all be in terrible danger if he did. But could she convince him? Could she even get to see him and how did she go about it? If only there were someone she could turn to for help.

She woke on Sunday morning with the answer clear in her mind. She knew exactly what she must do. Getting up, she dressed quickly and went out to walk the mile and a half through the East End streets to St Jude's Church. Father Gerard would surely know what to do. He always seemed to have the solution to her problem.

The church was pleasantly cool and peaceful. The early morning Mass was quiet, as usual. Kathy sat close to the front and knelt, closing her eyes and inhaling the familiar scents of incense, flowers and candle wax which took her back to her childhood. It was as though Mum had spoken to her through her dreams last night, telling her what to do and directing her to St Jude's and now she had the comforting feeling that her mother was close.

Father Gerard spotted her at once, though he gave only the merest flicker of surprise. When Mass was over, Kathy remained in her place until everyone else had gone, knowing that he would be back. Sure enough, after a moment or two she felt his light touch on her shoulder.

'Kathy, child, so you're back. It's good to see you, but I hope this is only a fleeting visit.'

She looked up at him. 'No. I'm afraid it's not, Father. I've been back in London for a while. I should have come before. I'm sorry. You'll be thinking I only come when I need help.'

He slipped into the pew beside her. 'So you need help. I'm happy that you feel you can come to me.' He looked into her eyes. 'Has something bad happened?' She nodded. 'Then maybe you'd better join me for breakfast,' he said. 'My housekeeper doesn't arrive until nine o'clock so we shan't be disturbed.' He took her arm. 'Come, child. It's bad for the digestion to talk about problems on an empty stomach.'

In the presbytery kitchen, Father Gerard, now devoid of his chasuble, tied on one of his housekeeper's aprons and began to make a breakfast of porridge and toast. He brewed a large pot of tea and as they sat opposite each other he urged Kathy to eat.

'Come along child. You look as though a puff of wind would blow you right up to heaven,' he said. 'Get that breakfast eaten. We can talk about whatever's on your mind after.'

Kathy felt better after she'd eaten. As she pushed away her empty plate Father Gerard nodded his approval and poured her a cup of tea.

'Right, that's better. You've colour in your cheeks again. Now, what can I help you with?'

She took a deep breath. It was hard to know where to begin. 'My stepbrothers, Charlie and Bill are in prison,' she told him. 'On remand, awaiting trial for murder.'

He nodded. 'I know, Kathy. I read about it in the papers and I remembered what you told me.'

'Charlie sent Jeff Slater to Beckets Green to get me to give a statement to the police, to give them an alibi. I was to say that the man – Gus Norris, was still alive when they left him.'

The priest frowned. 'Slater – he was the man who assaulted you?' She nodded. He looked incredulous. 'You're telling me that he came to Beckets Green to ask you to lie for them – after all that had happened?'

'Yes.'

'But you refused of course?'

Kathy bit her lip. 'It wasn't as simple as that. Jeff said that Charlie was threatening to turn King's Evidence and that he, Jeff would get the blame if he did. He said there'd be a contract out on him. That means—'

Father Gerard held up his hand. 'I know what it means, but I can't believe that you were willing to lie for him.'

'I wasn't! He threatened me, though. You see, when I went back to Magpie Farm there were things I didn't tell the Spicers,' she said. 'I didn't lie – just left the worst – the part about Jeff out. I was so ashamed. I know I should have been honest with them.' He nodded and Kathy went on, 'Jeff had learned that Chris Spicer and I were becoming close. He threatened to go to him with his version of what happened between us. He said he would make it look as though I was willing and – and. . . .' She broke off, hanging her head and biting her lip with humiliation.

'In other words, he blackmailed you.'

'Yes. I knew then that I had to leave – to come back to London. I couldn't involve the Spicers and I couldn't bear them to think badly of me – especially Chris. They would have felt I'd betrayed them.'

'So you came back to London and made your statement?'

'Yes, after I'd made a clean breast of things with Auntie Lena – Mrs Spicer. And in my statement I told the truth. I admitted that I'd seen the attack, but I wasn't there when they left their victim. Later I learned something that Jeff didn't know – that my statement didn't matter because there was another witness who is willing to testify, which means that the charge could be reduced to manslaughter and I won't be called to give evidence.'

'All the same, you should go to the police about the blackmail.'

Although she knew he was right, Kathy's heart sank. Jeff seemed to have ways of knowing exactly what she was up to. She said nothing.

Father looked at her enquiringly. 'But something tells me that I haven't heard the whole story. Am I right?'

'Yes. Charlie had sent me a visiting order. I went to see him in prison. He told me then that he had decided to turn King's Evidence so that he and Bill will get a lighter sentence. He insisted that he was about to turn over a new leaf after serving his sentence. He said he was doing it to make up for the trouble he caused me.'

'Really?'

Kathy took a deep drink of her tea. 'I found work and a place to live and I thought that was the end of it.' She looked up at him. 'I was wrong.' She recounted her suspicion that she was being followed home from work on several occasions, ending with last night's terror-filled encounter with Jeff.

'So unless I can persuade Charlie to change his mind, I'll be in constant fear of what might happen,' she concluded. 'And I haven't got a visiting order. I don't even know how to apply for one or what to do.' Her voice caught in her throat and tears began to well up and trickle down her cheeks. Father Gerard produced a large white handkerchief and passed it across the table to her.

'Dry those tears, Kathy,' he said. 'Go to the police. Go now.'

She shook her head. 'I daren't. Jeff would know somehow. You don't know what he's like. I have the feeling I'm being watched all the time.'

He sighed and sat back in his chair. 'I still think the police should be informed of this, but I can see how afraid you are.' He paused. 'As for a visiting order, I could easily get permission to visit Charlie as his priest. After all he and his brother were brought up Catholic. You and I will go along together and I will explain to Charlie the consequences of what he is about to do. It goes against what I feel is right. These evil people should be brought to justice, but not at the expense of the innocent. All we can hope is that they will get their just deserts in the end.'

'Charlie believes that turning King's Evidence will get him and Bill a lighter sentence.'

'When he knows that he will be putting his own brother's life in danger he might think again, although it goes against the grain to play into the hands of a blackmailer.' He looked at her. 'You and young Christopher Spicer – is it serious?'

She nodded unhappily. 'I love him very much. I have ever since I was a little girl. We were so happy, but that's all over now.'

He patted her hand. 'You deserve so much better than this, child, but don't despair. God has a way of answering our prayers in ways we least expect sometimes.' He glanced at his watch. 'I'll have to start getting ready for the eight o'clock Mass now, Kathy,' he said, getting up from the table. 'Leave it to me. I'll telephone the prison first thing in the morning and if you give me a number where I can reach you I'll let you know the outcome.'

Kathy scribbled down a telephone number and passed it to him. 'It's Kelly's newsagents shop. I'm there every morning till twelve,' she told him. 'Thank you so much, Father. I'm sorry to have taken up so much of your time.'

'Not at all, child. Go home and don't worry any more. You're not alone. You're in my prayers and I won't let anything happen to you, never fear.'

Kathy spent the rest of Sunday trying to relax. She felt so much safer now that she had spoken to Father Gerard. He had always been a tower of strength. He put everything in perspective for her. Halfway through the morning she went downstairs to the payphone in the hallway and dialled the number of Magpie Farm. She felt confident enough to assure Lena that she was well and happy. To her dismay a male voice answered.

'Hello. Magpie Farm.'

She recognised Chris's voice and panicked. She couldn't speak to him – not yet. Without speaking, she gently replaced the receiver and went back up to her room, shaken and upset.

She worked her evening shift at the café, always quiet on Sunday evenings and walked home afterwards without incident. She slept restlessly, her sleep disturbed by dreams of Chris, but when the alarm wakened her she remembered that Father Gerard was helping her now. Maybe this morning she would get a call from him with a day and time for the prison visit. The thought helped her to feel better.

At the newsagent's she arrived just as the daily papers were being delivered. Opening up the shop with her key she heaved the first of the bundles onto the counter and cut the string that bound them. Taking up her pencil she began to mark them. The first street finished, she loaded them into the paper-boy's bag. It was only then that an item in the 'stop press' of the *Daily Mail* caught her eye.

MURDER SUSPECT TURNS KING'S EVIDENCE. MANY ARRESTS MADE.

Kathy stopped in her tracks – stunned; she prayed that the news item referred to someone else. Holding her breath, she read the few red inked lines only to discover that her worst fears were confirmed; the item named Charlie and the Gus Norris case. There was no mistake. She was too late. He had gone ahead and done what he'd threatened. The die was cast.

CHAPTER SEVENTEEN

Kathy finished marking the papers in an agony of indecision. Charlie had no idea of the danger he had put his brother and stepsister in. All she could do was to get warning of the threat to Bill's safety to some-one – but who? And how would she do it? She was still agonising over the problem when Mrs Kelly came through from the back with two mugs of tea.

' 'Mornin' duck,' she wheezed. 'Woke up early this mornin' and couldn't get back to sleep again so I thought I'd get up and make us a nice cuppa.'

'Thanks, Mrs K,' Kathy took the mug from her and sipped it grate-fully.

The old woman peered at her. 'You're lookin' a bit pasty this mornin', duck. All right, are you?' She hoisted herself onto the stool behind the counter, wincing with pain. 'Ooh, me arthritis is giving me gyp this mornin',' she complained. 'Take my advice gel, don't get old. It ain't no picnic.' She pulled a copy of the morning paper towards her and began to scan it, slurping her tea with noisy satisfaction. Suddenly she gave an exclamation.

'Well, I'll be blowed! Look at this in the stop press! It's only what I'd've expected from one o' them Bradys, mind. *King's Evidence* indeed. Shoppin' all 'is mates to get orf – typical! Them two young buggers used to make my life a misery; they was always nickin' sweets an' fags, chuckin' stones and rotten fruit at me windows. It was almost worth 'avin' a war to get rid of 'em. I always knew they'd end up inside. Serve 'em right if you asks me. That Gus Norris weren't no angel, but he didn't deserve a bashin' up like wot they give 'im.'

Kathy felt the shop spinning round her. She held onto the counter to stop herself from falling and Mrs Kelly stopped talking and reached out a hand to support her.

' 'Ere, 'old up love. Oh, my dear lord!' She stood up. ' 'Ere, sit down gel an' put your 'ead between your knees. You've gorn as white as a sheet.'

Kathy did as the old woman advised until gradually the faintness passed off.

'Can I get you anything, duck? A drop o' water?'

'No, thank you,' Kathy said. 'I'm all right now. I – I think it must have been something I ate.'

'I knew you weren't right soon as I saw you.' the old woman fussed. 'Look, why don't you go 'ome and rest, duck? I'm 'ere now and you've done the papers. P'raps you'll feel better tomorrow.'

On the way back to the bed-sit, Kathy stopped at a call box and dialled the number of St Jude's presbytery. When Father Gerard answered she said, 'Father, it's me, Kathy. Charlie's already done it. We're too late.'

'I know child. I've just seen the morning paper.'

'What am I to do?' Kathy whispered.

'Why don't you go home to Beckets Green, Kathy? There nothing more you can do now.'

'I can't, Father. Nothing will ever be the same now. Besides, it said in the paper that the police have made a lot of arrests. That must include Jeff. I'll be safe now.'

'Will you at least go to the police about the blackmail?'

'I'll think about it, Father. Thank you for helping me.'

'That's what I'm here for, child. Don't forget to come and see me again soon.'

She smiled, knowing that he really meant 'Don't forget to come to Mass.' 'I won't forget, Father. Goodbye.'

On the way home she thought about Father's insistence that she go to the police about Jeff. True, it would probably count against him, but it would mean that she would be dragged into the case again – maybe called to give evidence against Jeff. All she really wanted was to try to pick up the broken pieces of her life and forget all about Jeff Slater and her stepbrothers. When things had settled down and the trial was over perhaps she could look round for a better job and somewhere nicer to live; perhaps even move to another part of

London – maybe out into the suburbs. Maybe – in time – she would even get over losing Chris.

She checked the time and saw that it was almost eight o'clock. James and Chris would have breakfasted by now and be out working on the farm. And Lena would not have left for school yet. This was a good time to ring. In the hallway of the house she found coins for the pay phone and slipped them into the box then dialled the number.

'Magpie Farm. Lena Spicer speaking.'

Kathy heaved a sigh of relief. 'Auntie Lena, it's me, Kathy.'

'Kathy – darling, are you all right?'

'I'm fine thanks. Is everyone there all right?' she said, trying to sound as normal as possible.

'Yes, we're all well. Kathy, I was so worried. Chris took a call last evening, but the caller hung up without speaking. He was sure it was you. Was it?'

'I'm sorry. I couldn't speak to him, Auntie Lena – not yet. Did you give him my letter?'

'I did and I have to say he was terribly upset. He couldn't understand why you didn't trust him enough to confide in him before. And even more upset that you felt you had to run away.'

'It – wasn't quite as simple as that. I don't want any of you dragged into this mess.'

'You're part of our family, Kathy. Your problems are our problems. Why don't you come home? I didn't give Mrs Trent your letter of resignation, Kathy. Your job's still open for you if you come home soon. Please – think about it.'

Kathy bit her lip to stop the tears from flowing. 'Maybe once all this is over,' she said tremulously. 'The trial and everything. As long as my name doesn't get into the papers. I couldn't face the rest of the village if that happened. I couldn't bring shame on all of you.'

'Don't be silly!' Lena sounded impatient. 'There's no shame in being called to give evidence. You're not the one on trial. Anyway we don't care what anyone says. Won't you at least tell me where you are?'

'I-I'll keep in touch.' Kathy couldn't take much more. She knew she must end the conversation before Lena could guess how upset she was. 'I've got to go, Auntie Lena,' she said 'Sorry, I haven't any more change. I'll ring again soon.' She stood in the hall for several minutes, trying to fight back the tears. Mrs Kelly had been right, a rest might help. She'd hardly slept at all last night and she still had her shift at May's café to do tonight.

Chris pushed his barely touched plate away from him. 'It's no use. I've got to go and find her.' He pushed his chair back from the table and stood up.

Lena shot James a worried look. 'Sit down and finish your lunch,' she said. 'You've hardly touched it. In fact you've hardly eaten anything since yesterday.'

He pushed a hand through his hair exasperatedly. 'I don't know how you can calmly sit there and eat,' he said. 'God only knows what's happening to her. Why didn't you make her tell you where she was living? How can you be so complacent about all this? Those stepbrothers of hers are about to turn King's Evidence and spill the beans on the gang they were working for according to this morning's papers. She's a witness to what happened. Can't you see what that could mean for her?'

James laid down his knife and fork. 'Chris, do as your mother says and sit down. You're over-reacting. How can you accuse her of complacency? Can't you see how desperately worried she is? Kathy isn't a child. She's a grown woman and capable of making her own decisions. She's not a stranger to London and she's got a sensible head on her shoulders. I'm sure the police won't let anything happen to her.'

Chris began to pace up and down the kitchen. 'Why couldn't she have waited till I got back from the course? Why wouldn't she speak to me on the phone? She couldn't even trust me enough to let me know where she was going.' He shook his head. 'I thought she and I had something special, yet she could go off like this without a word.'

Lena saw the hurt in her son's eyes and her heart went out to him. Reaching out as he passed her chair, she touched his arm. 'Chris – something very traumatic happened to Kathy,' she said gently. 'She had a very bad time of it in London with her stepbrothers. Although she is innocent in it all, she's suffering a heavy burden of shame and guilt. That's why she couldn't face telling you. She told me she couldn't face seeing the look of disappointment on your face. Right or wrong, by not telling us she was trying to wipe the slate clean and make a fresh start.'

'She should have known it wouldn't have made any difference,'

Chris said angrily. 'I love her. I'd love her what ever happened. I always will.' He strode to the door. 'I can't just carry on as though nothing has happened – as though she never existed. And now she's in danger. I have to find her.' As he opened the door, James called out to him.

'Don't go off at a tangent like that, son. London's a vast city and we don't know where she is. It'll be like looking for a needle in a haystack.'

Chris turned at the door. 'I'm sorry, Dad. You'll have to manage without me for a few days. I'll make up the time when I get back, but I can't just stay at home imagining all sorts of things. I've got to do something.'

Upstairs in his room he pushed a few things into a hold-all. He was just zipping it up when there was a quiet knock on the door. A moment later Lena looked round it.

'Can I come in?'

'Don't waste your breath, Mum,' he said without turning round. 'I have to go and that's that.'

'I wasn't going to try and stop you,' Lena came into the room and sat down on his bed. 'I promise you, Chris that I feel really bad about Kathy. I promised her mother I'd take care of her and although she's grown up now I still feel committed to that promise. Listen, I really don't know where she is, but I'm afraid for her safety, too. It's a long shot, but there is someone you could try. When Mary was killed I went up to London with Kathy to the funeral. It was at St Jude's church in Hackney. Do you remember, it was the priest from that church who came here to break the news to Kathy?' Chris nodded, sitting down on the bed beside his mother.

'Yes, I remember. Father something – Gerald wasn't it?'

'Gerard. Father Gerard. I don't even know if he's still the priest there but I do know that if Kathy was in trouble he'd be the one person she could trust.'

Chris looked at her with hope in his eyes. 'Well, it's a starting point at least.'

'Take the truck,' Lena said. 'The tank's full of petrol. It's the pink industrial stuff of course, but I'm sure you'll have an explanation for that if you get stopped.' She put her hand in her pocket and handed him some notes. 'Take this. It's all I have in the house at the moment.'

Chris put his arms round his mother and hugged her. 'Thanks,

Mum. I'll pay you back. Sorry I've been a pain, but. . . .'

'I know,' Lena smiled. 'You love her. We all do. And once we've got her back with us, safe and sound we'll show her just how much.'

Exhaustion finally took over and Kathy slept all morning. She was surprised when she woke to see that it was half past two, and relieved to discover that she felt much better. The house was quiet and taking her things she went to the bathroom and ran herself a bath. There always seemed to be someone in the bathroom when she wanted a bath so it was pure luxury to be able to take her time. She washed her hair and went back to her room to make herself some tea and a sandwich.

Arriving early for her shift at May's she helped the café owner to peel potatoes and cut sandwiches for the evening rush. Wiping the tables, she picked up a late edition of the *London Evening News* that one of the customers had left behind. On the front page was the story of Charlie's turning King's Evidence and the dramatic outcome. It seemed that four nightclubs had been raided the previous evening and numerous arrests had been made, but no names were given. Kathy folded the paper, her heart cold with apprehension. Charlie had done this unaware of the threat it would pose to Bill. Would it really be carried out? She asked herself. Jeff seemed sure that it would. She felt partly responsible for not getting the message to him sooner.

The evening shift was busy. As she worked, she overheard snatches of conversation about the news. Many of May's customers knew Charlie and Bill and it was clear from what she heard that there was little sympathy for them. Clearly on their return from the war they had revived some long held hatred and made a lot of new enemies.

After washing up and tidying the café ready for the morning, May made the customary pot of tea and Kathy joined her at the kitchen table. The older woman eyed her speculatively over the rim of her cup.

'You all right love?'

'Me? Yes, I'm fine.'

'You've had something on your mind for days now.' May smiled gently. 'You're their little stepsister, aren't you?' She pointed to the newspaper. 'The Brady brothers.'

Reluctantly Kathy nodded. 'Yes, I am. How did you know?'

'When they had that shop in Kemsley Street I went in once. You were serving behind the counter. I recognized you. I used to know your mum. A lovely woman she was and you look a lot like her. Anyway, I knew them lads'd never get anyone who wasn't family to work for them, not with the reputation they've got round here.'

Kathy sighed. 'I was evacuated when the war broke out. I didn't see the boys for years. Then they suddenly turned up and Charlie said he was my legal guardian and I had to come back to London with them.'

May snorted disapprovingly. 'What a load of rubbish. They just wanted a free skivvy no doubt.' She looked at Kathy. 'By the way you speak, love, it sounds as though you were brought up by some really nice people.'

'I was,' Kathy said, a lump in her throat. 'The best. They were like my own family. I got a scholarship to high school and I had to give up a place at college to come back here with the boys.'

May shook her head. 'A cryin' shame if you ask me.' She stabbed a finger at the newspaper on the table between them. 'Well, it seems like they've got their come-uppance now all right and not before time.' She sighed. 'Even with King's Evidence I reckon they'll go down for a good long stretch. What are you going to do love – go back to your foster family?'

Kathy shook her head. 'I can't, not after all this. Everyone will know now that the Bradys are my stepbrothers.'

'Don't see why,' May said. 'You don't even have the same surname.'

Kathy didn't want to go into her disastrous relationship with Jeff and the stain she felt it had left on her character, so she just shrugged. 'I'm all right here. I've settled in now,' she said lightly. 'I'll keep in touch with my friends – maybe go and visit sometimes, but I'm a Londoner at heart.'

She got up and began to put on her coat ready to leave. Her words were light and casual, but May wasn't fooled. She'd heard the catch in her voice and seen the brightness in her eyes.

'Poor little kid,' she muttered as she put the catch on the door for the night. 'Her whole life ruined by them two evil no-good crooks.'

Chris parked the truck in a quiet road close to the church. He'd taken five hours to get to London and another hour finding his way out to Hackney. Even driving at the farm truck's top speed he couldn't have made the journey in less time. It was now seven o'clock. He walked round the corner and knocked on what he hoped was the door of the priest's house. After quite a long interval it was opened by a rather fierce looking woman wearing an outdoor coat and a brown felt hat. She looked him up and down suspiciously.

'Yes?'

'Can I speak to Father Gerard please?'

'No, you can't. He's out at a meeting and not expected back till late.'

Chris's heart sank. 'I suppose I couldn't come in and wait?'

The woman looked scandalized. 'No, indeed you can't,' she said. 'I'm Father's housekeeper and I'm just off home now. I can't clear off and leave a stranger in his house.'

'Of course not. I quite understand,' Chris said. 'You said he'd be back late. How late?'

'I'm sure I can't say,' the woman said. Then, relenting a little she added. 'I should think it'd be half-nine to ten or thereabouts.'

'In that case can you tell me where I could find a place to stay? I've travelled quite a long way.'

The woman's attitude seemed to mellow a little. 'Well – there's The Feathers public house in the next street,' she told him. 'I think they put people up and do a bit of catering sometimes.'

'Thank you very much. I'll try them. Thanks for your help.'

As Chris turned the corner he was just in time to see two young lads with a piece of hosepipe and a can, attempting to siphon off his petrol. He broke into a run and shouted at them but they threw down his petrol cap, grabbed their equipment and ran off. Getting into the driving seat, he realized that if he was to stay the night he was going to have to find a secure parking place for the truck. Otherwise he would run out of petrol before he could get home and he had no petrol coupons with which to buy more.

The landlady at The Feathers provided him with a bowl of passable soup and a plate of corned beef sandwiches then at his request she showed him to a small but clean room on the second floor for which she asked him to pay in advance. Chris handed over the money and asked if there was a secure car park. She escorted him round to the yard at the back where a large Alsatian dog was chained to a kennel.

'We let Rex loose at night,' she explained. 'No one's got past 'im yet.' She threw the dog a biscuit and by the look of his large teeth Chris didn't doubt her. Rex was a far cry from docile old Winston, the farm Labrador.

'You've got to watch it round 'ere,' the landlady told him. 'They'd nick the fillin's out of your teeth if you let 'em.'

He drove the truck round to the yard and parked it neatly in the corner furthest away from Rex's kennel.

At half past nine he walked round to St Jude's presbytery again and knocked on the door. There was no reply and he was just turning away when a voice called out.

'Hello there! Can I help you?'

He turned to see a small man in dark clerical clothes walking up the steps. He held out his hand to Chris. 'I'm Father Michael Gerard.'

Chris shook the warm dry hand. 'How do you do, Father. I am Christopher Spicer from—'

'From Beckets Green,' Father Gerard finished, nodding and smiling. He took out his door key and began to open the door. 'And very glad I am to see you my son. Come in and we'll talk.'

As Kathy began the walk home she realized how tired she was. Although she'd had a sleep during the day she had slept hardly at all the previous night and she'd hardly eaten anything all day, which made her slightly light-headed.

For the first time she made herself face the future. Now that Charlie and Bill along with all their cohorts were likely to be locked away for a long time was nothing to keep her here in London. She had told May she was a Londoner at heart, but it wasn't really true. The city seemed alien to her now. The bomb-damaged East End was dirty and broken down; its people weary and dull-eyed. Perhaps it always had felt like that, she couldn't really remember.

She could try another town; train for a better job. Maybe she could be a nurse where accommodation would be provided while she was training. Perhaps hotel work would suit her. She was deep in thought as she turned the corner of Charter Street – almost home – if you could call it home.

As she stepped into the circle of light from the street lamp her arm was suddenly grasped and she was jerked into the shadow of a door-way by a man with the brim of his hat pulled forward and a scarf covering the lower half of his face. As she opened her mouth to scream his hand shot out and closed over her mouth, half stifling her.

'*Shut up!*' Her eyes widened as she recognized Jeff's muffled voice.

'Right. We're going to your room. Any noise and you've had it.' He pushed her hard against the wall, his hand still over her mouth as he withdrew something from his pocket. She saw with mounting horror that the object he held under her nose was a closed cut-throat razor. 'Know what this is, Kath? I'm not joking,' he said breathlessly. 'I'm desperate. I'm on the run now and I need you to help me. You owe me that. It's your fault I'm in this mess. Now walk. One squeak – one false move and you get it so don't try anything.'

His arm tight around her waist as he frog-marched her to the house. She hoped desperately that they would meet someone – one of the other tenants, in the hall or on the stairs so that she could somehow get help, but no one was about. On the top landing she fumbled in her bag for her key. He prodded her in the back.

'Get on with it.'

Inside the room he snatched the key from her, locked the door and pocketed the key then he pulled off his scarf and hat and threw them on the bed. She was shocked by his appearance. He looked haggard; his eyes were bloodshot and he clearly hadn't shaved for a couple of days. His jaws were dark with stubble. His clothes were dirty and crumpled too, as though he had slept rough. Gone was the suave, sophisticated Jeff she had once known, so immaculate and well turned out.

'What are you staring at?' he growled. He looked round the room. 'Got anything to eat?'

Trembling, she shook her head. 'Nothing much. There's some bread and marge and half a tin of Spam.'

'That'll do. And make some tea. I haven't eaten anything since yesterday.' When she hesitated he pushed her shoulder. 'Well, don't just stand there, *do it*!'

Her heart in her mouth, she hastily spread the bread and cut thick slices of the meat. When the kettle boiled she made tea. Then she watched as Jeff ate like a starving man. She longed to ask questions, but was afraid of his reaction. He had said he was on the run. Was he hoping to hide out here in her room? And if he were caught here would she be implicated? As he drained the last of his tea she plucked up her courage.

'Where are you going now?'

He laughed. 'You mean where are *we* going.'

Her blood froze. 'I – thought you'd been arrested with the others. The paper said. . . .'

'You *hoped* I had, you mean. Well lucky for me I had a tip-off and got out through the kitchen at the Starlight Room just as the fuzz dropped in for their little visit.' His lip curled. 'I should have known the balloon was about to go up when the boss left in a hurry.'

'He left? So he's on the run like you?'

'On the run? Do me a favour!' Jeff said bitterly. 'Got tipped off by someone inside is my guess. On a private plane to God knows where – his villa in Spain unless I'm very much mistaken. Never said a word to anyone. Just left the rest of us to take the rap.' He looked at her and withdrew the razor from his pocket. Kathy shrank back in horror. He laughed. 'Don't worry, I'm only going to use it to shave. Where's the bathroom?'

'On the floor below,' she said, swallowing hard.

'Right. Go and see if the coast is clear. I need a wash and shave.' Kathy's hopes rose, while he was in the bathroom she could telephone the police. But, as though he read her mind he said. 'You needn't get any clever ideas. You're staying with me. I'm not letting you out of my sight.'

'You won't get away with it,' she said with a bravery she didn't feel. 'When I don't go in to work in the morning someone will come looking for me.'

'Ah, but you won't be here, will you?' he said with a smile. 'You're going on your honeymoon, my darling – with me as your blushing bridegroom.'

She stared at him. 'H-how. . . ?'

'I've got the car parked round the corner,' he told her. 'Soon as I'm ready you and me are taking a trip. Anyone stops us we're just married.' He pulled the flashy signet ring off his little finger and grabbed her left hand. 'Here's the proof.' He slipped the ring on to her third finger. 'Right, now – no more time to waste. Get out there and see if anyone's about.'

In Father Gerard's study Chris took the chair offered him and watched as the priest opened a cupboard and took out a bottle of whisky and two glasses. He poured a generous measure and passed it to Chris.

'Drink that, son. You look as though you can do with it,' he said.

Chris took a sip and felt the fiery liquid warm and calm him. 'Thank you, Father,' he said. 'The reason I'm here is that I'm looking for—'

'For Kathy,' Father Gerard finished for him.

Chris leaned forward. 'You know where she is?' he asked hopefully.

'Not where she lives,' the priest said. 'But I do know where she works in the mornings.' He paused to take a sip of his own whisky. 'You know of course that as a priest anything told to me is in strictest confidence.'

Chris's heart sank. 'Does that mean you're not going to help me?'

Father Gerard smiled. 'I know that you mean a very great deal to Kathy,' he said. 'Do you feel the same about her?'

Chris nodded. 'I love her. We love each other.' He shook his head. 'I don't understand why she couldn't have trusted me. She wrote me a letter about the horrible things that happened to her when she was with her stepbrothers, but as I see it that was when she should have turned to me for help and comfort instead of running away.'

Father Gerard sighed. 'It's complex; Kathy was brought up to be a good Catholic and to live by her mother's standards in spite of their poverty,' he said. 'Mary taught her to value things such as truth, loyalty and faithfulness. What happened to Kathy was not her fault. She was the innocent victim. She trusted the wrong people, but she can't help feeling the shame and the guilt of it. She probably always will. At the moment she feels unworthy.'

Chris shook his head angrily. 'But that's *rubbish*!' He bit his lip. 'Sorry, Father, but it makes me so angry to think of her hiding away in shame for something she couldn't help. And now that her stepbrother has turned King's Evidence she could be in danger. Please, will you at least tell me where she's working?'

Father Gerard took a thoughtful sip of his whisky and considered for a moment. 'I'll tell you because I know she needs you,' he said at last. 'Because I'm convinced that you love her and because I, too, am deeply uneasy about her. If you can persuade her to go back to Beckets Green with you please do so – and as soon as possible.'

Chris leaned forward. 'I will. I promise.'

'The newsagents shop where she works is in Charter Street. I'll give you directions. It's called Kelly's. She starts work there at five every morning.'

'I can't wait until morning,' Chris said impatiently. 'Do you think the owner of the shop would know where she lives?'

Father Gerard shook his head. 'Who knows? I don't even know whether she lives on the premises, but it's worth a try.' He smiled apologetically. 'I'm so sorry I can't disclose any more, Christopher. When you see Kathy will you tell her that her younger stepbrother has been moved to another prison. She'll know what that means.' He laid a hand on Chris's shoulder. 'And be assured that my prayers go with you both.'

Chris found Mrs Kelly's shop without any trouble. It was closed of course and the rooms above were in darkness. After getting no reply from the shop door he found another door next to the shop window. Hoping it led to an occupied flat above he rang the bell. When there was no reply, he began to thump the door hard until eventually a voice from above his head called out.

'Who's that makin' all that racket? What d'you mean by it, banging on my door fit to wake the dead?'

'Is that Mrs Kelly?'

'What if it is?'

'I need to speak to you,' Chris said. 'Can you come down?'

The old woman coughed. 'Not on your nelly! If I opened that street door you'd be in and rob me of everything I've got. I'm ringin' the police.'

'No! Please don't do that,' Chris said. 'What I want is Kathy O'Connor's address. I'm her boyfriend.'

'Oh yeah? If you was you'd know where she lived, wouldn't you? Get orf and let me get back to sleep.' She began to close the window and Chris called out in desperation.

'Please – it's very important. I have to find her. Father Gerard at St Jude's Church sent me to you.'

There was a pause then the old woman leaned out and peered down at him. 'Oh, all right then. It's number thirty eight Denver Street.' She waved a hand. 'Left at the end of this street then first left again. Now clear orf!' She shut the window with a bang.

Kathy averted her eyes as Jeff stripped off his shirt and washed. With the bathroom door locked and the key in his trouser pocket there was nothing she could do. He dried himself on her towel then took out his razor, opened the blade and began to shave, using some shaving soap left on the shelf by one of the other tenants. She watched in fascination as he swept the blade up his throat in long strokes and down each cheek, shaking the soap off after each stroke. When he'd finished he splashed his face with water and patted it dry once more on her towel, which he then flung in her direction.

'Thanks for the loan,' he said. 'I feel more myself now. I had to kip in the car last night.' He began to button his shirt. 'Right, no more time to lose, we'd better get cracking.'

'I'm not coming,' Kathy said.

He took the key out of his pocket. 'Oh yes you are.'

She thrust out her chin. 'You can't make me.'

'Want to bet?' He fingered the razor again, opening it and running his thumb along the blade.

'If I scream someone will come,' she told him. 'There are about four other people living here. You'd have to kill me in front of them. There'd be witnesses. You'd never get away with it – even if you escaped they'd catch you.' She swallowed hard. 'And – and you'd *hang*!'

For an instant she had the satisfaction of seeing fear in his eyes then he laughed. 'But you'd be dead, my lovely, so where would the satisfaction be in that?'

'But I'm no good to you dead, am I?'

He drew in his breath sharply and the look on his face made her shrink back. Opening the door suddenly he grasped her wrist, twisting it viciously. 'Get down those stairs!' he hissed. One hand in the small of her back he pushed her towards the staircase. '*Walk*!'

She stumbled and almost fell, but he was behind her, one hand grasped her upper arm, so tight that she almost cried out with the pain. Out in the street he turned her to face him. His eyes glinted angrily in the lamplight.

'Try anything like that again and you'll feel the back of my hand, Kath,' he said. 'I'm past caring now. You're right, damn you. I need you alive. You're my ticket out of here and you'll do as I bloody well say or else.'

Round the next corner a dark blue Hillman saloon was waiting. He opened the passenger door and pushed her unceremoniously into the seat. As he joined her she said.

'This isn't your car.'

' 'Course it isn't. I'm not stupid. Wouldn't get far in a red sports job, would I? Had to – borrow this.'

She guessed correctly that he meant 'steal'. 'Where are you going?'

'Dover,' he told her, starting the car. 'By morning we'll be in France.'

'You need passports for that,' she said triumphantly. 'I haven't got one.'

He patted his jacket pocket. 'All taken care of. I've got one with the wife included – courtesy of a mate of mine.'

'But the photographs. . . ?'

'Sorted. Remember all those lovely days out we had beside the sea? I've got lots of photos of you, darling. They brought back some lovely memories, and only took a minute to substitute for the original.'

He revved the engine and put the car into gear then they were moving, the tyres screeched as he let off the handbrake and stepped on the accelerator. Kathy's heart sank. There was no hope now. It was all over.

CHAPTER EIGHTEEN

Chris hurried along the street, turned the corner and broke into a run as a sudden sense of urgency took hold of him. As he turned into Denver Street, a large saloon car roared towards him almost mounting the pavement as it screeched round the corner. He jumped back from the edge of the kerb, but in that instant he saw the face of the passenger illuminated fleetingly by the light from the street lamp. In that moment he recognized the terrified face of Kathy and he was sure she recognized him. He called out frantically, '*Kathy!*'

Before it had time to disappear he quickly memorized the registration number. He'd always prided himself on being good at that and remembering digits in pairs always helped. He raced after the car as it squealed round the corners of the narrow streets. He must see which direction it took when it reached the main Hackney road, after that he would telephone the police – give them the car's number and direction, then he would go and get the truck. He'd be miles behind by that time, but he had to try to follow.

There was a telephone box next to the tube station. He slipped inside and dialled 999, hastily giving the make and registration number of the car in which Kathy was being abducted and the fact that it was heading eastward. At first the policeman who answered seemed sceptical until he mentioned the fact that Kathy was the stepsister of the Brady brothers, awaiting trial for murder, after that Chris had his full attention.

'Sounds like he's heading for Dover, sir,' he said. 'Don't worry, all the ports are covered. He won't get far.'

Leaving the telephone box, Chris ran all the way back to The Feathers to get his truck, only to find the steel-barred gates of the pub yard closed and padlocked. Rex, the guard dog paced up and down inside, baring his teeth and growling. Inside the pub he begged the landlady who was just locking up for the night to open the gates for him.

'I have to have my truck,' he told her. 'My girlfriend is being kidnapped.'

She stared at him. 'You *what*?'

He shook his head. 'I haven't time to explain. She's being abducted in a car. I've telephoned the police, but I can't just wait around and do nothing. I've got to follow them.'

Something about the desperation on his face seemed to galvanize her. Taking the keys from their hook behind the bar she followed him out into the street. Unlocking the padlock, she spoke softly to the dog, taking a handful of dog biscuits from her apron pocket and holding them out to him. When he came to her she grabbed his collar.

'OK, get cracking,' she ordered Chris as the dog barked and leapt at him. 'He's got the strength of a horse and I can't hold him for long.'

Chris found his keys, unlocked the truck and clambered in. A moment later he was driving out of the yard, calling his thanks to the still bewildered landlady and heading eastwards.

Jeff drove like a madman and for most of the time Kathy had her eyes shut convinced that they were both going to be killed. She'd been sure it was Chris who had called out her name as they drove out of Denver Street, but now, the more she thought about it, the more she knew it must have been wishful thinking – a trick of the light – her imagination. Chris was back in Beckets Green, she told herself. She was never going to see him or feel his arms around her again.

Jeff had been driving for about half an hour and Kathy's head was nodding with fatigue when suddenly a loud expletive from him jerked her awake and made her look at him.

'What is it?'

'Petrol!' he said, thumping the steering wheel. 'Look at the bloody gauge! It was full yesterday – plenty to get us down to Kent, but now the tank's really low. Some thieving bastard's siphoned it off.'

Kathy could almost have laughed at the irony of it, but at the same time relief overwhelmed her. They would not get to Dover and the ferry so there was still hope. But what was to happen now?'

Jeff made a quick decision. 'Reckon I've just about got enough to get us to Virginia Water,' he said. 'We'll hole up at Maple Lodge. The boss left in too much of a hurry to ask me for the keys back. There are a couple of cars in the garage. I can siphon the petrol from one of them and we'll move on as soon as it gets dark tomorrow night.'

Kathy stared at him, her stomach churning. Maple Lodge! How could she bear to be in that house with Jeff again after what had happened the last time she was there?

He turned the car at the next junction and headed towards Surrey. After about ten minutes he pulled over and reversed onto a wooded track. Stopping the car, he turned to her.

'The radiator's overheating and I need to let it cool down. Take your shoes off.'

'Why? What for?'

'I might have to go and look for some water and I don't want you trying to make a run for it.'

He snatched her shoes and threw them out of the window into the dense undergrowth then he got out and opened the bonnet. Steam billowed out. He unscrewed the radiator cap and let out a scream of pain as boiling water spouted up his sleeve. Swearing he pulled off his jacket and rolled up his shirt sleeve. As he joined her in the car Kathy saw that blisters were already forming on his right hand and forearm. He glared at her.

'Well don't just sit there. *Do* something!'

'Have you got a first aid kit?' she asked.

'*Have you got a first aid kit!*' he mimicked. 'What do you think I am, a bleedin' doctor?'

'You should keep it covered,' she told him. 'It needs hospital treatment.'

'Oh yeah? A right little Florence Nightingale you are!' Wincing, he rolled down his sleeve and buttoned the cuff. 'This is all I bloody need.'

They sat on for awhile, waiting for the radiator to cool then Jeff got out and opened the boot, returning with a length of rope.

'Give us your hands,' he ordered.

She shook her head. 'No! You're not going to tie me up!' She snatched at the door handle, but as she opened the door his hand caught her a ringing blow across the side of her head.

'Sit still and do as I say,' he barked. 'It's only while I go and find some water. Don't be so bloody awkward.'

Her head still ringing, she allowed him to tie her hands together and then her ankles. Tears poured down her cheeks. What would be the end of this? There were telephones at the house. Jeff would not risk her using them so would he keep her tied up when they got there? And if the police came – would he use her as a hostage? She thought about the razor in his pocket and the threats he had made, knowing he was desperate enough to carry them out. The hours in front of her would be a nightmare of uncertainty.

Jeff took a can from the boot and disappeared down the track. About half an hour later he reappeared and emptied the contents of the can into the car's radiator, closing the bonnet and climbing back into the driving seat.

'Had to walk flamin' miles,' he complained. 'Finally found a pond.'

'Are you going to untie me now?' she asked.

'I wish you'd stop your bloody whining.' He sighed. 'I'll do your hands. You can do your own ankles. My hand is giving me hell. I just hope there's some burn ointment in the bathroom at Maple Lodge.' He switched on the ignition and pulled the starter. The engine coughed and died. He tried again and swore loudly as the same thing happened. Kathy's heart began to quicken with hope. If he couldn't start the car they couldn't go to Maple Lodge.

'Flooded the carburettor now I shouldn't wonder,' he groaned. He tried once more and the engine sprang to life. He let out his breath on a sigh of relief.

'Phew! About bloody time!' Putting the car into gear he nosed it out of the rutted track, bumped over the grass verge and onto the road. They were on their way.

Chris was lost; somehow he'd missed a turn a couple of miles back and now he hadn't a clue where he was. It was almost midnight and pitch dark. There was no one about to ask for directions. Nothing for it but to keep going and looking out for signposts. He'd always known there wasn't much hope of catching up with the car he'd seen. His only hope now was that the police would be waiting at Dover and would pick them up before the ferry could leave.

Suddenly he saw a sign ahead and slowed down to peer through the windscreen. To his dismay it read,

Staines
County of Surrey.

He was going in the completely opposite direction! He stopped the truck and laid his head down on his arms over the steering wheel. How could he be so *useless*! Kathy could be anywhere by now. Who was that man driving the car? Was he one of the gang the police were after? Was he the monster who had assaulted her? His blood ran cold at the thought.

He drove on slowly, looking for a place to turn the truck. He might as well head back to Hackney for all the good he was doing. Peering through the windscreen he looked for a lay-by then suddenly, ahead of him, he was surprised to see a dark-coloured car emerge from the trees on his left. He dipped his headlights automatically and braked, then the breath caught in his throat. It was a Hillman saloon just like the one he had seen being driven away with Kathy in it. As it turned onto the road he leaned forward, squinting to read the number plate in the dipped beam of his own headlights. His heart leapt. It *was* the same car. Clearly it hadn't been heading for Dover after all. What a stroke of luck! Perhaps the police had given chase and the driver had changed direction to shake them off. He hung back a little, thankful that he was driving a farm truck and not a saloon car. He was less conspicuous in this.

The road twisted and turned and the car in front of him drove at speed. Several times he lost sight of it but usually caught up with it again, catching sight of the red tail light just as it rounded the next bend in the road. Then suddenly the car was gone. Perplexed, he drove on for a mile or two, pressing his foot hard on the accelerator to get the maximum speed out of the old truck, but the Hillman was nowhere in sight. Eventually he came to the conclusion that the driver must have turned off somewhere.

Turning the truck round he headed back the way he had come, driving slowly this time, peering carefully to right and left. Suddenly he spotted it, lights out, parked a few yards into a driveway that looked as though it belonged to a house, set well back from the road. He drew into the grass verge, killed the lights and switched off the engine. After a moment's consideration, he took a torch from the truck's tool box and pushed it into his pocket.

The ornate wrought iron gates stood open. A sign swinging from a post beside them read Maple Lodge. He approached the car cautiously. It was empty. He looked around. All was quiet, the deep night-time silence of the countryside that Chris knew so well. An owl hooted and the wind sighed softly in the trees, but apart from that there wasn't a sound. Keeping close to the shadow of the shrubbery at the side of the driveway he edged his way slowly up the drive till he came in sight of the house; it was an opulent mock-Tudor style building. Like the car, it was in darkness. If Kathy was in there he had to get her out. He *would* get her out – somehow.

As Jeff drove in through the gates of Maple Lodge, the car's engine spluttered twice and cut out.

'Well, at least it got us here,' Jeff said. 'Pity we couldn't've got further in out of sight but I'll move her as soon as I've put some juice in the tank.' He turned to Kathy. 'Get out.'

She looked at him. 'I've got no shoes. You threw them away.'

'So what d'you want me to do, *carry* you?' He reached across her to open the door and she shuddered with revulsion as his body pressed against hers. 'Get out,' he ordered. 'What's a few scratches? If you had this arm you'd have something to moan about.'

She stepped gingerly out onto the gravelled drive, but the next moment Jeff had grabbed her arm and was frog-marching her towards the house, ignoring her cries of pain as the sharp stones cut into the soles of her feet. In the porch he held her arm in a vice-like grip as he fumbled for the keys and unlocked the door then he pushed her into the dark hallway and slammed the door behind them.

'Better not put any lights on,' he said under his breath, 'Best not to risk arousing suspicion – never know who's about.' He pushed her towards the back of the house and opened a door. Now that Kathy's eyes had adjusted to the darkness she saw that they were in the study.

'You can wait in here while I see to the car.' While he spoke he was testing the window locks. 'Yeah, they seem OK,' he muttered.

'Can I use the lavatory?'

'Hell, no!'

'But I *need* to.'

'Hard luck. I'm takin' no chances with you, sweetheart.' He pointed to a leather armchair. 'Why don't you relax for a bit? Might take me a while.'

'Can I at least have a light on?'

He hesitated then went to the desk and turned on the green shaded desk lamp. 'There,' he said. 'That'll do you.' He pointed to the two large Chinese vases that stood in the hearth. 'If you need a pee use one o' them.'

She stared at him. 'I *couldn't*!'

He shrugged. 'Suit yourself. I'm off.' He slipped quickly through the door and she heard the key grate in the lock. She was a prisoner.

Chris saw that the drive ended in a circular carriage sweep. To the right was a large garage, built separately from the house and big enough for at least four cars, he guessed. The door was the kind that folded back in sections. As he watched a man emerged from the front door of the house. Chris shrank back into the shrubbery and watched as he went to the garage, unlocked the door and pushed it back. It opened easily and silently and Chris registered that it was obviously well oiled and maintained. Inside the garage were two large expensive looking pre-war cars. Chris was puzzled. If the man was going to substitute one of these for the Hillman why had he left it blocking the drive? Then he guessed. It had run out of petrol and he was about to do what those two young thugs were trying to do to the truck earlier – siphon off some petrol! There wasn't a moment to lose. He sprinted quietly across the space between shrubbery and house and saw to his relief that the man had left the front door ajar. No doubt to save time later. It meant that Kathy was locked in somewhere inside. In the dark hallway he risked switching on his torch briefly, just to get his bearings. He tried one or two doors and found them unlocked, the rooms inside in darkness. Then, turning a corner he saw the thin line of dim light under a door. His heart leapt. He turned the handle. The door was locked, but briefly shining his torch he saw to his enormous relief that the key had been left in the lock. He turned it – opened the door and. . . .

'*Kathy*!'

Exhausted and dishevelled, she had never looked more lovely to him. She spun round and her eyes widened in disbelief.

'Chris! So it *was* you!'

He crossed the room and hugged her briefly. 'Are you all right?'

'Yes. What's happened? Where's Jeff? How did you know where to find me?'

'He's in the garage. I think he's siphoning petrol. There's no time for explanations. We need to get out of here – and quick!'

Hand in hand and their hearts in their mouths they ran through the house, expecting at any second to encounter an irate Jeff blocking their way. But as they reached the front porch there was still no sign of him. Looking from right to left Chris said, 'Right, run across to the shrubbery as quietly as you can.

Kathy did her best in spite of her painful feet and together they reached the shelter of the shrubbery safely. Chris paused and listened, then turned to Kathy.

'Go on up to the road,' he told her. 'The truck is parked on the grass verge, key's in the ignition. Get in and start the engine. You know how?'

'Yes.' She nodded. 'But what are you going to do?'

'Just do as I say. I'll be with you in a few minutes.'

'Let's just go.' She held onto his hand. 'Don't take any risks, Chris – please.'

'Just do as I say,' he told her. 'I promise you it'll be all right.'

He watched for a second as Kathy made her way through the shrubbery then he turned back. Inside the garage he could see that Jeff was busy with a length of hosepipe and a can, kneeling at the back of the larger of the two cars with his back towards him. To help him see he had a lighted hurricane lamp standing on the floor beside him. His heart hammering in his chest, Chris took a deep breath and, grasping the garage door handle firmly he pulled. It rolled easily across the gap and he winced as it made a louder noise than he expected. There was a yell of alarm from Jeff, but by the time he was on his feet the door was shut. Chris locked it and pulled out the bunch of keys still hanging from the lock, hurling it with all his might into the shrubbery. Then he took off as fast as his feet would carry him up the drive to the road where Kathy had the truck's engine ticking over nicely.

She edged over into the passenger seat and looked at him, weak with relief as he let in the clutch and pressed his foot down hard on the accelerator. After a moment she asked him, 'What did you do?'

'Locked him in the garage,' he told her. 'The keys were still in the door. He obviously wasn't expecting company. There's probably a window he can climb out of, but at least it will give us a headstart. He's got to put petrol in the tank of the Hillman, too. It all takes time.'

'How did you find me?' she asked.

He smiled. 'I did a bit of detective work – went to see your friend, Father Gerard. No, he didn't tell me anything you'd said to him, but he did tell me where you worked in the mornings. The old lady there told me where you lived. I was on my way there when I saw you in the car.'

She sighed. 'If you'd been just a few minutes sooner – or later.' She shuddered. 'I dread to think.'

'By the way, Father Gerard told me to tell you that your stepbrother Bill has been moved to another prison,' he told her. 'He said you'd know what that meant.'

She nodded. 'There were threats against him.'

'Well, as soon as we've put a safe distance between us and your abductor I'll find a phone box and ring the police.'

Kathy laid a hand on his arm. 'No – don't.'

He frowned at her. 'You want him caught and punished, don't you?'

'It's not as simple as that.'

He glanced at her. 'But he abducted you. What was that about?'

'He had a stolen dual passport,' she told him. 'He wanted to pass me off as his wife. He was planning to get on the ferry for France.'

'A bit naïve of him. He wouldn't have got far. The police told me that all the ports are being watched.'

She shot him a worried look. 'You – you've already spoken to the police?'

'Obviously – when I saw him driving off with you earlier.' He shook his head. 'What did you expect me to do?'

'No, no. You were right. I can't tell you how grateful I am to you for rescuing me, Chris.' She bit her lip. 'But now my name will be in the papers. I'll have to go to court and give evidence against Jeff.' She looked at him, her eyes huge with dread. 'It's what I've always dreaded. The thought of reliving it all – of everyone knowing.'

He pulled into the side of the road and drew her into his arms. 'My poor Kathy. I understand, darling, of course I do. The police will pick him up anyway and everyone knows that you've done nothing wrong. There is no way he can escape what's coming to him and you know that we're all behind you. The most important thing now is to get you home.'

She looked up at him. 'Home?'

'Home to Beckets Green, to Magpie Farm. Home to the family.' He searched her eyes. 'It's what you want, isn't it? It's what I want – to have you back with me, where you belong.'

'I have to be at work at five o'clock,' she said dully.

Chris stared at her for a moment then he laughed uncertainly. 'Darling – you're still in shock. It's already two, you'll be in no state to work in three hours' time. We'll go back to Hackney and get your things. You can explain to your employer and. . . .'

'No, Chris.' She looked at him, her eyes wide and clear. 'We can never be together now. We come from different worlds, there's no getting away from that. I can never forget the things that have happened and there's worse to come. It's better this way. You deserve better than me.'

He shook his head. 'You're tired and traumatized. You're not thinking straight. You can't go back to that place – you can't live like that.'

'I'll find something better,' she told him. 'I'll make some kind of life. You're not to worry about me.'

'Not to worry about you!' He pushed his hand through his hair in desperation. 'Damn it, I love you, Kathy, that's why I'm here. I'll always love you and want to be with you. There'll never be anyone else for me. Don't you know that after all we've been through tonight? Doesn't it tell you anything about me? Can you honestly look me in the eye and tell me you don't feel the same?'

Her eyes filled with tears. 'No, I couldn't lie to you, Chris. I love you more than anything in the world – which is why I'm letting you go. Please take me back to London now. If you love me please try to understand.'

Chris drove the rest of the way back to Hackney in silence. He could not understand. He did not believe that she could possibly mean what she said. Father Gerard had said that she would probably never quite recover from her ordeal, but all he wanted was to help and protect her. And he was sure he could. Surely if they loved each other they could conquer anything together.

He followed her up the stairs to her mean little top floor bed-sit and looked around him with distaste.

'Do you really want to stay here, Kathy?' he asked. 'Do you really prefer this to the place where you grew up? Is the thought of being with me so terrible that you'd rather stick it out here on your own?'

She rounded on him and he saw that her face was stained with dirt and tears. 'Why do you have to make it so *hard*?' she sobbed. 'I'm setting you free; free to live *your* kind of life – to find the kind of girl you deserve – that you're meant to have. A girl who's had the same kind of background as you.'

He grasped her shoulders. '*Free!*' he shouted. 'How can I ever be free? Don't you know that you stop being free the moment you fall in love with someone? I'll never be free any more, Kathy. And neither will you.'

He felt her stiffen under his hands and he relaxed his hold on her. 'All right. I'm sorry.' He took a step back. 'I still think you're wrong. I always will. And I want you to know that I'm not going anywhere. I'll be there, waiting if you change your mind.' He took one last step towards her and his voice broke as he said, '*Please* change your mind, Kathy.' He took her face between his hands and kissed her, his tears wetting her face then he turned abruptly and left.

Kathy stood motionless, listening as his footsteps clattered down the uncarpeted stairs. In the distance she heard the front door slam then the floodgates of her pent-up emotion broke and she threw herself on the bed, weeping until she thought her heart must break. Chris had come to rescue her. He had risked his own safety for her and now she had sent him away. *But he'll be all right,'* she told herself. *I'm doing the right thing. I'm not good enough. It's for his own good and he'll see that one day.* But the pain of sacrifice in her heart just grew and grew until she thought it would choke her. The thought of going on alone frightened her. Suddenly she felt weak and lonely and vulnerable.

Somehow she managed her morning shift at the newsagent's. Old Mrs Kelly was concerned about her, asking frequently if she was all right and insisting on making her a sandwich and a cup of tea before she went home.

'If you take my advice, gel, you'll get a few hours sleep before you go to work this evening,' she said. 'You look fair done in to me.'

On her way back to the bed-sit, Kathy realized that she would have to move sooner than she had intended. Now that Chris knew where she lived he might easily come looking for her again and now that she had made her decision she had to stick to it. They both had to forget and move on. She couldn't take any more of Chris's pleading looks. She wasn't strong enough.

CHAPTER NINETEEN

It was towards the end of Kathy's shift at May's café that two police-men, one of them in plain clothes came in, asking for her. May showed them through to the storeroom at the back of the kitchen and fetched Kathy, giving her a meaningful look.

'Miss Kathleen O'Connor?' The plain clothes policeman inquired. Kathy nodded, wondering wearily what could possibly have happened now. The plain clothes man made brief introductions.

'I am DS Brian French and this is PC Forbes. I'll have to ask you to accompany us to the police station, Miss O'Connor. There are some questions we need you to answer.'

The room began to spin and the man asked. 'Are you all right, Miss?'

Kathy nodded, taking a deep breath.

'I'm sorry to have to ask you. I understand you suffered a nasty ordeal last night.' When she did not reply he went on. 'Is it convenient for you to come with us now?'

'I think so.'

'You are not in any trouble and I promise you it won't take long.'

May gave Kathy an encouraging pat on the shoulder as she passed through the café, whispering softly, 'Good luck love.'

The ride in the back of the police car took only a few minutes. When they arrived at the station she was taken into an interview room furnished with a table and four chairs. Kathy felt as though she was walking through a living nightmare.

DS French joined her accompanied by a young police woman equipped with a shorthand pad and pencil. They sat down opposite her.

'You are Miss Kathleen O'Connor?'

'Yes.' Kathy wondered how many times she was going to have to confirm her name. He went on, 'Am I right in thinking that you are the stepsister of the Brady brothers?' She nodded. As if she could ever forget it.

'We were informed last night by an anonymous caller that you had been abducted in a dark-coloured Hillman saloon car travelling eastwards. Was that information correct?'

'Yes.' Kathy sighed.

'I take it you knew your abductor.'

'Yes. A man called Jeff Slater. He was an – acquaintance of my stepbrothers.'

The policeman smiled wryly at the description. 'And also on the run as I'm sure you also know.' He glanced up at her. 'Why do you think he chose to abduct you in particular?'

Kathy's heart skipped a beat. 'I think it was as some sort of reprisal for Charlie Brady's turning King's Evidence.'

'I see. May I ask where he took you?'

Kathy's heart was sinking fast. The police were obviously testing her. There was no way she could avoid being involved now. 'He had a stolen passport for a married couple,' she said after a pause. 'His plan was to drive to Dover and board the ferry to France, passing me off as his wife.'

'And he forced you to go with him?'

'He had an open razor,' she said dully. 'He threatened me with it.'

'I see. So what made him change his mind about going to Dover?'

'The car ran out of petrol so he decided to go to Surrey instead – to the house of his – of someone he knew.'

'We know who the owner of the house is,' the policeman replied. 'We would very much like to interview him but he seems to have taken an extended foreign holiday. So what made Slater think he could get petrol there?'

'He had keys to the house and he knew there were other cars in the garage. He meant to siphon petrol from one of them.'

'I see. So – while he was organizing this, what happened to you?'

'He locked me in a room at the back of the house.' In spite of her exhaustion, Kathy was suddenly on her guard. She could not have Chris involved. 'He left the key in the lock on the outside,' she said firmly. 'I-I managed to escape.'

The policeman nodded. 'The old trick eh? Sheet of paper under the door – push the key out and – bingo!'

'Something like that.'

'Careless of him. What then?'

'He was in the garage,' she said. 'I managed to close the door on him and lock it then I ran away as fast as I could. It wasn't easy. He'd thrown away my shoes.' She slipped off one shoe and displayed the bruised and lacerated sole of her foot.'

DS French raised an eyebrow. 'All the way back to Hackney from Surrey on feet like that?'

'I was lucky. I got a lift.'

'You didn't happen to get the name of the person who gave you the lift – or the registration number of the car?' Kathy shook her head. 'That was risky, Miss O'Connor.'

She sighed. 'After what I'd just escaped from?'

He nodded. 'May I ask why you didn't come straight to us?'

'I just wanted to get home.' She looked at him. 'Besides, I didn't want to have to give evidence in court. My stepbrothers have already involved me in what they did. You must have seen the statement I gave. I didn't want to be mixed up in any more of it. I just want it all to be over.'

'You do know that not reporting an offence like this could have seen you charged with obstructing the course of justice?'

'No!' She swallowed hard at the lump in her throat. Was there no end to this? 'I didn't know. I thought you'd have enough to charge Jeff Slater with anyway.' Tears began to trickle down her cheeks. 'Have you caught him? What has he said? Is he denying all knowledge of me? Is it because of him that I'm here?'

'Miss O'Connor!' The policeman stopped her. 'I have to tell you now that Slater is dead.'

Startled, Kathy looked up at him, the breath catching in her throat. '*Dead*? But how?'

'As you've already told us, he was siphoning petrol from one of the cars in the garage. He was in a hurry and he must have been careless,' he explained. 'The petrol caught fire. The firemen found the remains of a hurricane lamp among the debris; he probably knocked it over.'

Kathy shook her head bemusedly. 'But how was he found?' she asked.

'A passer-by saw smoke and called the police and fire brigade, but there was a car blocking the entrance to the drive which delayed the appliance from getting in. While they were trying to move it one of the cars in the garage exploded. Slater was alive when they got him out, but he died on the way to hospital, mainly from smoke inhalation and shock.' Kathy was silent, waiting for what she'd just heard to sink in. The policeman went on, 'It was later discovered that the registration number on the car blocking the drive was the same as the one that had been telephoned to us earlier. Naturally we were afraid that you might have been injured too. We've been trying to track you down all day. It's a relief to find you safe.'

Still stunned, Kathy looked up. 'So – what happens now?'

'You're free to go, Miss O'Connor,' DS French said with a gentle smile. 'We'll see that you get home safely. And if I were you I'd take tomorrow off and get a doctor to check you over, especially those feet.'

She stood up on shaky legs. 'Thank you. I'll be fine.'

DS French walked out to the front office with her. 'Have you any idea who it was who telephoned us to say that you were being abducted?' he asked.

She shook her head. 'A neighbour perhaps – someone who recognized me.'

'And you saw no one?' Again she shook her head. 'You're very young,' he said kindly. 'About the same age as my own daughter. Don't you have any more family?'

She shook her head. 'There was only my mother. She was killed in the blitz. My only real friends are the people I was evacuated with in Northamptonshire.'

He patted her shoulder. 'Then if I were you I'd go and stay with them for a while. At a time like this you need your friends. Goodnight, Miss O'Connor. And thanks for your co-operation.'

Once back inside her room, Kathy lay down on the bed and tried to take in what the policeman had told her. There was so much more they could have asked her about Jeff. So much more she could have told them about him, but there was no point any more. Jeff was dead. It was still hard for her to take in. Now what she had been through need never be made public. Tears of exhaustion and relief trickled down her cheeks to soak into her pillow. She felt free for the first time in ages. But free for what? Where did her life go now? She had thrown away everything that was worth living for.

walked up to the top field. The scent of new mown hay was heavy on the air and somewhere above a skylark was singing his heart out, a tiny speck high in the clear blue sky. Coming over the ridge she saw patient old Bunter standing still in the shafts as Chris pitch forked the last of the hay onto the cart. He looked tanned, his thick fair hair bleached golden by the sun and Kathy felt a lump rise in her throat and tears pricking her eyelids. How could she ever have sent him away – this man she loved with all her heart and soul?

She called his name and waved. He looked up, shading his eyes against the sun's low glare. Then he saw her and gave a great whoop. Dropping his pitch fork he sprinted across the field and gathered her into his arms.

'Kathy, Kathy, Kathy! Is it really you?' he mumbled into her hair. 'Have you come home to me?'

She took his face between her hands and kissed him. 'Yes, I've come home,' she said. 'I couldn't do it, Chris. I couldn't live the rest of my life without you so I'm afraid you're stuck with me now.'

He looked into her eyes for a long moment. 'Oh, you silly, *silly* girl,' he said. 'Don't you know that being stuck with you is the only thing I've ever wanted? I've missed you so much that I thought I was going out of my mind.'

'I've missed you too,' she said. 'I love you so much, Chris. Please don't ever let me go away again.'

He laughed. 'I won't. Don't worry!'

'Chris – I've got so much to tell you.'

'And you've got all the time in the world to do it.' He kissed her. 'But not now. All that can wait. Tonight I just want to hold you and love you and look at you – just to convince myself I'm not dreaming.'

A long time later they walked back to the farm hand in hand, Bunter trundling the hay cart and the western sky filled with rose-coloured promise behind them.

SCOTTISH BORDERS COUNCIL

LIBRARY &

INFORMATION SERVICES

*

Kathy stepped down from the bus outside the Turf Cutter's Arms and crossed the road to walk down the lane to Magpie Farm. She'd worked her week's notice at both the newsagent's and the café but she hadn't telephoned Lena to say she was coming. She refused to allow herself to examine her motives for this. Maybe she wanted to see the unguarded expressions on their faces when she appeared unannounced. Maybe she still couldn't quite believe that anyone really wanted her.

The bag she carried contained only the few basic belongings she had taken with her. She supposed the rest were still at the cottage unless Lena had given up on her by now and given them away to the church jumble sale.

It was a warm evening and she stopped to rest for a moment outside the gate of Shepherd's Cottage. Looking over the neatly trimmed hedge she saw that the front garden was ablaze with summer colour and the rose that climbed over the porch was a profusion of fat pink blooms. Clearly someone had been caring for the garden in her absence. Perhaps someone else lived there now. Or perhaps Lena had rented it out as a holiday cottage as she had once intended. Kathy picked up her case and walked on.

At the back door of the farm house she paused in an agony of indecision. She really should have telephoned to say she was coming. This was so inconsiderate. A loud bark made her turn and Winston came galloping across the yard towards her, his tail wagging and his tongue lolling in a grin of welcome. She bent to pat him.

'So you remember me, Winnie,' she said. 'Well, at least you're pleased to see me.' Taking a deep breath she opened the door and went in. Standing in the shadow of the little entrance lobby she saw that Lena was putting the finishing touches to supper. Her back was to Kathy as she stood at the Aga. James was washing his hands at the sink. She was about to break the silence and announce her presence when the door to the hall opened and Elaine stood in the doorway, her mouth agape with surprise. She let out a loud yell of delight.

'Kathy!' She closed the space between them at a run and threw her arms around Kathy, hugging her so tightly that she took her breath away. 'Mum! Dad! Look who's here!' she called.

But Elaine's joyful cry had already alerted them. Beaming smiles on both their faces they waited to greet their surprise guest, James with a towel slung across his shoulder, Lena wiping her hands on her apron. Elaine refused to allow them to get a word in as a torrent of remarks and questions tumbled over each other.

'Have you come home for good?'

'You better had or we'll just have to take you prisoner!'

'Your job at the post office is still open you know.'

'And Chris has been keeping the garden at the cottage in good order for you.'

Laughing, Lena gently drew her daughter away. 'Let poor Kathy get her breath,' she said. 'Come and sit down. I'm sure you're dying for a cup of tea.'

But James had seen Kathy's eyes sweeping the room and he knew who she was looking for. 'It's good to see you, love,' he said giving her a brief hug. 'And the person you're looking for is on the top field,' he added in a whisper. 'We've been haymaking all day and he's finishing off.'

Lena cut in. 'Yes – why don't you go and fetch him down for supper?'

'I'll come with you,' Elaine offered.

'No, Elaine.' Lena shook her head at her. 'I think Kathy would prefer to go alone. Besides, I need you to lay the table for me.'

Elaine shrugged. 'Oh – I get it. Off you go then.' She turned with her characteristic impish grin. 'But don't keep him out there too long snogging his face off. I'm famished.'

Lena walked out to the yard with her. 'Are you really home for good, Kathy?' she asked. 'Chris was devastated when you wouldn't come home with him last week. He's even been talking about emigrating to Australia.'

Kathy shook her head. 'I've had time to think,' she said. 'I thought I was doing the right thing in setting him free.' She smiled wryly. 'I know now that I'm not noble enough to make that kind of sacrifice.'

'He told me what you said.' Lena looked at her. 'Kathy, you're not responsible for the unfortunate turn your life took. You're still the same girl you've always been. The girl Chris loves.' She patted Kathy's cheek. 'Go and find him now,' she smiled. 'And never mind Elaine. Take as long as you like.'

The sun was a huge golden ball low in the summer sky as Kathy

D0298724

Pride of Peacocks

By the same author

King's Walk

Pride of
Peacocks

Jeanne Whitmee

ROBERT HALE · LONDON

© Jeanne Whitmee 2003
First published in Great Britain 2003

ISBN 0 7090 7448 4

Robert Hale Limited
Clerkenwell House
Clerkenwell Green
London EC1R 0HT

The right of Jeanne Whitmee to be identified as
author of this work has been asserted by her
in accordance with the Copyright, Designs and
Patents Act 1988.

4 6 8 10 9 7 5 3

For Leslie

WESTMEATH COUNTY LIBRARY

852.100|AF

Typeset in 11/14½ Plantin
Derek Doyle & Associates, Liverpool.
Printed in Great Britain by
St Edmundsbury Press, Bury St Edmunds, Suffolk.
Bound by Woolnough Bookbinding Limited.

CHAPTER ONE

'CAN'T YOU do anything right, girl?' Bess Markham snatched the cloth from Rose's hand and began rubbing the brass beer taps furiously.

'No wonder your ma got fed up with you,' she snapped, her face red with temper and exertion. 'She knew a good-for-nothing when she saw one. Worst day of my life when she lumbered me with you. You're worse than useless. *You listenin' to me?*' She leaned forward to glare into Rose's tear-filled eyes. 'You want to think yourself bloody lucky you got that job at the Co-op, my gel. Just you watch you don't lose it, 'cause if you do you can find some other mug to take you in – right?'

Rose nodded.

'All right then, get your face cleaned up and get yourself off to work. You can come back here and finish cleaning the snug in your dinner hour.'

Rose climbed the stairs to the tiny room she had occupied since she had first come to The Duke's Head as a six year old. Pouring some water into the chipped bowl on the washstand she scooped it up and splashed her face. In the grey-spotted mirror on the wall her reflection looked back at her. How she despised the pale oval face with its red nose and puffy eyes. Would things ever be any different? she asked herself despairingly. Would *she* ever be any different, or would she be bullied and ground underfoot for the rest of her life? Taking up a comb

5

she dragged it through her lank fair hair, then, with a last look at her dejected reflection, she grabbed her coat and ran down the stairs, scuttling out through the pub's back door into the alley with a hasty backward glance. But, to her relief Aunt Bess was busy with the drayman down in the cellar.

Rose had been at The Duke's Head with her Aunt Bess for twelve years, ever since that Saturday afternoon when her mother had dressed her up in her best clothes and marched her round to Wetherby Street to throw herself on her sister's mercy.

'I'm at my wits' end, Bess. I've lost my job and now I've got to get out of the room as well. If you could just take her for a few weeks – just till I get another job and a nice place. She's always liked you,' she wheedled, shooting a warning glance in Rose's direction. 'And as soon as I'm on my feet again I'll come for her.'

Bess strongly suspected that there was a man – or men at the root of it and made no bones about voicing the fact. But Sally turned innocent blue eyes on her with a look of reproach. '*Bess*! Do you really think I'd give up my kid for some bloke? It's breaking my heart, parting with her. I'm gonna miss her something chronic. I'll give you whatever I can towards her keep and I'll come and take her out every Saturday – *promise*. You know I wouldn't never let you down.'

Rose had cried herself to sleep that night. Although her mum and Aunt Bess were sisters they were not at all alike. Mum was pretty and slim, where Aunt Bess was fat and bad-tempered. Life with Mum was never dull. When she had money there were sweets and something nice for tea. Even when they were hard up Mum would make it fun. They would hide from the rent man, stifling their giggles as they hid in the cupboard till he went away. True there'd be only be bread and marge for supper, but there was always a cuddle and a goodnight kiss. But that was before Mum started bringing the men home. After that everything changed.

Rose would be woken up in the middle of the night and

moved out of the bed on to the sofa. The room would be full of whispers and the smell of beer and an alien male smell that made Rose uneasy and afraid. But even that was better than the bleak little attic room at The Duke's Head with its bare floor and torn wallpaper; the unkind remarks and the stinging cuffs round the ear. Not to mention the endless chores Aunt Bess made her do early in the mornings and after school.

In the beginning Mum had come every Saturday as she had promised. Rose would always be ready and waiting. Wearing her best coat, her hair combed and tied back neatly with a ribbon she would stand on a chair to watch from the window. When Sally appeared round the corner she would jump down excitedly and run to let her in. Mum would take her to the pictures or Up West to look at the shops. They'd have tea in a café, with buns and sometimes an ice cream. But after the first few weeks the visits dwindled to once a fortnight, then once a month. After that, Sally would often fail to show up without any explanation. Rose would stand at the window hour after hour, her legs aching and her heart growing heavier; knowing deep inside that her mother wouldn't come but refusing to give up hope. Her ears would strain to hear the high heels come tapping down the street. She would close her eyes and picture her mother coming round the corner, a jaunty little hat perched on her bright gold hair and her scarlet mouth smiling. When she opened them to find the street still empty she would trail dejectedly up to her room to cry herself to sleep.

Finally even Rose had to admit that she'd stopped coming altogether. By now she was nine. When nothing had been seen nor heard from Sally for six months, Bess sat Rose down and forced her to face the unpalatable truth.

'You got to accept it,' she said sternly. 'Your ma ain't coming back for you no more and that's the top and bottom of it.' Her lip curled cynically. 'I'm obviously not gonna get no more money for your keep neither. I've written to the last address she

7

gave me but the letter came back with 'gone away' written across it.'

'She hasn't gone away for good though! She *will* come back for me,' Rose protested. 'She promised!'

Bess laughed. 'Promises are like pie crust – made to be broken,' she said. 'And there never was a truer word as far as your ma's concerned. Face it, Rose. She's no good – never was. Now she's lumbered me with you. Can't keep away from the fellers, that's her trouble.' She gave a derisive snort. 'You saw that silver fox fur she was wearing last time she come? Didn't get *that* with no fag coupons, I'll tell you! No, man-mad, our Sally. How do you think you got born? And you can bet your sweet life that's what's happened this time. She's met a bloke with a bit of cash and she don't want him to know she's got a kid. So you better make your mind up that you live here now. But I'll tell you this – from now on you'll earn your keep, my gel. It's that or the orphanage.'

Rose left school two months after her fourteenth birthday. She was glad to leave. She'd dreamed of the day when she could get a job so that she could earn her keep and have a bit of independence. Her dream was that if she saved hard enough she'd even be able to afford a room of her own so that she could leave The Duke's Head and Aunt Bess for good. But things didn't quite work out like that. As she had grown older her aunt had become more and more demanding. Up at 5.30 every morning, Rose was obliged to put in three hours of cleaning before she went to her job behind the provisions counter at the Co-op. Aunt Bess never missed an opportunity to remind her of the debt she owed; that she'd been housed, clothed and fed for the past eight years. When she came home on a Friday evening her aunt would be there, hand outstretched for her unopened wage packet. The only time Rose had asked tentatively for some pocket money Bess had tipped the money on to the table and asked, 'How much do you think I've spent these past eight years

keeping you in food and clothing? A pretty penny, I'll tell you!' She jabbed the eighteen and sixpence from Rose's pay packet with a derisive finger. 'And how long do you think it'll take you to repay me at this rate, eh?'

'I do work here as well,' Rose pointed out boldly.

Bess's face darkened. '*Work*! Is that what you call it? Flappin' round with a duster like Lady Muck? Most of what you do has to be done again. You're about as much good at real work as your ma was. Only work *she* was ever willin' to do was on her back.' She wagged a finger in Rose's face. 'An' if you ever start that caper, my gel, you'll be out of 'ere so fast your feet won't touch the ground. So let's hear no more about no pocket money! You get clothed and fed. What more do you want?'

By now Rose was aware of why her mother had brought men home. She was also aware and deeply ashamed of the fact that she was illegitimate. Everyone at school had known and she'd been called names and bullied because of it ever since the day she first started. Only once had she ever asked Aunt Bess about her father and had received a slap across her face for her pains.

'Don't you never mention the word "father" to me,' Bess had shouted. 'Kids like you don't have no fathers. Not ones who wants to know them, leastways. Get used to the fact that you ain't got no father, nor ever will 'ave. You asked for the truth. Well now you've got it!'

Rose had known better than to bring up the subject up again.

By the time Rose was seventeen she had been promoted to the cash desk at the Co-op. She loved sitting in the little office, taking the money and making out the divi slips, screwing it all into the wooden containers and sending them down the chute to the counting house. Mr Perkins, the manager, had raised her money to thirty shillings a week and, on her birthday, Aunt Bess had announced that she could have two and sixpence a week pocket money. But she was to save it up and use it to buy her own clothes.

On Saturday evenings, some of the other girls from the shop went dancing or to the pictures. Several times they had asked Rose to join them but she was never allowed to go. Aunt Bess needed her to help out in the bar in the evenings. In the end the girls stopped inviting her. It seemed to Rose that she was fated never to have a life of her own at all.

All that year there had been talk of war. Rose heard the men talking about it in the public bar at The Duke's Head. The customers at the shop were full of it too. From what Rose could gather, this man called Hitler in Germany, seemed determined to cause trouble. At first she couldn't see how it would affect her. After all Germany was a long way away. But Aunt Bess seemed troubled.

'My Ernie got wounded in the last lot,' she said, as she pulled a pint for one of her regulars. 'Don't seem five minutes ago neither. What do they want to go startin' another lot for? You'd think they'd've learned their lesson.'

'Well, old Chamberlain is doing his best,' the man said. 'But I doubt it's gonna be good enough.' He took a pull at his brimming tankard and smacked his lips appreciatively. 'It'll be a damned sight bigger do than last time if it does come to it,' he said, with a shake of his head. 'They got a fearsome stock of weapons, them Nazis. Planes and tanks and such. You see them on the newsreels at the pictures. Hoards of 'em.' He sucked in his breath ominously. 'No, Adolf Hitler means business all right. World domination, that's what he wants. I reckon poor old London will be bombed to smithereens,' he added gloomily.

'Smithereens? *London*? Never on your life.' Bess retorted. 'They wouldn't dare.'

'You bet yer life they would,' the man assured her. 'Like I say, it'll be a different kind of war to the last. We'll all be in it this time. Tell you something else an' all: they'll start off here in the East End; put the docks and the railways out of action.' He swallowed the last of his pint and slapped his tankard down on

10

the bar. 'Old Hitler and 'is lot are all set to walk in and take us over.'

'Huh! Like to see 'im try takin' me over,' Bess said, but in spite of her sharp tone a shudder went down her spine and her cheeks paled.

Listening to it all, Rose began to see just how all their lives would be affected if war came. The customers at the Co-op talked of food shortages and of all the children being sent away to safe places in the country. Secretly she wished she were young enough to go. Once, when she was ten, she'd been on a Sunday School outing to Kent. The blue skies and green trees had entranced her. To see cows and sheep grazing in the fields had been a revelation. And the hedgerows and flowers were like something out of a picture book – only better.

At the Co-op the talk of food shortages gathered momentum. 'Farmers will need to grow as much food as they can,' Mr Perkins said. ' 'Cause there'll be nothing coming in from abroad.' He raised his eyes to the ceiling. 'God knows how we're all going to manage. Let's just pray it don't come to it, that's all.'

Rose heard some of the girls at the shop talking excitedly of going into the women's services. She didn't fancy that. Shy and quiet, she'd always felt she was 'different' and the thought of all that close proximity and lack of privacy frightened her. She supposed she'd just stay here, working at the shop and The Duke's Head and living with Aunt Bess.

September came and the Sunday morning when they all clustered round the wireless in the public bar to hear Mr Chamberlain's announcement. Some of the men had brought their wives along and you could have heard a pin drop as they all listened, heads bowed and faces grave at the news that England was indeed at war with Germany. It was the culmination of everyone's worst nightmare. Afterwards, silent and subdued, they all wandered home to their Sunday dinners, wondering how much longer they would have the luxury of meat and two veg on their plates.

But, in spite of all the apprehension and the frantic preparation, very little happened during those early months. There were tears and sad faces as the children went off to the railway station in neat crocodiles each day, their gas masks in cardboard boxes strung around their necks and labels tied to their coats. There were inconveniences like the blacking out of windows and the ugly brick air-raid shelters that sprang up at the end of every street. But apart from that, life went on much as before. Like everyone else, Rose grew accustomed to seeing windows criss-crossed with sticky tape and front doors masked by ugly brick blast walls. There were jokes about bossy air-raid wardens, who, intoxicated with the heady power invested in them, delighted in the shout of *'Put that light out'* whenever so much as a chink of light appeared after dark. Certain foods became short and Mr Perkins at the Co-op worried about his customers.

'We'll certainly have rationing before long,' he predicted. 'And maybe it'll be for the best. Put a stop to some of this black market carry-on.'

1940 came in uneventfully. Some of the children who had been evacuated even came home again. The summer came and in August, the cheering news of the RAF's bombing of Germany. Then, just as people were telling each other that it would all be over by next Christmas the terror began.

The blitz, when it came, was sudden and terrible; much worse than anyone had imagined. And the East End caught the worst of it. Night after night Rose and her aunt slept in the shelter at the end of the street. And when it became clear that the flimsy structure did not offer enough protection, they resorted to the Underground. Packed in like sardines with their thermos flasks, sandwiches and blankets, hundreds huddled together for warmth and reassurance as the fury raged overhead.

It was early the following spring when Aunt Bess dropped her own bombshell. 'I've had enough,' she said, as she closed

the door one evening at closing time and shot the bolts. 'Twenty-five years I've stood behind that bar. I reckon I've done my bit. Now it's time to think about myself.' She looked at Rose as she began to pull off her apron. 'I've made my arrangements. I'll be going to live with Grace Jarvis, my friend down in Devon. She runs a little post office and general store. The girl who worked for her has gone off into the ATS. She can do with my help so I'm off as soon as I'm packed and ready.'

'Oh!' Rose stared at her, a cold feeling in the pit of her stomach. 'So – where am I going, Aunt Bess?'

Bess shrugged. 'How do I know? You're nineteen now. You're a woman. It's up to you to make your own arrangements. I can't ask Grace to take you in too, can I? She ain't got room.'

'No – but. . . .'

'The brewers are closing this place for the time bein', but you can stay on here for a couple of weeks, till you find yourself a room or something,' Bess told her. 'I daresay they'll be putting another landlord in.' She cast a glance round the public bar with its cracked ceiling and boarded-up windows. 'If it's still standing,' she added wryly. 'So o'course, you're gonna be out one way or another anyway.' She eyed Rose dispassionately. 'Come on, gel, don't look like that. You're not a kid any more. You'll be all right.'

'Yes. Yes, I know,' Rose said, swallowing the lump in her throat. 'I'm sure I'll find something. It's just – I was wondering about Mum. I've been thinking a lot about her since the war started.'

'Your mum!' Aunt Bess gave a derisive snort. 'You don't imagine she'd want you back again, after all these years, do you?'

'No, I just wondered where she is – if she's all right,' Rose said.

'You can rest assured that wherever she is our Sal will be all right.' Bess said scathingly. 'Lookin' after number one as usual I shouldn't wonder. One thing's for sure, she won't be bother-

ing herself about you! Probably forgot she ever 'ad a kid!'

Rose watched in silence as, over the following days, her aunt went about the business of winding up her life at The Duke's Head, adding day by day to the pile of boxes and suitcases accumulating in the back hallway, waiting for Carter Patterson to collect them. In spite of spending night after night in the shelters, Rose went to work each day just as everyone else did. Even though the Co-op had been bomb blasted and had its windows boarded up it was business as usual. Try as she would she could see no prospect of finding somewhere to live. By the time the first weekend came round she was beginning to feel desperate. She had asked around but so many families were bursting at the seams with bombed-out relatives. It seemed there were no rooms to let anywhere and already she was becoming resigned to the fact that the Underground would probably soon be her only home.

Then, one morning as she was leaving the pub on her way to works she saw a man putting up a poster on the wall opposite. It read:

JOIN THE WOMEN'S LAND ARMY.

Beneath was a picture of a smiling young woman in jodhpurs and a green jumper, holding a little woolly lamb under each arm. Rose had heard talk of the Women's Land Army of course, though not as much as she had heard about the other women's services. Some of the girls from the shop had joined the ATS or the WAAF. Two had gone into jobs in a munitions factory. They came back smartly dressed, boasting about the good wages they were earning and the special make-up allowance they received. In spite of the smart uniforms and other incentives, Rose had never fancied the women's services or working in a factory. But, as the days passed, she began to wonder if it was the only alternative to being homeless.

Looking up at the smiling girl in the poster, glowing with

health and vitality, her heart lifted. She had a sudden vision of life in the country; of fresh air and green fields and, best of all, no sleepless nights and the horrifying prospect of being killed or buried alive in the bombing. Rose went along and registered that same afternoon. There was no point in thinking it over; in a couple of weeks she would be homeless. At least this way she would have a job and somewhere to live. Soon she received her uniform. Trying it on in her bedroom she thought that already she had taken on a new persona. The breeches and jumper looked strange on her and when she added the thick greatcoat and wide-brimmed hat it was as though a stranger looked back at her from the mirror. Aunt Bess's reaction was blunt and to the point.

'Well, it ain't exactly the height of fashion is it?' the sniffed. 'But then I daresay where you're going it won't matter much what you looks like.'

On the night before Aunt Bess left for Devon, there was a sudden and bewildering change in her attitude towards Rose. When she closed the door of The Duke's Head for the last time she looked thoughtfully at her niece as she took off her apron.

'Sit down,' she said. 'I think we should have a bit of a talk.'

To Rose's surprise, her aunt poured two small glasses of whisky from the last bottle on the shelf and pushed one across the bar towards her. 'Get that down you, gel.'

Rose lifted the glass to her lips and took a sip. The taste and the way it burned her throat made her pull a face. Bess laughed. 'Never mind the taste. Just get it down. It'll do you good. God knows when we'll be tastin' it again anyway.' She tossed her own whisky down in a single gulp and replenished her glass. Rose knew that her aunt had already had quite a lot of whisky that evening. The regulars had been buying her farewell drinks ever since opening time.

'You been a good gel since you've been with me, Rose,' Bess said surprisingly. 'I know I've been hard on you, but it ain't done you no harm.' She pursed her lips. 'I hope you don't hold

it against me. You ain't been unhappy here at the Duke's, have
you?'

Slightly embarrassed, Rose shook her head.

'Well, now we're partin' company, and the Lord above knows
when – or even *if* – we'll meet again, I'd like to put things
straight between us.'

'Straight?' Rose was even more bewildered.

Bess nodded. 'There's something you got a right to know.'

Rose looked up expectantly. 'Is it about Mum?'

Bess sighed. 'I s'pose it is, partly.' She took a deep breath.
'You asked me once about your father.'

Rose's hand went instinctively to her cheek as she recalled
the stinging slap she had received for her pains. 'You know who
he is?' she asked cautiously.

Bess sighed and drained the last dregs of whisky from the
bottle into her glass. 'Oh, I know all right,' she said wryly. 'No
use pretendin' any more. My Ernie was your dad.'

Rose stared at her. 'Your – your *husband*? The one who. . . ?'

' "The one who ran off and deserted you". Yes!' Bess said
brutally. 'When I found out he and your ma were carryin' on, I
threw 'im out. I never knew she was expectin' then. That come
afterwards – when she come to me cryin' her eyes out and askin'
if I knew where he was – desperate for help.'

'And he was. . . ?'

Bess laughed. 'Long gone! Neither of us 'as ever seen hide
nor hair of him from that day to this,' she said bitterly. 'Left
your ma with a kid on the way and me with this place to keep
goin'.'

A lot of things suddenly became clear to Rose. 'So that's why
you hate her,' she whispered. But Bess was shaking her head.

'Hate her? Lord love you, no.' Her face softened in a way
Rose had never seen before. It was almost as though it was made
of wax. 'I was ten when she was born and I loved her the minute
I saw her. Like a pretty little doll, she was. But them looks was
her downfall later on. Started even before she'd left school. Men

couldn't keep their hands off her. And she never done nothing to discourage them neither. I suppose I was jealous if I tell the truth. Never was no oil paintin', me. Our mum sent Sal off to a job in service to try and keep her on the straight'n'narrow. Soon after that I met my Ernie and it looked like it was my turn to catch a bloke. We got married and set up here at the Duke's and life was all right till Sal came home in disgrace after bein' caught with the son of the house. Seems it weren't her fault this time and I felt sorry for her. I made the mistake of offerin' her a job here.' She sighed. 'I should'a known what would happen. Like all the others, Ern couldn't resist her. I come home one afternoon and found them in...' She sniffed. 'Well, you know.'

Rose swallowed hard. 'I'm sorry, Aunt Bess.'

Bess looked up. 'It ain't your fault,' she said with a shrug. 'But that's always the way of it, more's the pity. *The sins of the fathers* the Bible says, don't it? Never been truer words spoken. That's life.' She put her glass down on the table with a thump. 'Well, if it's done nothing else, this war has done one thing: it's given folks like you and me a chance to make a fresh start. So, I want to wish you luck in the Women's Land Army, Rose. I reckon you'll do all right. You're used to hard work.' She grinned. 'You got to admit I taught you that if nothing else.'

'I hope you get on all right down in Devon, too,' Rose said.

'I'll like it all right,' Bess said. 'Got to, ain't I? Tell you the truth I'm sick of London. Mucky and dangerous. It ain't the place it used to be. Never will be again if you ask me. No, we're better off out of it.' She stood up, stretching stiffly. 'I'll give you one bit of advice, gel,' she said. 'Don't you let no one put you down. It's one thing takin' it from the person what brought you up, but when it comes to them outside, you're as good as the next man – better than most an' don't you forget it. You stand up for yourself. If you don't you'll get put on for the rest of your life.' Then to Rose's astonishment she put her arms around her and clasped her close. 'Be a good gel,' she said huskily. 'P'raps you could drop your old aunty a post card when you get there

and let me know you're all right.'

'I will,' Rose said.

After she was in bed, Rose thought about her aunt's revelation and the mellowing of her attitude. She wished it could have come sooner. Life would have been so much more bearable when she was growing up if she'd had a little warmth and affection. But at least she knew now that her aunt had some feeling towards her. The newly acquired knowledge that Ernie Markham was her father meant little to Rose. After all, she'd never set eyes on the man – never even seen a photograph of him. She had been registered in her mother's name. She was Rose Meadows and as far as she was concerned it was the only name she had.

She was sent to Yorkshire for her six week's training and enjoyed it more than she had expected to. There were a dozen girls at the hostel, sent out in pairs each day to different farms; taught to milk the cows, hoe weeds, cut sprouts and cabbages and dig carrots. At the end of each day, Rose's back ached and her hands were sore, but the camaraderie of the other girls was something she had never known before. Here they accepted her. There was no one to see her as 'different' or to ask her awkward questions about her parents. It was just as Aunt Bess had said – a new start. By the time the training period was over she could already feel that her body was stronger and fitter. Looking in the mirror she saw changes too. Her cheeks had filled out and had colour in them and her eyes sparkled with fresh air and exercise. She looked forward to her first posting.

Peacocks Farm, sounded lovely. Rose visualized it all the way to Suffolk on the train.

There would be a thatched farmhouse with latticed windows. Maybe she would be met at the station by a pony and trap, driven by the farmer's handsome son or maybe his plump, motherly wife. The farm kitchen would smell warmly of newly baked bread and fruitcake and the sheets on the bed would be

lavender-scented. She was a little disappointed by the fact that she was to be the only landgirl on the small farm. She'd grown used to the company of the other girls and she knew she'd miss them. Still, they'd promised to keep in touch. It would be nice to get letters from them and it wasn't as though she wasn't used to being on her own.

852.100 |AF

As the train rattled through the Suffolk countryside Rose wished it was summertime. From the train window she saw sheep, huddled together like bundles of dirty rags to shelter from the drizzling November rain under bare hedgerows. There were puddles in the empty fields and the leafless branches of the trees swayed and bent in the wind.

At Ipswich she was directed to the bus station. It seemed there was no railway station at Weston St Mary. It was quite a long walk to the bus station and the rain had soaked right through Rose's coat by the time she got there, only to find that she had just missed the hourly bus. In a steamy buffet she bought herself a cup of tea and a bun.

The bus set Rose down at the end of a muddy lane in the murky half-light of late afternoon.

'You'll find Peacocks about a mile up there,' the conductor told her in what to Rose was an almost unintelligible Suffolk accent. 'You can't miss it. There's a big oak tree by the gate.' He handed her case down to her and added with a wink, 'Rather you than me, love. A right miserable old bugger, Bill Peacock.'

Rose's heart sank. So she was coming to work for a farmer who was an old misery? Still, he couldn't be worse than Aunt Bess.

The rain had stopped but the narrow lane was slippery with mud and heavy going as Rose trudged along with her heavy suitcase. Presently she heard a tractor coming up behind her and drew into the hedge out of the way. The tractor stopped and she looked up to see a burly young man looking down at her.

WESTMEATH COUNTY LIBRARY

'Afternoon. You the new landgirl?'

'Yes. Am I right for Peacocks Farm?' Rose asked.

'That you are.' He smiled and bent forward to hold out his hand. 'Give us your case and hop up here. I'll take you there. I'm Harry Owen, Bill Peacock's cowman,' he said, when she was settled precariously beside him.

Rose saw that Harry Owen was a young man in his mid twenties, powerfully built and quite good-looking with thick, dark hair and brown eyes. He looked fit enough to be in the services, but she reminded herself that as a farm worker he would be exempt.

'Have you worked at Peacocks Farm long?' she asked, as they trundled along.

He shook his head. 'Only for the past year. My dad used to farm over at Melton Beeches. When he died he left the farm to my half brother. I tried to join the army but I got directed here instead.'

Rose was silent, wondering why Harry didn't work alongside his brother on the family farm. 'Is Mr Peacock nice to work for?' she asked.

Harry laughed. 'Depends what you mean by "nice".' His smile vanished. 'Bill's wife died about eighteen months ago. It hit him badly and he was all set to retire, but what with the war and everything he wasn't allowed to. It's only a small farm now; two hundred acres. The government requisitioned the rest to make an airfield for the RAF. It's mainly arable with a small herd of cows. I look after them and help generally around the place.'

'Are you the only one working there?'

'Oh no. There's Fred Beasley and Jack Griggs. They're both getting on, older than Bill, I shouldn't wonder, but they can still put in a good day's work.'

Rose was still thinking about the bus conductor's remark. 'But he – Mr Peacock – is all right, is he? To work for, I mean.'

Harry sighed and chewed his lip. 'Oh yes.' He glanced at her.

'He's just let himself go a bit since he lost his wife, that's all.'

'Has he got any family?'

'No. Jack and Fred are always trying to get him to go down The Grapes for a pint and a game of dominoes of an evening, but he won't budge, daft old devil.' He grinned at her. 'I reckon you're just what he needs to cheer him up.'

When Rose jumped down from the tractor in the farmyard the mud almost covered the tops of her boots. Harry handed her down her case.

'There you go then. Best o'luck. See you tomorrow I daresay.'

She watched as the tractor trundled away, then began to pick her way across the yard to where she could see a dimly lighted window. As she reached the back door, a dog's frantic barking made her start. Through the gloom she saw that a black and white collie was chained up to a kennel. Tentatively she reached out a hand for the dog to sniff.

'Come on then,' she said softly. 'I won't hurt you.' Apparently reassured, the dog lost interest and returned to its kennel.

The back door was ajar and Rose stood in the doorway and called tentatively, 'Hello! Is anyone there?'

From where she stood, she could see that the kitchen floor was stone flagged. The walls had once been whitewashed but were now dark with smoke and grease. Hams and a brace of pheasants hung from the blackened beams of the low ceiling, but on the far side of the room a huge black range threw out a welcoming warmth.

'Who the hell might you be?'

A man opened the door opposite, his bulk filling the door-way. He wore brown overalls and the largest boots that Rose had ever seen. Grey hair poked out in wisps from under a greasy cap, the peak of which hid his features from view.

Rose cleared her throat. Surely the man could see who she was by her uniform. 'I'm Rose Meadows. Your new landgirl,' she said, trying to sound confident.

Bill Peacock looked her up and down. 'Don't know what the

hell use they think a slip of a girl like you's going to be about the place,' he said, pulling off his cap and scratching his head. 'Still, can't argue with the Min of Ag, can we? Life's not yer own these days! I suppose you'd better come in then. And for Christ's sake shut that bloody door. That draught's enough to cut a bloke's ankles off.'

Rose felt like reminding him that it was already open when she arrived, but thought better of it. Closing the door and stepping into the room she saw that the dim light came from an oil lamp on the table in the centre of the room. One end of the table was covered by a greasy newspaper and stacked up in several piles were dirty dishes from what looked like a week's meals. Her heart sank as she stood there clutching her suitcase.

'Where am I to sleep?' she asked.

Without replying, Bill Peacock picked up the lamp and turned to walk through the door. Rose followed him through a gloomy oak-panelled hall and up two flights of stairs. At the top Bill opened a door.

Under the sloping eaves was a tiny room furnished with a single bed, a chair and, under the dormer window, a rickety table bearing a basin and jug. The floor was covered with cracked linoleum. 'This'll do yer,' Bill announced. 'If it ain't to your liking there's always the barn. I'm sure the rats'd be glad of the company.' He laughed gruffly at the joke.

'It'll be fine, thank you,'

'That's good 'cause it's all there is. There's some sheets in the cupboard on the landing below. I'll leave you the lamp. Bring it down when you've sorted yourself out. After that you can come down and make the supper.' He turned on his heel and left her.

Rose found cold pork, bread and potatoes in the kitchen and put together a makeshift supper. Bill Peacock sat morosely opposite her at the kitchen table. He refused her offer of tea, clearly preferring the large quantities of ale with which he washed down his supper.

'There's a woman from the village, comes up once a week to

muck me out and do the washing,' he volunteered, as she cleared the table. 'On the other days, household matters'll be down to you.'

'But I'm a landgirl,' she told him. 'My job is supposed to be working on the farm.'

Bill looked up at her. 'Plenty o' that too, don't you worry. Think yourself too high and mighty to help out round the house, do you? That what they taught you at that there trainin' place, was it?'

'No, but. . . .'

'Long as you're 'ere, my girl, you'll do whatever work is required of you. Right? Or do you want me to complain to the *supervisor* or whatever her high-falutin' title is?'

'No. I. . . .'

'Right, then. That's settled. I'm now goin' to bed, girl.' He got up from the table and Rose noticed that he was slightly unsteady on his feet. 'Better get yourself off too. Five o'clock start in the morning. And there's the range to rake out and make up before that. You'll find the coke in the shed next to the barn.' He picked up the oil lamp and looked down at her. 'Your candlestick and matches are on the dresser.' At the door he looked back. 'Mind you washes up before you goes up.' He indicated the pile of congealed dishes on the table. 'There's a few more there needs seein' to while you're at it.'

That night Rose's teeth chattered as she listened to the mice scuttling and squeaking behind the skirting boards. The flock mattress was lumpy and she was sure it was damp. She'd already ascertained that there was no gas or electricity at Peacocks Farm. There was no bathroom either. The only water supply was cold and obtained from a hand pump at the big stone sink in the scullery. The only lavatory was across the muddy yard and devoid of light, and Rose suspected with a sinking heart that one of her more unenviable domestic duties was to be emptying the 'slops' each morning. Her dream of idyllic thatched farmhouses and apple-cheeked farmers' wives faded.

Peacocks Farm wasn't the posting she had looked forward to. Tears trickled down her cheeks to soak into the coarse calico pillowcase. She'd thought life at The Duke's Head with her Aunt Bess was hard, but her future on the farm with Bill Peacock as her boss promised to be even worse.

CHAPTER TWO

B Y THE time Bill Peacock came down next morning, Rose had been up for almost two hours. Unable to sleep, she had risen and hurriedly dressed. Downstairs in the kitchen she had raked out the ashes from the range and found the fuel store, then, finding a coarse apron hanging behind the scullery door she had set about cleaning the place. With hot water from the massive black kettle always on the range she scrubbed the floor, removing layers of grime. She washed the dishes on the dresser and wiped down the dusty shelves. Crumpling Bill's greasy newspaper 'tablecloth' and feeding it to the range fire she scrubbed the table, then found a clean gingham cloth in one of the dresser drawers and laid the table for breakfast.

Bill stood in the doorway blinking and sniffing the appetising aroma of bacon. 'We don't eat breakfast here till after milking,' he said, glowering at her ungraciously.

Rose picked up the plate of eggs and bacon. 'I see,' she said. 'So you won't be wanting this then?'

'Well, I might as well eat it seeing as you've cooked it.' He sat down and looked around him. 'You been busy then?'

'Yes, the place looked as though it could do with a good clean,' Rose said. 'I thought you said a woman comes to clean for you.'

'S'right. She was here last Monday,' Bill said, through a mouthful of fried bread. 'Meg Brown from down the village.'

What Rose had found in the kitchen and scullery had appalled her. Cobwebs in every corner and grime inches thick. Aunt Bess would have sacked the woman long ago for being so slatternly, but it wasn't her place to say so.

She pulled off her apron and began to pull on the brown overalls she'd been supplied with. They were several sizes too large and she had to roll up the sleeves and legs. 'Shall I help with the milking now?'

'Yes, you can give young Harry a hand,' Bill said, helping himself to a cup of tea.

'Right.' He hadn't asked if she had had any breakfast. 'I've fed the dog by the way,' she told him. 'What's his name?'

'It's a she and her name's Jess.' He stuffed in another forkful of bacon. 'She used to be our sheepdog but we ain't got sheep no more. Now she rounds up the cows for us at milkin' time. Good old lass, is Jess.'

'I see. I've made some sandwiches for my lunch. There are some for you, too, if you need them. They're on the dresser.'

Bill stared open-mouthed as she disappeared through the door. She was taking a lot on herself, wasn't she? Still, perhaps she wasn't going to be as useless as she looked after all. He looked round the kitchen. He might even save money, having her here.

Rose picked her way across the yard to the milking parlour and found Harry halfway through the morning session. She found a stool and bucket and immediately set to work. She'd discovered on the training course that milking was one of the jobs she liked best.

'You never told me what your name was last night,' Harry said, as he emptied his bucket into the tank.

'It's Rose' she told him. 'Rose Meadows.'

He chuckled. 'There's a name with a real country ring to it.'

'I suppose it is,' she said with a smile. 'I'd never thought of it like that before.'

'How did you get on with Bill then?'

Rose hid her face against the cow's warm flank. 'All right. Though he doesn't seem to have grasped that I'm a government employee, not a servant.'

Harry laughed. 'You'll have to keep him in his place.'

'He says he has a woman to clean for him twice a week, but you can't see what she's done.' His silence made her wonder if she might have made some sort of blunder. 'Do you know her?' she asked.

'Meg Brown? Yes.'

'Well, she doesn't seem to be making much of a job of it,' Rose told him. 'I got up early and cleaned the kitchen.'

Harry looked across at her in dismay. 'Don't know that was a good idea,' he said. 'You don't want to start cleaning for Bill as well,' he said. 'Before you know it he'll be taking you for granted.'

'I didn't have much choice. It was filthy. My aunt was very particular about cleanliness where there's food. I couldn't bring myself to eat anything that came out of a kitchen like that,' she said. 'It's a wonder he's not ill with food poisoning.'

After a morning in a sodden field picking sprouts, Rose was ready for her cheese sandwiches. Huddled in the shelter of the hedge she unwrapped and ate them, hoping as she did so that she would not be staying long at Peacocks Farm. Most of the other girls were posted to farms where there was proper accommodation for them, or to hostels where they would be sent out on a variety of work. She felt lonely and depressed. She couldn't say she was homesick: she had no home any more and she'd never been happy at The Duke's Head. But there was nothing to look forward to here except that lumpy bed. Not even a hot bath and the cheery company of people her own age.

At four o'clock, Harry arrived with the tractor and trailer to collect the sacks of vegetables. He offered her a lift back to the farmhouse.

'Want to come down The Grapes for a drink later?' he asked. 'You can meet Fred and Jack and some of the village folk. I'll

27

call and pick you up if you like.'

Rose shook her head. 'It sounds nice, Harry, but to tell you the truth I'm so tired I don't think I could. As soon as I've had my supper I'm off to bed.'

'OK. Another time then, eh?'

She smiled. 'I'd like that.'

On the kitchen table was a bag of shopping. Bill had obviously been to the village for supplies. At least he didn't expect her to do that as well. Rose put the food away in the larder, noting as she did so that here was another place that needed a good cleaning. This Meg Brown she kept hearing about must be the worst charwoman in the world.

By the end of the week, Rose had realized with dismay that Bill Peacock drank himself into oblivion every evening after supper. On the first evening she had taken hot water up to her room to wash off the day's grime. Coming down later to make herself a hot drink she found Bill slumped at the table, almost senseless. Being brought up in a dockland pub drunkenness held no mysteries or fears for Rose, it was simply a fact of life. Nevertheless she'd seen the misery it could cause.

'Mr Peacock!' She tried to rouse him, shaking his shoulder. 'Mr Peacock! Wake up. You'd be better off in bed.'

He grunted and looked up at her blearily. 'Wha'? Whadya want, girl?'

'Let me help you upstairs,' she said, taking his arm. 'You can't sleep here.'

He submitted complainingly to being helped upstairs, though it was no mean task for Rose. He was a big man and a dead weight. He leaned heavily on her as they made their way precariously up the stairs. Several times she thought he was going to fall, taking her with him, but at last she managed to get him into his bedroom on the first floor. Tipping him on to the big double bed she pulled off his boots and threw the eiderdown over him. He was rambling incoherently and she bent

over him, trying to make out what he was saying.

'May,' he slurred. 'Best woman a man could have – never be the same again – wish I could go too.'

She drew the curtains and tiptoed out of the room.

In the morning he seemed to have forgotten all about the previous evening and apart from being his usual grumpy self he had no symptoms of a hangover. But as she pulled on her overalls he made a sudden announcement.

'I've told Meg Brown she needn't come no more. From now on you can see to the house and that.'

Rose was taken aback. Her first instinct was to accept meekly, then she remembered Aunt Bess's advice and decided that if she were not to be taken advantage of she must stand up for her rights.

'*Me*? How do you think I'm going to have time for that, Mr Peacock? I've told you, I'm a landgirl, not a servant.'

'All right. Hold yer horses. I ain't finished yet. You can have Saturdays and Sundays off to see to the house.'

'But that's the weekend,' she pointed out. 'If I'm to clean for you as well as do the farm work I'll need at least one day off a week.'

His eyebrows shot up. 'My May never had no day off,' he said. 'Worked her fingers to the bone every day of the week for me, she did. Never complained neither.'

'But she was your wife,' Rose said. 'I'm not happy to work my fingers to the bone seven days a week for you, Mr Peacock. Besides, I'm not really allowed. Forty-eight hours a week, I'm supposed to do. Fifty in the summer. That's what I get paid for. So if I don't suit you perhaps I should get on to my supervisor and ask for a transfer.'

'All right – all *right*! You can have your day off,' Bill said grudgingly. 'Look, s'posin' you was to do the household chores Sat'days and Mondays? Special arrangement like, between the two of us. I'll see you right with a bit of extra money. Ten bob, say?'

Rose chewed her lip. It was true that she wasn't here to do domestic work. On the other hand, the weather was atrocious. She thought of the wind, cutting across the fields to sting her eyes and redden her nose; the way the rain soaked right through her clothes and the pain in her fingers, aching and bleeding from cutting cabbages and digging carrots. Maybe two days work in the house would make a welcome respite. And she couldn't deny that the extra ten shillings would come in useful.

'All right then,' she conceded. 'If that's what you want, I'll do it.'

Cleaning the house was a revelation to Rose. It had become clear that Bill ate, lived and occasionally slept in the kitchen where he still drank himself stupid each evening. The other rooms in the house were shut up and never used. In daylight she saw that his bedroom was thick with dust and she suspected that the sheets hadn't been changed for weeks. The reason soon became clear. The sheets she'd taken from the linen cupboard were the last clean ones in the house. In the washhouse that adjoined the kitchen, she lit the copper and gathered up all the dirty linen she found strewn about the house wherever Bill had discarded it. Later that morning she had a line of washing blowing in the overgrown garden at the back. She cleaned her own bedroom and Bill's, as well as the hall, landings and stairs, but when curiosity prompted her to open the door of the large room at the back of the house she stopped short in her tracks. The floor in here was stone flagged too, but the flags were overlaid with a beautiful blue carpet. The walls were hung with expensive wallpaper and at the window blue velvet curtains were looped back with tasselled cords. There were velvet-covered chairs, a *chaise-longue*, and an elegant china cabinet filled with delicate porcelain. But, most surprising of all was the piano that stood against one wall, music still open on the music stand. She tiptoed across the room to peer at the photograph on top of the piano. Smiling

out of a silver frame was a couple in wedding finery. A young woman, fair-haired and lovely, gazed up adoringly into the eyes of her groom, a barely recognizable Bill Peacock: slim and upright and twenty years younger.

Rose dusted the room reverently. It was clearly a room that May Peacock had created for herself and was obviously exactly as she had left it. When she had finished she tiptoed out again, closing the door softly behind her so as not to disturb May Peacock's ghost. Now she felt she understood Bill a little better. Rose had been at Peacocks Farm for almost a month before she accepted Harry Owen's invitation to join him for an evening at The Grapes. Getting ready that evening she was surprised to see that a change had taken place in her. Gone was her London pallor. Her cheeks had filled out and there was warm colour in them. Her hair too looked less lank and lifeless. After work that evening she'd taken rain water from the big tub in the yard and washed it, letting it dry as she cooked supper in the kitchen. In her tiny bedroom, she applied a little lipstick and combed her hair, which she normally wore tied back, into soft curls around her face. By the time she came downstairs Bill had already begun the evening's drinking.

'Why don't you come too?' she asked him.

He looked up and shook his shaggy grey head. 'Rather stay 'ere,' he muttered.

'It's not good for you, drinking alone,' Rose ventured.

'What would you know about it, girl?'

'I was brought up in a pub. I know all about what drink can do.'

'Then you must know that it's best not to come between a man and his bottle.'

Harry arrived at that moment and Rose knew that it was no use arguing with Bill. 'Goodnight then,' she said.

' 'Night.' He waved his glass in her direction.

'You'll be all right?'

31

'I was all right before you come, girl,' he grunted. 'Why shouldn't I be all right now?'

As she and Harry walked to the village she asked him if he knew about Bill's drinking.

'Everyone knows,' he told her. 'He's been like that ever since his wife died.'

'What happened?'

'No one really knows. She died in an accident. She never really settled here by all accounts,' Harry told her. 'She wasn't from round here. A town girl; a singer on the stage, some say. I don't rightly know how Bill met her.'

'He must miss her.'

'He won't let anyone help him. I know that,' Harry said. 'Plenty have tried and been sent away with a flea in their ear.'

The Grapes stood by the village green; a small sturdy-looking building with a thatched roof. In the bar, a bright fire burned and the locals were gathered round it, playing darts or dominoes or just chatting. Rose quickly saw Fred and Jack, who hailed her warmly.

'So he'm brought you out o' your shell at last,' Fred said. 'Good thing too. Everyone needs a bit o' company an' a laugh after a day's work.'

Rose took off her greatcoat to reveal a clean green jumper and her best pair of breeches. She glanced appreciatively at Harry. Now that they were in the light she saw that he was freshly shaved. He wore a tweed jacket and a neatly pressed pair of flannels. Not for the first time it occurred to Rose how good-looking he was with his thick brown hair and dark eyes. She realized that she still knew next to nothing about him. He didn't talk about himself. Over glasses of the local ale she tried to draw him out.

'Why don't you work on your family's farm, Harry?'

He shrugged. 'My dad was widowed. My mum was his second wife. When I was born, my half-brother George was fourteen and already helping Dad on the farm. By the time I was ten

32

George was married. He and his wife moved in and took over after my mum died.' He took a long draught of his ale. 'I reckon Dad never saw me as anything but a boy.'

'How old were you when he died?'

'Eighteen.'

'And he left everything to your brother?'

Harry shrugged. 'Maybe he meant to change his Will. Just never got round to it.'

'Surely your brother could have made sure you had your share.'

'He wasn't forced to, was he? Besides, Myra, his wife wanted me off the farm and she made no bones about saying so.'

Rose made no comment. She felt that Harry had had a raw deal, but it wasn't really her business.

'I got a lot to thank Bill Peacock for. It was him gave me a job and one of his cottages. That was when his wife was still alive. It was a big farm then – before the RAF took nearly half of it for the airfield.' Harry drained his glass. 'You got family?'

'There's just my Aunt Bess. My mum left me with her when I was quite small. I've never seen her since. I never knew my dad. I grew up in a dockland pub. Went to work at the Co-op when I left school. Then here.' She smiled. 'Not very exciting, is it?'

He met her eyes shyly. 'You've got a lot of future to look forward to. Your life's just beginning.' He picked up the glasses. 'Want another?'

Before she had time to reply, a disturbance at the other end of the bar made them look up. A dark gipsyish-looking woman who had come in earlier had clearly had a lot to drink and had become obstreperous. Someone was trying to quieten her but her voice could clearly be heard at the other end of the room. And to Rose's surprise she was pointing in her direction.

'That's her!' she shouted, waving a finger at Rose. 'That's the graspin' little bitch what done me out of my job. She knows what she's doing all right. Cleanin' his house and cookin' fancy

London grub for him.' Someone laid a hand on her arm and tried to lead her away.

'Come on, Meg. Time to go. . . .'

'Gerroff me! I'm 'avin' me say!' She shook off the hand that tried to calm her. 'She's after Bill Peacock!' Her voice rose. 'She knows there's money there, money and land. Stands to reason, don' it? Living in the same house, just her and him. Nothin' but a flimsy wall between 'em! What's the betting there's some *sleep-walkin'* goes on there after dark?' She threw back her head and cackled suggestively.

Rose felt her cheeks burn. She looked at Harry. 'I'm going,' she said.

'No. You sit tight,' he told her. 'I'll see to her.' He strode down the room and confronted the woman. 'Just you watch your mouth, Meg Brown,' he said. 'The young lady you're slandering happens to be my girlfriend and I won't have you making such nasty accusations about her.'

'Your *girlfriend*, is she? Got you too an' all, Harry Owen? Looks like one man's not enough for her! I seen her sort before. We got a name for 'em where—'

'That'll do now, Meg,' The landlord had come round the bar by now. Taking the woman by the arm he steered her firmly towards the door. 'I think it's time you went off home. Don't want to have to bar you now, do I?'

The room fell silent after Meg Brown's departure. Rose felt acutely uncomfortable, aware that everyone was avoiding her eyes. Was that what everyone thought? That she and Bill. . . . The thought horrified her. She looked at Harry, her cheeks crimson. 'Please – I can't stay after that,' she whispered.

'I'll take you home if you're really sure,' he said. 'But you don't want to worry about what she said. Everyone round here knows Meg Brown's spiteful tales. They know you're just doing a job of war work. They're not going to believe a word of it.'

'I still want to go,' she said.

As they walked back to the farm, Harry took her arm. 'Rose

– I hope you didn't mind me saying – you know, about you being my girlfriend. I reckoned it was the best way of shutting her up.'

Rose couldn't look at him. ' 'Course I didn't.' She was sure that half the girls in the village would have given anything to be in her shoes this evening. She'd seen the way they all looked at Harry. Far from helping the situation, she wondered if it might make things worse between her and the village folk. But she knew he'd acted with the best of intentions 'Is that what people really think?' she asked. 'About Mr Peacock and me? It's true that we live in the same house – just him and me.'

Harry laughed and squeezed her hand. 'Believe the drunken ramblings of Meg Brown? Not on your life. Besides, this is 1942, not *1842* – and there's a war on.'

But, in spite of his reassurance, Rose was disturbed. One thing she knew, it would be a very long time before she showed her face in The Grapes again.

Next morning she told Bill about the scene in the pub. 'You shouldn't have sacked her,' she said. 'Now she's spreading tales about me – blaming me for losing her job.'

'What tales?' Bill asked, looking up from his bacon and fried bread.

Rose coloured. 'Just saying nasty things – spiteful things.'

'You don't want to take no notice,' Bill said, with a dismissive wave of his hand. 'Meg Brown was a gypsy girl. She come here about eighteen years ago with her tribe, but they dumped her because she was expectin' a child out o' wedlock an' they knew the father weren't one of them, which made it worse. She's been here ever since, still livin' in the ramshackle old caravan they left her with down Heathersedge Lane – makin' a livin' as best she can and bringin' up her daughter.'

'Then it was unkind of you to sack her,' Rose said.

Bill grunted. 'That's a good'un! Didn't you say yourself that she were a slut – never done her work proper?'

'Well, I. . . .'

35

'There you are then. She took advantage of me – a lone widower. Serves her right. Maybe she'll have learned her lesson.'

Christmas was drawing near and Rose wondered if Bill expected her to take a few days' leave. Where would she go? She'd had one letter from Aunt Bess since she came to Peacock's Farm. She seemed to be enjoying her new life in Devon. After all the years at The Duke's Head she was finding it a novelty, having all her evenings free to sit by the fire and listen to the wireless. She wrote that she and her friend were going to spend Christmas with Grace's daughter and grandchildren in the next village. She didn't even ask what Rose would be doing. At last she summoned the courage to ask Bill what his plans were.

'Christmas?' he snapped, looking at her. 'Why, it'll be no different from any other day here. Why should it? I got nothin to celebrate, have I? It'll be work on the farm as usual.'

Her heart sank. At The Duke's Head there used to be holly and mistletoe, plum pudding and a turkey dinner. All the regulars would be cheery and even Aunt Bess would be in a good mood for once. Bill's Christmas sounded bleak. He was studying her face.

'I expect you'll be wantin' time off.'

She shook her head. 'I've got nowhere to go,' she said. 'Would you let me make a Christmas for you here?'

He grunted non-commitally. 'If you're stayin' you can do what you like, I suppose.'

'Could we ask Harry to join us? I think he'll be alone too.'

'I told you – do what the hell you like.' Bill said, getting up from the table. 'On'y don't expect me to be cheerful. Christmas means bugger all to me nowadays.'

But in spite of his gruff words Bill provided a fowl and even plucked and dressed it for her. Rose made mince pies and a pudding and invited Harry to join them. He blushed with pleasure.

'Thanks. I'd like that. I usually spend Christmas on my own,' he told her. 'George and Myra have got three kids and they don't want me round there, getting in the way.'

'I'd guessed that,' Rose told him.

'Tell you what. I've got plenty of evergreens in the yard at the cottage,' he told her. 'I'll cut some and bring them over for you to decorate the place with.'

Rose was giving the drawing-room its weekly clean the following Saturday when she had the idea. It was a shame to waste a pretty room like this. It would be the perfect place in which to celebrate Christmas. She wondered how to put the suggestion to Bill. Opening the lid of the piano she ran her duster over the keys. At The Duke's Head they had an old upright piano in the bar parlour. On Saturday evenings old Jerry Briggs, the knife-grinder used to come in and play for a sing-song. He'd taught her to pick out one or two tunes when she was a little girl and she'd never forgotten them. There was 'The Bluebells of Scotland' and 'Danny Boy'. Putting down her duster she picked out the first notes 'Danny Boy', singing along to the tune. *'Oh Danny boy, the pipes, the pipes are calling, from glen to glen and down the mountainside.'*

'Hold your noise!'

Startled, Rose jumped back from the piano. Bill stood in the doorway, his face chalk white.

'What the hell do you think you're doin'? Get out of here. No one's allowed in this room.'

'I was cleaning it,' Rose protested. 'I'm sorry I played the piano. I didn't mean—'

'It's *hers*!' Bill shouted. 'My May's. No one else touches that piano. Understand?'

'Of course. It was just. . . .' Rose stopped. Bill had turned away, but not before she had seen the tears in his eyes. She followed him through the hall into the kitchen where he lowered himself into a chair at the table, looking visibly shaken.

'Please, Mr Peacock. I didn't mean any harm. I'm so sorry.'

'I thought it was her,' he said. His voice was thin and shaky now. 'I came in quiet like and heard that song. She used to sing that sometimes of a Sunday night. For a minute – just for a minute – I thought she'd come back.'

To Rose's horror, he laid his head down on his arms at the table and began to sob.

The incident with the piano seemed to shake Bill out of his lethargy. As Rose was getting ready for milking next morning he said suddenly, 'I been thinkin' It's silly lettin' that room go to waste. What do you say we make use of it?'

Rose paused, halfway into her overalls. 'At Christmas, you mean?'

' 'Course. If we're havin' company we can't sit in the kitchen, can we?'

'Shall I light a fire in there?' she asked. 'To air it?'

'Do what you like.' Bill got up and reached for his cap. 'No use livin' in the past, is it?' Without waiting for her reply he pulled on his cap and went out into the yard.

Rose's Christmas preparations progressed. On the day before Christmas Eve, she discovered that there was hardly any flour left. Putting on her greatcoat and hat she took the stout shopping bag that hung behind the pantry door and walked down to the village. The village post office doubled as a general store. It stocked everything from firewood and candles to ladies stockings and headache pills as well as all the usual groceries. It never failed to fascinate Rose with its mingling odours of paraffin, ham and creosote. As she was coming out, her head full of the tasks she had yet to do, she ran headlong into Meg Brown. Trapped in the doorway and unable to avoid the woman she nodded and said, 'Good afternoon.'

Meg stood in front of her and looked at the bag of shopping. 'Makin' it all nice and cosy for Christmas, are you?' she sneered.

'You'n Bill, all tucked up nice together. You got it all worked out, haven't you?'

Rose's heart began to beat faster. There was an evil malevolence about the woman. It was in the twisted mouth and the flash of the coal-black eyes. 'I'm only doing my job,' she said.

'Doin' a bit more'n your job, if you asks me,' Meg said. *'Far and above the call of duty*. Ain't that what they calls bedding the boss?'

Rose tried to push past her. 'Please leave me alone,' she said. 'And stop spreading lies about me.'

Meg took a step forward, barring her way. 'Or else *what?*' she asked, her face pushed close to Rose's. 'Why would you get him to sack me if you wasn't planning to trap him yourself?'

Rose faced up to her adversary. 'He sacked you because you weren't doing your work properly,' she said bravely. 'No other reason. It had nothing to do with me.'

'Now who's lyin'. He told me himself it were you said I weren't cleanin' the place proper.'

'You weren't.'

Meg drew a deep breath and pressed Rose into a corner of the doorway. 'I'll tell you somethin', lady,' she hissed. 'You got trouble in your past and trouble in your future 'n' all. You might think you done well. You got money comin' right enough, but it won't bring you happiness. The man you give your heart to will break it in a million pieces. You'll be used and abused and brought to your *knees* 'fore you're done, my lady!'

The shop door opened suddenly and Mrs Maitland, the post mistress appeared, filling the doorway with her considerable bulk. 'What's going on here?' she demanded. 'Be about your business, Meg Brown, and stop harassing my customers.' Meg turned and flung off, muttering to herself. Mrs Maitland looked at Rose.

'You all right, m'dear?'

'Yes, thank you,' Rose said, her heart beginning to slow again. 'She hates me because she lost her job at the farm.'

'No doubt she deserved to lose it,' Mrs Maitland said. 'I was surprised when Bill Peacock gave her a chance. If she let him down then more fool her. She's got no one to blame but herself.' She looked at Rose's pale face. 'You look right shook up, love. Want to come inside for a minute? I could make you a cup of tea.'

'No, thank you. I'd better be getting back.'

Christmas was a great success. The farm work out of the way, Rose set about cooking the dinner. She'd decorated the kitchen and the drawing-room with the evergreens Harry had brought and the place looked quite festive. Harry arrived at twelve, scrubbed and groomed in his best suit and when Bill appeared, surrounded by a powerful aura of mothballs emanating from the suit he reserved for funerals, Rose was surprised to see that he had shaved.

Both men declared Rose's Christmas dinner delicious and afterwards they sat in the drawing-room till evening milking. The more Bill drank the more talkative he became, telling them outrageous tales of his youth when he and the other local lads got into mischief scrumping apples and even poaching the odd brace of pheasant from Squire Beech's land.

He explained to Rose that Squire Beech owned the huge farm that had once dominated the village. In years gone by he had provided employment for most of the village; the men on the farm and the women in the house and the dairy. Ten years ago when he died, his only son, Richard, had inherited it. Bit by bit he had rented out much of the estate to tenant farmers and now farmed what remained in a much more modest way than in his father's day.

After tea, Rose and Harry changed their clothing and went out to do the milking, leaving Bill alone with his whisky bottle and his reminiscences.

'I haven't seen him that cheerful or talkative for a long time,' Harry remarked as they worked together. 'I always said you were just what he needed to cheer him up.'

'He's had a lot to drink,' Rose said. 'Do you think he'll be all right?'

'I daresay he'll do as he always does,' Harry said. 'Drink till he can't stand then sleep till morning.'

He proved to be right. When they returned to the farmhouse they found Bill half asleep at the kitchen table. Together they got him upstairs and settled for the night. In the kitchen Rose made cocoa for them both.

'He can't go on like this,' she said. 'It's all very well, but what can it be doing to his health?'

'Try telling him,' Harry said. 'Whatever anyone says he'll drink.'

'Did he drink when his wife was here? Could that have been why she left?'

Harry shook his head. 'Anyone's guess. Might be partly the reason. Who can say? Bill's not one to talk about his private life.' He reached across the table to touch her hand. 'Don't let's talk about him all the time. Why don't you come across and see my cottage?'

Rose smiled. 'I'd like that.'

The tiny tied cottage that Harry rented from his employer was on the far side of the rickyard. It had a kitchen-cum-sitting-room on the ground floor with a lean-to scullery leading off it. Rose saw that it was spotlessly clean with the minimum of furniture and a homemade pegged rug on the stone floor. A staircase led up to the bedroom above. Harry nodded.

'There's only the one room. Go up and have a look if you like.'

In the bedroom, a dormer window looked out across the fields. As below, the room was sparsely furnished. There was a brass bed covered by a white quilt, a wardrobe, one chair and a washstand. Everything was neat and clean. Descending the

stairs again she smiled.

'You keep it all so nice,' she remarked.

'Myra let me bring some of the stuff from my room at home,' he told her.

'Did she?' Secretly Rose thought that was the least she could do. 'That was nice.'

Harry reached out and took both her hands. 'I haven't got much now, but one of these days I'll have more,' he said. 'When that time comes I'd like to think I'd have someone like you to share it with.'

She blushed. 'What a nice thing to say, Harry.'

'I've never known a girl like you,' he went on. 'Most of the girls round here are so silly, giggling and talking behind their hands. You're a girl a man can call a friend too.'

'Thank you.' Rose blushed, wishing he'd stop. It was getting embarrassing. Harry seemed to have marriage on his mind and for that there would have to be love. Love and trust. There had been very little love in Rose's life; she had loved only one person. And that person had let her down. Was that what love was like? If you gave it could you ever be sure you were truly loved in return? Was love so fleeting that it could be taken away without warning? Harry was her friend. That seemed safe and it was all she wanted – for now.

'Maybe we should go back and see if Mr Peacock is all right,' she said, gently pulling her hands away.

At the back door of the farmhouse, the moon and stars shining down out of a frosty sky Harry pulled her close and kissed her.

'Goodnight, and thank you for a lovely Christmas, Rose. It was the nicest one I can remember.'

The kiss was pleasant and later, as she lay in bed in her little room at the top of the house, Rose thought about it. It hadn't sent her senses reeling or her head spinning like kisses in the books she'd read. But Harry's arms around her had felt safe and warm. His body pressed against hers had felt powerful and

strong. She supposed she could go a lot further and fare worse, she told herself in her Aunt Bess's words.

CHAPTER THREE

A s spring came and the blitz on London and other cities raged on, Rose's thoughts were often with her mother. Where was she, she wondered? She thought about writing to Aunt Bess and asking if she had heard, or if she had an address. Maybe she should go to London and look for Sally herself. But where would she start? It seemed impossible. Every day in the papers there were pictures of the damage caused by the bombing. Was Sally still alive? Would London be completely razed to the ground? Could the great city ever be the same again? After the war, where would she belong? she asked herself. An unwelcome thought that she thrust aside, finding no answer.

Life on the farm was busy. With spring came ploughing and planting, hedging and ditching, which she learned from Fred, who was specially skilled at it. She and Harry worked well together and remained friends. Rose forgot her dread of encountering Meg Brown and began to go with Harry to The Grapes again. The young airmen from the RAF airfield crowded in on most evenings. They were a high-spirited bunch and livened up the atmosphere. In spite of living their lives on the brink of death they were always laughing, and enjoyed nothing more than to crowd round the piano for a sing-song. The landlord liked the extra business they brought

in and the regulars admired their bravery and their youthful enthusiasm.

One evening Rose noticed a very pretty girl mingling with them. She asked Harry who she was. He followed her eyes across the room.

'Oh, that's Imelda Brown,' he said. 'Meg's daughter. If I'm not mistaken she'd not old enough to be in here. Not that you'd know it.'

The girl wore a brightly patterned skirt and a blouse with a drawstring neck, provocatively worn off one shoulder. She had tumbling black hair and flashing eyes like her mother's. But where Meg's ink-black eyes were bitter and treacherous, Imelda's were the rich brown of treacle toffee and they sparkled challengingly as she flirted with the young airmen. Harry looked disapproving.

'Asking for trouble, that one,' he remarked. 'Like mother, like daughter.'

A few minutes later, Sid Tarrant, the landlord, spotted her and asked her to leave.

'Lose me my licence, that one,' he said to no one in particular as he escorted her off the premises.

Rose worked hard in the farmhouse, turning out cupboards and generally cleaning. She found it hard work, doing all the housework, the washing, ironing and cooking as well as the farm work, but she found she enjoyed it. It was different from the drudgery she had hated at The Duke's Head. There, Aunt Bess was for ever at her heels, chivvying her on. Here she had a free hand. She had never had a real home before and gradually, as she took pride in her work she began to think of the farmhouse as her home. In the beginning she had insisted on having one day a week off and working no longer than the regulation WLA hours. Now she happily worked all day on Sundays to keep up her own high standard.

She had discovered other rooms in the house that were never

used. The dining-room, furnished with the heavy furniture that had belonged to Bill's parents. And upstairs, a pretty little bedroom overlooking the garden that looked as though it had once belonged to a child. She cleaned them and closed the doors again without asking Bill any questions.

As the months went by and his living standards improved, Bill's general attitude mellowed, though he still drank every evening when the work was done. Rose had abandoned her efforts to get him to give up drinking, but she made sure that he had a good meal every night and gradually she saw an improvement in his appearance. He began to look less haggard. His colour improved and he even went down to the village barber to have his hair cut instead of hacking it off himself. His manners also improved. He began to say 'thank you' more often, and Mrs Maitland at the post office told Rose that he had even remarked that in Rose he had 'one in a million'.

It was late one evening when he had drunk himself into a reminiscent mood that he began to talk about his marriage.

'You do a grand job for me, Rose,' he said. 'My May did her best, bless her, but it weren't her kind of life and never could be.'

Very gently, Rose took away his whisky glass and replaced it with a mug of cocoa. 'How did you meet her, Bill?'

He smiled. 'It were Christmas time, 1925. I was already forty. Most of the lads I'd grown up with were married with families by then, but I'd had to look after my mum and dad when they got sick, y'see. Run the farm almost single-handed at one time, I did. We had more acreage then – sheep an' more livestock, an' what with one thing an' another I never got much chance to go out lookin' for a wife. Well, a few of us fellers went drinkin' this particular time an' we ended up goin' into Ipswich to the pantomime, just for a laugh, like. An' there she were, up there on the stage, bright as a button. Singin' and dancin' with her lovely legs and her pretty voice.' He shook

his head. 'Bowled over, I were. Couldn't think about nothin' else.'

'So what did you do?'

'I went back there every night,' he said. 'On me own, o'course. Didn't want the other fellers laughin' at me. I reckon they'd'a thought I was too old for that kind o' carry on.'

'What did you do, Bill?'

'I used to go round to the stage door an' wait, just to see her come out.

'You never spoke to her.'

'Not for a long time. I couldn't – never said nothin'. Then, after I'd been there night after night for I don't know how long, she noticed me. She come across and asked me who I was and what I wanted.' He blew out his cheeks. 'Well – I were proper tongue-tied, couldn't say a word for a minute. Then I found me voice somehow. We talked, and I finished up askin' her out.'

Rose was smiling. 'And she said yes?'

He nodded. 'I thought it were a miracle. Head over heels in love I was, by then. I met her out after the show every night after that, and gradually bit by bit I got her to love me back. When the panto finished she said it had to end. She said she had to go back to London. I asked her to marry me but she said she couldn't. Her career on the stage was all she wanted, so we said goodbye.'

'You must have been disappointed.'

'I was – broken hearted. Then, about a month later, she suddenly fetched up here on the doorstep one day; said she'd missed me so much she couldn't enjoy her work no more. She said if I still wanted her, she'd marry me.'

Rose saw the tears glinting in his eyes and swallowed the lump in her throat.

'That must have made you so happy.'

Bill pulled out a handkerchief and blew his nose loudly. 'Thought I was dreamin'. I couldn't believe it. I thought my

heart would fair burst for joy.'

Rose reached across and touched one of the big rough hands. 'What happened, Bill?'

He shook himself and sighed, his eyes clouded with pain as they returned to the present. 'She tried. Like I said she did her best. It weren't easy for her at first. There was Mum and Dad to look after, y'see. They were both invalids and they weren't the easiest to do with at the best of times. Then, a year after they both died, we had a child – a little girl. Jenny, we called her. Dear little thing, pretty as a picture, just like her mother. I thought she'd mend things for us like; help May to settle down now that we was on our own like. But Jenny took ill when she were three. Diphtheria, the doctors said. They done all they could but it weren't no good. Well, after we lost our little Jenny nothin' was ever the same again. All the life seemed to go out of May. It was like someone had switched off the light in her. Nothin' I did or said could make her happy no more. In the end she met some old friends when a touring company come to the theatre in Ipswich. Next thing I knew she'd left – gone back to London. There were a note on the table when I come in from milkin' one mornin'.'

Rose felt her heart twist with pity. 'And you never heard from her again?'

'I planned to go up to London an' find her,' Bill said. 'It were harvest-time, so I couldn't go right away. But before I could go I got a letter from her friend to say that May had been killed. Knocked down crossing the road. Killed instantly, so they said.'

'Oh, Bill, I'm so sorry.'

'I brought her home and buried her in the churchyard, along with our little Jenny.' He looked at her. 'No one round here knows what truly happened,' he said. 'You're the on'y one I've ever told. Everyone knows she were killed in an accident, but not the part about her leavin'.'

'I understand. I won't say anything.' Rose felt privileged that he should trust her enough to tell her what he saw as his shame-

ful secret – his failure to make the only woman he had ever loved happy.

Spring blossomed into summer and the countryside was a joy to Rose. This was the countryside she remembered, leafy and rich with colour; blossoming with flowers and new life. One evening, when she and Harry were walking home from The Grapes, he seemed preoccupied. It was still light although it was after half past ten. Double summertime helped the farmers to work longer and it had been almost nine before Rose and Harry had been free to go out. He paused by a gate just before they reached the farm and took her hand.

'Rose, there's something I want to ask you.'

She guessed what it was and her heart sank. She was fond of Harry and valued their friendship. If he asked her to take things a step further and she said no, it would spoil things between them and that was the last thing she wanted.

'Don't say it now, Harry.'

'You don't know what it is yet.'

'I think I might.'

He looked crestfallen. 'And you'd have to say no. Is that what you're trying to tell me?'

'I'd rather not have to say anything.' She took his arm. 'I love having you as my friend, Harry. I've never had a friend like you before; someone I can talk to, tell all my secrets and dreams.'

'But those dreams don't include me. Is that it?'

She shook her head. 'I didn't say that. I love it here and I'm really fond of you. I'm happier than I can ever remember being. I'd like to stay as I am – as we are for a while, before I think about changing things.'

'Does that mean that if I wait. . . ?'

'I don't know,' Rose said. 'All I know is that I'd like us to stay as we are.'

He drew her close and kissed her. 'I wonder if you know how

hard that is for me,' he whispered.

'Just for a while? Please, Harry.'

He looked down into her upturned face and sighed. 'All right. Just for a while.'

Summer was over all too soon. At harvest time the children from the school were given time off to come to help. Sometimes some of the young airmen came too and there was much laughter and practical joking as they worked hard in the fields from early morning till nightfall. Autumn came, all gold, blue and crimson, with the sharpness of early frost and bonfires in the air. Then, in December, came the news that Pearl Harbor had been bombed by the Japanese and America had entered the war. Spirits rose. England was no longer alone in the struggle.

At Christmas, Rose did her best to make it festive for Bill and Harry. She had persuaded Bill to let her lay their Christmas dinner in the dining-room, polishing the dark old furniture till it gleamed and getting out Bill's mother's best china and glass which she had discovered lurking in the bowels of the massive mahogany sideboard. In one of the drawers she found a yellowing damask tablecloth and washed and ironed it almost as good as new.

Spring came again and with it the spring planting and the usual crop of calves. Working alongside Harry in the cowshed, she admired his gentleness and skill with the beasts. There was hardly ever any need to call out the vet. Harry always knew what to do, even in the most difficult of calvings, and because of him Bill hardly ever lost a calf or was involved in any unnecessary expense.

The April sunshine showed up the accumulation of winter grime and Rose asked Bill if she could have a week free of farm duties so that she could do some spring cleaning. He complained at first, but she had come to realize that it was Bill's way not to give in without a struggle. She knew he would

say yes in the end, just as he always did. She waited – and he did.

It was almost lunchtime and Rose was just returning to the house from hanging out the bedroom curtains when an ancient Austin Seven chugged into the yard. She watched as a uniformed figure got out of the car and headed towards her.

'Good morning. I'm looking for Miss Meadows,' the woman said. She took a sheet of paper from her bag and looked at it. 'Miss Rose Meadows.'

'That's me.'

'Really?' The woman's eyes took in the print overall Rose wore, protected by a sacking apron tied around the waist and she frowned disapprovingly. 'I am Cynthia Fairfax, your WLA supervisor,' she said. 'Perhaps we could go inside and talk, Miss Meadows.'

The kitchen floor was freshly scrubbed and the range threw out a welcome warmth after the chill outside. 'Can I offer you a cup of tea?' Rose asked, rolling down her sleeves.

The woman shook her head as her eyes took in every detail of the kitchen; the newly whitewashed walls and range, gleaming like ebony with black lead. 'This isn't a social call,' she said frostily. 'Miss Meadows, you are a member of the WLA. May I ask what you think you are doing?'

'I asked Mr Peacock for a few days off to do some spring cleaning.'

'That is not what the government pays you for.'

'I know but—'

'Are you in the habit of doing Mr Peacock's domestic chores?'

'I help out around the house, yes. Mr Peacock is on his own and—'

'That is not your concern,' the woman said. 'If he needs domestic help then he should find it elsewhere and pay for it.'

'He did have someone but she wasn't doing the work properly.'

'As I said, that is none of your concern.' She put the sheet

back in her bag and closed it with a loud snap. 'I'm afraid I shall have to report this,' she said. 'It is a very unsatisfactory state of affairs. Clearly there is not enough work on the farm for you. I think we had better consider a new posting.'

'Oh no, please!'

The woman's eyes narrowed. 'Just what is your relationship with Mr Peacock, Meadows?'

Rose coloured. 'What do you mean?'

'This is most irregular. It could even be a disciplinary matter. I shall have to speak to my superiors.' She got up and began to walk out of the door, Rose hurrying after her.

'Please, Miss Fairfax, all I do is help around the house for Mr Peacock, nothing more. In fact – in fact. . . .' A desperate idea had suddenly occurred to her. 'I am engaged to be married to the cowman here, Mr Harry Owen.'

The woman stopped in her tracks, turning to look at her. 'I see. I presume that this Mr Owen will confirm that?'

Rose colour deepened. 'Well – yes, though he isn't here at the moment.'

'Where is he then?'

'He's – he's. . . .' Rose was still casting about in her mind for a plausible reason for Harry's absence when the roar of a tractor was heard and a moment later Bill's old Ferguson trundled into the yard, driven by Harry. He switched off the engine and jumped down. 'Any chance of a cuppa, Rose?' he called.

Cynthia Fairfax looked at Rose. 'Is this the Mr Owen you spoke of, Meadows?'

Rose nodded, her heart sinking.

As Harry approached, Cynthia Fairfax gave Rose no chance to get in first. 'Good morning. I am the WLA supervisor,' she said. 'I understand congratulations are in order, Mr Owen.'

Harry looked from one to the other and quickly assessed the situation. 'Oh! Yes, that's right,' he said.

Miss Fairfax looked at Rose's crimson cheeks and drew

53

herself up to her full height. 'I am not at all satisfied with this situation, Meadows,' she said. 'I shall make out my report and no doubt you will be hearing from us again. Good day.'

They watched as she got into her car and started up the engine. As the wheels began to revolve mud sprayed the little car, coating the bonnet and doors with rich brown slurry. Harry grinned as he watched her reverse and head for the lane, the wheels spinning in an effort to grip the slimy ground.

'Serves her right, frosty old cow,' he said. 'No wonder she's a *miss* with a face like that. Enough to turn the milk!' He looked at Rose. 'What did she want? And what was I supposed to get congratulated for?'

'She was mad because she caught me doing the housework. Then she hinted that Bill and me were. . . .' She broke off, blushing again.

'Damned cheek!' His face cleared. '*Oh*, I get it. To get off the hook you told her that you and me were going steady. Right?'

'Sorry, Harry. I didn't know what else to say.'

He grinned good-naturedly. 'It's a good job I come in useful sometimes, eh?' He slipped an arm round her shoulders and gave her a squeeze. 'Don't worry about her. How about putting the kettle on then?'

A week later, Rose received an official-looking letter to say that she was suspended temporarily while a new posting was being considered. It was suggested that she take some leave, making it plain that she was to spend it away from Weston St Mary.

Rose was devastated. Peacocks Farm had been her home for the past eighteen months, though to her, it seemed a lot longer. She had been happier here than anywhere else. She loved the work and the old house that felt so much like her own. She was fond of Bill and Harry and she had come to know and like the village folk. Now, just because of a little housework it was all to end.

'Where will you spend your leave?' Harry asked her.

Rose shook her head. 'I suppose I could write to Aunt Bess and ask if I could go down to Devon,' she said, though even as she said it, she knew she wouldn't. 'I might go back to London and see if I can find my mother.' Catching sight of his worried expression she added quickly, 'Don't worry about me. I'll be all right. I'll soon be getting another posting anyway.' She smiled at him wistfully. 'I'm going to miss you all so much.'

'There is an answer,' Harry said. 'If we were to get married they'd probably release you, especially as you'd be working on a farm.'

'No, Harry. That would be marrying for the wrong reason.'

'Not as far as I'm concerned, it wouldn't.'

'But for me, it would.' She took his arm. 'I'll stay in touch though. I'll write. You'll write back, won't you?'

'Of course. And Bill will have to send on your posting when it comes.'

'And if I'm not too far away perhaps we can meet up now and again.'

His face brightened. 'You'd really like that?'

'Of course I would.'

'I wish you weren't going.'

'So do I.'

When Rose left Suffolk she went first to London. At Wetherby Street, she found The Duke's Head still standing, though most of the streets around had been flattened in the bombing. The windows were permanently boarded up and the place looked run down, but it was business as usual. The new land-lady, a kindly middle-aged woman called Kate Simmons, agreed to let her a room for a few nights and she found herself unpacking her few belongings in what had once been her own room.

Downstairs, she asked Kate about the people she used to

know and she learned that a lot of the regulars had been killed in the bombing. Most of the younger men were away in the services, the children evacuated and the women working in munitions factories or on the buses. Rose asked if her mother had been round, looking for her, but the woman shook her head. No one had enquired, either for her or Aunt Bess.

It was a strange feeling, lying in what had once been her own bed that night. Rose lay thinking about the past, about her unhappy childhood and her mother's desertion. If it hadn't been for the war she would probably still be here with Aunt Bess. She would never have joined the WLA, gone to Suffolk and met Bill and Harry. The war had changed everyone's life and sometimes it seemed that nothing would ever be the same again.

For a week she combed the area, looking for her mother in all the places they had lived together. Many of them were bombed out of recognition and those that were still standing were occupied by different people. No one she asked had heard of Sally Meadows. It was as though her mother had vanished without trace.

When her posting eventually came, re-addressed from the farm, it turned out to be in Yorkshire. She found that she was to stay in a hostel where she would be allocated to different farms in the area. Clearly the powers-that-be didn't mean to let her get too attached to any one place again.

'*It's nice to have the company of other girls and at least I'm still on the same side of the country,*' she wrote to Harry. She wrote to Bill too, but never received any letters back from him. Harry wrote that Bill's drinking had increased since she had left, something which saddened her.

At the hostel, Rose found herself sharing a room with a girl from Liverpool. Nell Sutton was the eldest of a large family and the two girls quickly became close friends. After they were tucked up in their bunks at night they each talked about their backgrounds. Rose envied Nell her large family.

'I've never really known what it is to have a family,' she said. 'Aunt Bess wasn't much like family. More like a slave driver! I suppose the nearest I've ever had was Bill Peacock and Harry at the farm in Suffolk.' She went on to tell Nell all about Harry and his proposal.

'And you turned him down?' Nell asked incredulously. 'What's wrong, don't you fancy him?'

Rose smiled. 'I love Harry, but I'm not sure it's right. I liked things as they were,' she explained. 'He's the best friend I've ever had. I'm scared that things would change between us if we got married.'

'Why should they?' Nell leaned over from the top bunk to look down at Rose. 'I'll tell you one thing. If some smashing fella like that asked me I'd have him down that aisle so fast his feet wouldn't touch the ground!'

Rose laughed. 'Whether you loved him or not?'

Nell blew out her cheeks. 'If somebody half decent asked me I'd love him all right. All I want is to get away from our lot at home and have a place of my own,' she said. ' 'Course I love them all to death, but there is a limit! Do you know I can't remember a time when our mam wasn't having a baby and guess who took over the kids – Muggins!'

'But you wouldn't marry anyone just to get away from home?'

Nell raised an eyebrow. 'Wanna bet?' She leaned over to look at Rose again. 'Anyway, you say you do love this Harry bloke, so why don't you feel it's right? What's holding you back?'

Rose considered for a long moment. It was so hard to explain, even to herself. 'All the people who were supposed to love me have abandoned me,' she said at last. 'My dad ran off before I was even born, and my mum when I was little. Maybe there's something about me. Maybe I don't deserve to be loved. I just daren't risk it.'

Nell shook her head. 'If you ask me it's yourself you've got to

learn to love, kiddo,' she said wisely.

Just before Christmas, Harry travelled up to see her. She booked him a room at the pub in the village and found herself getting more and more excited at the thought of seeing him as the date drew closer. She couldn't wait to hear all the news from Weston St Mary and, as they sat together in the bar parlour of the Dog and Duck in the village, he filled her in on all the news. Apparently, the government had ordered Bill to grow twenty acres of sunflowers next season. The seeds were to be used for fodder, he explained, and the stems for paper. Jack Deacon from the garage had been had up for selling red petrol and one of his customers had been the vicar! She was sad to hear that Jess, the old sheepdog had died. But she was horrified to hear that Meg Brown was back working for Bill again. She imagined her sparkling, pristine kitchen gradually deteriorating into the slum it had been before.

'Surely he could find someone better than Meg,' she said.

Harry shrugged. 'Bill just doesn't seem to care much any more,' he said. 'I reckon he misses you a lot more than he lets on.' He took her hand. 'That goes for me too. Oh!' He pulled an envelope out of his pocket. 'I almost forgot. Bill sent you this.'

Rose opened the crumpled envelope and found a Christmas card with a robin on the front. Inside, Bill had written in spidery handwriting, *With best wishes to Rose from William H. Peacock*. Her eyes filled with tears as she put the card carefully away in her bag. 'Will you thank him for me?' she said. 'I'll treasure this.'

They enjoyed their brief time together and Rose went with him to the station to see him off.

'You've only got to say the word and you could come back, you know,' he said as they stood on the draughty platform together.

'I know, Harry.' She stood on tiptoe to kiss his cheek. 'I'd love to come back to Weston St Mary, but it could make things awkward for me with the WLA. Besides, I like it here. I'm

getting experience with other things, sheep for instance. I'm looking forward to the lambing soon after Christmas.'

'You mean you still don't love me enough to marry me?'

Her heart tightened and she slipped her arms around his neck. 'Oh Harry, don't say it like that.'

'What then?'

'It's so hard for me to explain. I don't want to lose you, Harry.'

'Then marry me,' he said. He squeezed her hand. 'You can bet on one thing, Rose: I'll never give up trying. Like it or not, I'm yours for ever.'

As the train steamed into the station, she clung to him as they kissed goodbye.

'I'll come again as soon as I can,' he promised, leaning out of the train window and reaching for her hand.

She walked along the platform still holding his hand till the train's gathering speed forced her to let go. She waved until it disappeared round the bend in the line, then stood there, her heart heavy with sadness and longing. She worried about Bill, living alone in the farmhouse that was gradually disintegrating around him again, drinking himself into oblivion each night to dull the pain that would never go away. Her heart ached for Harry, knowing that she should make him give her up so that he could find another girl, because she didn't dare to let herself love him the way he deserved to be loved. Perhaps she would never love anyone until she found her mother and was able to ask all the questions that remained unanswered.

Rose threw herself into her work. The winter lambing was hard, exhausting work, but she enjoyed it. At the hostel things were never dull. The girls were a lively lot. One of them had a wind-up gramophone and they would play the few records they had over and over, singing along. The favourite was, 'You'll Never Know'. That one meant something special to

Rose, though she never confided her feelings to anyone except Nell.

Seeing the seasons come around was something she had never noticed in London. There it was either hot or cold, wet or dry, and every spring in the country to Rose was like a miracle of renewed life.

Aunt Bess wrote to say that her friend Grace had sold the village shop and that they were to retire and move to a bungalow close to the sea. There were letters from Harry. He wrote that Bill had had a bad winter with several bouts of severe bronchitis. He was taking a long time to recover and wasn't fit enough to do much work on the farm. He managed to visit her again at Easter, but after that there was too much to do on the farm for him to be spared.

The summer came in with a warm spell and in June came the exciting news about D-Day. The girls celebrated with home-made cider smuggled in by one of them from the farm she was working on. Every evening they would cluster round the wireless to listen to the news. At last it seemed as though the end of the war was in sight.

It was in October that the letter came. Rose found it waiting on her bunk when she came in from her day's work. She recognized Harry's writing and tore it open eagerly. But, on scanning the first lines, she sat down suddenly on her bunk, biting her lip with dismay.

I'm sorry to have to tell you that Bill died early yesterday morning, Harry wrote. *I don't know what will happen to the farm. He had no family, as you know. I suppose it will mean I'll have to look for another job and a new home. That sounds selfish, doesn't it, at such a time? But it's something that worries me a bit. I've been happy here. If you can get to the funeral, Rose, it's next Friday. I know he thought a lot of you. He was always talking about you.*

Rose put the letter down as the tears welled up and felt in her pocket for a handkerchief. Poor Bill. Had he died alone? She hoped not. Harry didn't say whether he had been in hospital or at home. Nell came in and saw at once that something was wrong.

'What's up, kiddo? Bad news?'

Rose explained, showing her Harry's letter. 'Do you think they'll let me have time off to go to the funeral?'

Nell snorted. 'Let you? You're going, kid. If they won't give you permission just go anyway and to hell with the consequences!'

Rose travelled down to Suffolk the following Friday morning and Harry met her at the station.

'What's going to happen to the farm?' she asked him.

'I've been looking after things as best I can,' Harry said. 'But I can't carry on much longer. I've been offered a job with a cottage over at Benham Market and it's too far to keep coming over to Weston.'

The church was full for the service and afterwards Rose and Harry stood side by side at the graveside, the nearest to family that Bill had had since he lost his beloved May and little Jenny. As her tears flowed Harry's arm went round her shoulders.

'He's with them now,' he whispered. 'Don't cry for him.'

As there was to be no funeral tea afterwards, Rose had intended to catch a late train back to Yorkshire, but as she left the churchyard with Harry a man stepped up to them.

'Excuse me. May I ask if you are Miss Rose Meadows?' he asked.

'Yes.' Rose looked up in surprise.

The man held out his hand. 'I am Reginald Garrod of Sutcliffe, Sutcliffe and Garrod, solicitors. May I speak to you for a moment?'

She glanced at Harry. 'I'm afraid I don't have time, Mr

Garrod. I have to catch a train back to Yorkshire in half an hour.'

The man cleared his throat. 'It is rather important, Miss Meadows,' he said. 'Is there any chance that you could postpone your return to Yorkshire?'

'Not really, you see—'

'It really is a matter of urgency.'

Harry intervened. 'Perhaps you'd better, Rose. If you're worried abut where to stay, I'm sure Sid would put you up for the night at The Grapes.'

Rose was bewildered. It seemed it was all being taken out of her hands. She looked from one to the other. 'Well, all right then – if you think so.'

Sid Tarrant agreed to put Rose up for the night and opened up his private room for them to talk. As Rose sat opposite the man in his dark suit and sober tie she wondered what on earth he could have to say to her. Harry had mysteriously disappeared, muttering something about coming back later.

Mr Garrod opened the briefcase he carried and took out a document. Then he took a pair of gold-rimmed spectacles out of his pocket and placed them on his nose. Rose's nerves were stretched almost to breaking point by the time he looked up at her over the rims of his glasses.

'This is Mr Peacock's Will,' he explained. 'And I have to tell you that you are named in it as the sole beneficiary.'

Rose swallowed hard. 'Wha— what does that mean?' she asked.

'It means that you inherit all that Mr Peacock owned.' He consulted the Will which he had spread out on the table. 'Comprising the farm known as Peacocks Farm, the farmhouse and furnishings; all buildings, livestock and machinery.' He cleared his throat. 'There is also the sum of fifty thousand pounds, invested at the Ipswich branch of Martin's Bank.' He took off his spectacles and gave Rose a tight little smile.

'It seems that you have inherited a farm, Miss Meadows.' He

took out a business card and passed it to her. 'I am sure you will need time to assimilate the complexities of your new position, but when you are ready to make a decision as to the future of the farm I shall be at your disposal.'

CHAPTER FOUR

ROSE RETURNED to Yorkshire still reeling from the unexpected news of her legacy. She kept it to herself for a few days, but the following Sunday afternoon as she and Nell lay on their bunks alone at the hostel she confided in her friend.

'You're *kidding*!' Nell leaned over the edge of her bunk to stare incredulously into Rose's face. 'Blimey! Fifty thousand smackers and then whatever you'll get for the farm. You're rich, you jammy little beggar!'

'I'm not going to sell the farm,' Rose announced.

Nell dropped to the floor and stood staring at her. '*Not sell it?* What the hell are you going to do then?'

'Run it,' Rose said simply. 'I'll need the money to put everything in order again. I'm going to be a farmer.'

'Are you mad? You know what the life is like. Think what you could do with all that cash?' Nell sat down on the end of Rose's bunk. 'Listen, kid, I don't think you've given this enough thought. Just think – you could live a life of ease. Going to the theatre, buying clothes. You could winter in Monte Carlo –just like Anna Neagle in the films.'

Rose laughed. 'I'm no Anna Neagle! Can you imagine me living like that? Peacocks is the only place that ever felt like a real home to me. Bill understood that. I believe it's why he left the farm to me. The last thing I want to do is let him down and

sell it to some stranger.'

'It can hardly matter to him now, can it?' Nell sniffed. 'Oh, well, it's your funeral, you've got to suit yourself. But if you ask me you're off your rocker!'

'That's a shame.' Rose smiled. 'I was just going to ask you to come and spend Christmas with me. You won't want to do that if you think I'm barmy, will you?'

Nell grinned. 'Just you try and bloody well stop me. I'm going to have to come and see what it is that makes this Peacocks of yours so bloomin' attractive! And I wouldn't mind betting it's got more than a bit to do with that gorgeous hunk called Harry. Can't wait to meet *him*!'

Rose wrote to Mr Garrod to ask him to go ahead with whatever arrangements were necessary and gave in her notice to the WLA. She also wrote to Harry, asking him to move back into his cottage and take the job of farm manager. To her dismay and disappointment she received a rather stiff letter of refusal by return of post. Surely Harry didn't resent her for inheriting the farm? It even occurred to her that he might have been expecting to inherit it himself, but she pushed the thought aside. As far as she knew Harry didn't have a resentful bone in his body. He hadn't even shown any real resentment for the way his brother had treated him.

In mid-November, she said goodbye to Nell and all her other friends at the hostel in Yorkshire and took the train to Ipswich. She had written hopefully to Harry to tell him what time she would be arriving and although she hadn't asked, she half expected him to be at the station to meet her. When he didn't appear she took the bus to Weston St Mary, recalling with nostalgia that time four years ago when she had first arrived as the new landgirl.

She hauled her heavy case the mile from the bus stop in the village, feeling depressed and wishing Harry would come along on his tractor as he had that other time. Suddenly she realized

that things might never be the same and she wondered for the first time if she had made the right decision.

As she let herself in at the little-used front door of the farmhouse with the key Mr Garrod had posted to her, her heart sank even lower. She had expected it to have a neglected air but she wasn't prepared for the atmosphere that assailed her senses as she stood in the empty hall. The stone flags beneath her feet were beaded with moisture, the furniture dulled by a greyish bloom and in places the ancient flocked wallpaper hung in mouldy strips. A pall of musty-smelling damp and decay hung over the place and a huge lump rose in her throat as she stood looking round her. She said aloud, 'I'm here Bill. I'll never forget what you've done for me and I'll make Peacocks a home again, I promise. Everything's going to be all right.'

Over the weeks that followed, Rose worked as she had never worked in her life before, scrubbing every room and trying to restart the heartbeat of the old house and regain the order she had created before. Lighting fires in every room and throwing the windows open to the fresh air soon dispelled the musty smell and Mrs Maitland at the village store unearthed some tins of coloured distemper for her that had been hidden away at the back of her storeroom since before the war. Rose set to work stripping the walls of the main rooms of the crumbling paper and painting them in pastel shades.

Since Bill's death, Harry, Fred and Jack had been carrying out the necessary tasks and caring for the livestock, but to Rose's dismay Harry stopped coming after her arrival. Both the elderly farm hands made it clear to her that they wanted to retire as soon as other arrangements could be made and she conceded that it was only fair. Both had been past retiring age for some time. Meanwhile, to help her out they took it in turns to do the early milking after which Rose would make breakfast for them in the kitchen.

One morning as Fred sat tucking into his eggs and bacon, she

plucked up the courage to ask him about Harry.

'Fred – is there some reason why Harry never comes up to the farm any more?'

Fred paused, a forkful of bacon halfway to his mouth. 'Couldn't rightly say, miss. Reckon he's kept too busy over at Benham. Farmer Jarvis has always been one to expect his money's worth out of his workers.'

'But he must get some free time,' Rose said. 'We were always such good friends. I thought he'd at least have been to see me.'

Fred shrugged and looked embarrassed. 'Not for me to say,' he muttered.

'I wish you'd say if you know something, Fred,' Rose said. 'If it's something I've done I'd like to try and put it right.'

Fred paused. 'Maybe he reckons you're a cut above him these days like.'

'Oh, what *nonsense!*' Rose said, so vehemently that Fred looked up at her in surprise. 'Look, do you see him at all?'

'He still comes over The Grapes most Saturday evenings for a game of darts and a pint or two.'

'Then will you tell him I'd like to see him, please? No, tell him I need to see him. Please, Fred.'

'Right. I'll tell him next time I see him, miss. I can't promise anything, mind.'

Rose's first priority was the farm. As it was winter there wasn't a lot to do and the livestock had been depleted during Bill's last year. Bill had given up his sheep when the government requisitioned more than half his land. Now there was only a herd of about a dozen cows a few pigs and the hens. Fred and Jack had promised to stay on until she had found suitable replacements, but it wasn't easy to find farm hands with men still away at the war. At last she found two young men recently repatriated from prisoner-of-war camps in Germany. Neither was as fit as he might have been, their health undermined by what they had been through, but both were keen and willing and at least they were familiar with farm work. Rose helped

them get in the crop of winter vegetables and sow the winter wheat, wishing as she struggled with Bill's old Ferguson tractor that Harry was here to help.

Although Fred assured Rose that he had passed on her message to Harry, he did not get in touch or come to see her, and by early mid-December she had resigned herself to the fact that he wasn't coming. Then, one Sunday afternoon when she was shutting the hens up for the night something made her look up. The light was fading and a dark figure standing by the rickyard gate made her start.

'Who is it?' she called. 'What do you want?'

'It's only me – Harry.' He started to walk towards her. 'Fred Beasley said you wanted to see me about something.'

She felt her heart quicken as she fastened the henhouse securely and brushed her hands on her apron. 'Harry – please, come in. It's cold out here.'

In the kitchen, Harry looked round, noticing the newly whitewashed walls and the gleaming range. 'Looks a sight better than the last time I was here,' he observed. 'You've been working hard. But then it's yours now.'

'I think I worked as hard when it wasn't,' she said, the barbed remark stinging her. 'It's good to see you, Harry. Why haven't you been before?' She watched as his mouth set in the familiar stubborn line she remembered. It was clear that he was uncomfortable in her company and she wondered why. 'It's manners to wait till you're asked.'

'I did write and tell you I was coming.' He simply shrugged and, knowing that they could beat about the bush all afternoon she decided to be direct. 'Harry, do you resent me for being left Peacocks?'

'*No!*' His eyes met hers with a startled expression and his cheeks coloured hotly. 'Why should you think that?'

'You've been funny with me ever since Bill's funeral. What was I supposed to think?'

'It's just. . . .' He shook his head. 'Things are different now.'

'How – *different?*'

'We were equal once – both working for Bill on the farm. Now you own it.'

'And I offered you the job of manager.'

'I know.'

'So are you saying you don't want to work for a woman? Or is it just because it's me?'

Harry shook his head angrily. 'Don't pretend you can't see, Rose! It's like I said: it's different now. Everything between us has changed.' He looked at his feet. 'I understand now why you wouldn't marry me.'

'What do you understand? What are you getting at, Harry? Do you think I said no to your proposal because I was *planning* for Bill to leave me the farm?'

He raised his chin defiantly. 'Some might see it that way.'

She was shocked. 'Couldn't you *tell* what a shock it was to me on the day of the funeral? Did you think that was all an act?'

'How should I know?'

Rose swallowed hard at the hurt that rose chokingly in her throat. 'And that's what you truly believe, is it?'

'I don't *want* to believe it. But that doesn't change anything. Now you're an employer and I'm an employee. We're—'

'Yes, you said – *different*,' Rose said bitterly. 'I'm the same as I've always been, Harry; it's you who have changed.'

'It was you who said no when I asked you to marry me,' he reminded her. 'I take it that hasn't changed either.'

'Suppose it had?' she challenged.

'Then folks would think I'd married you to get the farm. Anyway, you made it pretty plain before that you didn't want me.'

'I see. So your offer is withdrawn?' When he didn't reply she asked, 'How many other people in the village believe I used my womanly whiles to get Bill to leave the farm to me?'

'No one's suggesting you did that.'

70

'Aren't they? It seems to me that's exactly what you're suggesting. And if it's the general feeling I'd rather know.'

'I haven't discussed it with anyone, but you know how folks talk.'

'I'm learning.' The silence between them filled the room like a fog. 'Well, I suppose there's nothing left to say,' she said at last. 'Obviously I'm not the sort of woman you took me for and you don't want to know me any more.'

'I never said that. It's just – I think with things being as they are, maybe it's best we each know our place.' At the door he hesitated, turning towards her again. 'But if you ever want me – ever have need of my skills I mean, you only have to send word.'

'Thank you, but I don't believe I shall be troubling you.' Bristling with hurt and anger, Rose brushed past him and opened the door. The moment he had passed through it she slammed it shut and leaned against it, hot tears stinging her eyes. '*Damn* you, Harry Owen!' she said between clenched teeth. 'Hell will freeze over before I ask *you* for any help!'

As Christmas approached there was a lot to do. Nell was due to arrive on the 20 December and Rose wanted everything to be spic and span. Having a friend to stay in her own home meant more to her than she could say.

She had prepared the little room at the back of the house for Nell, the one that had once belonged to Bill's little daughter. Very carefully she packed the child's toys and clothes and put them away before cleaning the room, airing and making up the bed.

On the day of Nell's arrival, she hired the village taxi and went to meet her in style at the station. Back at the farm, Nell was taken on a conducted tour. She looked around her critically.

'It's a nice old house,' she said. 'But it's very old fashioned. What will you do with all this old furniture? Some of it looks as

71

if it came out of the ark!'

'Even if it was possible to buy new it'd look out of place here,' Rose said. 'What it really needs is some even older pieces.'

'Even *older*?' Nell stared at her in horror.

'In the deeds it says that this house was built in 1769,' Rose told her. 'So I thought it would look nice if I got hold of some furniture that old too. The kind of thing that would have been here then.'

'Well, rather you than me,' Nell remarked. 'If I was you I'd start by putting in some lecky and a bathroom and some proper running water. Replace that old range with one of them Agas like they had at the hostel. Hot bath whenever you want one. Think of the work you'd save too.'

Rose laughed. 'I daresay you're right. I'll have to look into all that. There's so much to do and a lot of it is going to have to wait till the war's over. Oh, Nell, I'm looking forward so much to making it nice.'

Nell wrinkled her nose. 'Well, I think you're mad! All that hard slog! Up at the crack of dawn to do the milking. Out in all weathers, trudging through the mud in your wellies. I'd have thought you'd have had enough of all that. With what you've got you could get a nice little semi in the suburbs. Close to all the dance halls and cinemas. If I was you I'd think carefully, pet. You're only young once. Out here you're going to be buried alive.'

But only the next afternoon Nell was to be proved wrong. The girls were coming downstairs when Nell looked out of the landing window and gave a little scream.

'There's a feller coming up the drive on a horse!' she squeaked. 'All done up in a hacking jacket and breeches. Proper gent. Not bad-looking either.' She turned to Rose. 'Not that Harry, is it?'

Rose joined her at the window in time to see the man dismount and approach the door. 'No, it's not Harry. I don't know who it is.'

'Shall I answer the door and pretend to be the maid?' Nell giggled. And before Rose had time to reply she had run down-stairs and was opening the door. From the bend in the stairs Rose heard a deep, educated voice say, 'Good morning. Miss Meadows?'

'I'll just see if she's at home, sir,' Nell said. 'Would you like to come into the drawing-room and wait?' She ushered the man in then joined Rose on the stairs.

'Says his name's Richard Beech,' she hissed. 'Comb your hair and put a bit of lippy on. He's a bit of all right.'

'What does he want?' Rose asked.

'What the hell does it matter? Go and flutter your eyelashes at him, kid. You'll soon find out.'

In the drawing-room, Richard Beech was standing with his back to the fireplace. He was a tall, well-built man with finely chiselled features and greying hair. When she entered the room he smiled warmly.

'Miss Meadows. I thought it was time I called and made myself known to you.' He held out his hand. 'Richard Beech.'

She shook his hand. 'Please sit down, Mr Beech. It's good of you to call. So you are the squire.'

He laughed. 'Hardly. All that is a bit archaic nowadays. Most of my land has been sold off over the years. Death duties and all that. Though I still have a fair estate to manage. I hear you intend to stay here and run Peacocks yourself.'

'That's right.'

'Very commendable.' He cleared his throat. 'You have a – fiancé in the forces perhaps? Someone who will be coming home to help you?'

'No. I'm hoping to manage by myself.'

He looked surprised. 'Really? You're very brave.' He looked at her. 'You're sure you'll be able to cope? It won't be easy, you know.'

'I've been used to farm work since the beginning of the war,' she told him. 'I first came here as a landgirl.'

'Quite. But if I might say so, it's a far cry from owning and managing a farm.'

She felt her hackles rising. 'I feel quite confident that I can do it,' she said firmly.

'I'm sure you can. All I'm saying is that if ever you want to sell Peacocks I would be happy to make you an offer. I knew, of course, that Bill Peacock had no family and I quite thought. . . .' He left the sentence unfinished. 'The northernmost boundary of your land borders mine, you know.'

'I know,' Rose said. 'The twenty-acre field, you mean. It gets so boggy in the winter that half of it is under water. It's because of your stream. If you were to pipe it I could probably grow another ten acres' more wheat up there.'

Richard Beech's eyebrows shot up. 'Really? I shall ask my manager to look into it at once.' He smiled. 'We must stick together, we farmers. Now that it looks as though the war will soon be over the government will surely have plans for us and we must be ready for them. I know that much of Peacock's land was requisitioned by the government. Remind me of how many acres you have now.'

'Only two hundred. So obviously I intend to get the very best I can out of it,' Rose told him. His patronizing attitude was beginning to irritate her. 'It's mainly arable, but I plan to increase the dairy herd next year. And perhaps go in for more intensive poultry.'

'I see. Well, I wish you the best of luck.' He stood up and she suddenly remembered her duty as a hostess. 'I'm sorry Mr Beech, can I offer you something – a cup of tea?'

'Thank you, no. This is only a flying visit and I'm forgetting the real reason for it. It occurred to me when I was out riding that you might be interested in a little party I'm giving to see in the New Year. May I send you an invitation?'

Rose blushed. 'Well I – don't know many people here yet.'

'Then this would be an ideal opportunity for you to meet them, don't you think? I'll ask my secretary to run over with an

invitation for you tomorrow.' He stood up. 'Now I'd better be going. I rode my mount quite hard so I mustn't let him get chilled. Good day, Miss Meadows. I hope we shall meet again soon.'

Sure enough next day Rose received the invitation to attend a New Year's Eve party at Weston Manor hosted by Mr Richard Beech. At the breakfast table, an impressed Nell ran a thumb over the embossed print.

'Well, well! Looks like you're about to start moving in elite circles now, kid. Will your Harry be there?'

'I shouldn't think so. And he's not *my* Harry.'

'OK. Pardon me I'm sure, for askin'.' Nell looked at her. 'I was hoping to meet him. Don't tell me you and him have fallen out?'

'He doesn't want to know me now that I'm Peacocks' owner,' Rose said.

'I see. How did that go down?' Nell peered closely at her friend. 'It hurt, didn't it? I can see it did. Well, never mind him and his stupid pride. You've got other fish to fry now.' She looked critically at her friend. 'But we're going to have to take you in hand first though. Get something done about your hair for a start. I don't reckon you've had it cut since last summer. And the decorating and carrot-digging hasn't done a lot for your hands. Then there's the question of what you're going to wear. You can't go in brown overalls and your wellies!'

Rose shook her head. 'Oh, I think I'll just say I can't go. I didn't take to his lordship all that much. Patronizing and over-bearing.'

'What you mean is that he made you feel small. I could see that right off, and we're not having it!' Nell said decisively. 'You're going to that do or my name's not Nell Sutton!'

'But what kind of people will be there?' Rose protested. 'They'll all be so – so upper class! I won't know how to talk to them – what to say.'

'They'll only be farmers. You know about farming, don't you?' Nell laughed. 'Come on, kid. Show 'em what you're made of! You're as good as any of them. After the war things are gonna be different when it comes to class, you mark my words. It's gonna be them that *do*, not them that *are* that matter.' She got up from the table. 'Come on, kiddo. We're going into Ipswich right now to get you sorted. I'm really looking forward to this. Nothing I like more'n spending other folks' money!'

Ipswich was bustling with late Christmas shoppers and Rose found herself pulled along by Nell who, now that she had the bit between her teeth had no intention of taking no for an answer. Outside the smartest hairdresser's in town she paused.

'Mmm. This one looks about right.'

'It looks terribly expensive and I'll never get an appointment this close to Christmas,' Rose said. But Nell took her arm and dragged her inside.

'If you don't ask you don't get,' she said, marching purposefully up to the reception desk.

As luck would have it there had been a cancellation and Rose was ushered along to a cubicle. Nell hovered in the background as the hairdresser settled Rose in the chair and draped her in the protective cape.

'What did madam have in mind?' the girl asked, lifting the heavy blonde hair and twisting it this way and that between her fingers.

'Short,' Nell said. 'You know, like Ingrid Bergman's in "For Whom The Bell Tolls".'

Rose's shocked eyes met Nell's through the mirror. '*Oh!* I don't think. . . .'

But the hairdresser was nodding approvingly. 'A bubble cut would really suit you,' she said. 'Your hair does have some natural movement and if it was cut really short it would spring into the shape nicely. What do you say?'

'She says *yes*,' Nell put in.

Rose gave up, closed her eyes and listened apprehensively as the scissors snip-snipped through her hair. When at last she opened them and looked in the mirror she gave an involuntary gasp of surprise. The short crop emphasized her high cheek-bones and delicate jaw-line. The eyes that looked back at her through the mirror looked wide with astonishment. The hair-dresser had been right. Relieved of the weight the hair curled close to her head and framed her face in elfin tendrils. Nell was beaming at her.

'There. What did I tell you? You're gonna knock 'em dead at that party, kid.' She took Rose's arm. 'Come on, we've got to find you the right frock now.'

They found a smart little shop in the same street as the hair-dresser's and there in the window Nell spied exactly the kind of dress she had in mind. With a squeak of excitement she grasped Rose's hand and pulled her over to the window.

'Oh my God, look at that. It was *made* for you!'

Rose looked. In the small window was a single dress draped tastefully over an antique chair, its wide skirt spread out. The tiny black velvet bodice was held up by a single diagonal diamante strap and the full skirt sprang out from a tiny waist to just below the knee.'

'It's much too grand,' Rose said.

'No it's not. It's got a short skirt,' Nell argued. 'So it can't be called a formal evening dress. Cocktail is what they call it. It's just right for this do at the manor.'

But Rose was shaking her head. 'I don't know. . . .'

'Well, I do. Trust me. I don't read all them fashion maga-zines for nothing. At least come and try it on.' Nell was dragging her towards the shop door. 'Come on. And don't say you haven't got enough clothing coupons, because I've got all mine.'

Half an hour later, they were on their way to the bus station, Rose carrying a shiny bag with the name of the shop on it. She still felt apprehensive. Never in her life had she paid as much

for a single garment and she had certainly never worn anything as glamorous as the dress. She felt dazed, still unsure of how Nell had talked her into buying it.

The other girl's enthusiasm had been infectious. 'You look smashing,' she'd said, her eyes shining as Rose emerged from the fitting-room in the dress to stand apprehensively before the cheval mirror. 'You've got to have it. You'd be mad not to.'

'Have you seen the price?' Rose whispered. But Nell waved away her doubts.

'What's the use of money if you can't enjoy spending it? The best of it is that you won't need any jewellery. Now – what about shoes?'

Shoes were found to match the dress by which time Rose had given up arguing. Back at the farm, alone in her room, she put the dress on a hanger and hung it on the outside of the wardrobe, standing back to look at it with trepidation. She had known that her life was changing when she moved back to Peacocks but it was only this afternoon when she stood before the shop mirror wearing that dress that she realized that a whole new future was opening up to her. The thought frankly terrified her.

Nell had to return to Yorkshire on the day after Boxing Day. Rose went with her to the station to see her off. Standing on the platform, Nell hugged her friend warmly. 'Thanks for a lovely Christmas, pet,' she said. 'I'm gonna miss you. Think of me up to me eyes in muck-spreading when you're hob-nobbing with the elite,' she joked. 'And don't forget to write and tell me all about the party. I want to hear everything, mind, from the other guests and what they wore, the eats and drinks. I bet there'll be caviar and champagne.'

'Don't,' Rose said, her stomach quaking. 'I'll be too nervous to eat anything anyway. But I will write and tell you all about it, I promise. I just wish you were coming too.'

'Me?' Nell laughed. 'The only way I'd be at a do like that would be washing up in the kitchen.'

'That's not fair. You know so much more than I do. You've got a natural flair,' Rose told her.

'No use having the flair without the money to back it up, pet,' Nell said good-naturedly.

'Oh, Nell, you make me feel guilty.'

Nell gave her hand a squeeze. 'Guilty nothing. Listen. I haven't said so before, but I really admire you for what you're doing. It takes real guts to take on a farm single-handed.'

'You said I was mad,' Rose reminded her.

'Yeah, well I still think so, but that doesn't stop me admiring you sticking to your guns. You deserve to have that money, but don't forget to have some fun with it too, pet, will you?'

The train steamed into the station and Nell began to collect up her belongings. She boarded the train and leaned out of the window. 'When this war's over it's people like you, with guts and determination, who are gonna run things. Not the bloated plutocrats. Just you wait and see.'

Rose waved till the train was out of sight then turned away with a heavy heart. She was going to miss Nell with her home-spun philosophy and her earthy sense of humour.

Rose had ordered the village taxi for nine o'clock on the evening of the 31st. The invitation said eight o'clock, but Nell had advised her that it would be better not to arrive too early. When she was ready she stood before the mirror in the bedroom, her knees knocking. What to wear over the dress to travel to the manor had been a problem. The only coat she possessed was a serviceable navy gabardine mackintosh, and that was hardly suitable. But during her clearing out she had found an embroidered shawl that had probably belonged to Bill's wife. Nell had pounced on it, proclaiming it to be 'just the ticket'. Together they washed and ironed it, delighted to see the colours come up brilliantly against the black silky material.

As the taxi drove up the long tree-lined drive of Weston Manor, the elderly taxi driver reminisced. 'Before the war

79

this place used to be ablaze with lights on New Year's Eve,' he said. 'The cream of county society would be invited. Fireworks – dance bands – the lot.' He sighed. 'That was when the old squire and his missis were alive, o' course. Still, maybe by next year, the war'll be over and Mr Richard will get wed and start pushin' the boat out again like his dad used to.'

Rose asked him to return for her just after midnight and he drove away, leaving her standing at the bottom of the steps feeling lost and very small.

A maid in uniform opened the door to her and took her shawl. 'Who shall I say has arrived?'

'Miss Rose Meadows,' Rose said. Her knees had begun to tremble again at the thought of entering a room full of strange people, but at that moment Richard Beech himself appeared and came towards her smiling. He looked very distinguished in his dinner jacket and black bow tie.

'Miss Meadows! Rose, how good of you to come.' His eyes swept over her appreciatively. 'And how delightful you look.' He offered his arm. 'Do come and meet the rest of my guests.'

When she first entered the large room, Rose was dismayed to see that most of the women were wearing full-length evening gowns. But, on closer inspection, she saw that most of them were far from new and – most probably in Nell's opinion – hopelessly out of vogue. Richard Beech escorted her round the room, introducing her to everyone and she soon realized that most of his guests were wealthy farmers or prosperous businessmen and their wives. She found the men pleasant and courteous while the women tended to be aloof and condescending.

'So you were a member of the Women's Land Army, Miss Meadows,' a middle-aged woman in a purple bias-cut dress said, looking at her as though she half expected her to have straw in her hair. 'And what did you do before that?'

'I helped my aunt to run a pub in the East End,' Rose said

truthfully. 'And I worked in the local Co-op.'

The woman laughed delicately. 'Oh, I see.'

'What did you do?' Rose countered. 'Before you were married, I mean.'

The woman blushed and turned away. 'Well, *really*!'

Rose felt a hand on her arm and looked round to see Richard smiling down at her. 'Do come and have a drink.'

As they moved away, Rose said quietly, 'I'm sorry but I think I've just offended one of your guests.'

Richard chuckled. 'I heard. That was Susan Gerrard. Her husband owns a large cattle feed mill.' He bent his head to whisper, 'She was a parlour maid before the war – until she married her employer's son. But that was twenty years ago and she doesn't care to be reminded of it.'

Rose blushed. 'I'm sorry, Mr Beech. But she did ask me first.'

'Don't worry about it. And perhaps you could call me Richard now that we're close neighbours.' He smiled as he handed her a glass of wine. 'Perhaps you'd like to see the house?'

Weston Manor was a beautiful house with richly furnished and well-proportioned rooms. Richard took her to the far end of the hall and opened a door that led into a large empty room that ran the entire length of the house.

'This is where my parents used to give parties,' he told her. 'It has always been known rather grandly as the ballroom. It's far too splendid for these days of austerity.'

One end of the room had tall windows that reached the floor, curtained with rich, gold velvet curtains. There was a fine, white marble fireplace with a gilded over-mantel and at the far end of the room Rose could make out the shape of a grand piano, shrouded in dust sheets.

'My mother used to play beautifully,' Richard said, following her gaze.

'It's a beautiful house. When was it built?'

'1710, during the reign of Queen Anne.'

'It's very elegant.' Rose looked up at the high moulded ceiling and the crystal chandelier that hung from the centre, its splendour reflected in the mirrors. 'Peacocks is old too,' she told him. 'Of course, it's only a farmhouse, not built for gracious living like this; 1769, is the date in the deeds. That makes it—'

'Georgian,' he supplied. 'George III to be exact. You won't go putting in too many mod. cons., will you?'

Rose blushed, annoyed that he should assume that she was ignorant and insensitive. 'I see you have electricity,' she remarked. 'And I'm sure there must be a bathroom somewhere, if not two. There must be running water and something more modern than a fire to cook on as well, I shouldn't wonder.'

He had the grace to look abashed. '*Ah!* I'm sorry. I wasn't aware that Peacocks didn't have those basics.'

'Oil lamps, wash stands; cooking on an old range. There's a tin bath hanging on a nail in the wash house, The nearest apology for a mod. con. is a pump over the scullery sink which at least saves me from having to fetch water from the yard.'

Richard looked shocked. 'My dear girl! I had no idea things were so archaic over there. You're practically in the stone age! You must let me advise you on the best workmen in the neighbourhood. And now I think we'd better rejoin my guests before they send someone to look for us.

The furniture in the large drawing-room had been pushed back against the walls and the carpet rolled back for dancing. After the buffet supper, which was laid out in the dining-room, Richard put records on his radiogram and several couples began to circle the floor to dance music. Rose danced with an elderly farmer; after that with a man who told her he owned a farm machinery plant in Ipswich. As the music stopped she glanced surreptitiously at her watch and saw that it was almost half past eleven. Another half-hour and she could go home, she told herself with relief. This really wasn't

her kind of entertainment at all. She went in search of a glass of lemonade and, as she came back into the room, a favourite of hers was being played. 'You'll Never Know'. It had been a great favourite with the girls at the hostel and suddenly she felt a wave of nostalgia, remembering how they would all sing along to it. Would she ever fit into her new life, she wondered? She didn't belong among people like this and they knew it. But would she ever be accepted in the village community either?

'You haven't danced with me yet. May I?' Richard took her hand and led her on to the floor. He was a good dancer, holding her firmly and moving with confidence. He smelled pleasantly of aromatic pipe tobacco and some spicy kind of cologne.

After they had danced in silence for a few minutes, he looked down at her and said quietly, 'You were looking a little pensive just now. I rather sense that you haven't altogether enjoyed this evening.'

She looked up at him. 'Oh *no*! I mean, yes, I have. It's just—'

'All a bit strange for you?' he guessed, drawing her close again. 'I understand. And of course most of the people here this evening are much older than you. This is the kind of party I need to give for business reasons,' he explained. 'And because I need to return hospitality.' He looked at her again. 'I do hope it won't put you off accepting invitations from me in the future.'

She shrugged, shaking her head slightly.

'How are you getting home?' he asked.

'I came in Mr Gidding's taxi. He's fetching me just after midnight.'

'Why don't you let me telephone him not to come?' he said. 'I'll happily run you home so that you can stay on a little later. People tend to relax more after midnight.'

Rose bit her lip. 'I think I'd rather leave the arrangement as it is,' she said. 'I have to be up early in the morning. Midnight is really very late for me.'

'Then perhaps you'll let me call on you at the farm again,' he

suggested. 'We could talk more easily if there weren't so many people present.'

She wondered what there could possibly be for them to talk about. 'Perhaps,' she said noncommittally. 'The farm and the house keep me very busy.'

'Exactly.' He looked thoughtful. 'Rose, it occurs to me that you have an enormous task ahead of you. I wonder if you realize quite how difficult the months ahead will be.'

'You think I won't cope?' There was a hint of challenge in her voice that did not escape his notice. He smiled.

'I can see that you're a very determined young woman. But don't be too proud to ask for help, Rose. There's a lot I can do to help you. I hope you'll allow me to.'

'You're very kind. Thank you – for what you've just offered and for inviting me to your party. I really have enjoyed myself very much.'

The large grandfather clock in the hall began to chime the hour. Someone turned off the music and everyone fell silent. Then, at the first stroke of midnight a cheer went up and everyone began kissing each other and shaking hands, then all joined hands for 'Auld Lang Syne'. Rose was about to slip quietly away and find her wrap when she found herself firmly held by the shoulders.

'I have a feeling that 1945 is going to be a very special year.' Richard smiled down at her. Then, to her surprise, he bent and kissed her lightly on the lips.

'Happy New Year, Rose.'

CHAPTER FIVE

T HE FIRST weeks of the New Year were busy for Rose. There was so much to do. Richard had been right when he had suggested that she hadn't realized quite how much. In the end she gave in and reluctantly accepted his offer of help after which things began to move quite fast. By the time the first spring lambs were in the fields and the winter wheat was sprouting, the house was beginning to look and feel more like a twentieth-century home.

The two new farm hands, Geoff Green and Peter Palmer were proving to be a good find. Both were young and strong and, as the weeks passed, the health and vitality that had been impaired by their imprisonment returned to normal. Geoff still lived with his elderly parents in the village, but in March Peter married Irene, his fiancée and Rose offered them the cottage that had been Harry's. In return, Irene was happy to help out in the house, leaving Rose time to cope with the accounts and the seemingly endless paperwork that the ministry demanded.

As the weeks went by Rose listened eagerly to the news each day on her radio. After almost six long weary years it looked as though the allies were going to win through. The war really would be over soon. As blackouts came down spirits rose in anticipation of the end. In March there was news that the allied forces were closing on Berlin. British and American troops

liberated the ghastly Nazi death camps. Mussolini and his cohorts were tracked down and executed. Then news broke that Hitler had committed suicide. There was a new, relaxed feel to life. Now it was surely only a matter of time.

In April, Rose went to her first cattle market, hoping to buy more cows. She would have appreciated Harry's help and advice but would have died rather than ask him. They had seen each other occasionally in the village since that December day when he had come to the farm. When they met they passed the time of day politely, each as stubborn as the other, neither of them making any move to renew their friendship. Once again Richard offered his help, suggesting that he sent his own cowman to the market with her, but this time Rose was adamant, knowing that in this she must make a stand. If she knew nothing about building and by-laws, at least she had learned a little about livestock.

When the bidding began in the cattle ring, Rose plucked up her courage. She was nervous, surrounded by older and experienced male farmers who nudged one another and eyed her with vague amusement as she stood on tiptoe to see the animals for sale. But some of Harry's experience had rubbed off on her and when two heifers and two cows in calf were paraded round the ring she cleared her throat and bid for them in as strong a voice as she could muster A few minutes later she found to her delight that they were hers.

Later, as she ate a sandwich lunch in a nearby pub, one of the older men whom she recognized as coming from a neighbouring farm, came up beside her.

'You chose well there, Miss Meadows, if you don't mind me sayin' so,' he said. 'Come early summer you'll have six beasts for the price of four. Good milkers too by the look on 'em. Well done, lass.'

His words made her blush with pleasure and, encouraged by the compliment she went back to the market after lunch and bought two dozen pullets for the new hen house she'd had built,

riding home on the bus afterwards with a feeling of satisfaction and achievement.

Nell kept in touch regularly with letters and had promised to visit on her next leave, but suddenly on 13 May the announcement came that Germany had surrendered unconditionally. The war was over. Nell wrote to say that she would be leaving the WLA and was thinking of getting a job in a factory in her native Liverpool, but she promised to come and spend some time with Rose at Peacocks before that happened.

When the taxi dropped Nell off in the yard the first week in June she stood staring around her in amazement. 'I can't believe it,' she told Rose,who ran out to meet her. 'Last time I was here all this was a sea of mud. And just look at the house. It's been painted.'

Rose laughed. 'That's not all. I've been busy trying to drag Peacocks into the twentieth century since I took over. Wait till you see inside. No more washstands and oil lamps. We've got running water now and a proper bathroom.' She tucked her arm through Nell's. 'There's an Aga in the kitchen and your precious 'lecky' in every room.'

Nell was taken on a conducted tour of the house, exclaiming as she went, 'How did you do it?'

'I got the Aga and the bathroom suite from a sale of equipment saved from bombed-out houses. I heard about that from Richard Beech.'

'What about the tradesmen though?' Nell asked. 'Everyone says how hard it is to get anything done these days.'

'Richard lent me some men from the estate. He helped me get planning permission too. That was something I hadn't thought of. He's on the local council, you see.'

'Oh! I *see* all right.' Nell's eyes widened. 'The fog's clearing now. But I thought you didn't go much for him. You said in the letter you wrote about the New Year party—'

'I know,' Rose interrupted. 'It's true that I didn't enjoy the

party. For a while I thought I'd never fit in here. I don't seem to have much in common with anyone. But Richard has been so kind and helpful; I don't know what I'd have done without him. I've paid for all the work, mind,' she added quickly 'He's already done more than enough and I don't want to be beholden to anyone.'

They were sitting at the kitchen table over tea. Nell took a sip of hers, smiling sceptically at Rose. 'Mmm. Interesting. So, you see a lot of him, do you?'

'He drops in sometimes when he's out riding.'

'Sometimes? Like what – every day?'

'Oh no. More like once a week – even less. And don't look at me like that, Nell Sutton. He's a fellow farmer and a neighbour. That's all – although. . . .'

'But he'd like to be more. Am I right?'

'Well – perhaps.'

'But you don't fancy him?'

Rose sighed. 'Maybe I'm being ungrateful, but I can't help feeling that he's just waiting for me to trip up and fail.'

'If he thinks that why is he going out of his way to help you get on your feet?'

'He offered to buy Peacocks from me when I first came here. Maybe he thinks I'll sell if he's nice to me, and he wouldn't want to take on a run-down place, would he?'

Nell raised an eyebrow. 'That's a bit cynical, isn't it?'

'Oh, all right, I daresay you're right. You know me. I've always been slow to trust people.'

'What about Harry? See much of him, do you?'

Rose shrugged. 'Not much.'

Seeing Rose's closed expression Nell decided that Harry was a tricky subject. 'Well, by the look of things you've been going at it flat out since Christmas,' she said. 'You must be about ready for a bit of a break. We're gonna have some fun while I'm here, kid. And I don't want to hear any arguments!'

Rose laughed. 'All right. Whatever you say.'

'So, what do you normally do in your spare time?' Nell asked. 'I suppose Richard takes you out to posh restaurants.'

'No; he does not.'

'But you've been out with him.'

'No. Oh, he's asked me but there never seems to be any time.'

Nell's eyes narrowed. 'You haven't been out at all, have you?'

'Not since Richard's party.'

Nell stared at her. '*New Year*! That's months ago! What do you do with your evenings?'

'Fall asleep mainly,' Rose answered with a wry smile. 'It's early to bed and early to rise in the country.'

'Well, I know all about that, but it never stopped us in the past, did it? You're entitled to some fun as well.'

'It was easy when it was a bunch of us girls all together,' Rose said. 'It's not so easy to go into a pub alone. Women who do that round here get a reputation.'

'Well, now that I'm here we'll have to change all that,' Nell told her. 'You know what they say about all work and no play! What do you say we give that village pub the once over?'

Rose found that The Grapes was much the same as she remembered it. Sid, the landlord greeted her warmly.

'Wondered when we'd see you in here,' he said, as he served their drinks. 'But from what I hear you've been too busy up at the farm.'

Rose laughed. 'News travels fast in Weston.'

'Does that.' Sid passed the drinks across the bar. 'By the sound of it Peacocks don't know what's hit it since the new mistress took over.'

As they settled at a table near the fireplace, Nell raised an eyebrow. 'Looks like you've been setting the tongues wagging.'

Rose smiled. 'That's village life for you. At least you can't say no one takes an interest.'

There were few customers in the bar until nine o'clock when the pub filled up with airmen from the local airfield. The

atmosphere lightened noticeably as one of them sat down at the piano and began to play.

Nell grinned. 'This is more like it,' she said. 'I was going to suggest getting the bus into Ipswich, but things are looking up now. That good-looking feller with the bedroom eyes hasn't stopped eyeing you since they came in. Do you know him?'

Rose glanced across the room to where the young airman stood resting his arms on top of the piano. 'I've seen him once or twice. I think he was one of those who helped out at harvest time.'

Nell picked up both their glasses. 'Right. What'll you have?'

'Oh, just a lemonade,' Rose said. The man Nell referred to had been in civvies on the few occasions she had seen him before. Now, she saw to her surprise, he wore a squadron-leader's uniform. As Nell had observed, he certainly was handsome; too handsome perhaps, she told herself, as she turned her chair a little so as not to meet his bold stare. But the small gesture did not put him off and, as Nell waited to be served at the crowded bar, he left the others clustered round the piano and crossed the room to her.

'Hello there. I haven't seen you in here for ages. I thought you must have been posted elsewhere. You're a landgirl, aren't you?'

'I was. I live at Peacocks Farm now.'

'Really?' That's the farm that joins the airfield. I heard the old fellow had died.'

'That's right. I inherited the farm.'

'*Really?*' Without being invited, he pulled Nell's chair round and sat astride it, looking at her so directly that she felt herself blushing. 'So are you his daughter?'

'No, she isn't – *if* it's any of your business.' Nell stood glowering down at him. 'And you happen to have pinched my chair.'

'I'm sorry.' The airman stood up at once. 'Please, let me buy you both a drink.'

Rose began to shake her head but Nell chipped in, 'OK, don't

mind if we do. I'll have another half of shandy and Rose'll have a lemonade.'

When he had gone to queue up at the bar Rose looked at her friend. '*Nell*! You're awful,' she chided. 'I'm sure he didn't mean to be nosy.'

'I bet he thought we were a couple of dim oiks with straw behind our ears,' she said. 'P'raps he'll show a bit more respect now. You're too open, Rose, you don't want to go telling your business to everyone.' She took a sip of her drink. 'Anyway, who does he think he is, chatting up anyone he fancies just because he's got a posh accent and an officer's uniform!' She glanced across the room as she did so. 'Mind you, he is a bit of all right if you like that type.'

When he returned he put down the tray of drinks and introduced himself. 'Squadron Leader Mark Elliot. Sorry, I should have said before.' He held out his hand to Rose, raising an eyebrow enquiringly. 'And you are. . . ?'

'Rose Meadows.' She shook his hand. 'And this is my friend, Nell Sutton.'

'Rose. It suits you. So – would that be Miss or Mrs?'

Nell gave him a warning look. 'You're doing it again.'

He laughed good-naturedly. 'Just don't want to be treading on any toes, that's all. Is it OK if I join you?'

Without waiting for an answer he pulled up a chair from the neighbouring table and sat down between them, but it was soon clear that he had eyes only for Rose. He had the bluest eyes she had ever seen and when he laughed they danced and crinkled up attractively.

'You used to come in here with a big chap,' he said. 'Husky-looking type.'

'Harry,' Rose said. 'Harry Owen.'

'Right. Boyfriend?'

'Just a fellow farm worker.'

This piece of information seemed to please Mark and he moved a little closer. He had a relaxed manner and before Rose

realized it she found herself telling him all about her modernization of the farm and her ambitions for the future.

'So what's next on your agenda?' he asked.

'I need to get a car,' she told him. 'I can drive a tractor of course, but I'd need a licence to use the roads so I'll have to take lessons first.'

His eyes brightened. 'I could teach you if you like,' he offered. 'I've got a smashing little MG sports. She's a nippy little crate and only just pre-war. May '39. Goes like the wind. How about I come and take you for a spin some evening?'

'Oh, I don't know.' Rose was aware of Nell's raised eyebrows but she refused to look at her. 'I don't get much time. . . .'

'You said yourself you needed lessons. At least let me take you for a run in the car? Got a phone number?'

'No.'

Mark caught Nell's sceptical look. 'I'd ask you too, Nell, but she's only a two-seater.'

Nell shrugged. 'No need. I'm off home in a few days anyway.'

The airman at the piano suddenly started playing 'We'll Meet Again' and everyone in the bar joined in loudly so that conversation became impossible. Nell, fortified with two pints of shandy sang along enthusiastically and Mark drew his chair a little closer to Rose's and draped his arm along the back, his fingertips touching her shoulder. His touch sent a tiny shiver down her spine and she coloured, giving him a shy, sidelong glance. He smiled disarmingly into her eyes and leaned closer.

'Song's rather apt, wouldn't you say?' he whispered.

She smiled and looked at her watch. 'I really do have to go now.' Mark looked disappointed.

'Look, I'll come and pick you up next Tuesday.'

'Well, I. . . .'

'About seven, all right?'

Rose hesitated. 'Oh, all right,' she laughed. 'Why not?'

As they began the walk back to Peacocks Nell said, 'You want to watch yourself with that one. Heartbreaker if ever I saw one.

By the way, you were getting some filthy looks from that old biddy through in the other bar. She was with a tarty-looking young girl and she was looking daggers at you too. Do you know them?'

Rose nodded. She too had seen the dark eyes burning into her as she talked to Mark. 'That's Meg Brown and her daughter Imelda,' she told Nell. 'Meg used to be Bill's cleaning woman. She was swindling him. The place was filthy. I persuaded him to sack her and she's had it in for me ever since.'

'Looks like you've made an enemy there,' Nell said. 'She's a gypsy, isn't she?'

Rose nodded. 'They say she had the child by a local man years ago and her tribe abandoned her. She's lived here ever since. The way she looks at me gives me the creeps. Talk about the evil eye.'

'You don't believe in all that rubbish, do you?' Nell scoffed. 'All the same, I'd watch her if I were you.'

They walked in silence for a while. It was a beautiful evening, the sky clear and full of stars and a full moon rising. Suddenly Nell said, 'Why do you want to do this, Rose? I mean, I know I've said it before, but it's not much of a life for a young girl like you. All the responsibility and the hard work.'

Rose sighed. 'I know you think I should sell up and have a good time with the money, but the truth is I've never owned anything before. Never really belonged to anyone or any place.' She shook her head. 'It's hard to make you understand. I was just a kid that no one really wanted. My mum abandoned me and I never even set eyes on my dad. You can't imagine how much that hurts. You come from a big, loving family.'

Nell laughed. 'A big *noisy* family you mean. Most of the time I bend over backwards to get away from them.'

'But you belong. You've got – I don't know – *roots*. You know who you are.'

'And you want to be Miss Rose Meadows, Lady Farmer. That's going to be your new identity, is it?'

'It's more than that,' Rose said. 'I want to be someone – a real someone, to have a place in the world. Bill Peacock was the nearest thing I ever had to a father. He did me the honour of trusting me with everything he'd worked for. That means so much to me: I can't let him down.'

Nell tucked her arm through Rose's. 'Well, you know best, kid,' she said. 'But don't let life pass you by while you're doing it, will you.'

Rose half expected Mark Elliot to forget all about inviting her for a drive the following Tuesday, but sure enough soon after seven o'clock a racy little red sports car roared up the lane and stopped outside in the yard, beeping the horn loudly. Rose grabbed a warm jacket and went out.

'I didn't think you were serious,' she said, taking in the car's sleek lines and shiny lipstick-red colour.

He adopted a wounded expression. 'Not serious! Ask anyone and they'll tell you that Elliot's word is his bond. Besides' – he leaned across to open the passenger door – 'you didn't think I was going to pass up a chance to go out with an attractive lady farmer, did you?'

The car sped off down the lane, the wind rushing through Rose's hair and taking her breath away. Mark glanced at her. 'Super little bus, isn't she? Soon as we get a straight run I'll open her up and show you what she can really do.'

Rose wasn't too sure about that but she said nothing. If he wanted to show off, then let him. 'What do you fly?' she asked.

He grinned at her. 'Spits mainly. Never been a plane like a Spitfire. You haven't lived till you've flown one.'

'Have you been in the RAF long?'

'Went in straight from school,' he told her. 'I was eighteen and I'd been in the ATC for two years, so I got a head start.'

'Battle of Britain?'

He nodded. 'Lucky to come through in one piece. Not that I didn't have a few prangs. Lost a lot of good pals too, and a lot

more were crocked up one way and another. Some physically, some with their nerves shot up.'

Rose shuddered. 'It must have been awful.'

He turned to her with a grin. 'Awful? No. Best time of my life in spite of everything.'

They had reached a long straight stretch of road and with a sidelong glance at her Mark pressed his foot down hard on the accelerator and the little car leapt forward with a furious roar. Rose felt the breath catch in her throat and her hands clutched surreptitiously at the sides of her seat. She was determined not to show the real fear she felt at the reckless speed of the car as it hurtled through the leafy summer countryside. Suddenly Rose saw a level crossing looming up ahead of them and glanced at Mark, biting her lip as he showed no signs of slowing down. Then, just when she thought they would certainly crash through the gates he braked ferociously, bringing the car to a halt inches from them.

When he turned to her, his eyes were ablaze with exhilaration. 'How about that then? Fun?'

Rose swallowed hard. 'It was very – fast,' she said breathlessly, trying to stop her voice from trembling.

He threw back his head and laughed. 'Do you realize that we touched eighty back there? That's the best I've got her up to yet! I've got to hand it to you, Rosie, most girls would have been yelling for me to stop.'

A goods train rumbled past and the gate keeper came out to open the gates, giving Mark a disapproving glare as he did so.

'Tell you what,' Mark said, as he started the engine again, 'I think you deserve a drink after that.'

Five minutes later he drew up on to the forecourt of a tiny thatched pub with pink-washed walls and a swinging sign with a picture of a Cavalier.

'The Hat and Feathers,' Mark told her as he opened the door for her. 'Best beer for miles around.'

Inside a log fire burned cheerfully in an open fireplace. A

group of locals were playing darts in the far corner, but apart from them there were no other customers. Mark settled her at a table by the fireplace and carried the drinks over.

'Tell me about yourself,' he invited. 'We've only talked about me so far. I don't know a thing about you except that you used to be a landgirl and now you're the owner of Peacocks Farm.'

Rose laughed. 'That's about all there is really,' she said.

'Come *on*, there has to be more than that. I'd say by that attractive slight accent you've got that you hail from London. Am I right?'

'I was born there. Lived there with an aunt till I joined the WLA. That was soon after the blitz started. My aunt decided enough was enough. She gave up the pub she ran and went to live in Devon.'

'And you joined the WLA?'

Rose nodded. 'I loved it.'

'And you were posted here to Weston St Mary?'

'Yes. I was the only landgirl at Peacocks. Poor Bill had let things slide a bit. His wife and child died tragically and he'd taken to the bottle.'

Mark smiled at her. 'Don't tell me – you shook him out of it; persuaded him that there was more to life?'

'I don't know about that. I tried to make the place more homely for him. We had some nice Christmases when I was there. I like to think I helped him get over his despair a bit. But I got posted to Yorkshire after a while and I think he let things slip again after that. He got ill. . . .'

'Died and left you the farm,' Mark finished for her.

She nodded. 'So now I want to make it a success again. I'm sure that's what he would have wanted.'

'Good for you. What about your folks though? You must have a mother and father somewhere – family?'

'No. No one. There's just me, apart from Aunt Bessie and I think she was glad to be rid of me.' She put down her glass and looked at her watch. 'Thanks for the drink, Mark, but I think I

should be getting back now.'

'Sure.' He swallowed the last of his own drink and held out his hand. 'And I promise not to speed on the way home,' he said with a twinkle. 'You hid it well, but I know you hated it really.'

When the little red car drew up in the yard at Peacocks the moon had risen casting its silver light over everything. Mark switched off the engine and slid his arm along the back of her seat.

'Funny how moonlight makes everything look beautiful,' Rose said, looking round the yard.

'You don't need the moonlight,' he said softly, cupping her chin and turning her face towards him. 'You'd look beautiful in any light. I fact I'm deeply in danger of becoming bewitched.'

Rose laughed. 'Bewitched?'

His eyes were solemn as they looked into hers. 'You haven't any idea how lovely you are, have you, Rosie? That's what makes you so irresistible.' He bent forward and took her head in his hands, lacing his fingers in her hair. Then he kissed her. It was a light kiss, tender, almost tremulous and it made her heart contract and her knees turn to water. She would have liked him to kiss her again, but he released her suddenly and got out of the car. As he helped her out he held on to her hand.

'Can I see you again, Rosie?'

'Yes. If you want to.'

'Friday – same time?'

Her eyes were shining as she nodded breathlessly. 'All right.'

'And maybe I could start teaching you.'

'Teaching me?'

'To drive.'

'Oh! To drive – yes.'

'Of course, to drive.' When he looked at her his eyes danced with mischief. 'What did you think?' He pulled her close and kissed her again, then turned and jumped into the car, driving off down the lane with a roar and a cheery wave.

For a long time after the sound of the engine had died away

into the distance, Rose stood at the door, her eyes dreamy and full of wonderment in the moonlight. Being with Mark had been exciting. Like his driving there was a hint of danger and unpredictability about him. It made her feel more alive than she ever remembered feeling.

She had just come in from the fields the following afternoon when Richard arrived. Tethering his horse in the yard he walked into the kitchen.

'Has your friend gone back, Rose?' he asked.

'Nell? Yes, several days ago.'

'In that case will you come and have dinner with me tonight?'

He had asked her many times before, but lately he seemed to have given up, so Rose was slightly surprised by the invitation. 'I don't know,' she began. 'I've had a hard day and I'm tired. I'm afraid I wouldn't be very good company.'

'You are always good company, Rose. I'd really like you to come. Please.'

'Where were you planning to go?' Rose asked. Her mind was racing ahead, wondering what she could possibly wear to a smart restaurant.

'I thought you might like to dine with me at The Manor.'

Rose's heart sank. 'Is it a dinner party?'

'Of course not.' He laughed. 'Just us – very informal. Do say you'll come, Rose. I know it's short notice but I really would like it. I've got something to show you.'

She relented. 'All right then, but I can't stay long. I've got to be up for milking in the morning. Peter's having the day off to go to the Suffolk Show.'

He smiled. 'I'll come and pick you up in an hour and I'll have you home by ten. How's that?'

She nodded. 'I'll be ready.'

She was slightly surprised when Richard came to collect her in the Land-Rover. She had put on the most dressy summer

dress she owned, one that she used to wear when she and her land army friends had gone to village dances. It was made of soft blue cotton. With it, she wore high-heeled sandals, which Richard eyed with some concern. As they bumped over rough ground on his estate she soon discovered why. The vehicle drew up by a hedge that bordered Peacocks Farm land. Richard switched off the engine and turned to her with a smile.

'Good job I always carry a spare pair of Wellingtons,' he said, reaching into the back. 'Here, put these on.'

Rose slipped off her sandals and drew on the boots, which were several sizes too large. 'What's all this for?' she asked.

He came round and helped her down. 'Just wanted you to see that I was as good as my word,' he told her.

She stood looking round her then it dawned on her. 'The stream,' she said. 'It's gone. You – you've—'

'Had it piped like I promised. Next year you'll be able to grow those extra acres of winter wheat.'

'Oh, Richard! Thank you. That's wonderful. I hope it didn't cost you too much.'

'Well worth it to earn a smile like that,' he said. 'Come on then, now for that dinner. Mrs Davies has pulled out all the stops this evening. I told her it was to be a celebration.'

An hour later as Richard passed her the biscuits and cheese Rose pushed back her chair and let out a sigh. 'No, thank you. I couldn't eat another crumb,' she said. 'Your Mrs Davies is a genius. Roast chicken and home grown vegetables – sherry trifle with cream – all my favourites.'

Richard picked up the wine bottle and refilled her glass. 'Well, you must help me finish this.'

'I should have given you dinner for doing me that favour,' she said. 'It's going to make all the difference, piping the stream.'

He took a sip of his wine and put the glass down. 'That wasn't my only reason for asking you here this evening,' he said. 'I've

got something to ask you, Rose. I don't need an answer right away, but I'd like you to give it some serious thought.'

'I'm intrigued.' Rose smiled. 'Whatever can it be?'

He stood up. 'Shall we go into the drawing-room?'

Mystified, Rose followed him across the hall and sat down on the sofa. He turned, his back to the fireplace, glass in hand, looking serious. 'Rose – we've known each other for a few months now and I think we have roughly the same aims in life.'

'Do we?'

'I think so.' He looked at her. 'I admire you very much. That's something I couldn't say about many of the young women I know. You have courage and integrity. You're brave and strong.'

Rose laughed. 'You make me sound like one of your horses!'

He frowned. 'Oh dear, do I? I'm sorry. This is something I'm not very used to – nor clearly very good at. What I'm trying to say, Rose, is that I've become – well, very fond of you over the past months and I'd feel privileged – no, honoured, if you'd agree to marry me.'

Rose almost dropped her glass in astonishment. For a long moment she stared at him speechlessly and when she did find her voice it came out in a husky whisper.

'I – oh, Richard – I don't know what to say.'

'Don't say anything.' He moved to sit beside her and reached out to take her hand. 'Not now. Just think about it. Ask yourself if you could possibly feel anything approaching affection for a crusty old bachelor like me. I must be something like fifteen years your senior. But I could give you so much, Rose. Comfort and security. A life of ease, because I hate to see you working your pretty fingers to the bone the way you do. Then there's affection, because as I said, I am fond of you, even if I haven't shown it. Even though you obviously didn't guess.'

Rose was acutely embarrassed. She could feel her cheeks getting redder by the minute and her mouth seemed to have dried up completely. 'I don't know what to say,' she said again,

feeling foolish and inadequate. 'I – I think I'd like to go home now if you don't mind.'

'*Rose.*' He was on his feet at once. 'I haven't offended you?'

'No, no! It's just so – so unexpected. I don't. . . .' She broke off, biting her lip. She was in danger of repeating herself and sounding like a parrot.

'I'll take you home,' he said, holding out his hand to her. 'You'll need time to think. I can see that it's come as a shock.'

On the way home she was silent. His proposal had been more than a shock to her: it was a complete bolt from the blue. Marriage to Richard was the very last thing she had envisaged, and the kind of life he was offering was total anathema to her. Her dream was to be independent and self-sufficient. But he was kind. He had helped her so much; she owed him something. But not this – not *marriage.*

He drew up in the yard and helped her down from the Land-Rover. Holding her upper arms he looked down into her eyes. 'I'll wait to hear from you then?'

'Yes.'

He bent his head and before she could back away his lips were on hers. She could feel the tension in his hands as he held her arms and when their lips parted she heard him take a shuddering breath as he pulled her close, folding his arms around her.

'For what it's worth, Rose, I've never felt as strongly as this about anyone,' he whispered. 'Goodnight, my dear.' He let her go reluctantly. 'Sleep well.' He got into the Land-Rover and drove away.

Rose let herself into the house and stood for a moment in the darkness, her hands clutching the back of a chair. If only there were someone she could talk to, someone whose advice she could seek. She didn't want to hurt Richard. He had been a good friend. And yet. . . . Thinking back over all that he had said one thing stood out. He had never said he loved her. The word he had used was 'affection'. Would it be a marriage of

convenience? Did he simply need a wife – someone to provide an heir to his estate and a hostess for social occasions? Or was it just that he was not very good at expressing his feelings?

'Oh, Bill,' she whispered. 'I could never have guessed that something like this would happen. Please, *please* tell me what to do.'

CHAPTER SIX

R OSE LOOKED forward to her first driving lesson with Mark much more than she would have admitted. For the two nights since her dinner with Richard she had lain awake, wondering what she could possibly say without hurting or offending him. The driving lesson with Mark would be something to take her mind off it.

On Friday afternoon she went into Ipswich and had her hair cut. She also treated herself to a pair of well-cut trousers and a pretty pink sweater, suitable, she told herself, for driving a sports car.

She was watching from the bedroom window at seven o'clock and when the little red car appeared her heart gave a little flip. She ran down at once and climbed into the passenger seat beside him. He looked at her appreciatively.

'You're looking very lovely this evening,' he remarked. 'Off we go then. I know just the spot to put you through your paces. I've brought some L plates.'

They arrived at the place Mark had chosen fifteen minutes later: a quiet spot with a long straight stretch of road. He got out of the car and attached the L plates. Rose had butterflies in her stomach as she got into the driving seat. But as Mark talked her through the controls it all seemed fairly straightforward, until she put the car into gear and pressed her foot down on the

accelerator. When the car leapt forward with an angry roar Mark laughed.

'Atta girl! Into second – foot off the gas a bit.'

Swallowing her apprehension she did as he said and, coaxed along by him she got the hang of it quite quickly and was driving along the quiet country road with confidence. Mark complimented her.

'Hey! You're a real whiz at this. You'll get your licence in no time. Now, it always helps to have a destination, so how about driving us to the nearest hostelry for some refreshment?'

'If you tell me the way,' she laughed.

Half an hour later they were seated in a small village pub enjoying sandwiches and beer. 'I don't think you really needed to learn to drive at all,' Mark teased. 'You were having me on. Go on, admit it.'

'I told you, all I've driven is the farm tractor,' she protested. 'But I love driving your car. Can I drive it all the way back to the farm?'

'Not tonight,' he said. 'Better walk before you can run.' As they drove back to Weston, Mark began to sing. He had a pleasant tenor voice and soon Rose found herself joining in. They sang 'The White Cliffs of Dover' and 'A Nightingale Sang In Berkley Square', two of Rose's favourites. She told him how the girls at the hostel would sing along to the wind-up gramophone and what fun they'd had.

'Do you miss all that?' he asked her, picking up the nostalgic note in her voice.

She nodded wistfully. 'The WLA was hard going at times, but the company was wonderful. I was lonely when I was growing up. I'd never known friendships like that before. I think it was probably the happiest time of my life.'

'Are you lonely now, Rosie?' he asked quietly.

She considered for a moment, then nodded. 'People here have been kind and helpful. And there's Nell of course. You met her in The Grapes that evening. But she's gone home to

Liverpool now so I won't be seeing much of her. Anyway, she has her family.'

'And you have no one?'

'No.'

'I know the feeling, Rosie. My own parents were killed in the blitz.'

She looked at him. 'Oh, Mark. I'm sorry.'

He reached for her hand. 'We're a couple of orphans then, eh? But a girl like you must have hoards of friends.'

'Not really. Running the farm takes up most of my time. There isn't much left for socializing, so yes – life can be lonely.'

'Not any more though.'

'No?' She looked at him.

'You're forgetting something.'

'I am? What?'

'Me, of course. You've got me now.'

She laughed. 'Have I?'

'If you want me.' He drew the car into the side of the road and switched off the engine. 'I'm not joking, Rosie. OK, you're thinking we hardly know each other, but I've wanted to get to know you right from the first time I saw you. I've been biding my time and waiting for an opportunity to get to speak to you.' He looked intently into her eyes. 'Do you know what I'm saying, Rosie?'

She swallowed hard, unable to answer such a direct question. 'I – I don't know.'

'I think you do. I've never met anyone like you before and now that I've found you I don't want to let you go. Is there any chance you might feel the same?'

Her heart was beating so fast she felt sure that he must hear it. 'Isn't – isn't it a bit soon?'

'How long does it take to decide that you're attracted to someone? How many times do you have to be with a girl to know that she's just what you've been looking for all your life? My mind's made up, Rosie. It was made up the moment I set

eyes on you.' He leaned towards her, one hand cupping her cheek, the other stroking her shoulder.'

She laughed shakily. 'You don't know what I'm like. For all you know I might have terrible faults.'

'Like what?'

'I don't know – a horrible temper,' she said, unable to take her eyes off his mouth as it came closer.

He laughed softly as his lips brushed hers. 'Fire eh? I like fire. It's warm, and when it flares it's exciting – like *this*.' His mouth crushed hers and his arms went round her, drawing her breathlessly close. For a long time neither of them spoke, then Mark whispered in her ear, 'I'll ask you again – just once. I'm not going to pester you. If the answer's no, just tell me and I'll leave you alone. Do you feel this – this magnetism that I feel?'

'Yes,' she murmured, winding her arms around his neck. 'Yes, I do.'

He kissed her again. 'That's what I hoped you'd say. Shall we go back to the farm now?'

She looked into his eyes and saw the unasked question there. Her heart raced. She was terrified and excited all at the same time and she knew instinctively that to refuse him now would be to lose him. There was only one answer. 'Yes,' she whispered, leaning her forehead against his. 'Yes. Let's go.'

Mark left as dawn was breaking. She stirred as he was crossing the room on tiptoe, his shoes in his hand. 'Mark?'

He came back and leaned over to kiss her. 'Got to go, sweetheart – have to be gone before your workers start arriving. Can't start the village tongues wagging, can we? But I'll be back later. That's a promise.'

She slipped her arms around his neck and drew him down to her, nuzzling his neck dreamily. 'Not yet. Stay a bit longer.'

He groaned. 'Don't! You have no idea how tempted I am but I mustn't.'

'Last night was – was. . . .'

'Yes, wasn't it!' He laughed and planted a kiss on her fore-head. 'But we have a whole future ahead of us. A million more nights to enjoy. See you later, darling. Be good.'

When he'd gone she lay watching the sky lighten, thinking about the night they'd shared. She felt different, transformed in ways she could never have imagined. She had never known that she was capable of passion before; how the fire of it could unleash all her inhibitions and make her do things that made her blush at the memory. Mark was so strong, so ardent and powerful. He had made her feel special and irresistible, the most beautiful woman in the world, the only one he truly wanted. She'd had no idea that physical love could be so wonderful. And what had he said? *A million more nights to enjoy.* The thought gave her a thrill of expectation as she turned over to snatch another hour's sleep.

From that night Rose's life changed. She felt alive – had bound-less energy and enthusiasm for her work on the farm. The wheat and barley crops planted in early spring were growing well and her small herd of dairy cows were yielding well. Soon there would be two additions to which she looked forward.

Mark came as often as his duties allowed. When she heard the sound of his car in the yard, followed by his cheery call at the back door her heart swelled inside her with love. The nights they shared were full of ecstasy, the sweet scents of summer floating in at the open window heightening each sensation. Each dawn when he left her she felt torn in half.

The only thing marring her pleasure was Richard. His proposal was at the back of her mind all the time, though she told herself she had nothing to feel guilty about. He still paid her occasional visits and although he never mentioned it, she knew he was waiting for her answer. Soon she would have to tell him about Mark. It was unfair to keep him waiting any longer.

As it happened she didn't have to.

Mark arrived unexpectedly early one evening, surprising her

as she was climbing out of her overalls after milking. He breezed in, his face wreathed in smiles.'

'Come to Norwich with me,' he said, standing in the doorway. 'We could have a meal and go to a little club I know. They have roulette and baccarat. It's the most enormous fun. Hurry up. Get your glad rags on while the engine's still warm.'

She laughed. 'Mark! You're mad! I can't just walk out like that. Besides, we'd be so late getting back.'

He looked crestfallen. 'Oh, come on, Rosie, I was counting on you. Where's your sense of fun?'

'I've got a cow due to calf at any time,' she told him. 'I'm sorry, darling, but I can't go so far away at this time.'

'Cows are animals. They manage by themselves, don't they?' he asked. 'Just let nature take its course.'

'I can't afford to risk it,' she told him. 'Have you any idea how much a cow costs? She's one of my new ones too.'

He pulled out a chair and sat astride it, resting his chin on his folded arms. 'So – we can't go anywhere then?' he asked, sulkily.

'I could cook you a meal and later perhaps we could go down to The Grapes,' she suggested. 'Don't look like that. It can't be helped. If only you'd given me some notice.'

'Would that have made your bloody cow less pregnant then?' He stood up, his lower lip thrust out, looking so much like a spoiled five year old that Rose laughed.

'I can't believe you're being so moody,' she said. 'You should see your face.' She crossed the kitchen and put her arms around his neck. 'Oh, I'm sorry, darling. I'll make it up to you later.' She kissed him. 'Come on. We can go another time, can't we?'

Before he could reply, a cough from the doorway made her turn. Richard stood at the open back door. She took her arms from Mark's neck and moved away guiltily.

'Richard! I didn't see you there.'

'Clearly.' His voice was tight. 'I called on the off chance. Perhaps I should have sent word first.'

'Not at all. You're always welcome.' Rose took a deep breath and did her best to recover herself. 'Mark, this is Richard Beech from the Manor,' she said. 'Richard, have you met Squadron Leader Mark Elliot?'

'I'm afraid I haven't had that pleasure,' Richard said drily.

Neither man made any move to shake hands. 'Well, I'll go,' Richard said. 'I can see that you're busy.'

'*Richard*!' She ran after him into the yard, catching up with him as he reached the Land-Rover. 'I've been meaning to come and see you. There's something I have to—'

'*Don't*!' He turned and held up his hand. 'I'm not so stupid that I need it spelling out for me, thank you, Rose.' His mouth softened into a smile. 'There's no need to look so embarrassed. You are a free agent after all. I'll see you again some other time.' He got into his Land-Rover and switched on the ignition. 'Goodbye.'

She went inside feeling bad. As she closed the door Mark looked at her expectantly. 'What was all that about?'

She shook her head. 'Richard has been very kind to me.'

'So?'

'I think he's – well, a bit sweet on me. I don't like the thought that he might be hurt.'

'*Sweet* on you? What does that mean?'

'He helped me a lot with modernizing the house. More than he needed to.'

'In the hope that he might get you into bed.'

'*No*!'

He laughed. 'Come off it, sweetheart. That's what men do.'

'Is it what *you* did?'

He shrugged. 'Probably – to start with.' He moved closer and put his arms around her, pulling her hard against him. 'But that was before I fell in love with you,' he said, his lips against her ear. 'You see, men aren't always as clever as they think. We get trapped by your wicked feminine wiles. Then it's all up with us.' He kissed her, and went on kissing her until her head swam.

'So you can tell that old fellow he's had it, my angel. Anyway he's old enough to be your father! Now, where's that meal you promised me?'

Rose's heart lifted as she cooked a simple supper. At least one thing was off her conscience. Richard now knew where he stood. And he hadn't seemed too upset. After they'd eaten she went out to the byre and looked at Kerry, the cow that was close to calving. The early signs were there, but she knew from experience that it would be some time before the calf would be born. Maybe she could spare an hour.

They drove down to The Grapes. Rose drank only lemonade and she found it difficult to relax. By half past nine she was looking at her watch every few minutes.

'I really should get back, Mark,' she said at last.

He sighed. 'What is it *now*?'

'Kerry. I think it's time I checked on her again.'

'All this fuss over a bloody cow!' He got up reluctantly. 'OK, if you must. You're lousy company tonight anyway.'

As they drew up in the yard she looked at him. 'Are you coming with me? I might need some help.'

'*Me*?' He stared at her, aghast. 'God no! I can promise you I'd be no bloody good to man or beast as a midwife. I'll give it a miss if you don't mind.'

'You're not staying then?'

He shook his head. 'There's another pint with my name on it down at the pub. I'll see you anon, my love.'

She watched as he drove away, her heart heavy with disappointment.

In the byre, Kerry's labour was well under way, but the animal seemed to be straining abnormally. She seemed distressed too, lowing plaintively with each contraction. Rose decided to go to the cottage and get Peter before it got too late.

Peter and Irene had already gone to bed when she knocked, but Peter came down, hurriedly pulling on his overalls and came back to the byre with her. He could see at a glance that

110

all was not well.

'Will you get me a bucket of water and some soap? I'd better try and find out what's going on,' he said. 'I don't like the look of that straining.'

After Peter had examined the cow he looked at her doubtfully. 'I'm no expert but it feels to me like a breech,' he said. 'I'm sorry, Miss Meadows, but this needs more skill than I've got.'

Rose's heart sank. 'Could you go to the phone box in the village and ring the vet?'

'I could, but he's got to come all the way from Woodbridge. It'll take him ages to get here, even if he's available. What it really needs is someone who can turn the calf. I don't know enough to risk it.'

It took Rose only a moment to make up her mind. 'Do you know Jarvis's farm at Benham?'

' 'Course.'

'Harry Owen's cottage?'

'I know where he lives, yes.'

'How long would it take you to get there?'

'About ten minutes on my bike.'

'Will you go and get him for me, Peter? As quickly as you can?'

' 'Course I will.'

It felt to Rose like an eternity as she waited with the distressed beast. She talked soothingly to the animal, trying to calm her, but it was clear by the way she was rolling her eyes that she was on the point of collapse, exhausted by unproductive straining. Rose was upset by the cow's obvious distress and terrified of losing her.

At last she heard the sound of a vehicle in the yard and looked out with immense relief to see Peter and Harry getting out of a pick-up truck and crossing the yard towards her. Harry looked dishevelled, as though he had risen hurriedly from bed. With the briefest of nods at her he got to work at once, pulling off his shirt and asking for fresh water and soap.

111

Rose refilled the bucket and carried it across the yard, then sat down on a bale of hay biting her lip anxiously as she watched. Harry worked hard, the sweat standing out on his skin as he struggled to turn the calf. Eventually he called to Peter to get the rope that hung behind the byre door. He attached it to the calf's legs which were now protruding and both men began to pull. Moments later the calf was delivered and Rose helped Peter to rub the new arrival with handfuls of straw.

'Thank you, Harry,' she said, looking up with tears in her eyes. 'A lovely little heifer too. Just what I'd hoped for.' She looked at Peter. 'Thank you, too, Peter. Why don't you go home to bed now? And don't worry about the morning milking. I'll do it.'

'Don't you bother yourself, miss, I'll be fine,' Peter said. 'Still time to get a couple of hours' shut-eye. I'll just get my bike off the back of the truck and I'll be off' He glanced at the tiny brown and white calf, smiling as the little creature struggled bravely to get to its feet. 'A good night's work, I reckon. Always gives you a lift, the birth of a healthy calf. 'Night then, both.'

When he'd gone, Rose looked at Harry who was doing his best to wash himself in the water left in the bucket. 'Come inside and have a proper wash,' she invited. 'I'll make you a hot drink and something to eat before you go.'

In the farmhouse kitchen, Harry looked around him. 'This looks a bit different to when Bill was alive,' he said.

'Thanks. I've done my best,' Rose said with pride. 'I've got running water now and electricity. You can use the bathroom if you like. First on the left at the top of the stairs. There's plenty of hot water.'

When he came back downstairs she had a pot of tea waiting and a plate of bacon and eggs keeping warm on top of the Aga.

'You shouldn't have bothered,' he said, buttoning his shirt. 'Won't take me long to get home in the truck.'

'It'll save you the trouble of making breakfast,' she said. 'It's already beginning to get light.'

'The house looks a treat,' he remarked. 'Poor old Bill would hardly recognize it.'

'The one thing I really need is a telephone,' she said. 'Tonight has taught me that. I don't know what I would have done without you, Harry. I could have lost both cow and calf.'

He nodded. 'It was a nasty one, but not all that unusual. They'll do fine now.'

'Thanks to you.' She watched him eat for a moment. 'Are you happy at Jarvis's?' she asked.

'I suppose so – whatever happy is.'

'I would have liked you to stay on here, Harry.'

'We all have to move on.' He laid down his knife and fork and took a drink of his tea. 'I've been thinking about emigrating as a matter of fact,' he said, after a moment.

Rose looked at him. 'Emigrating? Where to?'

'Australia. It's a great country for farming by all accounts and there's talk of a government scheme.' He lifted his shoulders. 'Opportunities out there for a bloke like me. Who knows, I might even have my own farm one of these days. There's nothing here for me any more.'

'You'll be missed, Harry,' she said softly.

He drained his cup and shook his head at her offer of a refill. 'Not by anyone who matters.' He got up from the table. 'Thanks for the breakfast. I'll be getting back now.'

Rose went out to the truck with him, shivering a little in the chill morning air. 'Thank you again for all you did last night,' she said. 'If ever there's anything I can do to repay you. . . .'

'I doubt there will be.' He slammed the truck door and looked at her through the window. 'Bye, Rose.'

After the truck had rattled away across the yard and disappeared down the lane she stood for a long moment watching the grey and pink-streaked sky turn to azure blue. A blackbird began to pipe its clear, liquid notes, then one by one others joined in, joyfully heralding another day. She took a deep breath of the sparkling clean air. It was a time when she loved

to be awake. Dawn: so full of promise. A new beginning, fresh and pure. If only one could always make the most of it.

She crossed the yard to look in on the new calf and its mother. Both looked contented, their ordeal forgotten, the little one feeding blissfully.

Making her way back to the house she thought about how much her life had changed since she first came to Peacocks. Changed for the better, of course. As a child, growing up with Aunt Bess at The Duke's Head she would never have dreamed that one day she would be so lucky – have so much. Yet at the back of her mind was a niggling feeling that she could have done better, a feeling that she'd let some important opportunities slip through her fingers.

CHAPTER SEVEN

MOVING INTO high summer meant hard work on the farm. There was hay-making and rick building, new calves to wean, root crops to lift and the prospect of harvest looming large.

Mark was petulant when Rose worked late into the evening. 'Why do you employ farm hands and do the work yourself?' he asked.

'I can't leave it all to them,' Rose told him. 'They work hard, but if they see me taking it easy they'll lose interest. I never ask them to do anything I'm not willing to do myself.'

'Very noble,' he sneered. 'If they don't want the work, get someone else in. There are plenty of men being demobbed and looking for work.'

'Not men like Peter and Geoff. They're good workers. I know what I'm doing, Mark. This is a busy time. It won't last for ever. You could always help instead of complaining.'

But farm work did not appeal to Mark. More often than not he'd fling off in a huff to The Grapes, returning at closing time contrite and affectionate to beg her forgiveness. Usually she surrendered, but one evening when he returned Rose was tired and merely irritated by his facetious behaviour.

'I'm exhausted, Mark,' she said, pushing him away. 'It's hot and we've been working since first light. It'll be the same tomorrow. I need my rest.'

His face dropped. 'We'll all get our *rest* soon enough,' he snapped. 'I'm sick and tired of you working all the time. You used to be fun. Now the farm comes first all the time. Do you think I came through a war for this?'

'I have to earn my living,' she told him. 'I was lucky enough to inherit this farm. It was badly run down and I mean to make it successful again.'

'And what about *me*? What about us?'

'I thought you'd understand,' she said, wearily. 'Life can't be fun all the time, Mark. We all have to take the good with the bad.'

'Not when it's bad *all* the time.' He strode to the door. 'All right, you get your rest, Rosie. But don't bother to come looking for me when the harvest's over. I might just be sick of waiting!'

For a long moment after the door had slammed behind him, she stood listening. She heard him rev the car's engine and roar off angrily. She was wretched at the thought that she might have lost him. Even more wretched that he refused to understand why she had to work. She felt angry and frustrated. Didn't he love her enough to bear with her for a few weeks?

In her weekly letter to Nell she wrote all about the row. Nell wrote back by return saying that she was well rid of him – that she could have told her long ago that Mark was no good. It didn't help. It wasn't what Rose wanted to hear. Two weeks went by and the hard work continued, but Mark was never far from Rose's thoughts. Every day she half expected him to come back, begging to be forgiven. He never came. Then one evening Richard called on her with disquieting news.

'He's deceiving you, Rose.' He stood facing her across the kitchen table. 'Believe me, my dear, it's taken a lot of heart-searching for me to come to you with this, and I don't want you to think I'm here out of spite. But I can't stand by and see a girl like you made a fool of.'

She was shaking her head as though to rid herself of the unwelcome words he was speaking. 'You must be mistaken.'

'Do you think I'd be here if there was any doubt in my mind?' He reached across the table to touch her arm. 'Please – sit down and hear me out.'

Slowly she sank on to a chair, but mainly because her legs suddenly refused to hold her up.

'I don't go the The Grapes very often,' he began. 'But that particular evening I'd arranged to meet my farm manager there to discuss a change of feed supplier. I'd been tied up in Ipswich all day and it was the only chance I'd get to see him.'

'Can you get to the point, please?'

'Right. It was quite late when I drove round to the car park at the back. I caught them in the beam of my headlights.' He broke off, shaking his head apologetically. 'I really hate having to tell you this, Rose. It's so sordid.'

'Go on,' she said, her face stony. 'If you want me to know you're going to have to tell me all of it.'

He sighed. 'It was Elliot. There was no doubt – and a girl, the one who's always hanging round the village in provocative clothes. The daughter of that gypsy woman.'

'Imelda Brown, you mean. So – what were they doing?'

He winced. 'Do I really have to spell it out to you?'

She looked at him levelly. '*Yes!*'

'They were. . . .' – he swallowed – 'in a passionate embrace. The point is, Rose, he was being unfaithful to you and I felt you should know.'

'So now that you've told me I'd like you to leave, please,' she said.

He looked at her for a long moment. 'Rose – my dear, please believe me when I say that I did not want to upset you. It is with the best of intentions that I'm telling you this.'

'Of course.'

'If there's anything I can—'

'There *isn't*. Please, Richard, will you go – *now*?'

'Very well.' He got to his feet, looked at her for a moment, then quietly left.

It was only when she was quite sure he'd driven away that she released the torrent of emotion she'd held in. Laying her head down on her arms she sobbed till her chest ached and she thought her heart would split in two with the agony of it. When there were no more tears she got up, made herself a pot of tea and tried to think what to do. Should she face him with it? Or should she just not see him again, even if he came asking for forgiveness? It seemed that Nell had been right. And yet she couldn't help remembering how happy they had been, of the long blissful nights they had shared and the beautiful things he'd said, the undying love he had declared to her again and again. Had it really all been false – just words? How could he so easily make love to someone else, so soon? The hurt of betrayal burned into her heart until she was forced to rush upstairs to the bathroom, physically sick with the pain of it. The days passed and she did nothing. Mark did not appear. She told herself that the hurt would grow less, but instead it grew and festered like some monstrous poisonous mushroom till it filled her whole being and she could think of nothing else. She went through the days like an automaton, hardly ate or slept, the same questions echoing through her mind again and again. Was it really all over between them? She was desperate to know, but only Mark could give her the answer.

It was as she was helping Irene with the sterilization in the milking parlour that Peter's wife mentioned the harvest supper.

'It's a week on Friday. We always have it in the church hall. I expect you remember.'

Rose did remember from when she was at Peacocks when Bill was alive. He had never gone to it though and consequently neither had she.

'You will come this year, won't you?' Irene was saying. 'Folks'll expect you to be there. Everyone takes something – a

pie or a dish of some kind – some fruit or veg. We have a smashing time.'

'Well, I don't know.'

'I'm on the committee,' Irene told her. 'So if you were to tell me now what you'll make you could have the choice. See, we try to organize it so we don't get too much of one thing.'

It seemed churlish to refuse so Rose agreed. 'I'll make an apple pie,' she volunteered.

'Lovely!' Irene smiled. 'I'll make a note of it. Ted Mott's two sons usually come and play their piano accordions so we can dance,' she said. 'There's always plenty of cider and beer and everyone gets quite merry. Well, we deserve it after the slog of harvest, don't you reckon?'

The harvest supper was two weeks later. Rose made her apple pie and took it across to the cottage for Irene to take down to the hall where the ladies of the committee were setting everything up. At seven o'clock she went along herself. The church hall looked festive, decorated with sheaves of corn and garlands of leaves. Dishes piled high with fruit and vegetables, which would later be sent along to the local children's hospital adorned the platform at the end. The supper was as sumptuous as rationing would allow, with everything either home-made or home-grown. Afterwards the Mott brothers got out accordions and the tables were cleared away for dancing.

Sid, the landlord of The Grapes, was running the bar and when Rose went up to buy herself a drink he asked her if she was all right. He'd seen her once or twice in the village lately and her pale face and haunted eyes disturbed him. He'd guessed that it might have something to do with Mark Elliot. He'd seen him flirting with the flighty Brown girl at the pub and knowing both of them well he knew it would not have stopped at harmless flirtation. Rose shook her head.

'No, I'm fine, thank you, Sid. Just tired after harvest like everyone else.'

As she turned away she saw Mark coming through the door with a bunch of other young airmen. Her heart gave a lurch and she felt the colour flood her cheeks as she turned away, looking for somewhere she could escape to. Taking her drink to a table in the furthest corner she sat down and hoped not to be noticed. But when Mark went to the bar she saw Sid speak to him and nod in her direction. For a moment she panicked, looking around for the nearest exit, but there was no escape. A moment later a shadow fell across the table and she looked up to see Mark looking down at her.

Hello, Rosie. Long time no see. Harvest all in then, is it?'

'Yes.'

He nodded towards the empty chair opposite. 'Anyone's?'

She shook her head.

'Mind if I sit down?'

'Of course not.'

'I'm honoured.'

She ignored the sarcasm.

'I didn't expect to see you here. You being so busy.'

'You know I'm not like that. It was harvest and—'

'Well, never mind. You're here now.'

She took a sip of her drink. 'You haven't been wasting your time.'

He raised an eyebrow. 'What does that mean?'

'I heard you were seeing someone else,' she said, without looking at him.

'Really? I wonder who could have told you that.'

'Is it true?' She raised her eyes to his.

He shrugged. 'I've dropped into The Grapes with the lads most evenings. How could I help *seeing* people?'

'You know what I mean. Don't be cruel, Mark.'

'*Cruel?*' His face darkened. 'You don't think you were cruel to me?'

'Not deliberately. I had work to do. I hoped – I *expected* – you to understand.'

He drained his glass and looked at her for a long moment. 'Let's get the hell out of here,' he said suddenly. Taking her hand he pulled her to her feet. As they picked their way through the dancers, Rose caught a glimpse of Imelda. She was dancing with Mrs Maitland's son, Tom. The girl saw them leaving and Rose couldn't mistake the look of anger in the girl's eyes.

Sitting outside in the car, Mark asked her, 'Right, who's been telling tales?'

'It doesn't matter.'

'Well, as a matter of interest, who am I supposed to be seeing?'

'As if you didn't know! Imelda Brown.'

He threw back his head and laughed. 'Melly. You know what they call her?'

'I don't think I want to know.'

'*The local lads' salvation*, among other, less polite things.'

'So you're denying it?'

He took her face between his hands. 'Listen, Rosie, you hurt me. You made me feel unwanted. What did you expect? I was looking for a diversion to take my mind off it and everyone knows that Melly's always eager for a bit of fun. That's all it was. And it was Beech who came running to you with it, wasn't it? Lord of the bloody manor Beech!' He shook his head. 'He actually had the damned nerve to warn me off. I can't believe you're taking it all so seriously. There's only one reason why he'd come to you with a tale like that and I think you know it.'

Tears welled up in her eyes and spilled over. He cupped her chin, raising her face. 'Hey! What's all this?'

'Oh, Mark. I've been so miserable, thinking of you and – and her. . . .'

He pulled her close. 'You silly girl. You're the girl I love. I wouldn't have been so angry if you hadn't meant so much to me. I thought you were going off me, that's all.'

121

'But I—'

'Shhh. You talk too bloody much.' He pulled her close and kissed her until all the misery she had suffered – all her fears – were forgotten.

A little later as they sat close together, her head on his shoulder, Mark said, 'I've got something to tell you. I'm getting demobbed soon.'

She looked up at him. 'Does that mean you'll have to leave Weston?'

'Well, what do you think? There's nothing here for me, is there?'

'So – what will you do?'

'Have to look for a job.' He sighed. 'It won't be easy. As I told you, I went into the RAF straight from school. Flying's all I know and there'll be hundreds of chaps looking for jobs with civil airlines.'

She thought about it for a moment. 'Harry's leaving too,' she said. 'He's talking of going to Australia.'

'Harry Owen. When did you see him?'

'On that night when we had the difficult calving. Peter and I couldn't manage on our own so Peter went over to Benham to fetch Harry. He told me afterwards that he's thinking of emigrating.'

Mark sighed. 'It's certainly an idea. We may have won the war but this poor old country's on her uppers.'

'That's no reason to leave,' Rose said hotly. 'It seems to me that if we stuck by our country through the war the least we can do is to help get her back on her feet again now.'

'Spoken like a true patriot,' Mark said with a wry smile. 'It's all right for you, my sweet. You have your own farm and a living at your fingertips. How would you feel if you were in my position?'

'What would you do if you went to Australia? I mean – Harry would go into farming, but—'

'Whereas, I'm good for nothing. Is that what you're saying?'

'Of course not.'

'Nevertheless, it's not far from the truth. I suppose I could learn farming.'

'You wouldn't need to go to Australia for that.'

He looked at her. 'I'm young and strong. There must be plenty I could do around a farm.'

She laughed. 'I don't think you'd make a very good stockman.'

'All right – fair enough. Maybe I'm no good with animals, but I could drive a tractor and learn how to plough and....' He laughed and began to break into song, 'sow. And reap and mow – and be a farmer's boy-oy-oy-oy-oy – and be a farmer's boy.'

She laughed with him in spite of herself. 'Are you saying you want me to give you a job?'

He stopped laughing, flushing warmly. 'God *no*! That was the last thing I had in mind.'

'It is an idea though,' she said thoughtfully. 'I couldn't pay you what you're earning now of course, but I could offer you—'

'*It's out of the question, Rose!*' he interrupted quickly. 'Bloody hell, I couldn't let you employ me.'

'Why not?'

He shook his head. 'I just couldn't, that's all. I'd feel like a – oh, I don't know. Just don't let's talk about it. It's not going to happen yet anyway. I'll worry about it when it does.' He looked at his watch. 'Do you want to go back in there and dance?'

'Not really.'

'What then? Want to go into town?'

'No.'

He searched her eyes. 'Shall I take you home then?'

'Please.'

The evening had the chill of autumn about it but it had been a humid day and Rose's bedroom felt cosy and warm. She drew the curtains but before she could reach out for the light switch Mark drew her into his arms and kissed her passionately.

123

'God, I've missed you, Rosie,' he whispered into her hair. 'There's no one quite like you. There never will be.' He began to caress her, his breath warm against her neck, and her body seemed to melt into his as they sank together on to the bed. She could hardly believe that they were here, together again, all their past troubles forgotten. It was the answer to all her prayers. Now all she wanted was to keep him with her – to make him so happy that he wouldn't want to leave her again.

His lovemaking was urgent and sweet and later as she lay with her head in the hollow of his shoulder he said, 'I love you, Rosie.'

'I love you, too.'

'Do you think there's any chance we could make a go of it, you and me?'

Her heart gave a lurch as she turned to look up at him. 'Make a go of it – what do you mean?'

He laughed and gave her a little shake. 'I'm asking you to marry me, stupid!'

Her first instinct was to say yes at once. She loved him more than words could say, but could he really settle down to life on the farm with her? He had led a life full of excitement and risk, adventure and glamour. Would he grow tired of her and the dull routine of country life?

'Does it really take this much thinking about?' he asked, looking down at her.

'Not for my part. I love you, Mark. You know that. There's nothing I want more than for us to be married. It's just. . . .'

'Just what?'

'Is it *really* what you want? Farming is a very different life from what you're used to.'

'It's you I want to marry, not the farm. Besides, the war is over. Life's going to change for everyone.'

'But I'm afraid you'd soon get bored. First with the farm and then, eventually, with me.'

He drew his arm from around her abruptly. 'You've got no

faith in me, that's the trouble. He swung his legs over the side of the bed and began to pull on his clothes. 'I shouldn't have asked you, Rose. Forget it.'

'*Mark*!' She was at his side instantly, her arms around his neck. 'Please don't take offence. I'm only being practical. We have to think it through properly if it's going to work.'

He held her at arms' length and looked into her eyes. 'You could always sell the farm, Rosie.'

She looked up at him, her eyes widening and her heart plummeting at the thought. 'No, Mark. I'll never do that. If that's a condition—'

'No, no. Of course it isn't.' He pulled her close. 'Look, if you want us to stay here then I'll learn. I'll do anything you want. I won't let you down, I promise.'

Rose sighed and relaxed against him. Deep inside she wasn't entirely convinced, but she ignored her misgivings. Never in her life had she felt so loved; so warm and safe; so *important* to someone. Nothing else mattered.

Mark and Rose were married four weeks later by special licence at the register office in Ipswich. Apart from Rose's employees, whom she swore to secrecy, they told very few people. Rose wrote to Nell with the news, but as her friend had just begun a new job she wasn't able to come and celebrate with them. Two of Mark's RAF colleagues were witnesses and after the ceremony the four of them had lunch at The Golden Lion Hotel.

When they arrived back at the farm Mark had a surprise for his new wife. There, in the corner of the living-room was a gleaming radiogram, delivered while they were out.

'Now we can dance whenever we like,' he said, putting a record on the turntable. 'I've got all your favourites; the ones you used to like when you were in the WLA. Like this for instance.' The romantic strains 'Long Ago and Far Away' filled the room. Mark closed the lid and held his arms out to her. 'May I have the pleasure, Mrs Elliot?'

Later, when Rose had gone upstairs to get ready for bed Mark decided to go for a walk. At the bottom of the lane he paused to let a Land-Rover pass. To his surprise the vehicle pulled up a few yards along the road and a figure got down from the driving seat. At first Mark couldn't see who it was.

'Elliot!'

'Who is it?'

'Beech. Richard Beech. Have you just come from Peacocks Farm?'

'I have.'

'I was under the impression that you'd decided to leave Miss Meadows alone.'

'And what business is it of yours whether I have or haven't? Did you think I'd take any notice of your pathetic warning?'

'I happen to have a great deal of respect for the lady. She deserves better than you. I know that you have been deceiving her.'

'And I know that you've been running to her with tales. It's a good job she had more sense than to believe you.'

Richard took a step towards him, his face red with anger. 'Leave her alone. Do you hear me? I won't warn you again.'

'I'm shaking in my shoes!' Mark laughed. 'Leave her alone, eh? And who's going to make me?'

'I am, if necessary.'

'Why is that, I wonder? Could it be because you've got designs on her yourself? Is that the only way you can attract a woman, Beech? By telling tales like the school sneak and throwing empty threats around?'

Furious, Richard threw a punch at him but Mark stepped back out of the man's reach. 'Steady, Beech,' he said, stifling his laughter. 'If you hit me I shall be obliged to hit you back and you don't want to find yourself spending a night in the police station, do you? As it happens you're in luck. I'd thrash you here and now, but I wouldn't want anything to spoil my wedding night, now would I?'

Richard staggered back, his colour fading. 'Your *wedding* night?' he echoed.

Mark nodded with satisfaction. 'Rose and I were married this morning; so you see, Beech you're on shaky ground. I think you'd better keep your mouth shut or you'll be guilty of trying to come between man and wife and I'm sure an upright citizen like you wouldn't want that on your conscience.'

Mark turned and began to walk back up the lane, leaving Richard shaken and speechless at the roadside. Before the hedge hid him from view he turned. 'Rose was getting ready for bed when I left her,' he said. 'Mustn't keep the lady waiting, must I?'

CHAPTER EIGHT

E ARLY WINTER that year was mild and Rose and Mark made the most of the fine weather to make excursions to places of interest that Rose had always been too busy to visit before. She loved the coast; Lowestoft and the quaint little town of Aldeburgh with its fishermen's cottages and shingle beach. She loved the mysterious Brecklands with their atmosphere of wild antiquity. At the end of the year, Mark was finally demobbed and they went shopping for a new wardrobe of civilian clothes for him.

Christmas came. The happiest Rose had spent since she had been here at Peacocks when Bill was alive. She cooked a sumptuous dinner and Mark's present to her was a border collie puppy from a litter Peter's bitch had given birth to on the day they were married. She hugged the little creature in delight.

'We'll call him Raff,' she announced. 'And maybe when he's grown up we'll teach him to work the sheep.' At Peter's suggestion, Rose had decided to reintroduce sheep to Peacocks. With his help she had bought two dozen in-lamb ewes and put them on the pasture that bordered Richard Beech's land.

But after Christmas the honeymoon had to come to an end as farm life began to be busy again. She had decided to invest some of last year's profit in having the milking parlour mechanized, which would make life so much easier. There was the sowing of winter wheat and in the first week of February the

lambing began, a task which Rose and Peter shared, staying up on alternate nights in the lambing shed.

The long overdue telephone was installed at the farmhouse and, best of all, Rose received her new driving licence which meant she could set about looking for a serviceable vehicle for the farm.

Mark began to show signs that he was feeling neglected again. In spite of his promises to learn farm work he showed very little interest. He grew petulant when Rose tried to arouse enthusiasm in him.

'Why not help me find a pick-up truck,' she suggested. 'I've seen a couple advertised in the local paper and I'd appreciate your advice.'

He agreed half-heartedly, but in the end it was Geoff who helped her choose and buy the truck. When the men arrived to fit out the milking parlour she thought he might be interested in that.

'You like machinery. It's something you understand. Why don't you let the men show you how everything works?' she said. 'Then you'll know how to fix it if things go wrong. It would really help, Mark.'

Reluctantly he went to the parlour, got in the way and stood around looking resentful. He made no secret of the fact that he found the cows repellent and really wanted nothing to do with any of it. Rose disguised her disappointment, hoping that soon he would find something that appealed to him.

The first quarter's telephone bill astonished Rose. She looked up at Mark in dismay over the breakfast table. 'I can't have made this many calls,' she complained. 'Have you been using the phone a lot?'

'I've used it, yes.' He threw down his newspaper. 'What have we got the bloody thing for if it's not to use?'

'But who could you have been calling to run up a bill like this?' she asked.

He turned to her angrily. 'Perhaps you'd like me to put

tuppence into a box every time I make a call – and keep account of all the numbers so that you can check them off.'

'No. It's not that; it's just that I like to know what I'm paying for.'

'Do you go out of your way to make me feel like a *kept man*?' he shouted. 'Or does it come naturally to you?'

'Please, Mark, don't be so touchy. You must remember that the farm is a business, like any other. I have to keep proper accounts. And the telephone is part of the business now.' She reached out to touch his arm but he pushed her off.

'OK, I understand. In future I'll go down to the village and use the phone box at the post office.'

'There's no need for that. Don't be silly.' But he had gone, slamming the kitchen door behind him.

Rose telephoned to ask for a run down of all the calls made and found that the one Mark used the most was to a bookmaker in Ipswich. Although it disturbed her she said nothing to him at the time, afraid that he would be angry again.

It was soon after that he suggested they open a joint bank account and when Rose refused they had their first serious row. He accused her of not trusting him and she felt obliged to tell him she knew about his gambling. He stared at her incredulously.

'You checked up on me? You actually asked for a run down of my telephone calls?'

'You couldn't tell me and I needed to know, Mark,' she protested. 'I've told you before: I need to know where all the money goes to.'

'And did you ring the bookie to ask how much I'd won?'

She shook her head.

'Well, if you had you might have seen that I'd made a profit.'

'That's not the point.'

'I don't see why. What else do you call spending money on a new farm truck, a mechanized milking parlour, all those blasted sheep?'

'That's called investment, Mark, to improve the farm. I invested the profit I made last year.'

'So? That's no different to what I've been doing,' he insisted. 'You could come unstuck. You could lose money – don't say you couldn't.'

'Well, yes, I admit it's possible. But I wouldn't have taken the risk without being confident that I could make it work.'

'Exactly!' he said triumphantly. 'I only gamble on hot tips and if you want to know, I almost doubled my money last month.'

Rose gave up. Clearly there was no way she could make him see the difference between gambling and investment. And, truth to tell, she loved him too much to try. They made up their quarrel and to her relief Mark was his old sweet, loving self again.

'You work too hard,' he told her, as they lay in bed together early next morning. 'Can't you get someone else in to help so that we can spend more time together?'

She wanted to point out that if he were to help more they would have more time, but she knew better. She thought about what he had said as she went about her work that day. Since his demobilization he'd had all kinds of plans – he'd talked of approaching the civil airlines about a job. At one point he'd become wildly enthusiastic about running a freelance pilot agency, which he could run from home, turning one of the farm buildings into an office. They would make heaps of money and have things they wanted that wouldn't entail touching the income from the farm, he told her – holidays, smart clothes. But somehow none of the plans ever came to anything – mainly because he didn't even try to put them into motion. She began to wonder if it was her fault. The farm did take up a lot of her time. If she had more help perhaps she could concentrate on trying to motivate him. Then something happened that gave her an idea.

Irene's mother died suddenly and, on the evening of the

funeral, the girl knocked on the kitchen door and asked to see her. Rose invited her in and made a pot of tea.

'I was sorry to hear about your mother,' she said. 'If there's anything I can do to help. . . .'

'Well, that's why I'm here,' Irene said. 'I don't know how my poor dad will manage all on his own,' she said. 'He'll rattle round in that big house on the Woodbridge road – three big bedrooms. He's talking about selling up and I know he doesn't really want to. We – Peter and I thought. . . .'

'You thought what, Irene?'

'Well, we thought that if we went there and lived with him, Dad wouldn't have to move out of his home,' she said. 'He and Mum had been there ever since they first got wed, so it'd be a big wrench for him to leave. Oh, it wouldn't make any difference to our work here,' she added hurriedly. 'But if we didn't live in the cottage. . . .'

'You're saying you'd need more money?'

'Oh no. We wouldn't be paying Dad any rent. We'd probably live a lot cheaper than we do now. Dad would lend us his old motorbike to come to work on. It's just that Peter's worried that we wouldn't be so near at hand for you to call on.'

'You must do what you think is best for your father, Irene. I certainly don't want to lose either of you.'

Irene looked relieved. 'Thank you, Mrs Elliot. That's a load off my mind and no mistake.'

She got up, but stood hesitantly biting her lip until Rose asked, 'Is something else troubling you?'

'Not troubling me exactly.' Irene cleared her throat. 'We heard the other day that Harry Owen is out of work,' she said.

'But I thought he was settled at Jarvis's. Anyway, he told me he planned to emigrate to Australia.'

'That's right. He really meant to go an' all. He'd sent for all the papers. But he changed his mind at the last minute. Trouble is that the Jarvis's son-in-law has come back from the war crippled. He couldn't do his old job in the building trade so,

133

thinking Harry were leaving, Mr Jarvis offered them his job and the cottage that went with it.'

'I see.'

'It made me wonder if you might be needing any extra help here,' Irene said. 'You know, what with the new flock and so on. He could have the cottage too, if we're movin' out.'

Rose looked thoughtful. 'Leave me to think about it, Irene,' she said. 'Thank you for telling me.'

Rose said nothing to Mark, but drove over to Benham late the following afternoon to call on Harry. She found him at home in the cottage he was soon to vacate, making himself a meal. He looked surprised to see her.

'Come in. It's good to see you, Rose. I meant to write and congratulate you on your marriage, but somehow. . . .' He shrugged. 'You know how it is.'

'Irene tells me you've given up your plan to emigrate.'

'That's right.' He turned away, picking up the kettle. 'Will you have a cup of tea?'

'Thank you. That would be very nice.' She sat down at the deal table. 'What made you change your mind, Harry?'

'Just seemed a long way away,' he said. He took mugs from the dresser hooks and set them out on the table.

'And you're about to lose your job and your home.'

He flushed. 'Bad news travels fast in Weston, doesn't it?'

'Irene only told me because your old cottage at Peacocks is about to be vacant again.'

He looked up sharply. 'Peter and Irene are leaving?'

'Not exactly. They're going to live with Irene's widowed father.'

He frowned. 'There's no job with the cottage then?'

'I need a farm manager. Someone I can trust, so that I can take a little more time off.'

'To be with your new husband?'

'Yes. I've bought some sheep. Just a few to begin with, but they've already lambed. I've always wanted to start them again

and I know you like sheep. As to wages, what are you getting now?' He told her. 'Then for the extra responsibility I'll pay you twenty per cent more.'

He paused, turning away to pour water into the brown teapot warming on the range. 'Well – I don't know.'

'It's not enough?'

'It's not that; the money's fine.'

She watched him pour out two cups of tea, never once raising his eyes to hers. The tension between them was palpable. 'Harry, is something wrong? Is there something you're not telling me?' He was silent and she asked, 'Is it to do with why you didn't go to Australia?'

'Do you really need to ask?' he said.

'I'd like to know.'

'All right then. If you want the truth I'll tell you: when I heard you'd married *him* – Elliot – I reckoned that sooner or later you'd be needing a friend.'

'What on *earth* do you mean?' It was her turn to colour.

He shook his head. 'I've got to say what's in my mind right out. I haven't got the fancy words for wrapping things up. I'm sure you know what you're doing and I respect your choice. You must love and trust the man or you wouldn't—' He broke off, lifting his cup and taking a great gulp of the scalding tea.

'I do love and trust him,' she said. 'I've heard the stories people take great delight in putting around about him. And I've heard his explanation. That's good enough for me. And if you don't mind me saying so, Harry, I think it's between Mark and me.'

'Of course.'

She sipped her own tea, studying his face doubtfully. 'So, will you take the job of farm manager at Peacocks.'

He looked up at her, startled. 'You're still offering – after what I said?'

'Of course I am. You're a reliable, competent worker, Harry. You taught me much of what I know. I can't think of anyone

better. So what's your answer?'

'Just one question.'

'Of course. As many as you like.'

'Who'd be my boss. You or him?'

'Me, if you want to call it that. Mark has nothing to do with the farm.'

'Right. Well, I'll . . . think about it.'

'When will you let me know?'

'Would the end of the week be all right?'

'That will do perfectly.' She got up. 'Thank you for the tea.' At the door she paused to look back at him. 'I hope you'll take the job, Harry. You were right about one thing: I do need your friendship. I always will.'

He nodded. 'Thanks. That's good to know.'

But Harry didn't wait until the end of the week. Two days later he knocked on the kitchen door early in the evening. He was freshly shaved and wearing his best suit. Rose invited him in.

'I've made up my mind,' he told her without preamble. 'I'd like to accept the job.'

She couldn't conceal her delight. 'Oh, Harry, I'm so pleased!'

'When would it be convenient for me to move into the cottage?'

'Irene and Peter are moving out at the weekend,' she told him. 'Why don't you go across and have a word with them about it now?'

'Thanks, I will.'

'Will you have a cup of tea with me to seal the deal?'

'No. If you don't mind I'll get on with making my arrangements.'

She stood at the door and watched him cross the yard, regretting his stiffness but congratulating herself that she was getting an ideal manager. As she turned back in she saw Mark standing in the doorway.

'Tell me I'm wrong!'

'Wrong. About what?'

'Tell me you haven't really offered that lout the job of farm manager.'

'He's not a lout. He's an intelligent man and a good worker. I thought you wanted me to take more time off so that we could be together.'

'I do. I never thought you'd want him hanging round the place though.'

'He's having the cottage but he certainly won't be *hanging around* as you call it. Anyway, what can you possibly have against him?'

'Just don't like the fellow,' Mark said sulkily. 'Every time I see him in the village he glares at me as though he'd like to kill me.'

Rose laughed. 'It's your imagination. Harry's a bit dour, that's all.'

'Well, just make sure he keeps out of my way.'

'It's going to make such a difference, having Harry to take care of things.' She went to him and put her arms around his neck. 'Just think – no more late nights. I'm going to have so much more time. I won't get so tired either. Shall we go out tonight to celebrate? There's a good film on at the cinema in Ipswich.'

He shook his head. 'I promised some chums I'd go over to Norwich for an evening at a club there.' He looked at his watch. 'Actually, it's time I was getting ready.'

'Shall I come too? I could be ready in no time.'

'Not tonight, sweetheart. It's chaps' only stuff. You'd be bored to death.' He slipped his arms around her waist and drew her close. 'Tell you what though, we'll go out tomorrow night; anywhere you fancy. A meal and dancing if you like. Just the two of us.'

She pressed her cheek against his. 'Oh Mark, that sounds lovely.'

He kissed her. 'Just one thing, darling, I haven't had time to

go to the bank today and the car's almost out of petrol. Could you let me have twenty pounds?'

'For petrol?' she asked, crestfallen.

'I've used up all my petrol ration and I have to get the black market stuff from a bloke I know in Snape. You know how much it costs.'

'I can't, Mark. I haven't that much in the house.'

His face darkened and he took a step back, letting his arms drop to his sides. 'What you mean is that you *won't*! I'm only asking for a loan for Christ's sake!'

'I know and I'd give it to you if I had it, Mark. If there's no petrol in the car you could take the pick-up if you like.'

'The *pick-up*?' he sneered. 'I wouldn't be seen dead in that thing. No, don't you worry about me. I'll ring a pal and get a lift over to Norwich.' At the door he turned. 'And before you start nagging again, I'll use the village phone box. Oh, and don't wait up. I'll probably be late.'

True to his word, Mark was late home. In fact he didn't come home at all that night, but drove into the yard as Rose was leaving the house to begin milking next morning. It occurred to her to wonder how he had managed to buy petrol when he hadn't any money, but she hadn't the heart to ask.

It became the pattern over the weeks that followed. At least twice a week he'd disappear to stay out till dawn, returning home to tumble into bed and sleep till afternoon. He became morose and moody until she felt she hardly knew the man she had married. The time they'd planned to spend together somehow failed to materialize and her suggestions that they go out together was met with impatient dismissal.

The pace of life on the farm quickened as the year matured and Rose had many an occasion to be thankful for Harry's help and support. Then something happened that caused her the greatest concern of all.

Her monthly bank statement failed to tally with her own calculations. She sat in the small room she used as an office,

poring over her receipts and trying to make sense of it, puzzling over how she could have miscalculated so badly. Then she turned to the sheaf of cancelled cheques, leafing through them one by one until she spotted something that made her blood freeze. There was something slightly odd about the signatures on half a dozen of them. It was not her own. It was certainly similar, but it was definitely not her hand. The worst thing was that all the forged cheques were for large amounts and made out to cash. After a moment's thought she picked up the telephone and asked for the bank's number, but at that moment Mark came in. Seeing the statement on the table and the sheaf of cancelled cheques he crossed quickly to the desk.

'Don't, Rose!'

She looked up at him. 'Why?'

At the other end of the line a voice answered. 'Martin's Bank, Can I help you?'

Before she could reply Mark quickly put his hand down on the receiver rest, cutting off the call. 'Leave it. Look, I can explain.'

'These are yours?' She picked up the cheques, looking up at him incredulously. 'You *forged* my signature?'

'Well, what the hell did you expect?' he said defensively. 'You keep me on such a tight rein – won't even lend me a few lousy quid for petrol when I ask you. I ran up a few debts and I knew it'd be no use asking you.'

'So you went behind my back. How *could* you, Mark?'

'Our marriage was supposed to mean we were equals, but since we've been married you have all the say. You hold the purse strings. Sometimes I feel I can't *move* without your sanction.'

'That's hardly true,' she countered. 'It seems to me you do exactly as you like. You never do a stroke of work here. You haven't even tried to get a job. You gamble as though you're a millionaire and you blame me for it all!'

'It's not like that. A man needs to *feel* like a man.'

139

'Then he should behave like one!'

'What about you behaving like a woman?' he returned. 'How am I supposed to fancy you when you come in stinking of cows and God knows what else. It's either that, or you're too damned tired. How long is it since we made love, Rose?'

'Perhaps that's because you seem to prefer spending the *days* in bed instead of the nights. I got a farm manager in so that we could spend more time together, but you prefer to go out without me.'

'If I asked you to go to Norwich you'd only make some excuse. It'd be too far; there'd be the milking or the lambing, or Christ knows what else to do. I'm sick of it, Rose. Sick and tired of it.' He turned and flung out of the room, leaving her shaking and upset.

By the time she came in from milking that evening he had left. His car had gone from the yard and there was a scribbled note on the kitchen table. It simply said,

Gone to find a job.

Rose went upstairs wearily, changed and had a bath. She began to make a meal, then abandoned the idea, her appetite gone. Mark hadn't gone to find a job, of course. Where would he find one at this time of day? It was far more likely that he was at his gambling club again. She sat down at the kitchen table, her head on her arms, wondering what had become of the dreams she had had, of the handsome debonair man she had married. Was it really all her fault?

A knock on the door made her start. She got to her feet and went to answer it. Outside, to her surprise, stood Meg Brown.

'Evenin', Mrs Elliot.' The woman's dark eyes glinted and her tone made it clear that it wasn't a social visit. 'I'll come in if you don't mind,' she went on. 'I think you'n me have got to have a talk, and it's not somethin' as can be settled on a doorstep.'

Rose held the door open with a sense of foreboding. The woman walked in and pulled out one of the chairs eyeing the Aga. 'A cuppa tea wouldn't come amiss,' she said insolently.

'Perhaps you'd like to say what you've come for,' Rose said, standing at the end of the table.

The woman shrugged. 'Suit yerself. But you'd better sit down before I start. I reckon you'll need to.'

Rose sat down. 'What is it?'

'My Melly is expectin'.'

'Really? So what does that have to do with me?'

'A lot, seein' as your husband is the father.'

'Rubbish! I don't believe you.'

'Well you better, lady, 'cause it's true.'

'From what I've heard about your daughter it could be any of a dozen men.' The moment she'd said it Rose knew it was a mistake. Meg was on her feet in an instant, her eyes flashing malevolently.

'I told you once you'd had trouble in your past and you'd have more of it in your future,' she said. 'I knew then it were true and now you know it too. You'd do well to have words with that man of yours, 'cause he's gonna have to pay for this child – that is if you wants to keep it between the four of us, like.'

'Are you blackmailing me?'

'I'm askin' for what's right and fair for my girl. You just tell him that.'

'And if he denies it, as he certainly will?'

'Then you'll be doubly sorry,' Meg sneered. ' 'Cause I'll *make* you pay.' She looked round the comfortable kitchen. 'You landed on your feet all right, didn't you? Bill Peacock must'a left you well provided for and I know enough about him to know he never done that for nothing.' She stepped up so close to Rose that she could hear the angry breath hissing in her throat. 'No prizes for guessin' what you did to make him pay, eh? A lonely man what hadn't had a woman in years. We both know the truth o' that un, so don't you play the high and mighty with me. What goes around comes around I always say. That man you married is no good.'

Rose sprang to her feet, her heart thudding. 'How dare you!'

'He's a cheat and a liar,' Meg went on, undeterred. 'He's done my girl wrong and somebody's gonna pay for it. I don't care whether it's him or you, 'cause I reckon you're both as bad. A woman as can't keep her man in her own bed ain't much of a wife!'

The door, which Rose had purposely left ajar opened suddenly and Harry's bulky figure stood in the doorway.

'Get on your way, Meg Brown!' he thundered. 'And don't you ever dare come back here threatening Mrs Elliot or it'll be the worse for you.'

Meg got up, her dark face flushing angrily. 'Don't you worry, I've said my say and I'm goin'.' She turned away, muttering, 'Wouldn't stay in this place any longer than I had to.' She wagged a finger at Rose. 'Just you remember what I said, missis. You ain't heard the last of this. Not by a long chalk!'

Harry took her arm and bundled her unceremoniously through the door and across the yard. When he came back Rose still sat where she was, her eyes stunned and blank. Raff, the puppy, jumped up at her side, his brown eyes anxious as he looked up at her, aware that his mistress was upset.

'Are you all right?' Harry asked.

She picked Raff up and hugged the animal to her for comfort. 'Oh Harry, thank you for stepping in when you did.'

'Can I get you anything – a cup of tea?' She nodded and he went to the Aga and set the kettle on the hob.

'You – heard?' she asked painfully.

Harry shook his head. 'I heard her shouting right across the yard. I knew she was up to no good when I saw her arrive. I just thought I'd better come across and see if you needed any help.'

'Thank goodness you did.'

He made the tea, watching her as he did so. 'It's none of my business, but was she trying to get money out of you?'

Rose sighed. 'She made a lot of accusations – about me and about Mark.' She looked up at him as he handed her a cup of tea. 'Do you – have you heard anything about us in the village?'

Harry sat down at the table, avoiding her eyes. 'You know what villages are,' he said.

'You can tell me, Harry. Have you?'

He shrugged. 'I never listen to tittle-tattle – and neither should you. Hot air, that's all it is.'

Rose shook her head. 'Not this time.'

'Look, it's none of my business, Rose, but if I ever hear anyone say a word against you I'll put them straight. And you know I'm always here if you need me, don't you?'

She reached out to touch his hand. 'I know you are, Harry. You're a true friend. But I'm afraid there's nothing you can do to help me out of this one.'

CHAPTER NINE

ROSE LAY awake night after night, her mind in turmoil with Meg Brown's accusation and demands. True, Mark had been seen with Imelda but that was before they were married. He'd sworn to her that it was just a flirtation – because of their quarrel. And she'd believed him. Surely he hadn't continued to see the girl? The thought of his betrayal cut her to the heart. The pain was with her all through her waking hours as she went about her work, eating away at her peace of mind, driving her mad with doubt and despair. But she knew she must keep her emotions in check and look at Meg's accusations sensibly. She must be sure of the truth before the woman came back making more demands. Before she faced Mark with the accusations she must somehow satisfy herself that the girl was indeed pregnant. The whole thing could be a trick dreamed up by the devious Meg to get money out of them. But how was she to find out?

She was still no nearer the answer a week later as she was buying petrol at the filling station on the edge of the village. A familiar vehicle drew in behind her pick-up truck and Richard Beech got out.

'Good morning, Rose.'

'Good morning.'

'I've been hoping I'd see you.' He told the pump attendant how much petrol he wanted, then walked over to her. 'Your new

sheep have lambed well. You've got the basis of a nice little flock there.'

'Thank you.'

'And Harry Owen is back working for you, I hear.'

'Yes, I was pleased to get him.'

He lowered his voice. 'Rose, can we talk?'

She laughed. 'Isn't that what we're doing?'

'I mean privately. Come up to the Manor and have coffee with me.'

'I'm very busy, Richard. I was on my way into Ipswich. Some other time per—'

'It's important, Rose. Please.'

Something about the urgency of his tone quickened her heartbeat. 'You sound serious.'

'I am.' He handed over his coupons and instructed the attendant to put the petrol on his account. 'Will you follow me home?' he asked her.

'All right, if you insist.'

At the Manor Richard led the way into his study and closed the door. He offered her a seat and then pressed the bell for the maid.

'What is it, Richard?' Rose asked, looking at her watch. 'I've got to. . . .'

He held a finger to his lips as the door opened and a girl whom Rose recognized immediately as Imelda Brown entered. The girl wore a black dress the buttons of which were noticeably strained at the front.

'What?' she asked sullenly.

'We'd like some coffee please, Melly. And ask Mrs Davis if she has any biscuits.'

'All right.' The girl withdrew.

When the door had closed behind her Rose said, 'I didn't know she worked for you.'

'She's only been here a couple of months. I had no idea of her condition when I gave her the job. She'll have to go soon, of

course. Apart from the fact that she's totally unsuitable I can't have a heavily pregnant girl answering the door to visitors.'

'I suppose not.'

'I spoke to her about it a couple of days ago,' Richard went on. 'She made quite a scene. It was very embarrassing.' Rose could feel her colour rising as Richard leaned forward confidentially. 'She wept bitterly and complained that her mother was out of work and they needed the money. Eventually I relented and offered her casual work on the farm. She turned it down, saying it was too hard. I've always felt I owed a certain duty to my employees so I asked her whether the child's father was planning to marry her. She said. . . .'

At that moment the door opened and the girl came in with the tray of coffee. Without a word or look at either of them she put it down on the table and withdrew.

'What did she say?' Rose asked, holding her breath.

'That he was already married.'

'I see.'

'She added that he would, however, be supporting her and the child. Her mother had promised her that she would see that he did. She told me that the man's wife was well off and that if they didn't stump up her mother would make sure that their name would be mud in every village in the county.'

'Why are you telling me this, Richard?'

He sighed. 'My dear, I think you already know the answer to that.'

She put her cup down and stood up. 'Thank you for the coffee. I really must go now.'

Richard got to his feet. 'Rose, please, I had no intention of offending you. I want to help if you'll let me. What the girl said made it easy to put two and two together. It was blatantly obvious who she was referring to.' He looked at her. 'I'm right, aren't I?'

With a sigh of defeat she sat down again and he asked gently, 'Were you already aware of this?'

147

'Her mother came to see me last week, making demands, accusations and threats.'

'What does he say about it?'

'I haven't mentioned it – so far.'

His eyebrows shot up. 'You've said *nothing* to him?'

'I had to think what to do. I needed to make sure it was true first. It could have been a trick to get money out of us.'

'And now that you know it is true?'

Tears welled up in her eyes. 'I suppose I'll have to deal with it – somehow.' She swallowed hard and raised her face to look at him. 'But I'll do it in my own way, Richard. This is no one else's business and I hope you'll remember that.'

He looked shocked. 'You surely didn't think that I'd tell anyone?'

She shook her head. 'No, of course not. I'm sorry. I know you meant well, Richard, but please allow me to handle this in my own way.' She stood up. 'Thank you for – everything. I really must go now.'

He walked with her out on to the drive. 'Rose, my dear, I assure you that what we have just spoken of is between the two of us. And I want you to know that if there is anything I can do – anything, at any time – please don't hesitate to ask.'

'I'll remember.' She got into the truck and started the engine. 'Goodbye, Richard. And thanks again.'

All the way home Rose considered what she would say to Mark. He would be angry – sure to deny that he was the child's father, and furious with her for suspecting him. And perhaps he was indeed innocent. Rose wanted so badly to believe that. But whether he was or not her allegation would cause a terrible rift between them so maybe she would be wise to keep quiet for the present.

She went over the possible alternatives. It could be that the father of Imelda's baby was someone long since gone from the village. There was a strong possibility that the girl wasn't even sure who it was. Meg Brown was a devious woman. She knew

that Rose had money. She also knew how to poison people's minds with rumour. Perhaps for now it would be best to try to appease the woman and keep the matter to herself.

Heathersedge Lane was right on the village boundary. It led to one of Richard Beech's pastures. The field was fringed by hawthorn hedging and in the corner was a small pond overhung with willow trees. By the five-bar gate stood a cattle-trough and a pump. It was here that Meg Brown's caravan had been parked for the past eighteen years. Richard's father had always given permission for the gypsies to set up camp here and when the tribe had abandoned their disgraced daughter, old Squire Beech hadn't had the heart to evict her.

Dusk was falling as Rose parked her pick-up at the end of the muddy lane and picked her way through the puddles to the field. The caravan was an old gypsy 'varda' with wooden steps leading up to a half door. Its once bright red and blue paint was faded and chipped and the empty horse shafts were half buried in the long grass. There was smoke coming from the little iron chimney on the roof so Rose knew that Meg was at home. As she drew closer, she saw that the top half of the door was open and she could see Meg's shadowy form moving about inside. At the creak of the gate the woman looked out.

'What do you want?' she shouted. 'Come to see if we really eat hedgehogs, and slugs have you? Come slummin'?'

Rose swallowed her resentment and took a deep breath. 'I've come to talk to you.'

'Fine words don't butter no parsnips!'

Rose wondered briefly where the woman got all her platitudes from. 'I'm sure you agree that we need to talk,' she said. 'Is your daughter in?'

Meg shook her head. 'She's taken a job in the pub kitchen. Goes there after she's finished at the Manor. Workin' all hours till she drops, poor girl. In her condition too! Your man should be ashamed of hisself'

149

'Perhaps I could come in.'

The woman opened the lower half of the door and Rose walked up the steps and into the caravan. The first thing that struck her was the lack of space and she wondered how two adults could exist in such a confined area. On the other hand, it was clean. A lot cleaner than Meg had kept the farmhouse when she was employed there. There were lace curtains at the tiny windows and brightly coloured patchwork covers on the two benches that also served as beds. On a little wood-burning stove a pot was steaming and the aroma that came from it was quite appetising. Meg, who wore a sacking apron over her skirt and cardigan, stood with her hands on her hips, her mouth pursed and her dark eyes challenging.

'Well?' she said. 'Say what you've come for. No point standin' on ceremony.'

Rose took an envelope out of her coat pocket and handed it to the woman.

Meg looked at it, then at Rose before she tore it open. 'What's this supposed to be?' she asked, taking out the notes.

'It's to get things for the baby,' Rose said. 'It's not born yet and anything can happen, so there'll be no more until it is.'

Meg gave a bark of laughter. 'Huh! In other words it's hush money, right?'

'Not at all.'

'He's admitted it's his then?'

Rose shook her head. 'That money is a gesture from me. My husband knows nothing about it and I hope he never will.'

'Then you're even more of a fool than I took you for.' Meg stuffed the money into her apron pocket. 'So – what happens when the chavvy's born then? Melly won't be able to work and there'll be another mouth to feed. She'll be needin' things – a pram and cot. . . .'

'And where would you put those things in here?' Rose asked. 'I thought you carried your babies in a shawl tied around you.'

'*Did* you now?' Meg's black eyes glittered. 'And is that what

150

you'd do with yours – if you was woman enough to have one?'

'No, but—'

'My Melly's kid won't be no gypsy. He'll be more'n half josser, so just you think on. When he's born he'll be entitled to live in a proper house. That cottage you got up at Peacocks 'ud do nicely for Mel and *your man's son*. That way the little'un'd see his dad every day. Then o' course there'd be proper maintenance due, wouldn't there?' She moved to the door and flung it open. 'Don't think you're getting' off that lightly, lady. Don't you kid yourself that you can come round here with your paltry handouts and shove it all under the carpet. If you take my advice you'll get off home and have a chat with that man o' your'n. A real woman would'a taken a chopper to him by now!'

Rose walked back to the truck with a heavy heart. Meg Brown intimidated her. The woman brought back echoes of her downtrodden childhood with Aunt Bess and reawakened feelings she thought she'd buried years ago. As she climbed into the driving seat she found she was trembling. It had started to rain and she sat for a while watching the raindrops run down the windscreen, wondering what to do next. There was no denying now that Imelda certainly was pregnant. And even if Mark had nothing to do with it there was no way they could prove it. But deep in her heart all her womanly instincts told her that the child was his. It was time to stop burying her head in the sand and face the fact that she had to challenge him.

At the farmhouse, Rose sat up till after midnight, then went reluctantly to bed. It was almost 2 a.m. when Mark eventually came in. As he fell into bed beside her she knew that he was drunk and although she had stayed awake, all her courage screwed up to speak to him, she knew that in his present state it would be useless to try. She slept fitfully, rising at five to go out to the milking parlour. Harry was surprised to see her.

'It's my turn this morning.'

151

'I know. I couldn't sleep. I feel better out here.'

He peered at her with concern. 'Are you all right?'

She shook her head. 'Yes, I'm fine. Now that I'm here I may as well help you.'

The cows were already in their stalls and together they set about washing them down and applying the clusters to their udders.

'This is a lot different from when you first came here,' Harry remarked. 'Do you remember Bill's ramshackle old cowshed and milking by hand?'

'How could I forget? Sometimes I long for those days.' Rose's eyes filled with tears. She lowered her head to hide her face, but Harry had heard the break in her voice.

'Look, you're tired,' he said. 'You look dead on your feet. Why don't you go back to bed for a couple of hours? I'll see to everything here.'

She thought about getting back into bed beside Mark – of the unavoidable confrontation. Even worse, keeping things locked up inside herself for another day. The thought made the ache in her heart tighten like an iron band and she shook her head.

'No. I'd rather stay. Don't worry about me,' she said. 'A bit of a headache, that's all.'

Harry walked across the parlour and stood looking at her. 'It's something to do with the Browns, isn't it? Something that old witch said to you the other night.'

She tried to laugh. 'No, of course not. Do you really think I'd lose any sleep over Meg Brown and her rantings?' But even as she said the words they sounded hollow to her. When the milking was done and the cows released from the machine and herded back out into the yard Harry took her arm.

'Come and have breakfast with me at the cottage. You don't have to tell me anything you don't want to; I'm not going to ask any questions. Just let me make you some tea and a bit of a fry-up.'

She thought of Harry's sunny little cottage, so neat and

peaceful, then of facing a bad-tempered, hung-over Mark across the breakfast-table with the inevitable row. 'Thanks, Harry. That would be lovely,' she said.

Raff was waiting patiently for her outside the milking parlour. He jumped up for her greeting and trotted at her heels as they drove the herd back to their pasture, running out now and then to nip at the ankles of a straying cow. Harry laughed.

'He's coming on, getting to be a real working dog.' He grinned at her. 'At least, he would be if you didn't make such a fool of him.'

Rose was silent. Raff's love for her was constant and unconditional. No need for Harry to know that the dog's affection was the only kind she had now.

Inside the cottage, she sat at the table watching as Harry put a bowl of water down for the dog and set about making breakfast. She couldn't possibly tell him about her terrible dilemma and she knew he wouldn't press her. That's what a real friend is, she told herself. Someone who is always there no matter what.

They ate in silence. True to his word he didn't press her for a reason for her preoccupation. She felt stronger with hot food inside her and, as he poured her a second cup of tea, she made up her mind that she could put things off no longer.

'Can you manage without me this morning, Harry?' she asked. 'There are things I need to do.'

'Of course. You don't need to ask.' He looked at her. 'You'd planned to walk the crops with me later; do you still want to do that?'

'Yes. It's high time we did it. It might be later though. I'll come and find you if that's all right.'

'I'll look out for you. I'll probably be with the sheep. Mr Beech is having the shearers next week. I thought we might share them with him while they're here.'

'That's a good thought, Harry.' She smiled at him. 'What would I do without you?'

'Do you want me to drive over and ask him then?'

'If you would.'

They parted company and she crossed the yard, Raff at her heels. It was now or never. She could put it off no longer.

When she opened the back door. Mark was up and sitting at the table, his face was grey and his eyes bloodshot. A cup of strong black coffee stood on the table in front of him.

He looked up as the door opened. 'Where the hell have you been?'

'Doing the milking.'

'You lying bitch! You've been over there with that Owen lout. I saw you out of the window.'

'That's right. Harry offered to make me breakfast after milking. I had a headache. I didn't sleep last night.'

'Makes himself useful, doesn't he?' he sneered. 'A bit too useful if you ask me. No wonder you wanted him back in that cottage.'

'That's rubbish, Mark, and you know it. Harry is my manager. I have to see him every day. It was after two when you came in. I was in bed but I wasn't asleep, as you'd have known if you hadn't been so drunk. Did I ask where you'd been?'

'No, and if you had I wouldn't have told you. I've told you before, I won't have my life ruled by you.'

'Mark, stop this. I don't want an argument. We have to talk.'

He clutched his head. 'Christ! Here we go again. What is it this time?'

'I've had Meg Brown here, demanding money for the child her daughter is expecting.'

His pale face took on a greenish tone and for a second he stared at her open-mouthed. 'She said – what?'

'That you are the father of the child Imelda is expecting. She threatened – tried to blackmail me into giving her money.'

'You didn't give her any, did you?'

'Is it true, Mark? Is the baby yours?'

'If you've given her any cash she'll never be off our backs.'

'I asked you a question, Mark?'

154

'And I asked *you* one!'

'She threatened to spread vile rumours – about me. All of them untrue, of course, but mud sticks. I couldn't have that.'

'You're not telling me you gave in – stumped up?'

'I gave her a small amount to keep her quiet till I got at the truth. And now I want to know, Mark: are her accusations true?'

He got up and began to pace the kitchen. 'Oh, for God's sake, Rose, what do *you* think?'

'I don't know what to think. You've been seen with the girl in the past.' A lump filled her throat so that she could hardly speak and she burst out, 'Heaven knows, I don't *want* to believe that it could be true, Mark, but you've cheated me – told me lies – even stolen from me. What was I to—'

'OK!' He spun round to face her, his forehead beaded with sweat. 'OK, you asked for it so here it is: Melly's a lovely girl and I've seen her a few times, yes. Why? Because she's warm and loving and – yes – sexy. Something you know nothing about. If I've been seeing her it's *your* fault. If you'd been more of a wife to me it wouldn't have happened.'

'I've tried so hard, Mark. When we married I thought you loved me – that we'd be a partnership. I thought you'd help on the farm so that we'd have more time to be together. When you didn't I took Harry back to manage the farm for me. But by then you'd lost interest in me. Now I know why.'

'Yes, you know why!' he said brutally. 'You've never let me forget that you're the one with the money, have you? How do you think it feels to have to ask you for every penny I spend, like some snivelling kid? You wouldn't even have a joint account – didn't trust me enough.'

'What did you do to earn my trust, Mark? You spend money like water. If it were left to you I'd be bankrupt by now.'

'There you are! *You'd* be bankrupt. I don't come into it, do I?'

'You could have found a job if you didn't like farm work. You

could have earned all the money you wanted. The truth is, Mark, you don't care much for work at all, do you? Only money for nothing.'

'Being married to you isn't money for nothing, believe me!' He pushed a hand through his hair. 'God, it's so *good* to get this out into the open at last. Melly's ten times the woman you are.'

'I see.' She swallowed the pain his words inflicted. 'Do you love her?'

He stared at her. 'Whatever love is – yes, I suppose I do.'

'So you're admitting that her child is yours?'

He shrugged. 'Could well be. But why the hell did you give money to that old cow of a mother of hers? It was equal to admitting responsibility before you'd even spoken to me. The woman must despise you for the fool you are! And do you think poor Mel will get a sniff of it? Not a hope!'

Rose felt as though her heart was raw. How could he be so cavalier about the whole thing? Had he no feelings for her at all? 'Do you have any idea how I felt?' she shouted at him. 'Can you imagine what I've been going through for the past ten days? I tried to spare you. I wanted so *much* to believe you were innocent and that it was all a trick. I've been protecting you, Mark, because – because I loved you!' The last words came out on a choking sob as she sank on to the nearest chair, tears pouring down her cheeks.

He stood looking down at her with something like contempt on his face. 'Love me? Is that what you call it? You've treated me like a dog – *worse*.' He flung out a hand towards Raff who crept beneath Rose's chair. 'That animal gets better treatment than I ever did. You refused me any money, any freedom. I felt stifled – *suffocated*! You might as well have chained me up out there in the yard and had done with it. Well, I've had enough, Rose. I'm going.' He strode to the door.

'Going! Where?'

He paused at the half open door. 'Who knows? That's the beauty of it. But don't worry, I'm not going to ask you for any

cash. I had a big win last night so I'm independent of you. I bet that hurts, doesn't it? Not having me chained to you any more!'

She sat at the table as though frozen, listening to him banging around upstairs, opening and closing drawers. She had begun life with nothing, deserted, unloved and despised. Peacocks was the only home, all she'd ever had, that was hers. It was the one place she had ever felt she belonged. All through her life people had rejected her. And now her husband was doing it too. What was wrong with her? What could she have done to deserve being treated like this? Half of her wanted to throw her pride to the wind, run upstairs and beg him not to leave her, but the other half knew that it was useless. He didn't love her. He probably never had. He had simply seen her as a free meal ticket.

As he burst back through the kitchen door and threw his bag down on the floor she flinched as she had in years gone by when Aunt Bess had raised her hand to her.

'I'm taking a few essentials,' he said, standing over her. 'I'll send you an address as soon as I've got one and you can send the rest on by rail. I think that's the least you can do for me.'

He took his jacket from where he'd hung it over the back of his chair and slipped it on, looking at her. 'What this, Rosie? No more tears?' he mocked. 'Aren't you even going to beg me to stay?'

She felt ice cold and numb. 'I've got no more tears,' she said quietly. 'Do you want a divorce?'

'I'll leave all that to you,' he said, picking up his bag. 'Because frankly, the less I have to do with you, or this God-forsaken place in the future, the better I'll like it.'

As he slammed out of the back door it was as though the ice inside her melted and the floodgates opened. A cry of anguish escaped her and she clamped a hand to her mouth. Raff jumped up and peered anxiously into her face. She gathered the dog to her and buried her face in his soft fur. Outside in the yard she

heard the angry roar of Mark's car revving up and listened despairingly as the sound of the engine gradually faded into the distance.

He'd gone. Her marriage was over. Once again she was alone.

CHAPTER TEN

'*WHERE IS she? Where has he taken her?*'

Meg Brown stood at the back door, her hair wild and her dark eyes ablaze with anger. It was barely light and Rose had slept in snatches all night to be wakened by a frantic banging on the back door that sent Raff into a frenzy of barking. Now she stood half asleep in her hastily donned dressing-gown, her feet bare, looking into the enraged eyes of the gypsy woman.

'I don't know what you're talking about.'

Meg barged past her into the kitchen. 'Don't lie to me. Where is he?'

Rose resignedly closed the door. 'If you mean my husband, he isn't here.'

'Well I know that much! She never came home last night and this morning I found this note in the tea caddy where she knew I wouldn't find it till she was long gone.' She thrust a scrap of paper at Rose who took it and read the one brief sentence.

I've gone with Mark. Mel

Rose handed back the note and swallowed the lump in her throat. She was unprepared for the fact that Mark had taken Imelda with him. Knowing him as she did she would have

expected him to abandon her too when he knew she was pregnant. He must have meant it when he said he loved her.

'I don't know where he's gone,' she said. 'I'm sorry but I can't help you. Will you go now please?'

The woman stared at her. 'You tellin' me you let him go without askin' where he was going? What kind of a woman are you?'

'It's none of your business.' Rose went to the door and held it open. 'If you don't go now I'm going to telephone the police.'

Meg stood her ground for a moment, then, muttering, she crossed the kitchen to the door. 'This'll end in tears, you mark my words,' she said, as she came face to face with Rose. 'You're responsible for this. If anything happens to my Melly it'll be your fault.'

Rose rounded on her. 'My fault! I suppose your daughter had nothing to do with it. Stealing other people's husbands is all right, is it?'

'You can't steal a happy husband!' Meg said, thrusting her face close. 'You never pleased him. He despised you. You should'a heard some of the things he told Mel about you. A right good laugh they had behind your back, an serve you right if you ask me.'

'No one is asking you!' Rose felt the blood rush to her face as her heart began to hammer with anger. 'Is that what you taught her – how to break up marriages? Is that what you did? Whose husband was your child's father?'

'No one's!' Meg thundered, her face darkening. 'All right. You've asked for it so now you're going to hear it, lady. My Imelda's dad was Bill Peacock!'

'*No!*' Rose reeled back, her mouth dropping open with shock.

'Oh yes. He knew it an'all. The only reason he give me a cleaning job up 'ere was out of guilt.' She took a step towards Rose, her face menacing. 'My people abandoned me because I carried his child. But would he ever own up and see us right?

160

Would he hell as like! He'd taken up with that fancy actress woman by then. Didn't want me around, spoilin' things for 'im.' Her mouth twisted in a bitter smile. 'I cursed them then just like I cursed you. He lost 'em both in the end and serve 'im right, so you wanna be careful!' She swept an arm round the kitchen. 'This farm should be ours by rights. Mine and Melly's. That's the least he could'a done for us. Probably would an all if you hadn't come along with your smarmy ways. Gettin' round him and sneakin' into his bed.'

'How *dare* you say that! It isn't true. Anyway, I don't believe a word of what you say,' Rose said.

Meg shrugged. 'Don't matter to me whether you do or not. I'm used to not bein' believed. Who believes a gypsy? It's true though, about Bill, like it or not. Why would I lie after all these years? Fact is this place is bad luck for us. First me, now Mel. Looks like I've lost my girl and all because of you. You never belonged 'ere. Best thing you could do'd be to sling your hook!'

'*Get out!*' Rose opened the door to the hall and called to Raff who rushed into the kitchen barking and baring his teeth at Meg. Rose grasped his collar. 'Get out before I let him go!'

Clearly afraid of the dog, Meg opened the door and backed out. 'You'll be sorry for this. I always told you you'd 'ave trouble,' she shouted. 'And it ain't over yet lady. Not by a long chalk!'

Rose let go of Raff who leapt towards the door, but Meg had slipped out and slammed it before he could cross the kitchen. Frustrated, he threw himself at it, barking furiously until Rose called him off.

'*Raff!* Come here. It's all right. She's gone now.' She watched from the window as Meg crossed the yard and disappeared through the gate. Relieved, she went to the Aga and set the kettle on to boil. The encounter with Meg had left her shaking and her head began to reel nauseously. Suddenly overcome, she

rushed upstairs to the bathroom to heave wretchedly into the toilet bowl.

When at last the faintness eased and her stomach stopped churning she came down to the kitchen and sat at the table, her legs weak and her heart still lurching. *Bill – Meg's lover!* Father of the girl who had taken Mark from her. It was true that Bill never said a word against Meg, even though he knew she was taking his money for slipshod work. In those far off days he had been a lonely man, farming here at Peacocks with sick and elderly parents. Who could blame him for seeking the company of a young woman. Meg had probably been as pretty as Imelda at that age. She'd probably been as free with her favours too, so no one could ever prove that her child's father was Bill Peacock, and she must have been well aware of the fact. But a woman like Meg would never let anything go. She'd bide her time until the chance for revenge came and then wreak it with every ounce of her pent-up spite.

Rose went about her work that day like an automaton, wondering if she would ever feel better; ever lose the sick heaviness in her heart and feel happy again. She had postponed walking the crops with Harry the previous day, but she could put it off no longer. Any mildew or disease must be spotted and dealt with soon or they could lose a valuable crop. Once or twice during the morning she was aware of Harry peering at her curiously and eventually he asked her if she was all right.

'Look, I've brought some sandwiches and a flask of tea,' he told her. 'They're only cheese and not very fancy but you're welcome to share them with me.'

Rose shook her head. 'I'm not very hungry, thank you, Harry.'

'If you don't mind me saying so, you should try to eat something,' he insisted. 'You look washed out and I wouldn't mind betting you didn't have any breakfast.'

'Well, no.'

He shook his head disapprovingly. 'You should know better. You'll be ill if you don't let up.'

She gave in and smiled. 'All right then, Harry. Perhaps I will.'

It was a fine warm day, the sky a hazy blue that promised heat. Harry took off his jacket and spread it in a dry spot under the hedge. 'A good thing the haymaking's done,' he remarked. 'You can take it easy for a couple of weeks, but we'll have harvest on us before we know it.'

As she settled herself on the ground Harry looked up, shading his eyes against the glare of the sun.

'Look.' He pointed to a tiny speck high above them. 'A lark. Can you hear him?'

Rose listened and sure enough the bird's song could be heard, the pure clear notes rising and falling as he soared and dipped, joyfully riding the warm currents of air in the summer sky.

Something about the perfection of the summer day, the clear air and the elated birdsong brought tears to her eyes. Harry gently touched her hand.

'Something's wrong. What is it?'

'It's nothing.'

'Yes it is. You should talk about it – get it off your chest. You know it'll be safe with me.'

She swallowed hard at the sob that choked her throat. 'Mark has left me, Harry.' She turned to him, her eyes brimming with tears. 'It's over. My marriage is finished.' Suddenly it didn't matter any more who knew. Soon it would be common knowledge anyway, if it wasn't already. She had no pride left. She felt as though her whole being was racked with pain.

'The man must be mad! Did he give you a reason for leaving?'

She shook her head. 'It was me who brought things to a head. I daresay it's common gossip that he's been seeing someone else.'

163

Harry looked away, his face colouring. 'I told you; I never listen. . . .'

'But you must have heard rumours.'

'That gypsy girl – Meg Brown's daughter?'

'She's expecting his child. That was why Meg came to see me that night.'

He nodded. 'I thought as much.' He looked at her. 'He'll be back. How can he compare a girl like that to you?' The moment the words were out he looked away, his colour deepening.

'But he does, Harry,' she told him. 'He only ever wanted me for the money and the farm. He thought he was going to have an easy life. Imelda is much more his kind of woman. She must be. He's taken her with him.'

'Taken her?' His head swung round to face her, his eyes incredulous. 'Surely not?'

'It's true. Meg was up here at first light this morning. I daresay she's furious because she can't demand any more money from me now.'

'You gave her money?'

'To keep her quiet while I got at the truth. I needn't have bothered, need I?'

'Well, I still think he'll be back,' he said.

Rose shook her head. 'I wouldn't have him back now. His affair with Imelda was only part of it. There were other things before that. It's over, Harry. I'll have to make the best of it.' She glanced at him, wondering if she should confide to him the worry that had been nagging away at her mind for the past two weeks – the fact that she was almost certainly pregnant herself. But the moment passed and she said nothing. It was something she must come to terms with. No one could help her with that. Could gypsy curses really come true? she wondered.

By early evening she was so tired she could barely stand. She made herself a quick meal and fed Raff, then she climbed the

stairs to run a comforting warm bath. She had just stepped out and begun to dry herself when she heard heavy footsteps on the gravel of the front drive, followed by a loud knocking on the door. Pulling on her dressing-gown she ran downstairs and opened the door to find Tom Marler, the village policeman, standing on the step. At his side was Mr Gresham, the vicar. When Constable Marler saw her he removed his helmet and asked politely if they might step inside. She ushered the two men into the drawing-room, looking from one to the other apprehensively.

'I think you'd better sit down, Mrs Elliot,' the vicar said. 'I'm afraid we've got some rather bad news to break.'

Her mind full of foreboding, Rose sat on the edge of one of the chairs and looked at the policeman.

'What is it, Constable? Did I forget to buy a licence for Raff?' Her attempt at lightness faded as she looked at the two grave faces.

The policeman cleared his throat and opened his notebook. 'I believe your husband owns a red sports car with the registration NV 4832.'

'That's right.' Her heart began to grow cold. 'But he isn't here at the moment.'

'Mrs Elliot – I'm sorry to have to tell you that your husband's car was found at the bottom of the cliffs at Sizewell earlier today. We think it must have been there for several hours.'

She caught her breath. '*Mark*! Is he hurt – in hospital?'

'Your husband was nowhere to be found,' he told her. 'Halfway down the cliff we found the body of a young woman who has been identified as Imelda Brown. She must have been thrown clear as the car plunged over.'

Rose's heart missed a beat. 'Oh my God!'

'I'm afraid it looks as if she was killed instantly.' He cleared his throat again. 'Can you tell me if your husband was likely to have been driving the car?' When she looked bewildered he

added, 'Is there any chance that it could have been stolen?'

'No. He left here in the car yesterday.'

'And – forgive me for asking, but would he have had any reason to have the young woman with him?'

'Possibly. Her mother told me this morning that she was missing.'

'I see.' He made brief notes in the notebook, his face expressionless.

Rose looked at the two solemn faces and felt a chill run through her. 'So, if Mark wasn't there, where is he?'

The constable paused, glancing at the vicar. 'The car was half submerged in the water and the tide had been right in earlier. We think that as it was an open-topped car his body must have been washed out to sea.'

'When – when will you know?'

'If that assumption is correct it could be some time.'

The vicar looked at her ashen face and moved to her side. 'I'm so sorry, Mrs Elliot. Is there anyone I can contact for you?'

She shuddered. 'No, I have no one. No family. I. . . .' She felt the room begin to spin and clasped her hand over her mouth. 'I'm sorry – I. . . .'

'Have you any brandy? Can I get you anything?' He picked up her other hand and began to chafe it, nodding dismissively at the policeman. 'I'll stay with Mrs Elliot if you want to go, Constable,' he said quietly.

Rose took a deep breath. 'I'm all right. Please don't let me keep you, Vicar.' His face was concerned as he looked into hers. 'You really shouldn't be alone. Surely there must be someone who would come and stay with you. A friend perhaps?'

'There's Nell,' Rose muttered. 'But she's miles away in Liverpool and she's working.'

'Nevertheless, I'm sure when she hears your terrible news. . . .'

'Could you send a telegram for me?' Rose asked. 'I would like to see her.'

166

'Of course. I can do it by telephone immediately. Just give me the address.' When the vicar had gone she crept up the stairs, taking Raff with her. All night she tossed and turned, terrible dreams invading her sleep, waking her with gory images of violence and death.

It was dawn when the pain first struck. Low in her back, it nagged and gripped. She got up and went downstairs to make herself a drink and take some aspirin, but the pain grew worse, coming and going in spasms that spread through her body like fire. Looking at the clock at last, she saw that it was time to get up for the morning milking, but the moment she got out of bed it happened. The sudden haemorrhage took her completely by surprise. Shocked, she got back into bed and lay for a while, hoping the bleeding would stop, but it didn't and at last she was forced to face the fact that she could be having a miscarriage. A doctor! She must send for a doctor. Even now it might not be too late to save her baby. But when she stood up her head reeled so badly she was forced to sit down again.

At last with great difficulty, holding on to the banisters at every step, she managed to reach the bottom of the stairs. She made her way to the kitchen where the telephone was, each step agony, but as she began to lift the receiver she realized that she didn't know the number. She had always been healthy – never needed a doctor since she'd been at Peacocks.

She took the telephone directory from the dresser drawer and began to look for the number, but she began to drift, her eyes blurring so that she couldn't see the print. Pulling out a chair she slumped on to it. It was no good. She couldn't do it. She needed to lie down. She slipped to the floor, wanting only to float away to whatever fate awaited her.

She didn't know how long she had lain there, drifting in and out of consciousness, when she heard a vehicle draw up in the yard. Footsteps crossed the yard and someone knocked on the door. She tried to get up but sank down again, too

weak to stand. A moment passed then a dear familiar voice called, 'Rosie! Come on, pet. Don't mess about, let me in! I've been on that bloody train all night and I'm gaggin' for a cup of tea!'

When Rose opened her eyes the light bouncing off white walls dazzled her.

'Hello, pet. You're with us again then.' Nell's face swam into view and when Rose saw her familiar smile tears filled her eyes.

'Nell – thank God you're here.' Her hands went instinctively to her stomach. 'Have I lost the – the. . . ?'

'Yes, pet.' Nell grasped her hand in both of hers and held it tightly. 'I'm so sorry. The doctors did what they could but it seems it was too late.' She leaned forward. 'You never said in your letters that you were expecting. Anyway, where's Mark?'

The traumatic events of the past days flooded back into Rose's mind and she closed her eyes as a stab of pain went through her. 'He's gone, Nell.'

'But where is he? I'll get a message to him and—'

'*No!* You don't understand.' Rose pulled herself up in the bed and looked at her friend. 'He left me – but then he was killed. He's dead, Nell. The police came to tell me last night. They told me that his car went over the cliffs at Sizewell. Imelda was with him. Imelda Brown, remember? She's dead, too.'

'Oh my God!' Nell looked shocked.

Rose slumped back against the pillows. 'There's more – much more. There's so much you don't know.'

'So I gather, but not now, pet.' Nell squeezed her hand. 'You need to rest. You can tell me all about it when you're stronger.'

'But the farm! What about the farm? I have to get out of here – go home.'

'No you don't. I can stay on and take over. Harry and I will manage fine.'

'But your job?'

Nell pulled a face. 'That bloody factory drove me barmy. I gave it up last week, so my time's my own at the moment.' She grinned. 'It'll be just great to be working on a farm again. Just like old times, eh? I can't wait. All you have to do is get plenty of rest and don't worry about a thing.'

Rose sighed, weak with relief.

'Now listen, they'll keep you in here as long as you're poorly. But if you behave yourself and if there's someone at home to look after you, they might let you go home in a couple of days,' Nell told her. 'And I'll stay and take care of you for however long it takes.'

It was almost a week before Rose was allowed home again. Nell came to fetch her in the pick-up and had a sumptuous tea waiting for her back at Peacocks. It was only when they were sitting together later that evening that Rose told her all that had happened during her brief marriage to Mark. Nell was shocked.

'Well, I have to say now that I never trusted him,' she said. 'Though how he managed to pack so much into such a short time really takes the biscuit! Cheating and stealing from you ... and then to be carrying on behind your back! You poor kid.'

Rose shook her head. 'I've been thinking a lot while I've been in hospital. It wasn't all Mark's fault.'

'You what?' Nell's face was aghast.

'He went straight from school into the RAF,' Rose said. 'Then he led that hectic life; living on the edge of life and death – elated one minute, shattered the next. Making close friends only to see them shot down out of the skies and killed. How could anyone expect him to settle down to an every-day existence on a farm after that?'

'Plenty have,' Nell pointed out. 'Some of the fellers were married – had wives and kids to support. They couldn't afford to go off the rails.'

'Maybe they were different kinds of men from Mark.'

'You're actually making excuses for him!' Nell said. 'How can you do that? Did he know you were having a baby?'

'No.'

'Do you reckon it would have made a difference if he had?'

Rose shook her head. 'In all honesty, no. He took Imelda with him when he went. He said he loved her. I thought at the time he was just saying it to hurt me, but he must have meant it. Now he's gone and both of his unborn children too.' Tears filled her eyes again and Nell leaned forward to touch her hand.

'I know it sounds hard, but maybe losing the baby was best in the long run. Bringing up a child with no father is hard and what with the farm to run and everything. . . .' She broke off as tears slipped down Rose's cheeks.

'They're all dead because of me, Nell. If I'd been a better wife, if I'd trusted him more – done what he wanted. . . .'

'You're not to blame yourself.' Nell said sternly. 'However you look at it, he was a bad lot, Rose. What happened was his own doing, not yours.'

'I did love him though.' Rose covered her face with her hands. 'Oh, Nell, it still hurts so much.'

Nell put her arms round her friend and held her close. 'I know, pet. I know.' She rocked her until she felt the sobs subside, then took out a clean hanky and pressed it into Rose's hand. 'No more about him. Not now. What's done is done and you must move on. Listen, this place is yours. You've a nice home and a good living. Things could be a lot worse. And you've a lot of good friends here. Everyone in the village has been asking about you. And you've a real gem in Harry Owen. Maybe I shouldn't say this but he worships you, you know. You could do a lot worse than—'

Rose smiled in spite of herself. 'Nell Sutton! That will be quite enough of that!' She sighed. 'I know I must move on, but I'm afraid it'll be a long time before I could ever look at, or

trust, another man.'

Nell said nothing. Although neither of them had mentioned it they both knew that Rose would not be able to pick up the scattered pieces of her life until Mark's body was found and they could finally lay him to rest.

Nell stayed for three weeks and Rose missed her sorely when she'd gone. Harvest time came. Rose had recovered her strength enough by that time to begin working herself again. Then it was Christmas. Nell came back and the two friends celebrated together, neither of them mentioning Mark or the fact that his body had never been recovered. Nell now had a job with the Municipal Parks Department in Liverpool and was taking a horticulture course at night school. She had also met Gerald Denby, a horticulturist at the college she attended and the two were seeing each other regularly.

Imelda's death had affected Meg Brown badly. She could not hold down a job, even with the few people compassionate enough to tolerate her slipshod ways. Her appearance grew more and more wild and unkempt and she often appeared drunk, ranting and raving incoherently outside The Grapes on a Saturday night until Sid was obliged to send for Constable Marler to escort her home. Rose, feeling misguidedly responsible for her predicament, went to the caravan in Heathersedge Lane one evening to see if there was anything she could do to help the gypsy woman. Meg's dishevelled head appeared as she opened the caravan door a few inches.

'What do *you* want?'

'I came to see if you needed anything – if you were all right,' Rose said.

'It's yourself you should be worryin' about,' Meg snapped. 'You think you're a widow, but you ain't. That man o'yours ain't no more dead than what I am! He's comin' back into your life, and when he does you'll know worse sufferin' than you ever dreamed of. He *killed* my girl. That weren't no accident. But I'll

171

have justice on him if it's the last thing I do!'

Rose clapped her hands over her ears and ran from the field, wishing she hadn't come.

'That's right, you run, missis,' Meg shouted. 'You can run but you won't escape what's comin' no more'n what he will!'

Rose shuddered as she drove back to the farm. Meg's mind seemed to have become unhinged. She still blamed her for what had happened and it was clear that she would never be forgiven.

Spring came again and life was busy with ploughing and sowing. Then came lambing time and later the newest brood of calves arrived. Harry was a tower of strength, always there, ever watchful but never intruding. But somehow the joy had gone out of farming for Rose. Although a year had gone by she could not forget Mark; the love he had thrown back in her face and pain and disillusionment he had brought her. The house seemed full of the ghosts of past occupants: poor lonely Bill and his parents; his lovely young wife and the precious little daughter they had lost. Everywhere she looked there were reminders of her own brief, turbulent marriage to Mark and the terrible night she had learned of his death and lost their baby. She was a successful farmer and this was her home, yet her confidence and self-esteem seemed to have died along with all the other tragic figures who had lived here. Maybe Meg had been right, maybe Peacocks was an unlucky, cursed place.

On impulse she wrote to Nell, asking if there might be a suitable job for her in Liverpool. After all, she was a city child by birth. Perhaps a city would be the place to make a fresh start. Nell wrote back with the news that she and Gerald were engaged. She begged Rose to think again about leaving Peacocks, saying that it was where she belonged and she must not act rashly, but take plenty of time to plan her future. But a deeply depressed Rose read the advice to mean that she would

be in the way; a burden that Nell didn't need to spoil her happiness.

One Sunday afternoon, at odds with her own company, she walked over to Weston Manor to see Richard Beech. He had called to pay his condolences on hearing of Mark's death but since then he had not visited her again.

It was a beautiful afternoon and he seemed delighted to see her, inviting her to sit and have tea with him in the garden.

'It's good to see you, Rose,' he said. 'How are you?'

'I'm very well, thank you, Richard.'

'But. . . ?' He looked at her enquiringly as he handed her a cup of tea. 'I can see there's something on your mind. Can I help?'

'I feel I need to make a fresh start,' she told him. 'Since Mark's death I've been restless. I think I've put as much as I have into farming and it's time to move on.'

'So how do you think I can help?'

'Do you want – would you consider buying me out?'

His eyebrows shot up. 'Take Peacocks off your hands?'

She nodded. 'All my enthusiasm – all my confidence has gone. I keep waiting for the next disaster to strike.'

'But surely that's only natural after what happened. These things take time.'

She shook her head. 'No. It just seems to get worse. It will be a wrench, giving up Peacocks. It's meant so much to me in the past. I love the house – and the farm. It's just that there are so many unhappy memories there now.'

Richard looked thoughtful. 'Of course, there is another solution,' he said.

'Is there?'

'I did ask you before, but – you could always marry me.' Seeing the look on her face he added quickly, 'I know you said no before and I understood, but circumstances alter. I also realize that you can't remarry yet. But it might be something for you to think about, for the future. We could amalgamate

the two farms, let a manager – someone like Harry Owen –
live at Peacocks. He's a personable fellow: he's bound to
marry one of these days. You could then live here. It would be
a good economic proposition and I could offer you a good
life.'

She smiled wryly. 'Aren't you forgetting something?'

He flushed. 'I didn't like to mention it, but I am very fond of
you, Rose. I'm sure you know that. I'm equally sure that you
could find it possible to return my feelings – eventually.'

She sighed. 'It would be so simple if that were true, Richard.
As you say, it would be the perfect solution. But in any case, if
Mark's body is never recovered it might be a very long time
before I could be declared free to marry again.'

'I understand that.' He frowned. 'There is another consideration: is Peacocks yours alone, Rose? I mean, are you free to sell
under your present circumstances?'

'I don't know. It's something I'll probably have to have
advice on.'

'And I'd like you to think about sharing your life with me at
some time in the future, Rose,' he said. 'I really believe we could
be happy together.'

Returning home, Rose felt even more confused. Marrying
Richard was out of the question. She didn't love him and knew
that she never would. Apart from that, she didn't fit in with his
lifestyle or his circle of friends. If she were to marry him she
would be bored and lonely. And perversely, in spite of the way
she felt, she couldn't bear the thought of anyone else living at
Peacocks. Not even Harry. In fact, although she would barely
acknowledge the thought, the idea of him living there with a
wife, probably bringing up a family there gave her a twinge of
something she didn't quite understand. So what was there for
her in the future?

It was on the last weekend in September that Sid, the landlord of The Grapes, organized a trip to Norwich to see a
demonstration of wartime fighter planes. Peter and his wife,

Irene, were going, along with Geoff. On the Friday evening, Harry came across to the house and knocked on the half-open back door. Raff rushed out, barking excitedly and jumping up to make a fuss of his friend, then Rose, who was busy cooking supper, appeared, wiping her hands on her apron.

'Hello, Harry. Can I do something for you?'

'It's this trip to Norwich on Sunday,' he said. 'Irene can't go. Her dad isn't very well and she doesn't want to leave him. I thought you might like the spare ticket.'

Without even thinking about it, Rose shook her head. 'I don't think so, Harry. It's good of you to think of me though.'

'I think you should come,' he said. 'You never go anywhere these days. You never even came to the harvest supper. It's been all work and sleep with you since. . . .' He broke off, looking at his feet. 'Anyway, I think it'd make a nice break for you. And I'd be there to look after you.'

She was touched. 'Oh, Harry, how kind, but—'

'I'm not leaving here till you say yes,' he said stubbornly.

She laughed. 'I never knew you could be so persistent.'

He flushed. 'Of course, if you don't want – I mean, perhaps you wouldn't want to be seen with me.'

Something inside her stirred. Reaching out she took his arm and drew him gently inside the kitchen. 'Please sit down, Harry,' she said. When he was seated she said, 'I've been meaning to speak to you for weeks. I want you to know how much I appreciate all you've done for me over these past difficult months.'

He flushed even deeper, shaking his head. 'It's my job.'

'No!' She held up her hand. 'You've done much more than your job. I know you've looked out for me – done extra work when I haven't been up to it. And if you really think that I'm so shallow that I wouldn't want to be seen with you, then I'm disappointed. We're two of a kind, Harry. We always have been. Ever since the day I arrived at Peacocks you've always been there for me, in the background, solid and dependable. And if

you really want to take me to the air show then I'll be proud to be escorted by you.'

He got to his feet. 'You mean it?'

'Of course I mean it.'

'It'll be a good day out. I promise you.'

'I know. I'm looking forward to it.' She laughed. 'In fact, I can't wait!'

The following day Rose looked out her one and only suit for the occasion, a light-blue silk two-piece which she pressed carefully and hung up on the wardrobe door. Sitting down at her dressing-table she took a long hard look at herself. Since Mark had gone she'd let herself go, pulling on overalls each morning and thrusting her feet into Wellingtons. Her hair was quite long and hadn't seen the inside of a hairdresser's for months. She washed it and set it in pin curls like she and the rest of the girls had done in her Land Army days. Getting up early on Sunday morning she bathed, then rummaged in the dressing-table drawer until she found some make-up. She combed her hair out into a halo of curls and put on a little powder and lipstick, then dressed in her blue two piece and a crisp white blouse. Even she was pleasantly surprised at the transformation and when Harry came to call for her he flushed with pleasure at the sight of her.

'You look lovely, Rose,' he said.

She smiled as she locked the door behind her. 'Thank you. Shall we go?'

The crowd of people assembled at the pick-up point outside The Grapes greeted her warmly. There had been gossip about how pale and wan Rose Elliot had looked since her husband took off with the Brown girl and the pair of them had been killed. It was good to see that she was getting over it at last.

Sitting next to Harry on the coach, Rose was very conscious of the warmth of his arm through her sleeve. He'd thought of everything, even bringing boiled sweets to suck in case she was

travel-sick. As he offered them to her he smiled.

'It's so good to see you looking happy again, Rose.'

And as she took a sweet and popped it into her mouth she realized with a small surprise that she was.

The show was on a small airfield just outside Norwich and consisted mainly of Spitfires and Hurricanes, though there were a few other light aircraft and one or two German planes too. The noise of their take-off was deafening and most of the women put their hands over their ears. But once in the sky the expert flying and aerobatic tricks brought 'oohs' and 'aahs' from the crowd and made them hold their breath. To Harry's great delight, he felt Rose's hand slip into the crook of his arm as they stood watching together. He turned to smile down at her and pressed her hand against his side.

When the tea interval came, spectators were invited to go across to the hangars to meet the pilots and look at the aeroplanes more closely. Not many of the women were interested and Rose encouraged Harry to go off with Peter and Geoff. He was reluctant at first but at last she persuaded him, insisting that she would keep Mrs Maitland, the postmistress, company in the tea tent until he came back.

Harry had his head bent over a Spitfire engine displayed on a bench when someone touched his arm and he was aware of Peter standing next to him.

'They look so simple, don't they?' he said. 'You wouldn't think. . . .' He looked up and stopped speaking as he saw the troubled look on Peter's face. 'What's up, Pete? You look as if you've seen a ghost.'

'I have,' Peter whispered. 'Don't make it obvious but just take a look at the bloke over there in the flying suit – on the left of that little bunch – the one who's taken his helmet off.'

Harry followed Peter's gaze and caught his breath. 'My God! He looks just like. . . .'

'Not only looks like. It *is*!'

'But it can't be. He was killed – drowned.'

'Never found a body though, did they?'

The colour left Harry's face. 'What do we do now?'

'By rights we ought to go over and ask him what he thinks he's playing at,' Peter said. 'But if you ask me, she's better off without him. I vote we keep quiet.'

'I don't know.' Harry's mind was in a turmoil. Mark Elliot – alive after all! What would Rose do? Worse, what would she think of him if she found out that he knew and hadn't told her?

It was late that night as they walked back to Peacocks together. The coach had stopped halfway home at a pub where they had all had a snack meal and a drink. Back in the coach everyone was merry and sang popular songs the rest of the way home. Harry even managed to get Rose to join in and for her it was like old times in the hostel when she and the girls would sing along to the old wind-up gramophone. As he opened the gate and they walked into the yard she looked up at him.

'I've had such a lovely day, Harry,' she said. 'Thank you so much for taking me.'

'I've enjoyed myself too,' he said. 'The more so because you were with me.'

At the back door she turned to him. Standing on tiptoe she put her hands on his shoulders and reached up to kiss his cheek. 'You're such a good friend to me,' she said. 'There couldn't be a better.'

He had to fight down the urge to take her in his arms and kiss her properly. He might even have given in to it if it hadn't been for the image of that pilot, his fair hair tousled and his eyes bright with laughter as he had called out to a colleague. What a nerve he had, acting as though nothing had happened. He clearly didn't give a damn for the pain he'd caused. Thinking about it now made him wish he'd gone over and

punched his head in.

He looked down into Rose's shining eyes and his heart contracted. He'd loved her for years. Once she had almost been his. Only this morning he'd dared to hope that there might just be a slender chance for him again. Now, once again it looked as though his dreams were about to be shattered. Knowing Elliot as he did, he guessed it would only be a matter of time before he ran out of money and came back with some cock and bull tale about what had happened. And knowing Rose as he did, he guessed with a sinking heart that she'd take him back.

CHAPTER ELEVEN

H ARRY HAD been trying for weeks to persuade Rose that it was time for Raff to begin learning to work the sheep.

'He'll never be a real sheepdog, Harry,' Rose laughed. 'I've made too much of a pet of him for that. You've said so yourself.'

'Of course he will. It comes naturally to that breed. He's already very obedient so just let's give him a try. We need a sheepdog now that the flock is increasing and it seems daft to get another when you already have Raff.'

At first Harry had trained him out in the yard with a few commands and Rose had to admit that he had done well. He would sit and lie to command and was beginning to learn and obey the whistle signals, so that at last she had to give in and agree that the time had come to introduce him to the flock.

It was a crisp October morning when they walked him up to the pasture where the sheep were. Harry had already set up three sides of a pen with hurdles for the sheep to be herded into. When he was first let off his lead Raff went mad, racing round and round the flock until Harry shouted the command to lie. He was so excited that it took several loud commands from Harry before he finally obeyed, flattening himself to the ground, eyes bright and tongue lolling as he looked towards Harry, eager for the next command.

Rose watched from the gateway. If Raff became a good sheepdog she knew she would have to lose him as a pet. He would

have to go and live with his new master and become accustomed to the life of a working dog. Not to mention the diet. No more tit-bits and treats; no more sneaking upstairs to sleep on the rug beside her bed. She had mixed feelings of pride and regret as she watched Raff obeying Harry, eager to please, happy to be a grown-up working dog.

After that, Harry worked hard with the dog, taking him for regular training sessions with the sheep and gradually Raff became more Harry's dog than Rose's, moving to the cottage and being fed and cared for by his new master. Harry's one concession to her was that Raff should not have to live outside in a kennel. Instead,he slept in Harry's kitchen, always with one eye open, so eager was he to respond to his master's every wish.

Secretly Rose felt that the last link with Mark had gone. He had given her the puppy on their first Christmas together. Now, to all intents and purposes, Raff was lost to her too. She thought again about leaving Peacocks. There was nothing left for her here now. More and more over the months since she had lost the baby she had thought about her mother. If she returned to London perhaps she could trace her. Somehow deep inside, she felt that Sally was still alive. Perhaps she even regretted abandoning her daughter and longed to find her again too.

As they slipped into November, all the talk was of Princess Elizabeth's wedding. The newspapers were full of it. There were accounts of the dress, to be made of real silk and embroidered with thousands of pearls. There was speculation as to who would be bridesmaids and much interest over the list of crowned heads and important people who would attend this first great state occasion since before the war.

During the war and since, weddings had been improvised affairs with families pooling clothing coupons and mothers doing their best to create couture wedding gowns out of parachute silk; scheming and hoarding rations and points coupons

for months to provide a proper wedding breakfast. But in spite of the austerity that was still a part of everyday life no one grudged the princess her special day. Rather, everyone wanted to share in it and planned to gather round their wireless sets to listen to the ceremony broadcast from the Abbey, and later to put on their own celebrations.

Weston St Mary was no exception and a committee was formed to arrange a royal wedding day party in the village hall. There was to be a children's fancy dress competition and tea, a bonny baby contest and later in the evening there was to be a dance for the adults, for which a local band had been engaged. Everyone looked forward eagerly to the 20th.

Rose saw the celebrations as a secret farewell. Only Richard Beech knew of her plans to leave Peacocks. He had eventually agreed to buy the land and house from her when she was ready and they had decided on a price. She had only to say the word and arrangements for the sale would be put into motion.

Rose knew that she must tell Harry before the news leaked out. She planned to soften the blow with the news that the farmhouse would be his to live in for as long as he was there.

It was a week before the royal wedding when she went across to the cottage to break the news to him. Raff greeted her ecstatically when the door was opened, but Harry looked surprised.

'Rose. Come in. Is anything wrong?'

She stepped over the threshold. 'No. I have some news, that's all. I wanted you to be the first to hear it.' She looked around the small cottage living-room with its welcoming fire and comfortable chairs. Not many men were capable of making a house into a home, but Harry was the exception. She had no qualms of handing over her precious farmhouse to him. She sat down in the chair by the fire and Raff came and settled close to her legs. Harry stood with his back to the fire, looking down at her expectantly.

'Can I get you anything? A cup of tea?'

'No, thank you. I've come to tell you that I'm leaving

Peacocks, Harry.' There was no other way to say it, but she regretted her bluntness when she saw the look of abject shock on his face.

'Leaving! But why?'

'There's nothing for me here now. Even Raff isn't really my dog any more. Somehow it all seems flat and pointless.'

'How can you say that? What about Peacocks and all the hard work you've put into it? You've made the farm into a profitable business again.'

She sighed. 'Somehow, after all that's happened I've lost my enthusiasm for it.'

'What are your plans? Where will you go?'

'Back to London, probably. I want to try and trace my mother. She might have been killed in the blitz, I don't know. I haven't seen her since I was a little girl. I just need to find someone of my own again. Some roots, I suppose you'd call it.'

'Roots? I thought you felt you'd put down roots here.' He sat down in the chair opposite and looked at her, shaking his head. He knew that at this point he should tell her that he'd seen Mark – that he knew he was still alive. It had been worrying him ever since the day of the air show. But somehow he still couldn't bring himself to tell her. 'I don't know what to say, Rose.'

'It's not easy to explain. Since what happened – Mark leaving, and then losing the baby, I feel I don't know who I am any more. For a long time I had this odd feeling that I didn't really exist – as though if I looked into the mirror there'd be no reflection – nothing looking back. I still feel that to a certain extent. I really need to find myself.'

'And you can't do that here?'

'No. I've tried.'

He shook his head, unable to comprehend. 'But – what will you do about the farm?'

'Richard Beech has agreed to buy it from me,' she told him. 'He's eager to expand his farm and as Peacocks' land adjoins his

it's ideal. He'll take everything, livestock, machinery and all farmhands. No one will be out of work. I made one other stipulation, Harry, I want you to have the house, to live in as long as you work here.'

He seemed hardly to be listening. 'This is a blow. I can't imagine Peacocks without you. Nothing will ever be the same.'

'Yes it will, Harry. People come and go all the time. You'll forget me. Richard will make the farm even better. One day I know you'll meet someone you'll want to marry and you'll have a nice house in which to—'

He coloured and got up from his chair abruptly, turning away from her. She stopped speaking realizing that she was upsetting him. 'Harry – what is it?'

'For God's sake, Rose. Don't you *know*?' he said harshly, turning suddenly to face her. 'For a woman with deep feelings you can be very cruel!'

'*Cruel*? But—'

'Surely you must know what I feel for you.'

She lowered her eyes. 'That was a long time ago.'

'For you maybe. For me it's the same as ever.' His voice was hard and husky with pain. 'Over the years it's just grown stronger. I had to watch you marry Elliot – stand by while he betrayed and hurt you, and say nothing. I had to stand aside when you were ill and let your friend take care of you. I've tried my hardest to help when all the time I wanted to do – to *be* so much more to you. Don't tell me you didn't know – couldn't *see* how I felt.'

His vehemence shocked her. She'd never seen mild-mannered Harry so emotional before. She got to her feet. 'Harry, you've always been a wonderful friend and I appreciate you and all you've done. Perhaps if things had worked out differently our lives would have been—'

'I know.' He shook his head, recovering quickly. 'I'm sorry. That wasn't fair. I'm not blaming you. You can't force yourself to love someone. But I wish you weren't going, Rose. I still

think your future is here and I meant it when I said I'd miss you. Of course, it's good of you to think of the house for me, but I'm not sure I'll want to stay. This place will hold as many painful memories for me as it does for you.' He managed a stiff, controlled little smile. 'But thank you for coming to tell me first.'

'Oh, Harry!' She went to him and reached out for his hands, but he took only her fingertips, keeping her at arms' length. 'Harry, don't you think I'll miss you too?' she said. 'You've been my best friend – a part of my life – a very important part for years now. I couldn't bear to lose our friendship. Please say we'll keep in touch.'

'Of course we will,' he said.

'None of this is happening yet,' she said. 'Nothing's settled and it could be some time before I leave. There's the royal wedding to look forward to with all the village celebrations. And Christmas. We can still enjoy those things together, can't we?'

He sighed, wondering how he could bear the months to come, seeing her every day and knowing he was about to lose her for good. 'Of course.'

'You'll still take me to the dance?'

'Naturally.'

'And – please say you don't hate me.'

A small sound escaped his lips. '*Hate* you? How could I?'

'I'm not saying I'll never come back, Harry,' she said. 'Perhaps one day when I've got my life sorted out again I'll—'

He held up his hand. 'I know. We'll see. You must do what you feel is right.'

When she'd gone he closed the door and slowly went back to his chair by the fire. There'd be no other woman for him – ever. And soon she would be gone for good. Sensing his sadness, Raff came and sat by his side, leaning against his legs and looking up into his distressed face with compassionate brown eyes. Harry fondled the dog's ears.

'We're losing her, boy,' he said aloud. 'It had to come one day. And now it has.'

The day of the royal wedding was grey and cloudy, but the atmosphere in the village was electric with excitement. Richard Beech had invited Rose to go to the Manor to listen to the ceremony, but she had refused, preferring to listen on the wireless in the farm kitchen on her own. She was reminded painfully of her own simple wedding to Mark and wanted to be allowed the luxury of tears.

In the afternoon, she went down to the village hall to help with the children's tea. Richard had been asked to judge the fancy dress competition. He chose a miniature guardsman for the boys and a fairy queen for the girls and he asked Rose to present the prizes.

After they had cleared the hall and washed up, and the parents had taken tired offspring off to bed, Rose came home to change for the dance. Eager to make it a special occasion she had been into Ipswich the previous day to buy herself a new dress. She'd chosen a deep violet-coloured taffeta with a swirling skirt in the new length inspired by Christian Dior. She'd been to the hairdresser's afterwards and had her hair cut into a sleek shape with a little fringe and when she was ready and stood before her dressing-table mirror she was pleased with the effect. If she was to move back to London she must get used to taking more time and trouble over her appearance.

Harry looked handsome when he came to call for her, wearing his best suit and a white shirt, his unruly hair tamed with hair cream. The village hall was festive with bunting and balloons in red, white and blue. Sid from The Grapes had set up a bar and the ladies of the committee had laid out the buffet that had been contributed to by almost everyone in the village.

'We haven't exactly got a five hundred pound cake like what the royals had,' laughed Mrs Maitland, who had made a replica wedding cake as a centrepiece, two tiers of which were made of

cardboard. 'But I reckon the village has done us proud.'

Rose had the first dance with Harry and found that he was a surprisingly good dancer. 'My mother taught me,' he confided. 'She loved to dance, but my dad was never much of a dancer. I was just a kid at the time but you don't forget, do you?'

Richard Beech put in an appearance and asked Rose for a dance. As they circled the floor, he asked her if she had given any more thought to the sale of the farm, but she shook her head.

'I'd like to postpone making a decision on it until after Christmas if you don't mind, Richard,' she told him.

At the supper interval, Harry got her a plate of food while she kept a seat for him. When they had eaten he looked at her. 'There's something I want to tell you,' he said. 'Get your coat and we'll take a walk outside.'

The clouds had cleared and it was a frosty night, the sky clear and starlit. Together they walked across to the church and sat on the bench outside the gate.

'I just wanted you to know that I'm leaving too, Rose,' he said. 'So I won't be needing the farmhouse when you go.'

She was taken aback. 'Where are you going, Harry?'

'To Australia,' he said. 'I told you once before that I wanted to go and now there's nothing to hold me back. I can get an assisted passage and it shouldn't be hard to find work and make a life for myself out there.'

Something inside her sank like a stone. 'All that way. Are you sure, Harry?'

'Quite sure. This time I've made up my mind.'

'So – if I came back – you wouldn't be here.'

'Not any more. You see I have to find myself too, Rose,' he said. 'I've had my troubles in the past, as you know. I've never had any illusions about my future prospects in this country, and for a very long time I've known what I wanted. But as it seems I'm destined never to have it I've got to get right away and try to start again.'

For a moment she was silent, then she looked up at him and his heart lurched as he saw the tears glinting in her eyes. 'This is because of me, isn't it?' she said softly.

'It's because of circumstances,' he said. 'It's because of what life has done to us – to you and me. You mustn't blame yourself for anything, Rose. It's not your fault.'

'It all seems so final, Harry,' she said. 'Both of us going away – so far away.'

He slipped an arm round her shoulder and pulled her close to his side. 'Better this way,' he said. 'A new start for us both. Maybe we'll both meet someone we can really love and we'll live happily ever after like in the fairy-tales.'

'Life's not like that though, Harry,' she said sadly. 'I'm sure neither of us has any illusions about that.'

When they went back into the hall the supper had been cleared away, the lights had been lowered and the band was playing a popular romantic tune. Harry held out his arms to her. 'Just for tonight we can pretend, can't we?' he said. 'Pretend that everything's fine and enjoy ourselves.'

Harry's arms were warm around her and as they danced she laid her cheek against his. It was easy – so easy to pretend, and as she looked up at him she wondered for a fleeting moment what it would have been like if she had never met Mark – never married him. Life was such a tenuous affair. One moment – one chance meeting could change the course of it forever.

The music had just ended and the dancers were returning to their seats when there was a sudden disturbance at the entrance to the hall. A man's voice was heard shouting. A woman gave an alarmed scream and there was the tinkle of breaking glass. Then, as the crowd parted and the intruder was revealed, Rose caught her breath. The man who had pushed his way into the hall was clearly drunk. He was unshaven, his clothes were dishevelled and his hair long and untidy, but she recognized him instantly.

'*Mark!*' Her hand flew to her mouth and the word came out

189

in a strangled whisper as she reached instinctively for Harry's hand.

'I've come for my wife!' Mark's words were slurred as he stood swaying in the doorway. 'She's not at home so she must be here.' He began to search the room with bleary eyes. 'Where is she?'

Richard, who had been about to leave, stepped up to him and took his arm. 'Why don't we talk about this outside?' he said quietly. 'You're making a scene.'

Mark shook him off. 'What the hell has it got to do with you? Leave me alone, Beech! The peasants might think you're God almighty but you're nothing to me.' Suddenly he spotted Rose who stood frozen with shock. 'Time to come home, Rosie.' He began to stagger towards her. 'We've got some catching up to do.'

Harry joined Richard and they took one arm each before he could reach her.

'Don't be an idiot, Elliot,' Harry hissed. 'Can't you see you're spoiling everyone's evening?'

'Spoiling it, am I?' Mark scoffed. 'Well tough luck! It's nothing to do with you. Rose is my wife and she's coming with me. You can't stop us.'

'You're drunk. Are you going quietly or do you want me to get the police?' Harry said.

Her heart in her mouth, Rose quickly crossed the room. 'I'd better go with him,' she said, trying to hide her apprehension. 'Don't worry. I'll be all right.'

Mark grabbed her arm in a painful grip and pulled her towards the door. 'I should bloody well think so too! Let's get the hell out of here.'

Harry and Richard made to follow but she shot them a warning look, shaking her head. 'Leave it. I'll be all right, really.'

Reluctantly, they stood aside, but Harry slipped unseen into the porch to keep watch. As Rose went with Mark into the chill of the night her mind teemed with questions.

'Where have you been, Mark?' she said. 'All these months, and you were alive all the time! How could you do this to me? I thought you were dead.'

'*Where have you been? What have you been doing?*' He assumed a high-pitched voice, mocking her. 'Nothing bloody changes, does it? Still the same nagging wife!'

'Have you any idea what I've been through?'

'Can't be any worse than what I've suffered,' he said. 'Never mind all that now. Time enough for explanations later. Come on, we're going home.' Richard's Land-Rover stood on the forecourt and Mark pulled her towards it. 'Good of the Lord of the Manor to provide transport for us, isn't it?' he said.

Rose pulled her arm away and held back. 'No – you can't. You're not fit to drive. Besides, it's stealing.'

He rounded on her. 'Still calling me a thief? But surely you remember, Rosie – that's what I am! A liar, a cheat and a thief! Good enough to risk my life flying a Spitfire for my country, but not good enough for my tight-fisted, sanctimonious bitch of a wife to treat me as an equal. Well, from now on it's going to be different. I'm going to be the boss. Do you hear? It's going to be my *name* on the deeds of that farm and on the bank account.' He made a grab for her and she shrank back.

'*No!* You're drunk, Mark. You don't know what you're saying. You need to sober up before we can talk.'

'Come *on*, you stupid cow!'

Harry, who had been watching from the doorway sprang forward and put himself between them. 'You heard what she said. Leave her alone!' he shouted.

'Or *what?*' Mark challenged.

'Or you'll have me to deal with.'

'Oh *dear!*' Mark threw his head back and laughed. 'I'm terrified! How touching. My wife and the loyal, clod-hopping farm labourer. Or should that be *bed-hopping*? I bet you thought all your birthdays had come at once when I left the field clear for you. Well, the fun's over now, Owen. I'm her husband and I'm

191

back! So if you want a fight, come on: I'm ready.' He struggled out of his jacket and threw it on the ground, waving his fists about ineffectually.

'Don't be a fool,' Harry said. 'You'd only get the worst of it, the state you're in.'

But the remark only made Mark even angrier. 'You reckon? Come and find out then!' He made a reckless lunge towards Harry who stepped aside and watched him stagger into the wall.

Suddenly a woman's voice rang out stridently, startling all three of them.

'*So you've come back, you murdering rat!*'

Mark stopped in his tracks and spun round to face the wild-eyed woman who had emerged from out of the shadows. Her greying hair stuck out in a wild halo and to Rose's horror she raised a shotgun and levelled it at Mark.

'*Meg!*' she screamed. 'Please, Meg, don't!'

She made an impulsive move towards the woman but Harry caught her arm.

'Let me deal with her.' He took a tentative step towards the gypsy woman. 'Meg, this isn't the way. Give me the gun. He's not worth it.'

'You stand aside. I got a job to do.' Meg never took her eyes off Mark who stood as though rooted to the spot, his eyes wide with fear. 'I always knowed he'd show up here again one o' these days. Well, now he's got to pay for what he done. He killed my girl,' she said, her voice trembling with passion. 'He done it 'cause she carried his child an' he wanted rid of her. He weren't never in that car when it went over the cliff, the lyin' scum. When I saw him walking through the village, drunk as a lord and twice as cocky, I knew the time had come.'

Mark made a sudden desperate dash for Richard's Land-Rover and Meg fired. One deafening shot split the quiet of the country night. Rose screamed as she saw Mark fall and Harry shouted at Meg. But she had dropped the gun and stood staring impassively at the body on the ground.

192

'An eye for an eye, an' a life for a life. That's our law,' she said. 'Well, now justice has been done.'

Rose was on her knees beside Mark's body, calling his name and desperately feeling for a pulse. The almost point blank shot had hit him in the back and a pool of blood was rapidly spreading over the ground. Behind them a crowd of people who had rushed out of the hall at the sound of the shot stood huddled together, staring with horror at the scene before them.

After a moment Harry bent to touch her shoulder. 'Rose. Leave him,' he said gently. 'There's nothing you can do. Sid has gone across to the pub to telephone for an ambulance and the police.'

Slowly she stood up and turned to him. His arms closed around her and she laid her head on his shoulder, shaking with shock.

'Oh my God, Harry. Oh dear God!'

The ambulance and police came. Mark was pronounced dead at the scene and taken away. In the kitchen of the village hall, a policeman took statements from a stunned Rose and Harry. But Meg Brown was nowhere to be seen. She had melted into the night as suddenly as she had appeared. Only the shotgun lay on the ground where she had dropped it.

At the farmhouse, Harry made Rose a hot drink into which he had dissolved two aspirin tablets. She hadn't spoken since the police had interviewed her. Shock was making her shiver uncontrollably and her teeth chattered against the rim of the cup as she tried to drink. He helped her upstairs and she stood, passive and child-like as he unzipped her ruined dress, badly stained with dirt and blood. Wrapping her in her warm dressing-gown he gently lifted her on to the bed and lay down beside her, holding her close until, at last, to his relief, her tears flowed and her body shook with sobs.

Eventually she slept and he got up and covered her with the eiderdown. Downstairs in the kitchen, he looked for Nell's tele-

phone number and rang her. It was late but he knew she would understand. Shocked at his news, she promised to come as soon as she could get away.

He dozed uncomfortably in the chair by the Aga until it was time for milking, then, checking first that Rose was still asleep, he went to fetch Irene to sit with her until he'd finished the morning chores.

CHAPTER TWELVE

NELL STAYED with Rose for as long as she could, fending off the journalists who haunted the farm and village for days after the tragedy, taking notes from anyone who would talk to them. She promised to return later when Mark's body was released for the funeral.

At the inquest, a verdict of murder was brought in. As the shooting had been witnessed there was no police investigation. And no charges were brought as Meg's body had been found the morning after Mark's death, floating face down in the pond close to her caravan.

On the night before Nell was to return to Liverpool, she asked Rose what she planned to do.

'I've decided to stay on here,' she said. 'Before it all happened I was going to sell the farm, but somehow now everything has changed. I know some terrible things have happened here at Peacocks, but I have a strong feeling that the curse – if curse it was, has been lifted.

'Curse?' Nell looked at her askance. '*Rose*! For heaven's sake, this is 1947! You don't mean to tell me you believe in all that rubbish in this day and age?'

'I believe that there are people who have an evil influence,' Rose said. 'Did you know that Meg's people heard somehow about her crime and her suicide?' They must have read about it in the papers. They came and claimed her body for a funeral of

their own, but before they went they burned her caravan with all her possessions. You could see the blaze all over the village and when I saw it I had a powerful feeling that nothing else bad would happen at Peacocks. Meg has had her last revenge.'

Nell shuddered. 'So you're going to stay?'

'Yes. I feel more settled now. The dairy herd is doing well and the flock is growing. There's never been a better time for farming with all the government subsidies. Bill entrusted the farm to me and I feel I'd be letting him down if I ran away just because of the personal mistakes I've made.'

Nell nodded. 'And Harry?'

Rose looked up. 'Harry?'

'You know what I'm talking about,' Nell said. 'Are you really going to let him leave – go to Australia?'

'I can't stop him if that's what he wants. I don't have the right to.'

Nell shook her head. 'You know damn well it's not what he really wants, don't you? Well, *don't* you?'

'Then why is he doing it?'

'Do you want me to spell it out for you?' Nell gave a snort of exasperation. 'Because he can't stand seeing you every day and knowing you'll never be his!' she said bluntly. 'The man's head over heels in love with you. Don't tell me you don't know that? Anyone with half an eye can see it!'

Rose sighed. 'I've been so unfair to Harry,' she said. 'He all but told me some time ago how he felt and I didn't respond. I couldn't because at the time we still didn't know what had happened to Mark. He deserves better.'

'But he doesn't want *better*. He wants you!'

Rose gave her friend a wry smile. 'Nicely put.'

'So – what's stopping you now?'

'I said he deserves better and I meant it. Harry's a good man. He's loyal and true and he should have someone – someone whose first love he'll be.'

'First love or last. It's *you* he wants! Are you really going to

stand by and let a man like that slip through your fingers?' Nell took Rose by the shoulders and looked into her eyes. 'Rose – listen to me. How do you feel about Harry – *really* feel, I mean? Have you asked yourself? Have you actually sat down and thought it through? Will you miss him when he's gone?'

Rose sighed. 'Of course. Peacocks won't be the same without him.'

'That's not what I meant and you know it.'

Rose bit her lip. 'I'll miss him as a friend and companion. We've known each other a long time. We think the same – we like – *want* the same things.'

'And what are those things?' Nell asked.

Suddenly Rose's throat tightened and her eyes filled with tears. 'On the night Mark was killed Harry brought me back here,' she said softly. 'I was in shock and not thinking straight, but later I remembered him taking off my dress and wrapping me up. He lay on the bed and held me until I fell asleep. The dress was soaked with Mark's blood and he must have taken it away so that I wouldn't see it and be reminded, because I never found it afterwards. Irene told me later that he stayed downstairs all night in case I wakened.' She looked up at Nell. 'Yes, of course I love him. Who wouldn't? But I can't let myself admit it.'

'Why on earth not?'

'Can't you see, Nell? I ruined Mark's life. Maybe if I'd given him more responsibility – let him share more in the farm he'd have—'

Nell interrupted. 'Stop fooling yourself, pet. You know that's not true. He'd have bled you dry. He was a waster. Don't make him out to be something he wasn't just because he's dead.'

But Rose shook her head. 'Whatever you say I was the wrong wife for him. As a result I was to blame for that poor girl's death, not to mention poor crazy Meg's. I don't think I'm fit to be anyone's wife.'

'And you don't think you'll be ruining Harry's life by letting

him go to the other side of the world without you?'

Rose was silent.

Nell got up. 'Well, I've stuck my neck out far enough so I'm saying no more. I've got to go home tomorrow, but I do beg you to think carefully, Rose. The past is over and you have to move on and think about your future. And not only your future. Good men are hard to find. And real love – love that lasts is a rare jewel.'

'I didn't know you could be so poetic,' Rose said ironically.

Nell shrugged. 'Neither did I, so make the most of it!' She bent and kissed her friend's cheek. 'Don't leave it till it's too late, pet. You deserve happiness and I think you know where to find it.'

Rose gradually picked up the threads of her everyday life again after Nell had left. It was only then that she realized how much the farm meant to her. Working on the land and with the animals was wonderful therapy and helped her to heal. She went to see Richard and told him she had decided to stay after all. To her surprise he wasn't angry with her.

'I think you're doing the right thing,' he said. 'What you need at the moment is stability and whatever else has happened you've always had that at Peacocks. My other offer is still open if ever you change you mind about it,' he said with a wistful smile. But she shook her head.

'I'm better on my own for the time being, Richard. But I'll always feel proud and flattered that you asked me.'

Christmas was an occasion that Rose had no enthusiasm for. Nell had gone with her fiancé, Gerald, to visit his family. Harry went to spend it with his brother and family. As he said, once he had left for Australia it could be years before he saw any of them again. So Rose found herself spending Christmas Day alone with only Raff for company.

On Boxing Day evening there was a knock on the door and

when she opened it she was surprised to find Harry on the doorstep.

'I knew you were on your own and there's something I need to tell you,' he explained. 'I think we should have a talk.'

In the drawing-room, Rose offered him a chair by the fire and poured him a glass of whisky.

He came straight to the point. 'I've found your mother,' he told her.

Stunned, she stared at him. 'But how?'

'When I was in London, at Australia House, applying for my visa, I thought I'd do some searching. I wanted to save you time when you go back to London. I wasn't at all sure how to go about it, so first I checked church records. That wasn't easy, so many were lost in the bombing. When I drew a blank there I tried the local paper where they keep copies of all the back numbers and there I was lucky. I turned up the wedding of a Sally Meadows. She married Able Seaman Patrick Donovan of the Merchant Navy in May 1943. They still live in Hackney.' He fished a piece of paper out of his pocket. 'I didn't look her up, but I did check with the electoral roll that she was still at the same address and I've written it down for you.'

Rose stared at the paper. 'You're sure it's her?'

He smiled. 'There was a wedding photo in the paper. She looked so much like you that I had no doubt.' He looked at her. 'Will you go and see her when you move?'

'I don't know,' she said. 'Probably not. She might have other children. She was very young when I was born. Her husband might not know about me. It could be awkward for her. I'm glad she's still alive though. It's a comfort to know that she's there.' She looked at him. 'Thank you, Harry. It was so kind of you to go to all this trouble for me. Why did you do it?'

'I felt I owed it to you.' He looked uncomfortable. 'You see for weeks before Mark came back I'd known he was alive and I never told you.'

'You *knew*? But how?'

'That air show we went to. He was one of the pilots. Peter and I both saw him in the hangar when we went to look at the planes. We decided between us to keep it to ourselves. I know now that we were wrong.'

'You did it to protect me,' she said.

'Yes. But that's no excuse. I'm sorry.'

'It's over now, Harry. You did what you thought was best. You've nothing to reproach yourself with.' She refilled his glass and for a moment they were silent, sitting in the firelight.

She looked up at him. 'When do you leave?'

'In about ten days. I'm waiting for the list of sailing times.'

Her heart sank. 'I see.'

'I'll be glad when I'm on the boat now. Waiting about is nerve-racking.' He paused, then asked, 'When are you moving back to London?'

'I'm not. I'm staying on, at least for a while.'

'Oh. I'm sure that's wise.'

'Yes. I'm sure too.' She glanced at him. 'Harry.'

'Mmm?'

'I wish you weren't going.'

'It's best this way.'

'Is it?'

'I think we both know it is. You really should start looking for someone to take my place. Lambing time will be here before you know it now.'

'No one could ever take your place, Harry.'

'Of course they can. I know a couple of good lads in the village who could do with the work. If you like I could—'

'*Harry*!' she interrupted. 'I meant it when I said no one could take your place, and I wasn't talking about the lambing or anything else on the farm.'

He raised his head to look at her. 'I don't see. . . .'

'You were right when you said once that my roots are here. They are. That's why I've decided to stay. But you're part of those roots, a very important part. If you go it'll be like cutting

my right arm off' He made to speak but she held up her hand. 'Let me go on, Harry. It's so hard to find the right words. Just now, when you told me you'd found Sally, my mother, I knew quite suddenly that all that was in the past. It's dead and gone. My life – my past and my future – is here at Peacocks. But only – only if you are here to share it with me. Without you, it's meaningless.'

His eyes were round with surprise. 'You mean?'

'I mean that I love you, Harry. Really, truly love you. I know now that I always have. I was just too stupid to see it. I've made a lot of terrible mistakes in my life and if I let you go again it will be the worst mistake of all. So please, *please* don't leave me.'

In an instant he was out of his chair and pulling her to her feet. He crushed her close and she could feel his heart beating wildly against hers. 'Rose! Oh my darling Rose, do you really mean it?'

She reached up to kiss him. 'More than I've ever meant anything in my life.'

'So. . . .' He searched her eyes. 'Will you marry me?'

'Of course I will. And I want us to share everything. We'll own Peacocks equally.'

He held her at arms' length. 'Maybe that's something you should think carefully about.'

'No need. I'm sure it was what Bill had in mind. In fact, the more I think about it, the more certain I am.'

The wedding of Rose Elliot and Harry Owen was the event of the year in Weston St Mary. It took place on a beautiful June day at the village church with Nell as matron of honour and Peter as best man. Rose looked radiant in a dress of pale blue with her bouquet of pink cottage garden roses and Harry looked proud and happy at her side. Everyone agreed that they made a handsome couple.

After a quiet reception at The Grapes, Rose and Harry went back to Peacocks and in the late afternoon they walked together

hand-in-hand up to the sheep pasture with Raff at their heels. The sky was a wide blue arc above, the hedges were green with summer and from a tiny speck high in the heavens came the thin, pure song of a lark. Rose lifted her face to the warmth of the sun and slipped her arm through Harry's.

'This is all I want,' she said. 'You and me together at Peacocks – our farm. I'm so happy, darling. My only regret is that I made you wait so long.'

Harry bent his head to kiss her. 'You were worth waiting for,' he said. 'This moment is worth every day of it.'

Raff barked and ran ahead of them and Harry laughed. 'All right, boy,' he called. 'We're going home now. All three of us.'

WESTMEATH COUNTY LIBRARY

3 0019 00168146 3

/10S   M

WESTMEATH COUNTY LIBRARY

852,100	A F

1. This book may be retained for three weeks.
2. Thereafter, if not returned, fines at the appropriate rate, plus postage costs will be charged.
3. This book is due for return on the latest date entered below.

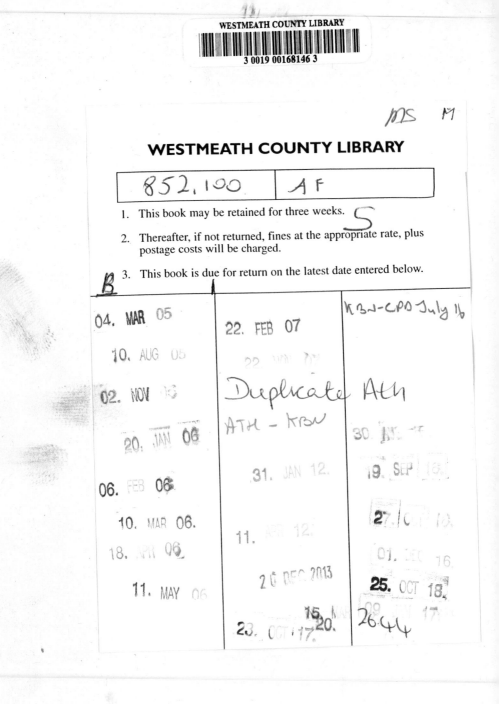

04. MAR 05   22. FEB 07   KBN-CPD July 16

10. AUG 05

02. NOV   Duplicate Ath

20. JAN 06   ATH - KBN   30.

06. FEB 06   31. JAN 12.   19. SEP

10. MAR 06.   27.

18.   06   11.   12.   01.   16.

11. MAY 06   2 DEC 2013   25. OCT 18

                    23. OCT 17 20. 26 44